**Sharon Ke**███████████████████████ **iting**
competition by describing her ideal date: being

just wandered into her dream job! Today she writes
for Mills & Boon, and her books feature often
stubborn but always to-die-for heroes and the
women who bring them to their knees. She believes
that the best books are those you never want to end.
Just like life…

**Kelly Hunter** has always had a weakness for fairy
tales, fantasy worlds and losing herself in a good
book. She has two children, avoids cooking and
cleaning and, despite the best efforts of her family, is
no sports fan. Kelly is, however, a keen gardener and
has a fondness for roses. Kelly was born in Australia
and has travelled extensively. Although she enjoys
living and working in different parts of the world,
she still calls Australia home.

# ITALIAN NIGHTS TO CLAIM THE VIRGIN

SHARON KENDRICK

# CINDERELLA AND THE OUTBACK BILLIONAIRE

KELLY HUNTER

MILLS & BOON

First published in Great Britain 2023
by Mills & Boon, an imprint of HarperCollins*Publishers* Ltd,
1 London Bridge Street, London, SE1 9GF

www.harpercollins.co.uk

HarperCollins*Publishers*, Macken House, 39/40 Mayor Street Upper, Dublin 1, D01 C9W8, Ireland

Italian Nights to Claim the Virgin © 2023 Sharon Kendrick

Cinderella and the Outback Billionaire © 2023 Kelly Hunter

ISBN: 978-0-263-30676-7

05/23

# ITALIAN NIGHTS TO CLAIM THE VIRGIN

SHARON KENDRICK

MILLS & BOON

This story was inspired by Il Giardinello,
the Umbrian home of my dearest friends
Guy Black and Mark Bolland.
In this exquisite setting I have enjoyed
countless laughs and good times,
delicious food, lively debate and stunning sunsets.
*Grazie, cari!* xxx

# PROLOGUE

ALESSIO DI BARI COULD cope with the fact that Nicola Bennett disliked him. He was used to women disliking him—usually whcn they finally realised he had no intention of budging from his negative position on matrimony, or indeed any form of long-term commitment.

And he was used to anger. Hot-blooded passion, which often ended up in the bedroom in a riot of hastily discarded clothing and warm, pulsating flesh. It made a welcome change from his infamously cold and scientific demeanour.

What he wasn't used to was indifference.

He frowned, because such a lukewarm sentiment was insulting—and it was definitely indifference which was filtering through the air towards him as he stood within the airy confines of the exclusive London art gallery.

'Would you like some coffee, Signor di Bari?'

Her eyes were glacial, he thought. Cool as ice. But then, everything about Nicola Bennett was cool. Her clothes. Her demeanour. Even her voice—every syllable carefully chipped out, as if she'd thought about each and every word she was uttering.

Alessio met the shuttered grey gaze which gleamed from her unmoving features, puzzled by his fascination for her. Because she certainly wasn't beautiful and neither was she particularly well-dressed—although he recognised that he had fairly exacting standards. Her plain white shirt and plain black skirt were undeniably smart but surely a little *dull*. Her shoes were sensible, *sì*, as were her neatly filed fingernails—but again, they were dull. Her only adornment was the thinnest gold chain he had ever seen—a modest piece of jewellery which glittered at the base of her long neck. Her pale hair was styled into a neat pleat at the back of her head and, because he had never seen a single strand of it out of place, he sometimes thought it looked more like a helmet. Nothing *feminine* about such a style as that, he thought disparagingly. Indeed, the only thing which marred her neat precision was the tiny rose-shaped birthmark on one side of her breastbone.

She was the most uptight woman he had ever met.

A pulse at his temple flickered.

*Very* uptight.

Yet at times, didn't he find his gaze inexplicably straying to that rosy little birthmark and wondering what her skin would taste like if he traced its raised surface with the tip of his tongue? Or imagine how it might be if he unclipped that severe hairstyle and let the blonde strands tumble in silken profusion over his fingers?

Again, he frowned.

What was *that* all about?

And since he was a scientist and therefore a man who abhorred the grey landscape of uncertainty, he always demanded answers to speculative questions. Perhaps it was because his busy schedule had been off the scale recently, with a new factory opening in Germany as well as another in his adopted country of America. But the subsequent stream of late nights and early mornings had led to an almost complete absence of leisure. Was it that which was responsible for him fantasising about the most unlikely of people, like the cool Miss Nicola Bennett?

'Shouldn't you be offering me champagne?' he drawled. 'Considering the significant hole which has blasted its way through my finances as a result of purchasing this overpriced painting.' He raised his eyebrows as he gestured towards the large canvas. 'Wouldn't you have thought your boss would have presented me with a hefty discount for being such a regular customer to his gallery, considering we've been friends for so long?'

But her implacable features barely moved and her polite smile stayed frozen in place. 'If you wait until the weekend, you'll get the chance to haggle with him in person,' she answered smoothly. 'He's due back from Argentina on Friday.'

'Unfortunately, I'm busy at the weekend,' said Alessio, but when he thought about the reason why, he could feel a trickle of distaste whisper over his skin.

'Oh, that's a shame.' She gave a small shrug, which rather distractingly drew his attention to the slender curve of her breasts, which were outlined in crisp white cotton. 'For what it's worth, I happen to think you've got yourself a bargain,' she added.

'Do you?'

'Of course.'

Silently, their gazes travelled to the oil painting which depicted a woman sitting beside a bathtub, wearing nothing but a man's shirt and the expression of someone who had just been sexually satisfied. Her dark hair was tangled, her thighs slightly open and a soft smile was playing at the edges of her lips. The artist was well known for portraits of his many lovers and it was an astonishing piece of work, yet there was something about the study which was uncomfortably intimate, which made the viewer feel almost like a voyeur.

Alessio couldn't imagine staring at a woman for long enough to paint her in such a situation—even if he possessed a shred of artistic ability, which he definitely didn't. He was the type of man who cut short post-coital reflection by going straight to the bathroom and dousing himself beneath the jets of a powerful shower and afterwards becoming engrossed in work—employing any method he could to avoid sentimental contemplation. It had been noted and complained about on more than one occasion, but he had no intention of changing his behaviour. Why should he?

He glanced at the smooth profile of the woman beside him, noting the faint flush of colour which was staining her creamy skin as she studied the painting. 'Do you like it?' he enquired.

'It's one of his finest pieces of work,' she replied carefully.

'That's not what I asked, Nicola.' He paused, his gaze flickering over her. 'You're a very evasive woman, aren't you?'

'Am I?' She raised a pair of neat eyebrows. 'That's news to me. I just happen to prefer landscapes, Signor di Bari, nothing more mysterious than that.'

'And you never call me Alessio,' he observed softly. 'Even though I've asked you to on more than one occasion.'

There was a pause.

'Because I prefer professional boundaries,' she answered crisply. 'I refer to all Sergio's clients using their titles and nobody's ever objected before. In fact, some people seem to enjoy the use of formality in an increasingly informal age.'

Her accompanying smile made her words seem light—almost flippant, but they were not flippant. They were... He narrowed his eyes. They were dismissive. *Sì.* Definitely dismissive. And so was she. He saw the way she glanced at her wrist, even though she was trying to disguise it by fiddling with the cuff of her white shirt, as if she were doing nothing more than innocently checking that the button was secure, rather than looking to see the time.

She was bored, he realised incredulously. And she wanted him gone. Alessio could feel a pulse thudding at his temple as a warm flame of anger heated his blood. Because for a moment it had felt as if Miss Cool was judging him, and that pressed all the wrong buttons to someone who had spent much of his life being judged. It took a moment for the feeling to pass and he gave an impatient shake of his head.

What was the *matter* with him? Since when had he started caring about what some unknown English shopgirl thought, and allowed it to impact his mood? She was nothing to him. Pity his poor friend Sergio Cabrera, who was forced to study her chilly countenance day after day.

Pity even more her boyfriend. His lips hardened. That was if any man would be capable of enduring the company of such a cold fish as she.

'Have the painting shipped to my Manhattan address, would you?' he clipped out, pulling out his phone to direct his chauffeur to pick him up from the Mayfair gallery.

'With pleasure,' she answered politely.

Alessio couldn't help thinking that a woman like this would surely be a stranger to pleasure. He certainly couldn't imagine her showing it. Why, a plank of wood would display more emotion than Nicola Bennett!

And speaking of pleasure...

He thought about the evening ahead and the plea made by a man who'd been pivotal during the construction of the latest di Bari factory. Karl Schneider was young and dynamic, determined to see as much of London's nightlife as he could during his brief stay in the capital. Last night had been all about the theatre and dinner at an award-winning restaurant, but tonight...

Tonight was something which needed to be endured. Alessio wasn't crazy about Soho, or nightclubs—and old-school drinking establishments staffed by partially clothed women were definitely *not* his thing. He sighed. But he would go along with it because business was business and he liked Karl.

Maybe the place would surprise him and prove to be the one bright spot in a week over which a heavy black cloud was looming. He had no desire to attend his mother's birthday party, but this was one of the few occasions in his adult life when he felt as if he had no choice—an unwelcome acknowledgement for a man for whom control had always been key.

With a brief nod to the cool blonde who was opening the door for him, he swept from the gallery towards his waiting limousine and slid onto the back seat. He wondered just what form the forthcoming 'celebration' would take. And he wondered just how bad it was going to be.

A ragged sigh left his lungs.

A whole weekend to endure, with nobody but his toxic family for company.

# CHAPTER ONE

THE SUMMER RAIN was torrential. It splashed up the back of Nicola's calves and dripped back down into her shoes, making them squelch as she walked. Already she was soaked to the skin and her flimsy umbrella was proving useless against the driving wind. Also, she was cold and very hungry and these were the factors which should have been her sole focus this evening, especially as she had a long shift ahead of her.

But it wasn't just that she hadn't had time to sit down and eat before coming here—all Nicola could think about was Alessio di Bari. No matter how hard she tried she couldn't seem to shift his image from her mind, or block out the memory of his mocking, silken voice.

She'd often thought he was a bit of a contradiction. His appearance did nothing to suggest he was a highly successful chemist, with factories dotted around the globe—and most people agreed that he looked more like a movie star than a scientist. He possessed a dark and sensual beauty which made her go to pieces every time he walked into the London art gallery where she'd worked for the past three years, often with a beautiful woman hanging onto his arm—although not lately, she noted. Gorgeous sensual creatures with legs up to their armpits and amazing boobs, often dripping with diamonds, which the Italian billionaire had probably lavished on them.

Nicola had never seen or met anyone like him. He exemplified power and strength and intellect. She'd seen the way people turned to look at him and she totally understood why—and it had nothing to do with his expensive suits or chauffeur-driven cars or private jets. But she hated the way he managed to storm his way into her thoughts, like some sexy, heat-seeking missile. Just as she hated his effect on her—although a lifetime of keeping her emotions hidden meant she was confident he had no idea about her feelings for him. She always put up her defences whenever he was around—yet somehow he managed to knock them down without trying, leaving her aching and vulnerable in a way which felt exciting, scary and unfamiliar.

She swallowed as his hard, chiselled features swam into her mind. Those bright sapphire eyes, set in skin of burnished gold. That mane of ebony hair which framed his face and that honed, muscular body, which no amount of handmade tailoring could disguise. Yet he had a particular skill in looking down his nose at her and Nicola resented him for that. Her carefully maintained poise always threatened to desert her whenever Alessio di Bari was around. She found herself wanting to touch him. To kiss him. To press his hard body close to hers and never let him go.

How insane was that?

Especially since she was that embarrassing thing which nobody of her age should be.

A virgin.

Snapped out of her thoughts by a buzzing sound from the depths of her handbag, Nicola sighed. She didn't have to look at her phone to know who was calling, which was why she chose not to ignore it. With a shiver, she sheltered underneath the dripping awning of a shop selling vintage comics and pulled out the vibrating handset.

'Nicky?' whined a familiar voice.

'Hello, Mum. Look, I can't talk for long. I've got to go to work. What's up?'

'It's Stacey.'

Of course it was. It was always Stacey. As ever, Nicola's heart plummeted at the mention of her brother's girlfriend. 'She's okay, isn't she?' she questioned urgently.

'Suppose so.' The deep inhalation of a cigarette was followed by a brief, rasping cough. 'Says she's fed up with the weather and thinking of going to Majorca. Apparently her auntie's got a time-share out there and says she can get her a job in some fancy café on the beachfront.'

Nicola bit back the obvious response that an eight months pregnant young woman with a lifelong aversion to work was unlikely to walk straight into a jammy job abroad—even if she could get a work permit sorted out in time, which Nicola doubted.

Clearing her throat, she attempted to project an air of calm. 'Mum, listen. Tell her everything's going to be okay. I've got some money I've been saving up for her and the baby and she's going to get it very soon.'

'She knows that. She wants to know why she can't have it. Now.' Another rasping cough. 'Says she needs furniture.'

Nicola bit her lip in frustration—because delayed grat-
ification was as alien a concept to her mother as it was to
her brother's girlfriend. She thought about Stacey's penchant for expensive make-up and handbags. Her love of
eating out, which went hand in hand with an inability to
cook anything more complicated than a piece of toast. 'I
know she does, but I'm scared she'll fritter it away before the baby's born,' she confided huskily. 'Look, I'll go
and visit her tomorrow and see what I can do. I'll reassure her and try to talk some sense into her, but I've got
to go now, Mum, or I'll be late for work.'

She cut the connection and hurried across the shiny
pavements which reflected the garish lights of the Soho
streets, which were unusually quiet tonight—presumably
because of the foul weather. At last she came to a halt in
front of the Masquerade club—its pink neon lights flashing flamingo-bright alongside a giant photo of a canal
and a gondola. A bouncer stood outside, mostly turning
people away because this was the current hot ticket in
town and the difficulty of gaining entry was one of the
things which made it so attractive.

One of the doormen nodded as Nicola entered, slipping through a discreet interior door at the back and taking the stairs to the staff changing room in the basement,
where she proceeded to get changed. It always took longer
to put on her outfit than to remove the clothes she'd arrived in and there was a reason for that. Try as she could
to break the habit, her movements were always reluctant because this costume was the last thing she would
ever have chosen to wear. In fact, if she didn't need the
money so desperately she would never have taken a job

like this. But it was relatively easy and, more importantly, the tips were excellent—and that was what had kept her here for the last five months, laboriously putting aside every penny she earned.

Pulling her blonde hair from its neat pleat and shaking it free, Nicola peered into the mirror. The club was supposed to be Venice-themed, which was why the menu was full of *cicchetti* and bottles of expensive Valpolicella and barmen dressed in stripey tops with distinctive hats tipped at jaunty angles. While the waitresses, of which she was one...

She sighed. No way would her appearance offend anyone's sense of decency. There was more substance to her costume than something you might see on the beach—it was just so ridiculously *tight*. Her breasts felt as if they wanted to burst right out of the sequined bodice and her tiny skirt of black and purple feathers left far too much of her fishnet-covered thighs on show. And as for her shoes...

She glanced down at the killer stilettos. Her shoes were crazy-high. At least the traditional Venetian mask meant nobody would be able to recognise her, which had been another of the job's enticements—not that she knew anyone who would be prepared to pay these kinds of overinflated prices for glasses of mediocre wine.

Going back upstairs, she picked up her tray and her electronic ordering pad and, walking into the dimly lit interior of the club, looked around. It was the usual selection of guests and they were nearly all men. Out-of-town visitors. A smattering of celebrities. A clutch of premier league footballers with a bevy of beautiful blondes hanging onto their every word.

The light on her electronic pad was flashing, instructing her to go to table thirteen—somewhat ironically numbered since it was the most prestigious table in the VIP section of the club. Nicola pinned a wide smile to her lips and swayed her hips, the way the manageress had taught her to, though the skyscraper heels made the movement feel very exaggerated and secretly she wondered if it didn't make her look rather ridiculous. But her smile froze the instant she saw the two men who were sitting on the raised dais. Or rather, when she clocked the one who was gazing rather moodily at the empty dance floor, his hard profile drawing the covert and not so covert attention of pretty much every woman in the place. Beneath her too-tight bodice, her heart squeezed out a painful beat and her skin grew clammy and cold.

It couldn't be.

It couldn't.

Fate would never be that cruel, would it?

Yet she of all people should know how cruel fate could be. Of course it was him. Who else would it be? Because if anyone was going to walk in and discover her secret job—wouldn't it have to be the man she hated and fancied more than anyone in the world? Who just happened to be one of the best friends of her powerful boss…

Her heart began to race, because her boss, Sergio Cabrera, was in many ways a highly conservative man—it was one of the reasons he'd taken her on as Chief Assistant in his London art gallery in the first place. He approved of her prim, neat image and the fact that she never came to work with a hangover or allowed her love life—which was non-existent anyway—to impinge on work. Wouldn't he hit the roof if he discovered that his loyal and supposedly very conventional assistant was spending her evenings draped in minuscule scraps of feathers and lace, selling overpriced glasses of champagne to wealthy punters?

He mustn't find out. And the only way he could would be if Alessio recognised her and told him—so she must make sure that didn't happen.

She needed to stay calm. The Italian billionaire wouldn't look at her face. They never did. And even if he did—*even if he did*—she was wearing a mask, wasn't she? An elaborate sequinned mask which had the ability to conceal most of her features. She even thought about slipping back into the rough South London accent of her youth, which she'd tried to leave behind—but something inside her baulked at that. She had come too far to ever go back—and wasn't there a bit of her which felt that if she did, she would be swallowed up by the horrors of the past all over again?

Anyway, Alessio wouldn't have a clue it was her. Why would he? She doubted he would have given her a second thought after leaving the gallery today—let alone remember her. Someone like her wouldn't even register on his radar. She would take his order and deliver it as quickly as possible, averting her eyes all the time. Then ask one of the other waitresses if they wouldn't mind swapping sections for the rest of her shift.

But her fingers were trembling and her heart was still pounding beneath her tight costume as she weaved her way through the tables towards the two men. And then, making sure she addressed the man who wasn't Alessio, she said quietly, 'What can I get for you, sir?'

Alessio wasn't really concentrating as the blonde waitress took their order and neither was he particularly engaged when she returned to the table with a bottle of rosé champagne, even though he could remember his companion only asking for two glasses of the stuff.

But he frowned as he watched her tear pink foil from the neck of the bottle, his attention caught by the way her thumbs began to ease out the cork, thinking how long her fingers were and how incongruous her sensibly filed fingernails seemed in comparison to her flamboyant outfit. He wasn't sure what made his eyes travel upwards, past the badge which said 'Nicky', past the creamy thrust of her cleavage to her long neck—his gaze stopping to alight on a tiny birthmark on her neck, shaped like a rose.

Something flickered in the depths of his memory.

*Shaped like a rose.*

She was focussing intently on the bottle, which she must have shaken because it had started to foam in a creamy cascade in a way which was exceedingly erotic. He could see her hand trembling as she splashed—yes, splashed—champagne into two tall goblets, but despite the mess she was making of the table, she was determinedly refusing to meet his gaze.

He could have let her go.

Maybe he should have let her go.

But his curiosity was stirred—which was rare—and so was something else. Something which felt like a fierce shaft of recognition and something else, too, something which felt uncomfortably like desire.

'Nicola?' he said softly. 'Is that really you?'

She lifted her gaze at last, and the eyes which met his were not so cool now, her glacial gaze melting into one of apprehension.

'Would there be any point in me denying it?' she said, her tone not quite as clipped as usual.

For a moment Alessio was so taken aback that he didn't answer. But it was less his shock at discovering her in such a bizarre setting which was responsible for his uncharacteristic hesitation, than the growing realisation that Nicola Bennett didn't usually do herself justice.

Not at all.

'I guess not,' he said slowly, his disbelieving gaze taking in her incredible body. 'Though it's proving a little difficult to get my head around. Seeing you here, like this.'

'I'm afraid I can't help you with that,' she said crisply as she began to mop up the spilt champagne. 'It is what it is.'

As she bent over the table her long hair swung like an armful of ripe corn—the coloured lights of the nightclub creating a neon kaleidoscope amid the thick and gleaming strands. Alessio's eyes narrowed, because he was baffled—and he was rarely baffled by a woman. He wondered why she hid that magnificent fall of hair—choosing instead that repressive helmet-like style which did her no favours. And why conceal that amazing body and achingly long legs beneath the type of clothes which made her look as if she'd taken a vow of chastity? For some bizarre reason he didn't actually *approve* of the skimpy outfit she was wearing tonight—but that didn't detract from the shimmering beauty she usually kept locked away.

Why did she do that?

His frown deepened.

And why the hell was she leading some sort of double life—working in a nightclub in an edgy part of the city, which was a world away from her sedate day job in privileged Mayfair?

She was staring at him—her grey eyes sending out a silent message which contained none of their usual enigma—as if daring him to interrogate her. And he wondered whether he might have done just that, if they hadn't been surrounded by other people, with the smoky note of a saxophone throbbing in the background, infiltrating the air with a layer of sensuality which only increased his feelings of disorientation.

'Hey, you two know each other, *ja*?'

Karl's voice broke the silence as he looked from one to the other of them—like somebody at a cocktail party waiting to be introduced—and Alessio responded with a lazy smile.

'We've met before,' he said carelessly. 'Though I wouldn't say we actually knew one another, would you, *Nicky*?'

He saw her throat work a little but that icy smile was back with all its chilly force.

'Not at all,' she said, with a quick smile. 'We've run into each other from time to time—but London is a much smaller city than people imagine, isn't it, Signor di Bari?'

She stared at a spot in the far distance. 'Oh, look. Somebody over there is signalling for a drink. Will you excuse me?'

He watched her go. Long legs in fishnet tights and a provocative flurry of feathers which adorned a deliciously high bottom, and Alessio found himself captured by another achingly sweet shaft of a desire which had been absent from his life for too long now. And he couldn't just blame overwork. Wasn't it also to do with his innate sense of boredom and cynicism, because women came on to him all the time? Because hadn't he reached the age of thirty-four with a sexual appetite which had lately grown very jaded?

He drank a mouthful of champagne, wincing at the inferior quality of the wine, before putting down the glass. He watched Nicola's elegant journey across the floor as she took the drinks order and then disappeared from the VIP section, instinctively knowing she had no intention of returning.

He wondered afterwards, if the dreaded weekend hadn't been approaching, whether he would have just let the matter lie. He could have stored the interesting and conflicting nugget of information about the cool Miss Bennett in the recesses of his mind, along with the many other of life's peculiarities which he'd picked up along the way.

But the weekend *was* approaching and he was increasingly focussed on what lay ahead. Various family members who hated one another—with a giant inheritance at stake, which exacerbated all the greed within his half-siblings which always simmered beneath the surface. If it hadn't been his mother's birthday he would have found an excuse to decline—but his refusal to attend would hurt her. And hadn't she been hurt enough during her foolish life?

He thought about the best strategy for coping with the ordeal. Perhaps he should have arranged to take a date with him but there was nobody he was interested in dating and it was too late now. What he needed was a woman who was suitably distracting, but who wouldn't get the wrong idea about his motives.

His lips curved into a hard smile because he'd suddenly had the most brilliant idea.

# CHAPTER TWO

'HAVE DINNER WITH me tonight.'

Despite the drawled delivery of his statement, the velvety words were more of an order than an invitation, but somehow Nicola didn't react. She didn't imagine many women would've refused a dinner invitation from Alessio di Bari—but those women weren't her. Because presumably they had nothing to lose, while she had so much.

So very much.

Surveying him from the other side of the gallery, she thought—not for the first time—how incredible the human body was. Inside you could be experiencing a cocktail of dread and unwanted physical attraction, while on the outside she was aware of appearing as composed as she always did. All those relentless years of training hadn't let her down. At least, not so far, she thought grimly, meeting a pair of blue eyes so bright they looked almost electric—which might account for the sparks which were fizzing over her skin.

Last night, she had worked the rest of her shift at the Masquerade club and although she had situated herself in the non-VIP section, she had been quaking with nerves, praying she wouldn't have to see Alessio again. And her prayers had been answered, because she hadn't.

When she'd peeped through the velvet curtain, he and his companion had no longer been there and she had heaved a great sigh of relief. He must have left soon after she'd served him the disgusting fizz they had the temerity to call champagne. He hadn't sought her out to say good-bye and she tried to convince herself she would hear no more about it. He would return to his fancy life in New York and next time he turned up to buy another paint-ing—probably with another luscious brunette hanging off his arm—he would have forgotten all about it.

Yet when she'd arrived at work this morning, some gut instinct had warned her that the Italian billionaire wouldn't just let matters lie. Deep down she had suspected she would see him today—and she had been right. Shortly after eleven he had walked into the gallery, dressed in a charcoal suit which made him look impossibly cool and a pale shirt which was open at the neck. His black hair gleamed and he glowed with health, as if he'd just returned from a fortnight at a spa. She, on the other hand, was pasty and panda-eyed, having barely slept a wink all night.

But fear and trepidation would not serve her well in this situation. He had seen a side of her she had never intended him to see and somehow that removed the ne-cessity to retreat behind the cool mask she always wore. It meant she was able to speak to him with a truth she would never have dared use previously.

'Why do you want to have dinner with me?' she said evenly. 'Are you planning to blackmail me?'

His evident surprise at her question did little to reas-sure her. Was that because the glint in his eyes remained as steely as ever?

'*Blackmail* you? *Madonna mia.*' Dark eyebrows were elevated in mocking query. 'You've been reading too many novels, *cara.*'

'I never read novels,' she replied repressively. 'I prefer facts.'

'Now why do I find that easy to believe? Although, actually, so do I,' he murmured.

'And is that relevant?'

'I guess not.' He gave a short laugh. 'Okay, Ms Prickly, I'll stick to facts. I would like very much to have a conversation with you.'

'Isn't that what we're doing right now?'

'Indeed we are. But another customer could easily walk in and interrupt us.'

'I might welcome an interruption.'

'And I might not.' He paused, and now the dazzling blue eyes were narrowed and determined. 'Nicola.'

Saying nothing, she waited for the inevitable.

'Or should I call you Nicky?'

Suddenly her hard-won aplomb drained away and Nicola felt herself grow tense. She could feel the approach of fear, because wasn't this like being back in the playground? And wasn't it disturbing how quickly those times could come flooding vividly back—as if the sophisticated veneer she had acquired over the years was melting away, like an ice cube in a warm drink? She remembered being the girl with holes in her shoes, her threadbare socks still damp from having washed them under the tap the night before. She remembered the tatty old lunchbox, which was always empty because she'd given her jam sandwiches to her hungry little brother.

But this was not the playground and she was no longer a schoolgirl—and even though this was the grown-up world, it could still be harsh and cruel. There was nobody to protect her now, just as there had been nobody to protect her then. Reflecting on the unfairness of life would get her nowhere—she needed to face the situation head-on and deal with it, same as she always had.

She knew that, in theory, there was nothing in her contract to say she couldn't get an evening job as a waitress—but she knew her boss would not be pleased. Because this was a world where image was everything. Crisp white blouses and neat black skirts were one thing—fishnet tights and feathery bottoms were a very different ballgame. That had been her choice and she had been found out, but she was damned if she was going to give up and buckle under—especially to *this* man.

She gave an exaggerated sigh. 'Look, why don't I save you the cost of a meal, Signor di Bari? If you want to tell Sergio about last night, than go ahead and tell him.' She shrugged. 'If he sacks me, he sacks me—I'll cope. There are always other jobs. But please don't start making veiled threats under the guise of asking me to dinner, because I can assure you that I'm not easy to intimidate.'

'Whoa! Easy!'

He was holding up his palms as if warding off an attack and the brief puzzlement on his granite features seemed genuine enough. And suddenly Nicola felt a rush of remorse—because that wasn't the most diplomatic way to speak to one of the gallery's best customers, was it? She had no right to be rude to him, just because she fancied him.

'Sorry,' she mumbled. 'I shouldn't have said that.'

'Do you always think the worst of people?' he questioned curiously.

She was tempted to tell him that yes, she did. She'd had plenty of reason to—and experience was a brutal teacher. But nobody wanted to listen to a sob story—especially not a man like him, who had wealth and privilege dripping from every pore of his body. Ever since she'd entered the hallowed world of selling paintings which cost more than an average house, Nicola had discovered that rich men—and women—thought everything in their world should be perfect. Their money was supposed to protect them from the cares which ordinary people suffered. They wanted sparkle. Magic. Not some glorified shop assistant pouring out her woes.

'I do tend to be a glass-half-empty sort of person,' she concurred wryly. 'But I'm always pleasantly surprised when I'm proved wrong.'

'So let me prove you wrong,' he said softly. 'Have dinner with me.'

'Why?'

'Because I find you intriguing.'

'I can assure you, I'm not.'

'Modest, too,' he observed.

She stared at him, trying to tell herself she didn't care what he thought of her, but it was hard to deny the sudden heat of her blood. 'Why?' she repeated steadily.

There was a pause. 'Because I have a proposition which might be of interest to you. And I don't think this is the right time or the right place to tell you about it.'

'Now who's being intriguing?'

'I know.' His sensual lips curved into a smile. 'It's an irresistible quality, isn't it?'

Suspiciously, Nicola identified his deliberate switch to charm, which did nothing to mask the steely resolve underpinning his words. Because that was something else she'd discovered about rich people. They were used to getting what they wanted, *when* they wanted it and she suspected that Alessio di Bari wouldn't go away until he had got what he'd come in for.

She couldn't imagine what his *proposition* was, but would it really hurt to humour him? Maybe even pretend to be flattered to receive an invitation from him—as she imagined most women with a pulse would be. She could come up with some cock-and-bull story about why she was moonlighting in the West End. She could explain that she needed new furniture. Which was true. Maybe even persuade him to keep her little secret to himself, so that Sergio would be none the wiser. She smiled and now it was *her* turn to switch on the charm—another lesson she had learned from watching other people. She tried to smile with her eyes, the way she knew you were supposed to—even though sometimes her eyes felt as empty as dry wells.

'Okay, then,' she said. 'Where did you have in mind?'

'My driver will pick you up.' He pulled his phone from his pocket. 'Let me have your address.'

'No.' Nicola felt a sudden flicker of apprehension as she imagined this powerful man turning up at an apartment which barely had enough room for one person, let alone two. But it wasn't so much that she was ashamed of her home—more that she couldn't contemplate all his powerful charisma being contained in such a modest space. It would be like trying to trap a hurricane in a matchbox. 'I'll meet you at the restaurant.'

His blue eyes narrowed. 'Are you always this guarded?'

'Always,' she affirmed coolly, plucking an ivory card from the edge of the glass desk and handing it to him. 'Here's my card, with my number. Text me the name of the restaurant when you've booked it.'

Alessio took the card, the brief brush of her fingers making his pulse rate soar, and he wondered how such an innocent touch could feel so unbelievably *erotic*. Was it because he'd never had to work this hard to get a woman to agree to have dinner with him which made her so fascinating? Or because he couldn't shift the memory of the way she had looked last night, in her fishnet tights and feathery miniskirt with that cascade of blonde hair gleaming down her back, which was a world away from today's buttoned-up appearance?

Reluctantly, he heaved out a sigh. 'As you wish. Seven-thirty okay? I have an early flight in the morning.'

'Make it eight-thirty, would you?' she amended crisply.

'Are you always this…*difficult*, Nicola?'

'I'm not being difficult. I…' Some of her composure seemed to leave her. 'I have a few errands I need to run after work, that's all.'

Shopping most probably, he thought, with the sudden beat of satisfaction—rushing to the nearest store to buy a new dress in order to impress him. But his mood had soured by the time his car drew up outside the gallery, because coming second to a bunch of *errands* was a novel experience for him. He gave a hard smile. Still. Let her play her little games. He rather relished the idea of having someone to cross swords with. It would certainly make a change from his usual dates, most of whom had taken submission to a whole new level. Even the smartest of women seemed to spend spent an inordinate amount of time trying to gauge his mood. Trying to work out how to become…

What?

Indispensable?

Probably. And from there they imagined it was one short step to getting a wedding band on their finger and a baby in the crib.

But no woman was indispensable and no woman was ever going to become his wife, because marriage was a flawed institution and one he despised. Yet no matter how many times he repeated his distaste at the thought of commitment, every woman thought she could be the one to change his mind.

Maybe that was the real reason why he'd been celibate for almost a year now, aware that the recent publicity surrounding his elevation to the super-rich list had made him something of a marital quarry. And, *sì*, his body might sometimes ache with a sexual hunger which was fierce and raw, but in a way it had been liberating not to have to meet a pair of reproachful eyes over his breakfast coffee when he explained he was going away on business. Or having to explain why he couldn't possibly commit to Christmas, when it was only July.

He spent the rest of the day in meetings, but when he returned to his hotel to change before dinner, he couldn't deny the unfamiliar ripple of excitement which had little to do with the proposition he was about to put to the enigmatic Miss Bennett. Standing beneath the powerful jets of water, he could feel the heavy throb of desire.

Did she have a man in her life? he wondered idly as icy droplets rained over his heated skin. His hair still damp, he walked over to the hotel window with its sweeping views of Green Park, bright with flowers on this warm summer evening. But he wasn't really concentrating on the view. His thoughts were still preoccupied with Nicola. Because if she *was* seeing someone, there was the very real possibility she might turn him down, and that was unthinkable. Pulling a silk shirt from the wardrobe, he felt the whisper of silk cool against his flesh as he acknowledged that he found her a challenge.

And he couldn't remember the last time *that* had happened.

# CHAPTER THREE

IT WASN'T WHAT Nicola had been expecting. A tiny restaurant in an unfashionable part of London, with a weathered sign which hung beneath the faded awning saying Marco's. She frowned as she checked her phone, wondering if she'd made a mistake. Whether the crazy thundering of her heart when she'd received Alessio's message had made her misread the text and brought her to a decidedly unflashy part of town. But no. This was definitely the right address.

So where were the neat bay trees standing sentry by the door? The bouncer discreetly keeping away the common people while making room for the press? Pushing open the door, she could hear the buzz of lively conversation as she stepped into a room to be instantly greeted by a beaming maître d'.

'*Buona sera, signorina.*'

'Good evening.' She gripped her clutch bag a little tighter. 'I'm meeting—'

'*Sì, sì.* I know exactly who you are meeting.' He gave a flourish of his hand. 'Come this way, *signorina.*'

Either the man was a mind-reader or Alessio had tipped him off, because she was being led past tables decked with old-fashioned red-and-white-checked table-cloths, adorned with small vases of plastic flowers—plastic!—towards a booth right at the back of the room. And Nicola felt her throat drying with a mixture of disbelief and longing, because there was Alessio di Bari, waiting for her. Waiting for *her*. It was like a scene from a film, or maybe a dream, and she could do nothing to prevent the sudden thundering of her heart. He was rising to his feet to greet her, looking impossibly gorgeous in a beautifully cut charcoal suit which defined the broadness of his shoulders, the long legs and narrow hips.

She tried not to feel nervous, but the truth was that she did—because this felt too much like a date and she'd given up on dates, a long time ago. Why had that been? she wondered fleetingly. When she'd realised that she didn't fit in anywhere? Not in the world she had left behind, nor the shiny new one she had embraced. When she'd accepted that on some level she had been disappointing the men who had taken her out for drinks, or dinner—because she wasn't what they expected. Despite her fancy job in one of London's most sophisticated galleries, she wasn't posh and she certainly hadn't been to the 'right' schools. She wasn't who she appeared to be from the outside.

*And she could never let them know who she truly was.*

But tonight definitely wasn't a date and it was perfectly okay to be nervous about what to wear, because she'd never been out with a man like Alessio before. In the end she had opted for an old but much-loved dress, which she had carefully maintained over the years. It had been very expensive and she had spent a long time saving up for it—but it was considered a 'classic', which wouldn't look out of place in even the fanciest of settings, and she'd certainly got a lot of wear out of it. Though judging by the rustic simplicity of the place she needn't have bothered—jeans would have fitted in much better.

Why was she even here, she thought crossly as she sat down, angsting about what to wear and wondering if she looked okay? Why had she docilely agreed to his request, instead of turning him down and calling his bluff? But as she placed her bag on the banquette she knew why—and it wasn't just because the Italian billionaire had discovered one of her secrets. Wasn't the truth a little more complicated? Hadn't the sheer force of his personality flattened her like a steamroller, so that she'd been unable to turn him down? And that was dangerous. *He* was dangerous.

'Nicola,' he said as he sat down opposite her. 'Thank you for coming.'

'I don't think I had a choice, do you?' she challenged pleasantly.

'I think we both know that's not true.'

'Whatever,' she said, with a careless shrug. But although this whole situation might not be to her liking, she couldn't deny the satisfaction she derived from this newfound freedom to speak to him exactly as she pleased.

In a rapid stream of Italian, he spoke to the maître d', who was hovering by his side, and, once the man had hurried away, he studied her from across the table. 'I've ordered for you. I hope you don't mind?'

She raised her brows. 'Why did you do that?'

'I didn't want to waste any time with protracted decision-making and I trust the staff's advice about what's the best thing on the menu.' He glittered her a look. 'Unless you have any allergies?'

'Only to arrogant men making decisions for me.'

'I can always call him back if you'd prefer something different.'

Nicola shook her head, though she wasn't quite as indignant as she would have him believe. Because she wasn't supposed to *like* a man behaving in such an outrageously masterful way. She was proud of her hard-won independence and his approach was so last century. So why was an unfamiliar softness beginning to unfurl deep inside her? Because it made a change to have someone else making a decision, or because his easy confidence made him seem even sexier?

She shook her head, sitting back against the banquette and looking around the room, which was preferable to losing herself in the brilliance of Alessio's electric-blue eyes. The place was almost full—mostly with young families—though there were several couples of differing ages. It was an understated place. Relaxed. People looked happy, she thought—as if they didn't have a care in the world—and suddenly she felt wistful. But she couldn't spend the whole evening looking everywhere except at Alessio and so, as the waiter poured wine and water, Nicola directed her gaze towards the carved contours of his beautiful face.

'This isn't a bit what I expected,' she said.

'No? Let me guess.' His hard blue gaze raked over her. 'Chandeliers and a hushed atmosphere? Waiters dressed like penguins and food which has been messed around with so much that it's unrecognisable?'

Biting back a reluctant smile, she shrugged. 'Something like that.'

'Formality and luxury have their place but so does this. They make the best home-made pasta outside Italy, which is why it's always full.' He lifted his glass, surveying her mockingly over its rim. 'Are you disappointed I didn't treat you to an evening of five-star excellence, Nicola?'

She watched him take a sip of wine, unwillingly fascinated by the gleam which highlighted his bottom lip, despairing at her sudden urge to drink in all his golden dark, masculine beauty. Because this wasn't why she was here. She wasn't supposed to be *flirting*. She shook her head. 'Not disappointed at all. I think it's a lovely place and very unpretentious.' She drew in a deep breath. 'But why don't we just cut to the chase? You obviously don't want to waste any time and neither do I. The venue is irrelevant. You still haven't told me why I'm here.'

'You don't think it has anything to do with your wit and your beauty?'

'Please don't insult me with sarcasm.'

'You don't like compliments?'

'I don't like prevarication, which you seem a master of.'

'I am a master of many things, *cara*.'

'As well as boasting, you mean?'

'Why is it considered a flaw to simply state facts?' He gave the flicker of a smile. 'Very well. Since last night I've been more than a little *puzzled* by your behaviour, Nicola.'

'Oh?'

'Mmm... Usually you come over as one of the most

buttoned-up women I've ever met—an attitude which is not without appeal.'

'Appealing to you has never been my intention.'

'And then I run into you,' he said, completely ignoring her intervention, 'working in a nightclub, looking—'

'Different?' she supplied, using the most innocuous word she could think of.

'You could say that.'

'Maybe I'm just one of those people who likes a little contrast in their life,' she said quickly, because the last thing she wanted him dwelling on was that frivolous little costume. She didn't want to think of that electric-blue gaze skating over her thighs and her bottom, or to imagine him following that visual assessment with the slow drift of his fingers... 'You know,' she added, helpfully, trying to ignore the lump which had risen in her throat. 'Someone who likes a bit of variety.'

The wave of his hand was impatient, as if her arguments had failed to impress him. 'No. It doesn't seem to add up,' he continued, his gaze burning into her like a laser. 'So why are you doing it, Nicola?'

'Isn't it obvious? I need the money.'

'But surely Sergio must pay you a decent wage.'

She wanted to tell him her finances were none of his business, but instinct told her that an alpha man like Alessio di Bari would persist until he got some answers. His curiosity was aroused and he would wish to have it satisfied, because he was a rich and entitled man and that was what men like him were like.

*So make the story real, but not too real. Be creative with the truth.*

Her mouth twisted into a smile edged with bitterness. Wasn't that the way the world operated? What she'd had to do countless times in the past when social services had come looking for her and her little brother. There was nothing wrong with admitting to problems in your life—you just had to convince the people in power that you could deal with them. 'I'm in debt,' she said baldly.

'Again, a little surprising,' he mused.

'Oh?'

He shrugged. 'That someone who always seems so cool and in control should allow her finances to get out of hand.' His eyes glittered as he circled the tip of his finger round the rim of his wine glass. 'How did that come about?'

'Oh, you know. I overextended myself with my mortgage,' she elaborated, really getting into it now. 'I was a bit too cavalier with the credit card—it's surprisingly easy to spend money you don't have, these days. Before I knew it, I owed the bank a shedload of money.' She paused, unable to keep a note of defiance from her voice. 'Something I don't imagine you've ever been familiar with.'

Alessio nodded as he acknowledged the accusation behind her words, but for some reason her easy assumption irritated him. Was she totally lacking in imagination? Did she think that just because he was a wealthy man, he'd never known hardship, or pain? He wondered how she might react if she knew the real story. But he didn't need to prove himself to her or tell her just how wrong she was. There was only one reason he had invited her here tonight and she had just provided him with the perfect opening.

'How much do you need?' he questioned suddenly.

'I'm sorry?'

'You heard me. Don't look so shocked, Nicola. I said, how much money do you need?'

Her neat blonde hair was gleaming in the candle-light, her grey eyes narrowed with the glint of suspicion. 'What's it got to do with you?'

'Because I could help you.'

'That's the whole point of having a second job! I don't need your help.'

'Are you sure?' He frowned. 'Because unless we're talking six-figure sums—and I imagine you might be in jail if you owed *that* kind of figure—it would be easy for me to give you the money you need. So I'll ask you again. How much?'

He could see her hesitation and the brief flare of silent desperation on her face before she blurted out a sum which was less than he'd spend on a weekend in Paris.

'That's nothing,' he said.

'Maybe to you it isn't—but it's certainly not *nothing* to me!' she declared fiercely.

'I could write off your debt in one fell swoop,' he said. 'In fact, I'd be prepared to double the amount. How does that sound?'

Now her grey eyes were as wide as saucers. 'But why?' she questioned breathlessly. 'I mean, why would you do that?'

He waited while two steaming plates of pasta were deposited on the table in front of them and, although it was his favourite *cacio e pepe*, he paid the food little attention. 'Because I need a favour.'

He saw the veiled look which obliterated the sudden spring of hope in her eyes and made them grow hard.

'What kind of favour?' she questioned woodenly.

The inference behind her question was deeply insulting and Alessio wondered whether working in a club like that had given her a jaundiced view of life. Did she really think he was offering her money to have sex with him? That he was the kind of man who needed to *pay*? His initial response to such a negative character assessment was one of anger, but there was something about the way she'd started biting her lip—a glimpse of unexpected vulnerability lying behind the suspicious mask— which made him soften his stance a little.

'Let me reassure you that what I am proposing is perfectly above-board,' he informed her coolly. 'You need something and I need something. Namely, a woman to accompany me to my mother's sixtieth birthday party next weekend.' He shrugged. 'It's a simple financial transaction, Nicola—nothing more complicated than that.'

'Oh, come on. I'm not completely stupid.' She had relaxed her frozen position but her gaze was still narrowed with suspicion. 'Are you trying to tell me there's nobody else you can ask? Surely you must have a little black book with hundreds of candidates more suitable than me.'

'Indeed I do,' he agreed softly. 'But the trouble with taking a lover on a gig like that is that she'll start to think it's significant.'

'She'll start to think it's significant,' she repeated slowly.

'Introducing her to the family. You know. Take a woman home to meet your mother and before you know it, she'll be trying on long white dresses and organising hen nights.'

'Oh, my goodness. How little you seem to think of my sex,' she breathed. 'Do you really imagine they would be so scheming—or so desperate—to want to be married to a man like you?'

'I hate to disillusion you, Nicola, but yes, they would. But let me be candid with you, and tell you that your fervent words give me a great deal of pleasure.' His voice lowered. 'Since they reassure me you won't be thinking along those lines yourself.'

'Too right I'm not. I'm not interested in marriage.' She pulled a face. 'And even if I *were* looking for a husband it would be someone who was the polar opposite of you!'

'Then why don't you think about my offer instead? You'll get flown out to Umbria—'

'Did…?' There was a brief pause and now she was sitting up very straight in her seat. 'Did you say Umbria?'

'*Sì*, the party is in Italy.'

'I know where Umbria is,' she hissed, before taking a big gulp of water. 'Why take anyone? Why not just go on your own?'

'I've come to the conclusion that wouldn't be the best option,' he said, without missing a beat. He certainly wasn't going to explain that, with a third party present, his poisonous stepfather and two half-siblings might be less inclined to stir up mischief and malcontent. That their company would *possibly* be more tolerable if it was diluted by another person. He wanted Nicola Bennett to agree to his proposal, not send her screaming in the opposite direction. 'All you need to do is to be polite and

charming for a few days. I'm sure even you could man-
age that.'

She raised her eyebrows. 'Surely that would depend on
how much time I'm expected to spend with you!'

'And since my mother is a stickler for convention,' he
murmured, biting back a reluctant smile, 'we won't even
have to be in the same room.'

'I should hope not!' she said, her voice rising with what
sounded like genuine horror, which Alessio also found
deeply offensive.

'And for undertaking a simple task in one of the most
beautiful regions of Italy, you get to write off your out-
standing debts and have enough left to provide you with
a cushion,' he continued, his voice dipping as he slipped
into the familiar role of negotiation. 'Think about that,
Nicola. No more having to work past midnight in some
questionable nightclub. No more worrying that someone
is going to rumble you to Sergio.'

His gaze dropped to her outfit. It was a perfectly re-
spectable dress the colour of vanilla ice cream, but that
was about all you could say about it. She obviously hadn't
decided to go shopping after work after all, he decided
wryly. Just as she hadn't loosened her glorious hair so
that he could feast his eyes on it again, but had tied it into
its usual forbidding pleat. He realised he'd only ever seen
her at opposite ends of the sartorial spectrum—repressed
or tarty—neither of which would work for the forthcoming weekend. And wasn't the truth that he was curious
to see what she looked like in something pretty? 'You'll
need some suitable clothes to wear, of course, and I'm
perfectly happy to foot the bill.'

Her grey eyes narrowed. 'You don't think my existing wardrobe will work?'

'No.'

'Do you…?' She seemed to steady her breathing. 'Do get off on being so insulting?'

'But you asked me a straightforward question, Nicola. I'm a scientist. I deal with facts. Would you prefer me to lie to you?'

'No. But I certainly think you could benefit from a crash course in diplomacy.'

Alessio studied her, aware that some of the layers surrounding her were being peeled away tonight, and that behind that glacial exterior seemed to beat the heart of a tempestuous woman. Was that really so? Unprepared for the sudden sweet ambush of desire, he leaned back in his chair. 'So what do you say?' he questioned unsteadily. 'Are you tempted?'

She shook her head. 'Not in the least.'

'Are you sure?' he persisted, recognising that her refusal was spurring him on, because how long since he'd had to fight for a woman? Fight for anything? 'You wouldn't have to strut around wearing that abbreviated feathery nonsense any more.'

'For all you know, I might enjoy dressing up like that.'

'But you don't,' he said suddenly, with a certainty which came from deep inside him, though he wasn't sure where. 'You don't enjoy men looking at you with hunger in their eyes and talking to your breasts, do you? In fact, I suspect that the prim Nicola Bennett I see at the gallery is a far more accurate reflection of your true character than the blonde showstopper in the skimpy outfit, swaying in her high heels.' He paused. 'Am I right?'

Nicola hesitated. Yes, damn him, he was totally right. But she didn't want him to be. She didn't want his perception or his understanding. She wanted him to vanish into thin air and take his ridiculously attractive offer with him.

But his words were buzzing around inside her head like a mosquito in a cheap hotel bedroom and she couldn't seem to keep her unwelcome thoughts at bay.

She thought about Callum and the mess he'd made of his life. How it hurt like hell to imagine her baby brother in a prison cell.

She thought about his girlfriend, Stacey, and the helpless little infant who would soon depend on her.

On all of them.

Soon she was going to have to help Stacey learn how to be a mother—and how could she possibly do that if she was working nights at the Masquerade club, with the inevitable lack of sleep which came with the job? The rocky road ahead was fraught with enough potholes already, but surely Alessio's offer was giving her the opportunity to smooth it out.

The waiter had reappeared and was looking questioningly at the untouched bowls of pasta in front of them, which smelt absolutely wonderful, though Nicola didn't recognise the dish.

'*Cacio e pepe*—pasta with cheese and pepper,' Alessio informed her, his blue eyes shadowed by the shuttering of his dark lashes. 'And I'd like your answer before we eat. Unfinished business spoils the meal, I always find.'

The delicious aroma wafted towards her, adding to the general overloading of her senses, and it took a serious effort for Nicola to get her head around this opportunity, which was hers for the taking. Alessio was prepared to give her double what she needed and all she had to do was spend a few days in Italy with him and his family.

*Double.*

How hard could it be?

But nothing was ever straightforward. If something sounded too good to be true, it was usually because it was. And still she wasn't confronting the most complicating factor of all. Her feelings for Signor di Bari. Or rather, her *sexual* feelings, which, no matter how much she wanted to, she couldn't deny.

She had spent her whole life terrified of intimacy because she had seen what the fallout could be—and her determination not to make the mistakes of her feckless mother had led to her keeping herself to herself. It was a habit so deeply engrained that she didn't even have to think about it. Her lack of engagement with the opposite sex came as easily as breathing—though up until now it had never been tested. And then along had come Alessio di Bari and blown all her preconceived ideas out of the water. He had set her blood on fire right from the get-go. Didn't that add an extra layer of danger to his proposal? Wouldn't increased proximity to his particular brand of arrogant charm only make her more susceptible to him?

Nicola's fingers tightened around her napkin. If it was just her, she would refuse—but it wasn't just her, was it? Could she honestly turn him down?

'Very well. I'll do it,' she said at last.

'*Madonna mia*... I don't think I've ever had to wait so long for an answer.'

She frowned. 'And we'll definitely be getting separate rooms?'

'Count on it, *cara*. Believe me, the thought of waking up to your disapproving expression doesn't fill me with any joy.' He picked up his fork. 'You need to be ready to leave on Friday.'

'And presumably you don't want me to mention anything about this to Sergio?'

'Probably better not to.' He glittered her a complicit smile. 'It might complicate matters if he knew we were spending the weekend together.'

'We're not spending the weekend *together*,' she corrected repressively. 'It's just a couple of days we need to get through as best we can.'

She saw him bite back a smile and wished he hadn't, because it made his features relax and she wondered if he was aware just how blindingly beautiful he looked in that moment.

'How severely you dent my ego, Nicola,' he murmured.

'If anyone's ego can take a little denting, it has to be yours.' Dragging her gaze away from him, she focussed instead on her plate of pasta. After sealing such an uneasy deal, some women might have been keen to get away, or have lost their appetite, but not Nicola. When you'd known real hunger, it always seemed like a sin to turn down a good meal.

Bending her head, she began to eat.

# CHAPTER FOUR

AS THE HOUSE came into view Alessio slowed the car, feeling an inevitable tension begin to creep into his body. His reaction to these surroundings was predictable despite his having stayed away for years, yet nobody could deny the beauty of the place. He gave a bitter smile. Least of all him.

With Nicola beside him, he had driven past tiny terracotta-roofed houses, clinging to the edges of dark green hills. His powerful car had passed through sleepy village squares, where locals drank tiny cups of coffee and exquisite churches rang out the Angelus. There were fields of cows the colour of caramel, and other fields splashed yellow by sunflowers or bright, scarlet poppies. Up here in the hills, it was more remote. His stepfather's estate was surrounded by forests in which wild boar roamed free and the sunsets over the distant lake were among the most beautiful he had ever seen. Yet Alessio wished he were anywhere else in the world than here.

But wishes rarely came true—that had been a lesson he'd learnt early on. In approximately fifteen minutes' time he would be driving through the electronic gates of his stepfather's enormous mansion, ready to face the in-

evitable family disharmony. He wondered why the hell
he hadn't just bought his mother an extravagant present
and taken her out to lunch next time he was in London,
or in Paris.

*Because she would never have forgiven you.*

*Because, despite her many flaws, she's still your mother.*

And didn't he sometimes despise that biological connection which could draw you back to the bitterness of
the past?

'Okay. So what do I need to know before we get there?'
asked Nicola, her crisp words breaking into his uncomfortable reverie. 'You haven't really said.'

He turned to look at her. He had been so deep in
thought during the journey that at times he had almost
forgotten she was there. He swept her an assessing look,
silently applauding his insistence she acquire the services
of a personal shopper, because the Nicola Bennett who
was outlined against the green and gold of the Tuscan
countryside looked like a completely different woman.
Her summer dress caressed the high curve of her breasts
and the floaty skirt outlined her slender thighs in a way
which was...

He swallowed. *Compelling.* There was no other word
for it. Her hair was piled on top of her head in its usual
helmet style, but it showcased her long and swan-like
neck. Suddenly Alessio found himself imagining how it
would feel to have her in his arms and the taste of her soft
lips beneath his. Suddenly he wanted to trail his tongue
over that soft flesh, only this time to find the rose-shaped
birthmark above her breasts and explore it. He wanted
to strip her bare and lose himself in the hidden and for-

bidden areas of her body and he wanted all these things with an urgency which took his breath away.

Yet she had done nothing to this incite the potent stir of desire which was heating his blood. She hadn't flirted, or chatted. In fact, she had been almost completely silent during the journey, which had pleased him—though conversely it had also irritated him that he wasn't having to bat off the predictable remarks women often made when you put them in a powerful car and drove through some very expensive real estate. He frowned. Even on entering his private jet, she had failed to make the usual calculating murmurs which always served to reinforce his many prejudices about her sex.

'What do you want to know?' he questioned silkily.

'Who's going to be there, for a start.'

'My mother, obviously. And my stepfather.'

'Okay. So did…?' She pushed her sunglasses further up her nose. 'You haven't really talked about them. Did your parents get divorced, or did your father die?'

Impatiently, he pulled over and killed the engine, tapping his fingers against the steering wheel. 'Why on earth is that relevant?'

'Because I'm going to be a guest in their home,' she said. 'I'm just operating on a need-to-know basis, that's all—I'm not interested in anything else. And it's useful to discover some of the background behind their relationship, should the subject come up.'

'I can assure you that there won't be any discussion about their relationship,' he said, with a short, cynical laugh. 'My stepfather's name is Edward Bonner. Lord Bonner,' he elaborated, because the man had always been a crashing snob and woe betide Nicola Bennett if she had the temerity to call him *mister*.

'You mean he's…he's a member of the aristocracy?'

He heard the note of apprehension which had entered her voice.

'I'm afraid so.'

'And he's English?'

'Yes. He's been married to my Italian mother for nearly thirty years.'

'Wow.' Some of her caution evaporated. 'That's…well, that's wonderful.'

'In what way is it "wonderful"?' he questioned sarcastically.

'To have such a long marriage. Especially second time around. You know the stats for *those*. Doom and gloom.' She hesitated. 'They must be very happy.'

His eyebrows shot up. 'Since you know nothing about the background, isn't that a somewhat naïve assumption to make—especially coming from a woman who says she isn't interested in marriage?'

'Just because marriage doesn't appeal to me personally, doesn't mean I can't appreciate one which has overcome the odds!'

Alessio didn't enlighten her. Why be the one to destroy her ideals? Let her discover for herself just where his family featured on the happiness register. He gave a bitter smile. Wasn't that what he was paying her for? To tolerate a weekend of dysfunction and make it more bearable. 'My younger half-brother and half-sister, Sebastian and Lydia, will be there. There'll be a quiet family dinner tonight and a big party tomorrow.' He started the engine again. 'Anything else you want to know?'

Yes, there was plenty, but his tone sounded so forbidding that Nicola shook her head as the car pulled away. What a difficult man he was turning out to be, she thought, tearing her gaze away from his wind-ruffled hair. Increased exposure certainly hadn't altered her negative opinion of him.

He'd barely said a word on the flight over, just buried himself in a heap of work—and she had taken the hint and kept quiet. He'd even taken a phone call from a woman and agreed that he'd take her out for dinner next time he was in Munich, which for some reason Nicola had found intensely irritating. Plus, he hadn't even remarked on her new clothes or changed appearance, which was oddly hurtful as he'd been so critical of it before. Especially as she had reluctantly accepted the ministrations of the personal shopper he had arranged to take her in hand.

Against the backdrop of one of London's glitziest department stores, it had been a surreal experience to realise that as many new clothes as she needed for the weekend were to be hers, with money no option. Imagine that. Nicola had blinked in disbelief at one of the price tags, while the stylist had been rifling through the rails. She'd seen these kinds of clothes on the women who came into the gallery but wearing them herself was a completely new experience. She wondered what it must feel like to have unlimited wealth at your disposal. Did you become blasé if you never had to think about the cost, and would that explain some of Alessio's cynicism?

Yet despite her inner pep talks, she could feel her palms

growing clammy as the powerful car whipped through the stunning Tuscan countryside and she thought about what lay ahead. Alessio's stepfather was a lord, which was a pretty big deal to someone from her background, and he was English. Did that explain Alessio's unique accent—the slightly crystal inflection which underpinned his sexy Italian drawl and made him so hard to pin down?

Nicola had done a lot of work on her own way of speaking and had smoothed out the worst of her early accent. But what if his family saw through her and realised the kind of person she really was? Suddenly, she was nervous. Because, yes, she was employed by a successful man and no stranger to the trappings of wealth—but those things had always been at a distance removed. Maintaining an air of confidence at an art show after-party with her influential boss was very different from spending a whole weekend under the microscope as a bogus date, with people who were of a completely different class to her. What if she let Alessio—or herself—down? What if she committed some terrible cringe-making gaffe, like the time she'd almost drunk the bowl of lemon water after eating shellfish, instead of dipping her fingers into it? Would that mean he wouldn't pay her?

Nicola's heart raced.

He *had* to pay her.

Because she had gone round to Stacey's bedsit last night, her stomach sinking as she'd registered the dirty dishes cluttering up the sink and general air of neglect. She had opened up the empty fridge, slotting in the cartons of soft fruit, olives and hummus she'd brought with her—which would hopefully tempt the pregnant woman into eating more than the biscuits which had been the only food on show.

It had taken an effort but Nicola had injected a note of forced jollity into her voice as she'd surveyed the sullen profile of her brother's girlfriend. 'I'm going to have a surprise for you after the weekend, Stacey,' she announced.

But Stacey had barely stirred from her rapt preoccupation with a TV programme about a family who seemed to be inexplicably cutting all ties with their English life to go and live in remote Spain. 'What sort of surprise?'

'Ah!' Nicola had waggled her finger in the manner of a cartoon fairy godmother. 'If I tell you now, it won't be a surprise, will it?'

For once, Stacey had turned away from the screen, a flicker of interest shining briefly in her eyes. 'Okay. I'm cool with that.'

And that was the trouble with money, Nicola decided. It had a power all of its own. It could change the way you felt and the way you reacted. Now she'd envisaged getting the life-changing amount Alessio had promised her she couldn't countenance *not* getting it. The thought of going back to the Masquerade club and dealing with all those leering punters filled her with dread.

But that wasn't going to happen.

She was a fighter, not a quitter. She was going to make this weekend work, no matter what they—or he—threw at her.

'We're here,' Alessio drawled as the car slowed in front of a giant set of wrought-iron gates and Nicola stared ahead. As the gates opened she saw a long path, which

led to an enormous cream mansion. Manicured lawns
were dotted with bronze statues which glinted in the afternoon sun, and there were flowerbeds bright with roses
and daisies. In the distance she could see a walkway
edged with the purple haze of lavender and imagined all
the bees buzzing contentedly there. But it was the house
itself which dominated everything. Flanked by the dark
spears of cypress trees, it was tall and statuesque, its soaring marble columns only adding to its majestic beauty.

'Oh,' she said, a little breathlessly.

He shot her a glance. 'Like it?'

On one level, yes, of course she did, for who could
fail to like such a magnificent pile? But she found herself thinking it looked more like a palace than a home.
'It's very impressive.'

'I think that's the whole point,' he said drily.

As the car drew closer Nicola could see an older woman
standing in the porticoed doorway, her black dress chic
and her hair neatly styled. 'Is that your mother?' she
questioned nervously.

'Actually, it's my stepfather's French housekeeper,
Genevieve.'

Inside, something in Nicola died. Gaffe number one.
Tick. 'I'm so sorry. I thought—'

'Don't worry about it.' He switched off the engine and
passed the car keys through the open window to a young
valet who had appeared from the back of the property.
'It's an easy mistake to make. Who could blame you for
thinking that the welcoming committee might actually
be a member of my family? No doubt my mother will be
inside.' His lips curved. 'With her husband.'

Did Nicola imagine the scorn in his voice? She thought about her own mother, who had a catalogue of defects as long as your arm. But Nicola couldn't imagine her not running out to greet her in person. What *had* she let herself in for? she wondered as the housekeeper inclined her head deferentially towards Alessio, before shaking Nicola by the hand.

'Your mother has asked would you please wait in the south sitting room,' said Genevieve, in her soft French accent. 'She and Lord Bonner will be with you shortly.'

They followed the housekeeper up the short flight of steps into the house and an entrance hall of breathtaking dimensions, where the air was thick with the scent of lilies. But Nicola didn't get the chance to study any of the priceless artworks which would have usually made her drool, because they were being led into a vast sitting room.

She glanced around the room, taking in the enormous marble fireplace, the floor-to-ceiling nineteenth-century portraits, and several sets of French windows, which overlooked a stunning garden. At Genevieve's suggestion, Nicola perched nervously on the edge of a velvet chair, but Alessio was pacing the room like a caged lion. As the minutes ticked by it became impossible to ignore the increasingly stony set of his features and implacable line of his unsmiling mouth, and although conversation was the last thing she wanted to engage in, she couldn't hold back the question any longer.

'Is everything…okay?'

Electric-blue eyes narrowed. 'I'm not sure I understand what you're asking.'

Why was he doing that remote thing, which made her feel so inadequate? 'I'm just not sure why we're being made to wait like this. I mean…surely your mother must be anxious to see you? I'm sorry,' she amended quickly when she saw his face darken. 'It's probably none of my business.'

'You're right, it's not,' he snapped, then seemed to relent. 'Don't worry about it, Nicola. It's a power thing.'

But before she could ask any more—which he obviously didn't want her to—they were disturbed by the arrival of the couple and Nicola scrambled to her feet, a little unsteady in the new pink espadrilles which matched her dress. Introductions were made and her first impression was that Alessio's mother, Rosetta, must have been an absolute stunner in her time because she was still a startlingly beautiful woman. She was petite and slim, her dark hair was threaded with silver and her bone structure was amazing. It was easy to see where Alessio had got his looks from, Nicola thought, even though his eyes were blue, not brown. But she thought the greeting between mother and son was decidedly subdued. From the lack of warmth in their embrace, they might have been casual acquaintances meeting at a cocktail party.

Rosetta's husband, Edward, was at least twenty years older than his wife, his upright stance suggesting a career in the military. But his faded grey eyes were calculating as they looked Nicola up and down and she wondered if he could see right through her. Did he realise that she'd been born in one of the roughest parts of London and that her early years had been total chaos? That she was the last person who Alessio would *genuinely* have dated?

'Please. Sit down. Let's have some refreshment.' Lord Bonner waved his hand and, as if it had been timed to the second—which it probably had—Genevieve appeared with a young maid, bringing in all the accoutrements for afternoon tea, which they proceeded to lay out on a beautifully polished mahogany table.

It felt strange to be offered scones and cake in the centre of Italy, but Nicola accepted only a cup of milkless tea, terrified of ladling cream and jam on the scone in the wrong order, which people seemed to get really exercised about in certain parts of England. She sat back while Alessio and his mother chatted about the family dinner that night, which would be followed by the bigger birthday party the following evening—all beneath the oddly unsettling and watchful stare of Lord Bonner. Nicola wondered if she was imagining the inexplicable undercurrents which were making the atmosphere around the small table feel so tense.

'So...' Rosetta plucked at her linen napkin nervously. 'Have you and my son been together very long, Nicola?'

Momentarily, Nicola froze.

*Why on earth hadn't they rehearsed the answer to this?*

She wondered what they would say if she told them the truth.

*No, I try to keep out of his way as much as possible because I find him arrogant and unbearable and he does dangerous things to my heart-rate.*

Or, even worse...

*Actually, he's paying me to be here.*

But her hesitation was due to more than her conflicting feelings. She simply didn't know how a woman in a loving relationship was supposed to respond to a question like that, because she'd never been in one before. The smile she directed at Alessio was uncertain. 'We've—'

'Known each other for quite a while, haven't we, Nicky?' Alessio glittered her a look which suggested she needed to up her game. 'What you might call a *slow burn...*'

Slow burn was about right—that was if the sudden rise of heat in her usually cool cheeks was anything to go by. 'That's right. We...erm...we met in London.' Nicola licked her lips. 'My boss has an art gallery and Alessio is one of his best friends, as well as one of our best customers.'

'But no purchase has ever seemed quite so valuable as you are to me, *tesoro mio*,' said Alessio smoothly, and he leant across the table and briefly squeezed her hand.

Nicola stiffened and not just because his unexpected touch had made her breasts and her tummy tighten. It was more to do with the sudden gleam which had entered Lord Bonner's eyes—as if he recognised that the gesture was meaningless. And suddenly she realised that he didn't like his stepson one bit.

'Ah, young love,' the baron said reflectively, giving a theatrical sigh. 'Always such a delight to witness. Thank heavens I've managed to talk your mother out of some of her more old-fashioned ideas, Alessio. I keep telling her she needs to move with the times. So we've put you both in the lake room. I think you'll be very comfortable in there.'

*'Perfetto,'* Alessio murmured, rising gracefully to his feet and holding out his hand to Nicola, and she was so discombobulated by what she'd heard that she took it, re-

senting the warm caress of his fingers, while somehow revelling in it at the same time. 'I think we might go and freshen up.' He turned to his mother. 'Mamma, perhaps we should have a few moments on our own before dinner? Is that something which is going to be possible?'

Nicola was aware of how nervous Rosetta seemed in response to her son's suggestion. Her beautiful dark eyes were clouded with apprehension and her expression was fretful as she looked at her husband, as if she wanted to say something but didn't dare.

'I'm sure that can be arranged,' said Lord Bonner smoothly.

After thanking their hosts, Alessio led her away, still holding her hand—with the older couple watching them in tense silence. They exited the grand sitting room to ascend a sweeping staircase to the first floor, but she didn't trust herself to say a single word until the door swung closed behind them and she found herself alone with the Italian billionaire.

Alone in an enormous bedroom, with an equally enormous bed.

And although her mind was buzzing with questions about why his mother seemed so jumpy and his stepfather so scary, there was really only one thing on her mind.

# CHAPTER FIVE

'THIS IS...*INTOLERABLE*!' Nicola declared, snatching her hand away from his.

Rather missing the rapid slam of her pulse beneath his fingers, Alessio watched as she plucked her sunglasses from the top of her head and hurled them onto the four-poster bed, where they sank into the luxurious brocade. He'd never seen Miss Cool lose her temper before. Never even imagined she was capable of it. It was like seeing a stone statue suddenly become flesh and he found he couldn't tear his eyes away from her tempestuous beauty.

'What's wrong?' he murmured, noting that a strand of blonde hair had broken free from its confinement. *At last*. It was the first crack he had seen in her armour and yet the subsequent kick of lust which powered through his veins bemused him. He had witnessed her in a night-club with little more than a flurry of feathers adorning her delicious bottom and her long legs encased in a pair of fishnet stockings—so why the hell did a fallen strand of hair suddenly seem so intensely erotic?

'You know exactly what's wrong, Signor di Bari—so please don't give me that wide-eyed look of bewilderment! I could just about forgive the episode of hand-holding downstairs, which I *suppose* was necessary to make our relationship seem more convincing, but not this. Definitely not this.' She glared at him. 'You promised me separate rooms. You promised! That was the only reason I agreed to come.'

'The only reason?' he echoed coolly. 'Are you sure about that? You don't think your big fat pay cheque might have something to do with it?'

'You said we wouldn't have to share! You told me your mother was old-fashioned about that kind of thing.' She looked at the enormous bed and then quickly turned away from it. 'I definitely didn't sign up for this!'

'And neither did I,' he said, thinking that her shudder might have been amusing, if it hadn't also been the strangest kind of *turn-on*. 'This wasn't supposed to happen.'

'Then why,' she said, 'has it?'

There was silence as Alessio felt his body tense, resenting the ability of the past to impact on the present. No wonder he had stayed away so long. No wonder his heart sank whenever he strayed into the poisonous atmosphere which surrounded his family. He thought how best to convey the facts, because, as Nicola herself had said, this was purely on a need-to-know basis. And he wanted her to know as little as possible. About him. About his life. Because knowledge was all about power and, ultimately, control and he was reluctant to relinquish either of those things.

'I suspect my stepfather is playing games and doing something designed to cause mischief. It's a particular talent of his,' he added acidly. 'My mother doesn't approve of her unmarried children sharing rooms with members of the opposite sex, and everyone has always gone along with her wishes.'

'Seems a little old-fashioned,' she offered cautiously.

'You could say that.' His mouth hardened. 'It's never really bothered me, because I've never brought a woman here.'

'Until now,' she said slowly.

'Until now,' he agreed slowly. 'In fact, this is the first time I've been here for years.'

'So what made you change your mind about coming?'

Alessio turned away from the hypnotic beauty of her grey eyes and walked over to the window, where the formal grounds outside the house contrasted incongruously with the wild forest beyond. But the stunning setting was lost on him—because how could you possibly appreciate beauty in such a hostile environment? He hadn't intended to tell her anything about his family dynamic, but now he recognised he couldn't keep her totally in the dark. She was an intelligent woman and if he wanted her co-operation, she would require some kind of explanation. Because wasn't he buying her compliance, as well as her company?

He turned back to face her, momentarily startled by how changed she appeared in the intimate setting of the bedroom. The errant strand of hair was still dangling around her flushed cheek, and he got a sudden idea of how she might look first thing in the morning. All creamy flesh and pale blonde hair spread across the pillow. Her curvy body soft beneath the sheet. His throat tightened. How the hell was he going to resist her when she was looking at him like that?

Across the vast expanse of the room their gazes locked, her eyes growing dark, and he heard the catch of breath in her throat, as if acknowledging the sudden pulse of attraction which was throbbing through the air between them. But he shook his head, closing his mind to the automatic parting of her lips, which were making him want to kiss her, and steeling his sudden desire as best he could. There were a million reasons why having sex with Nicola Bennett was a bad idea, and having to share a bedroom was adding an unbearable layer of temptation. But it would do him good to resist her. It was something he'd never had to do before—and wasn't he always keen to embrace the novel whenever it came his way?

'What's different is that it's my mother's milestone birthday, which means I needed to make an effort—and this is precisely why you are here, Nicola. To defuse the atmosphere. To give everyone something else to think about, other than the usual petty squabbling over their inheritance.' He paused, a wry smile touching the edges of his lips. 'But given my reputation as something of a commitment-phobe, you should be prepared for some fairly insolent questions about how serious our relation-ship is.' He raised his eyebrows. 'It might add a little more conviction if you could try not to recoil whenever I come near you.'

'I'll try.' She huffed out a sigh. 'But believe me, this is the last thing I wanted.'

'Ditto, *cara*. I'm not exactly jumping for joy myself.'

And wasn't that just typical of a woman? he thought. The moment he mentioned that he *didn't* want to be alone with her—she extended her bottom lip in a brief but unmistakable pout. Was she offended by his assertion that he didn't want to be alone with her? Did she *want* him to acknowledge the desire which was simmering between them, or pretend it didn't exist?

'Don't worry. Nothing's going to happen. We can put a line of cushions down the centre of the bed as a temporary barricade,' he suggested drily. 'If that'll make you feel better.'

'The only thing which will make me feel better is when I'm on that plane going back to England.'

He could see her gritting her teeth behind her lips and he felt another flicker of disbelief. Didn't she realise how many women would have moved heaven and earth to find themselves alone with him like this? Women who, by now, would have been showering him with hungry kisses and unzipping his fly.

'In the interests of authenticity let's at least try to be civil to each another, shall we?' he snapped. 'I'm going to take a shower.'

'Take your time.'

'Oh, don't worry, I will.'

After he'd gone into the bathroom, Nicola resisted the temptation to drag her hairbrush from her handbag and hurl it at the door which he'd slammed shut behind him. But instead, she sucked in a few deep breaths, in a futile attempt to calm herself. What was the *matter* with her? Was she, someone who was always so calm and collected, actually contemplating *throwing a hairbrush*? Why was she letting Alessio di Bari get underneath her skin like this?

She knew why. It was because she wanted him. The

truth was that she had always wanted him and being trapped like this meant it was getting increasingly difficult to hide that fact. Over the years she had deliberately put a stopper on her feelings, not wanting messy emotions to hijack the strange double life she had forged for herself. It had never been a problem because nobody had ever captured her imagination or her emotions before. But emotion was what was rushing over her now and it was powerful and all-consuming. She could hear the sound of gushing water from the other side of the bathroom door and the thought of Alessio standing naked beneath the shower was enough to send her senses into overdrive.

She imagined his bare chest.

Bare arms.

Bare bottom.

Imagined water cascading over all that darkly golden flesh. A tug of heat clenched low in her sex and suddenly she felt so weak she was no longer certain her feet would support her. Sitting down on the edge of the bed, she untied her espadrilles and slumped back on the mattress, her heart racing. She stared up at the enormous chandelier which was dangling from the ceiling, like a cascade of diamonds suspended in mid-air.

How was she going to tolerate an entire weekend if this was what it was going to be like? Because no matter how enormous the room—and it *was* enormous—there was still only one bed. How was she going to pretend she couldn't care less about him? She wasn't *that* good an actress. Even worse, she didn't actually know the protocol for sharing a room with a man, because she'd never done it before. Would he laugh if he knew the truth? Of course he would. She was a modern-day freak, which was why she always kept it quiet.

*Actually, I've reached the grand old age of twenty-five and I'm still a virgin.* She imagined the coolly questioning look she would direct at him before remarking, *I know. It is unusual, isn't it?*

Nicola had spent her whole life learning the kind of things which most people took for granted. She'd learnt how to read and write long after most girls her age. How to hold a knife and fork properly and iron out the harsh way of speaking which she'd picked up during her first few feral years. She had been a diligent student and largely successful in most things she had turned her hand to. She had studied on buses, on Tubes or whenever she got the chance. While her peers had been buying lipsticks and giggling about boys, she'd always had her head in a book. When she'd got the opportunity to work in the high-octane art world, she had diligently watched how other people behaved and successfully copied them. But inside she could feel like that little girl who sensed the whole world was against her.

But this was different. This wasn't something you could *learn*. You couldn't watch other women and mimic their actions when they were alone with a man. Because—unless they were engaged in one of those *ménage à trois* situations you sometimes read about—bedroom etiquette wasn't actually a spectator sport.

So how *did* you go about cohabiting with a man you weren't in a relationship with? She bit her lip. She supposed she would have to get undressed in the bathroom. Would he let her go first—or should she defer to him, since he was paying her? She was definitely going to wear the baggy T-shirt she'd brought from home—not the slippery and highly revealing nightgown, which the personal shopper had insisted she purchase.

Her eyes flickered towards the heavy antique furniture and the big vases of blousy roses which were dotted everywhere, their petals spilling onto the polished wood. She was feeling uncomfortably warm, so she undid a button on her dress, but that did little to cool her heated skin. Her thoughts were spinning so fast that Nicola shut her eyes in an attempt to block out some of the visual stimuli which were playing havoc with her senses. But the perfume of the roses was powerful and the warm Umbrian air which filtered in through the open windows felt deliciously soft on her bare arms.

She could feel her eyelids growing heavy and her limbs were growing heavy, too—as if someone had coated them in liquid gold and weighted them down to the bed. Suddenly, she realised she'd hardly slept a wink in the preceding days because she'd been so worried about Stacey and Callum, and also, of course, about this trip. But now all her worries were being dominated by her body's need for rest. They were seeping away, like raindrops on leaves, evaporating in the sunshine. For a while she drifted away on a fragrant cloud, until a sound started beckoning her reluctantly back down to earth.

It was a voice, she thought.

A gorgeous voice.

Silk and velvet. Crystal and gravel. And rich, like chocolate.

'Nicola.'

Nobody had ever said her name that way before. *Nee-co-la*. Caressing the three syllables and making it sound incredibly *sexy*. Was that air from the open window fanning her face, or was it something else? Instinct told her it was breath and so did the impression of someone bending over her. How did you realise someone was so close, when your eyes were closed and they weren't even touching you? Her lips seemed to be parting of their own accord and although afterwards she tried to tell herself she didn't know what she was doing, Nicola knew exactly what she was doing. Her hands were reaching up to encounter Alessio's shoulders and she gave a soft sigh of satisfaction as they made contact with the silk shirt covering his flesh. Because wasn't this what she had wanted all along?

For a moment she kneaded the silk-coated muscle, before letting her fingertips drift to his face. With the edge of her thumb she traced the curve of his jaw before allowing it to drift to his upper lip. She heard him utter something indistinct as she outlined the sensual curve and then her heart almost leapt out of her chest because suddenly his mouth was on hers and he was kissing her.

Hungrily.

Frantically.

And she was kissing him back. Her mouth was opening wider to allow his tongue to move inside and Nicola felt as if she had been touched by flame. As if a million stars had exploded. Liquid heat flooded her sex as he deepened the kiss and she moaned with a sense of disbelief. Because although she had been kissed by men before, nothing could have prepared her for *this*. This didn't feel like a clumsy intrusion—this felt like heaven. She could feel the warm drench of desire. The painful prickling of her breasts. The sweet longing pulsing through her body was so insistent that she began to writhe her hips in silent invitation.

*Take me,* she thought desperately. *Do what you want with me.* And just in case he hadn't got the message, she pressed her breasts against his chest and gave a little moan. And he responded. Pushing her back against the mattress, his hand moved to the front of her dress—undoing several of the buttons before slipping inside to her lacy bra. He didn't even touch her bare skin. His thumb just brushed over her peaking nipple through the lace and Nicola nearly passed out.

It felt unbelievable.

*Incredible.*

His other hand was on her knee, tiptoeing towards her thigh. Against his lips, Nicola held her breath as an unfamiliar pulse began to beat and, instinctively, she tilted her hips, imploring him to go further. To touch her where she most needed to be touched.

But just as suddenly as it had started, it ended. He pulled away and the absence of his lips and his body felt shocking, as if she had been deprived of something essential, and she made a small sound of protest.

'Open your eyes,' he said roughly.

But Nicola didn't want to. She wanted to keep them shut and carry on with what they were doing. She wanted to forget it was him and just enjoy the way he was making her feel.

'Open your eyes,' he said again, his voice even harsher.

What else could she do but obey that fierce command? Her lashes fluttered open to see his slashed features swimming in and out of focus. He must have been leaning over to wake her up when she had grabbed him, as if he were a lifeline. But he was clearly as affected as her by what had just happened. The pupils of his eyes were dilated, their wild blackness almost obscuring the bright blue.

'I'm perfectly happy to carry on with what we're doing, Nicola,' he said, once he had steadied his breathing. 'But I would prefer some kind of acknowledgement that it's me who is making love to you.' His eyes glittered—hard and bright. 'I would hate to think you're lying there fantasising about someone else. Particularly when you still haven't even said my name.'

And in a way Nicola was grateful for his words, because they killed her desire stone-dead. She swallowed. Well…maybe not *completely* dead—but enough to allow common sense to replace the debilitating sense of longing which kept her anchored to the bed. She wished she had the energy to get up, but she didn't. All she could do was lie there, heavy with heat and hunger as she tried to ignore the crazy pounding of her heart.

His words had made her angry, but his perception made her angrier still. No way had she been fantasising about anyone else—as if anyone else would ever get a look-in while Alessio di Bari had his tongue inside your mouth—but she *had* been just letting it happen and hoping her lack of engagement would absolve her of responsibility for what she was doing.

Yet guilt and fear were powerful motivators and those

were what sparked her response to him. 'Wait a minute. I don't think we should be doing this,' she managed, her breath leaving her mouth in infuriatingly short little bursts, while the tingling sensation in her breasts was almost unbearable.

Straightening up, he raked his fingers back through his damp hair, his lips twisting with disdain. 'All I did was try to wake you. As I recall, you were the one who eased me down towards your delicious lips and then lay there, just begging to be taken.'

His raw words were like a bucket of cold water to her senses. Nicola watched as he walked awkwardly towards the window as if something was obstructing his movement and a sudden rush of anxiety washed over her as she thought about what he'd said. Had she really made a pass at him? Grabbed him and forced him to kiss her? Oh, God.

'I didn't mean—'

'Relax, Nicola, I'm just trying to take some of the heat out of the situation' he said, his voice tinged with mockery as he turned to look at her. 'It was just one of those things, that's all.'

She nodded. He made it sound inevitable. Did women always want to have sex with him? As she stared at his powerful body silhouetted against the lush green countryside outside the sharp tightening of her nipples gave her the answer. Of course they did.

'It was?' she managed huskily.

'Of course. Or maybe it was my own fantasy, not yours,' he conceded, his blue eyes glinting with a spark of unholy humour. 'Waking sleeping beauty with a kiss.'

Nobody had ever called her beautiful before, nor described her lips as 'delicious', and Nicola was unsure whether to believe what he was saying. Probably safer not to. People paid you compliments when they wanted something, didn't they? And there was nothing she wanted—or dared—to give him.

So don't just lie there like a passive wuss. *Do* something.

Her prone position putting her at a distinct disadvantage, she rose from the bed with as much dignity as she could muster, smoothing down the crumpled skirt of her dress and tucking an errant strand of hair behind her ear. 'I don't know what came over me,' she said.

'Oh, I think you do,' he offered drily. 'Unexpected proximity coupled with a very powerful sexual chemistry. It's a potent mix and don't pretend you don't know *that*, Nicola. What we do about it, of course,' he added, after a moment's pause, 'is an entirely different matter.'

She stared at him blankly, as the meaning of his words sank in. Was he implying that they could have sex when they weren't even in a relationship? Didn't he realise he was dealing with the biggest prude in London? 'We do nothing, of course,' she informed him primly. And then, because his expression remained perplexed, she took pains to remind him. 'We have a plan, remember?'

'A plan?' he echoed non-comprehendingly.

'Didn't you say something about putting cushions down the middle of the bed?'

Thoughtfully, his eyes narrowed. 'And you really think that's going to work?'

'Why wouldn't it work?' she challenged. 'If it's what we both want.'

He seemed about to answer but maybe he thought better of it, because he firmed his lips as if he were trying very hard not to laugh and it took a moment before he had composed himself enough to speak. '*Certo, cara*—it will be exactly as you say,' he murmured. 'In which case, I'd better leave you to get settled in. This room is proving a little too…claustrophobic for my liking.'

She wondered if he'd forgotten his promise to show her around the estate before dinner, but maybe that was a good thing. 'As you wish.'

'I'm going downstairs to find my mother.' And then, as if he was determined to reassert his authority, his blue eyes glittered with familiar command. 'Make sure you're ready for cocktails at seven.'

# CHAPTER SIX

ALESSIO RETURNED FROM his meeting with his mother, walking into their room with his dark features set and brooding, and Nicola looked up at him with some alarm. Now what? she wondered.

'Is everything okay?' she ventured.

'Everything is fine,' he gritted back repressively, his drawled voice growing mocking as he began to unbutton his shirt. 'I don't know your views on voyeurism, Nicola, but I'm about to get changed, so...'

The thought of him stripping off his clothes was enough to send Nicola scuttling outside into the early evening sunset, where she settled herself on a wicker bench and willed the racing of her heart to subside. But the magnificent landscape didn't really register and neither did the book whose pages remained unturned, despite the glowing reviews on the front cover, no doubt courtesy of the author's friends. She couldn't stop thinking about what had happened between the two of them earlier, and kept wishing she could forget it.

But she couldn't.

Round and round in her head it played—an endless spool of provocation and frustration. Alessio had kissed her and she had responded in a way which had spooked her. Because it had been more than a simple kiss, even she knew that. It had felt as though he had flicked a switch—cracking open the stony darkness inside her and flooding her body with heat and desire. She had melted beneath his touch and prayed for him to carry on.

'Nicola?'

He was walking out onto the terrace to find her and Nicola's breath dried in her throat as she saw him in formal tailoring for the very first time. Hugging the contours of his powerful frame, the suit mirrored the blackness of his hair and against the white shirt his skin glowed like burnished metal. But something about his appearance was different—his golden dark beauty somehow compromised. It was as if a shadow had fallen over him. His eyes were cold, his mouth hard and unsmiling—and an instinctive part of her wanted to ask him what the matter was and then reach out and comfort him. But that wasn't why she was here, she reminded herself grimly—though his next words took her by surprise, even though they were delivered in something of a growl.

'You look…' He paused. 'Good,' he finished abruptly.

'Do I?'

Alessio nodded, the insecurity in her eyes making him realise this wasn't the disingenuous query of a woman who was regularly showered with compliments. But then, who would ever have imagined that Nicola Bennett could look like this? Not him and possibly not her either. High-end fashion suited her and the flower-sprinkled green gown hugged the soft curve of her breasts and hips. She looked like a meadow, he thought with sudden longing. Fresh and beautiful. Her long hair had been transmuted into fiery gold by the sunset behind her and it tumbled down to a surprisingly tiny waist.

Suddenly he wanted to bury his lips in those silken strands and to continue the lovemaking he had so reluctantly terminated. But he closed his mind to the unwanted trajectory of his erotic thoughts because her Cinderella-like transformation was not the purpose behind this visit. She was supposed to be a diversion, not a distraction. So what was happening? How come she was making him feel like…?

He shook his head with self-directed impatience.

Like an untried teenager and an experienced man all at once. That kiss had been heady. She had invoked a powerful and intoxicating hunger which had rolled over him like a heavy wave, until he had called a halt to it. And he had never done that before. Never stopped a session of sex just as it was getting started, not when he had wanted it so much. His tongue slid out to ease the dryness of his lips. Lust and restraint—another potent combination.

'Come on,' he said curtly. 'Let's go.'

She followed him down the sweeping staircase towards the garden, where he could hear the murmur of voices, and out onto the terrace. Only his two siblings were there, surveying their luxurious surroundings with an air of proprietorial satisfaction. The relationship between the three of them had always been non-existent at best and hostile at worst, but Alessio reminded himself that he was here to please his mother.

Yet he frowned as he recalled Rosetta's fretful demeanour during their meeting when, although free from the watchful presence of her husband, she had been unable to relax. He remembered the way her gaze had darted repeatedly towards the door and her refusal to disclose what was troubling her, no matter how gently he had persisted with his questions. But she was an adult, he reminded himself—and he could not help her unless she asked for help.

'Come and meet the others,' he said, touching his fingers to Nicola's arm, dipping his head to speak quietly into her ear. 'This probably won't be the friendliest of encounters, but I'm confident you'll be able to deal with it.'

But Nicola was finding it difficult to subdue her sudden clamour of nerves—despite Alessio's supposedly reassuring words, or the touch of his fingers to her elbow. The seeking gazes of the striking couple who stood drinking champagne in the dying sunlight were making her feel inadequate because they were everything she was not—and that pressed all sorts of buttons.

Both younger than Alessio, the man's upright posture was reminiscent of his aristocratic father, while the woman was tall and rangy with an expensive mane of streaked hair, which complemented her golden dress and diamonds. With their perfectly even tans suggesting a lifetime of leisure, they looked glossy and…well, just *rich*, really, with an air of wealth and privilege which went more than skin-deep. Alessio possessed it, too—but she didn't. No matter how many fancy clothes she was given, or how many articles on social etiquette she studied, inside she would still be the same Nicky Bennett. That insecure little girl with holes in her socks.

But she knew how to fake it to make it.

You painted on a smile and acted as if you didn't care.

'Nicola, meet Sebastian and Lydia, my brother and sister,' said Alessio, distracted by a sudden movement which made him glance back towards the house. 'Ah, I see my mother has just arrived and she's on her own. Would you excuse me for a moment?'

'Yes, of course.'

His eyes looked very fierce as he glittered a warning glance towards his siblings. 'Be nice to her, okay?'

'Alessio!' exclaimed Lydia, in mock horror. 'Would I ever be anything else?'

'Hello,' said Nicola into the silence which followed Alessio's departure, holding out her hand towards Lydia, and producing her best gallery smile. 'How lovely to meet you.'

But Lydia didn't shake it, instead she removed a glass from the tray of a passing waitress and pressed a flute of cold champagne into Nicola's fingers.

'Just to make it clear, we're Alessio's *half* brother and sister,' she elaborated smoothly. 'I don't think we should allow sentiment to get in the way of accuracy, do you? Same mother, different father.' Her eyes darted towards the French windows as if checking Alessio was still out of earshot. 'We were both born securely within wedlock, unlike your wunderkind boyfriend.'

At this point, Sebastian raised his sandy eyebrows. 'You do know he's illegitimate?'

Nicola was so tempted to say *and so am I*, but stopped herself. She wasn't supposed to be trashing her own reputation in order to save Alessio's—who probably didn't need her help anyway. 'Oh, I don't think that kind of thing matters at all any more,' she commented mildly.

'No?'

She saw a disappointed look pass between the pair before Lydia tried a different tack.

'You do realise this is the first time Alessio's ever brought a woman here?' she continued.

'Yes, he told me.'

'I suppose it must be because Papa has relaxed the bedroom rule.'

'I have no idea,' said Nicola, her cheeks flushing in the darkness, and she wished Alessio would come back.

Lydia glanced down at Nicola's left hand. 'Does this mean it's serious? That our famous billionaire sibling has found himself a prospective bride at last? I must say, you weren't a bit what I was expecting, Nicola—given that he usually has a penchant for firecracker brunettes.'

Her critical gaze washed over Nicola, who now was now feeling washed-out and inadequate as she silently compared herself to the vibrant firecrackers.

'I don't usually date men like him either,' she answered evenly.

'So. Tell me a secret.' Lydia took another large mouthful of champagne. 'How on earth do you put up with him?'

'I'm… I'm not sure what you mean.'

'Oh, come on. Isn't he a little *ostentatious* about all his wealth? I keep reading about his plane and his priceless artworks and his high-tech factories. I mean, I'm assuming his PR team make sure they position all that stuff in the press to enhance his reputation, but really…it isn't a terribly *classy* thing to do to keep banging on about how much you own, is it?'

Her verbal demolition was followed by an insincere smile which was making Nicola feel distinctly queasy but suddenly all her own perceived insecurities began to fade in the light of the other woman's words, because they rankled. How dared Lydia be so rude about Alessio in front of someone she'd met for the first time? Yes, her own family might have been dragged up from the gutter, with several members choosing to remain there—but nobody could say they weren't loyal. They all had each other's backs. And suddenly, out of nowhere, came a fierce desire to defend him from his viper-mouthed half-sister. 'I can't imagine for a moment that your brother gets people to plug him or his possessions,' she deflected coolly. 'According to my boss, he's a notoriously private man who likes to keep his life *out* of the papers.'

'Maybe he's got a lot to hide?' suggested Sebastian, with a short laugh.

'Who cares what he wants to keep secret? That's everybody's right, surely? Anyway, maybe it should be the other way round,' Nicola continued doggedly. 'If you turn the question round—how on earth does he put up with *me*? You'll have to ask him. But to spare my blushes, perhaps you'd better not do it within my earshot.'

At that moment Lord Bonner arrived and dinner was announced, and Nicola was grateful to be led away from the toxic pair towards a table at the far end of the terrace, which was covered in gleaming silverware and sparkling crystal. Tall candles were flickering in the indigo dusk, fireflies were sparking their tiny golden flames and the scent of the starry jasmine flowers was perfuming the air. It looked like a scene from an advert, or a lifestyle magazine—but it was hard to appreciate anything because she could sense a terrible tension bubbling beneath the surface as she took her seat between Alessio and his mother.

And now her inexplicable reaction to his half-sister made Nicola's face grow warm. Had she felt the need to defend him because they'd shared that red-hot moment in the bedroom? Why else would it be? Had their physical closeness helped forge a new kind of bond? But his terse nod of greeting made it clear he didn't share any such feelings and so Nicola sought to lighten the atmosphere around the table which was, after all, what she was being paid to do.

She made small talk. She was good at that. She enthused about the delicious food, which was cooked by the family's resident chef and served by a variety of young women from the nearby village. She sipped a little fine wine—but not too much, knowing she needed all her resolve to line up those cushions later. She needed a similar resolve when first Lydia, and then Lord Bonner attempted to interrogate her about her background. But Nicola was a deft hand at batting away unwanted questions like these and couldn't help notice Alessio's lazy smile as she stonewalled them yet again.

Only once, before *the incident* occurred, which was to derail the whole evening, was she momentarily wrongfooted. A simple dessert of cherries and ice cream was being carried to the table on a silver platter to whoops of childish delight from Lydia and Sebastian, when Alessio's mother suddenly turned to her and asked in a low voice whether her son was happy.

Nicola didn't hesitate. She didn't say she suspected

Alessio di Bari was a man fundamentally incapable of happiness, because that was not the answer any mother wanted to hear. There were many different grades of lies, she thought fleetingly—and if there was such a thing, then this was a good one.

'He is,' she said softly, her heart clenching with guilt as the beautiful Italian matriarch gave a trembling smile in response.

'It was worth it, then,' she said.

But Nicola didn't have time to ponder the meaning behind Rosetta's sad words because an unknown guest had suddenly arrived in their midst, followed by a flustered-looking housekeeper. Surrounded by a miasma of cigarette smoke, a statuesque redhead in a tight white dress came to a halt at the far end of the table. She looked at each one of them in turn, leaving Lord Bonner until last. And then she smiled with the look of a starving predator who had just spotted a piece of glistening meat. There was a split second of silence while everyone stared at the glamorous intruder, and then all hell broke loose.

Nicola heard Rosetta gasp and thought Lydia's and Sebastian's eyes were going to pop out of their heads as their father rose to his feet and made his way towards the stunning intruder, like a man who was caught up in the midst of a powerful spell.

'Monica,' he said, but the shock in his aristocratic voice was underpinned with something which sounded remarkably like triumph. 'This is…unexpected.'

'I guess it is.' She lifted one bare, bronzed shoulder and shot him another vermillion smile. 'You always said you wanted to show me your Italian home, so here I am,' she drawled. 'Show me!'

But Alessio was on his feet, too, his face thunderous, his fists white-knuckled and clenched by his sides. He surveyed his stepfather with a mixture of disbelief and contempt as his mother began to quietly cry. 'Get her out of here. *Now,*' he snapped from between gritted teeth and his stepfather nodded, as if unwilling to confront the ire of his furious stepson.

Alessio watched the couple depart before turning to his sister. 'Take Mamma to her room,' he instructed. 'I'll be along to see her in a moment. And, Nicola, go and start packing, will you? We're leaving.'

Nicola gazed at him blankly—but what else could she do but obey? She waited until Lydia had taken her mother away and only Sebastian was left, having watched the drama unfold, his head turning this way and that, like a spectator at a tennis match.

'Long time coming,' he said, his posh accent unsteady as he picked up his wine glass and drained it in one.

'I wouldn't know,' answered Nicola coldly.

But it seemed surreal to be back upstairs, pulling out all her new and mostly unworn clothes and layering them back into the plush leather suitcase which had also been purchased for this trip. It seemed that her brief tenure as Alessio's paid companion had come to an abrupt end. All that angst about sharing a bed had come to nothing.

Taking off the fairy-tale dress, she pulled on a denim skirt and a shirt and walked over to the window, where the almost full moon had turned the landscape into something magical. But just like magic, none of this was real.

The silvery light hid the weeds and snakes which lived in the shadows of the gardens. The seeming perfection was flawed because there was no such thing as perfection. Not in places, nor in people, she reminded herself bitterly. Especially not in people.

She heard the door open and close and when she turned around she saw Alessio standing there, just inside the room, his hard body unmoving. And if she'd thought his expression had been forbidding earlier, that was nothing to the anger which harshened his stony features now. But she wasn't here to analyse or offer an opinion. Matter-of-factness was what he needed, which might remove some of the heat from the situation.

'So, what happens next?' she said calmly.

At the sound of her words, his eyes cleared, as if he had only just remembered he was not alone. 'Just that?' He gave a short laugh. 'No other questions?'

'It's none of my business,' she replied.

'You're not curious about why my stepfather was openly flaunting his mistress in front of his wife?'

She shrugged. 'Even if I was, surely that's irrelevant?'

'*Certo.* Totally irrelevant. But I applaud your attitude, Nicola. Not many women would have resisted the temptation to dig deeper. It's one of the things which made me realise you would be the ideal candidate for what I needed.' His gaze was speculative. 'Your coolness. Your...' He hesitated, as if he could not find the right word in either English or Italian. 'You are an enigma,' he said at last. 'And that's why I felt it safe to employ you.'

Nicola didn't know if she liked the sound of that. He made her sound like a robot, but at least his words reinforced the transactional aspect of their relationship. 'Which brings me back to my original question,' she said crisply. 'What do we do now?'

'We're leaving, of course. I want my mother to come with us, but she is refusing.'

'Can't you...insist?'

'Don't you think I've tried?' he demanded. 'But short of forcibly bundling her in the car, she's going nowhere. She's waiting for my father to "come to his senses".' He gave a bitter laugh. 'And I refuse to hang around to witness any more of her inevitable humiliation. Plus, if the truth were known, I don't trust myself not to hit him, and I am not a violent man.' In the moonlight, his eyes were shards of pure silver. 'Still no questions?' he added roughly.

As his narrowed gaze bored into her, Nicola shook her head. If he thought she was fascinated by his dysfunctional family, he was wrong. Didn't she have one of her own to worry about, which made his look like amateurs? She thought about Callum pacing his prison cell and pregnant Stacey, watching TV in her poky bedsit, and as she realised she had only 'worked' for one afternoon and evening, a wave of anxiety washed over her. Because what if all this had been for nothing?

The words came blurting out in a rush before she could stop them. 'Are you still intending to pay me?'

Did she imagine his look of distaste? No, she was pretty sure she did not—nor the sudden scorn in his voice.

'Oh, yes, Nicola. Have no fear. I will pay you in full.'

'And...we're flying back to England tonight?'

'Unfortunately, no. I've sent the plane back to England and I won't be able to get it back until Monday.'

'Why not?'

'Because I've lent it to my London secretary. Her mother has been sick and they're flying her to France for the weekend.' He shrugged. 'Tomorrow, I can arrange for a commercial airline to take you home—but for to-night, we're going to have to find somewhere to stay.'

Nicola glanced down at her watch, startled to discover it was almost midnight. She swallowed. 'You mean, find a hotel?'

'That would obviously be impossible at this time of year and night,' he returned coolly. 'Fortunately, a friend of mine, Khaled—he's a sheikh actually—has a property up in the hills. It's just over the border, in Tuscany, and it's empty at the moment.' The smile he glittered her was edged with steel. 'We can go there, if you like.'

If she *liked*?

As if she had a choice.

Nicola bit her lip, telling herself this was going to be hell on earth. But no matter how hard she tried, she couldn't deny her sudden flare of excitement as she con-templated spending a night alone with Alessio di Bari.

# CHAPTER SEVEN

SECURITY LIGHTS BLOOMED by their feet and sound of barking dogs echoed in the night air as they weaved their way through the cypress-scented grounds, towards a stone cottage. Punching out the code on the keypad, Alessio opened the door and stepped inside.

'What is this place?' Nicola asked as he flicked a switch and light flooded through the room, illuminating the bare walls and deceptively simple furniture.

Alessio's eyes narrowed. 'Not what you imagined?' he suggested sardonically.

Defensively, she shrugged. 'When you said your friend was a sheikh, I naturally assumed—'

'Something on more palatial lines?'

'Well, yes.'

He put their cases down, assaulted by a sudden stab of recognition as he looked around, for it was a long time since he had stayed somewhere as small as this. Everything was bespoke and high-end, as befitted a property owned by a billionaire sheikh—but there was only so much you could do with dimensions like these and suddenly the fragment of a memory whispered into his mind.

His grandmother's tiny flat above the shop in the village square. The smell of Altamura bread wafting up from the bakery, the steaming pot on the stove and the distant view of the mountains. But his grandmother had left this world all too soon and his heartbreaking farewell to her had made him determined never to let anyone get close to him again. The only woman he had loved and trusted had not been around to enjoy the fruits of his success, cruelly cut down by an illness which had ravaged her. Sorrow mingled with regret and he tensed, because that was the trouble with memory. It dragged you back to places you didn't want to visit.

With an effort he forced his attention back to the matter in hand and met the curious grey eyes of his reluctant companion. 'Khaled offered to have someone open up the main house for us,' he explained. 'But since it's full of priceless artworks and I didn't want security swarming everywhere, I opted for the converted shepherd's hut instead. It's small, but as you see it's supremely comfortable.' He slanted her a look of mocking challenge. 'Any objections?'

'Would there be any point in me objecting?'

'What do you think?'

'I don't imagine you'd like to know what I think.'

A low laugh rumbled from somewhere deep inside him. 'Do you know, I think I prefer you feisty to enigmatic?'

'Which would only be relevant if I were looking for your approval, which I'm not,' she said, glancing around the room like a trapped animal, trying to work out the nearest escape route. 'So why don't I have a look around to see what the rest of the accommodation has to offer?'

'Be my guest.'

Arrested by the peachy curve of her bottom, he watched as she ascended the narrow wooden staircase but returned almost as quickly, not managing to conceal her expression of...

He frowned. He couldn't quite put his finger on it. Was it dread? Maybe. But could dread co-exist with the flash of excitement, or was he simply reading what he wanted to see in her grey eyes?

'What's the matter?'

'Nothing,' she said flatly.

'Bad news on the sleeping front?'

'You could say that. There's…there's only one bedroom and only one bed.'

'Would it reassure you to know that I've spent the majority of my life having to fight women off, not the other way round?' he boasted, before adding softly, 'Control has never been an issue for me.'

He saw her bite her lip before turning her back on him.

'I'm going to investigate the kitchen,' she said. 'See if I can find some tea.'

'Or wine?' he suggested, stretching his arms above his head and stifling a yawn. 'It's been a long day.'

Alessio sank down onto the small but sumptuous sofa before punching out a text to Lydia. He barely heard from his half-sister from one year to the next, and that suited him just fine, but it added to the already bizarre nature of the evening to see her reply come winging straight back.

Mamma's asleep now. Papa and that woman have gone to the gatehouse. You should have stayed, Alessio, you know you should.

Why was that? he wondered cynically. So that she and her brother could abdicate all responsibility while continuing to display their resentment towards him at all times? But a lifetime of deliberately blanking their vitriol made him reply with restraint.

He wrote back.

Whatever you need, let me know. Tell her to speak to my lawyers in the morning.

It was a forlorn hope. But as he slid his phone back into his pocket he found himself thinking about Nicola again, unable to shift the serene image of her face from his memory. Those icy eyes and pale hair and that shuttered way she had of looking at him. Was it her cool attitude which had so captured his imagination, or the erotic flame which had scorched his senses during that single kiss?

The tension between them had been escalating as they had driven through the Tuscan hills, the unmistakable weight of sexual awareness hanging heavy in the air. Surely she must have felt it, too—as tangible as the heat of his blood and fierce beat of his heart. He had waited for some kind of acknowledgement—the subtle brushing of her arm against his perhaps—but she had just stared in silence at the darkened Italian countryside, keeping firmly to her side of the car.

His leant his head back and closed his eyes. He had offered her this job because he'd known she would be perfect for it, but now he recognised there had been more to it than that. She intrigued him. Her aloof manner turned him on—and she had spiked a powerful surge of desire which had lain dormant for so long. But he had meant what he'd said. Control had never been an issue. Just because he wanted to have sex with Nicola Bennett, didn't mean he was going to, for wouldn't that create more trouble than it was worth?

Yet here, in this upmarket cottage with nothing but the velvety darkness outside, he could feel reason being defeated by the irresistible lure of arousal. He couldn't stop thinking about the way she'd kissed him, or the musky scent of her desire perfuming the air as his fingers had explored her. His throat thickened as he remembered the way she had parted her soft thighs and remembered, too, his idiocy in ignoring that silent invitation. Like some old-fashioned fool he had insisted she open her eyes and look at him. He had wanted her to acknowledge him and say his name—as if that actually *mattered*. And he had broken the enchantment. He had been left hard and full, and frustrated.

Just as he was now.

So deep was he in uncomfortable thought that he didn't hear Nicola return and when he looked up, she was placing a bottle of wine on the streamlined table, along with a single glass and a steaming mug.

'Here,' she said, pushing the bottle and corkscrew towards him.

'You aren't going to join me?'

She shook her head and pointed towards her tea, her voice faintly repressive. 'I'm fine, thanks.'

She sat down beside him, though he noticed that she perched as far away as possible, and he watched as she bent to remove her espadrilles, his gaze inexplicably drawn to her unvarnished toenails.

The wine was good but failed to relax him—and since Nicola's silence provided nothing in the way of diversion, Alessio couldn't stop going back over the evening. The ugliness of his stepfather's triumphant expression and his mother's inevitable tears. Had the festering sore at the centre of their marriage burst open at last, spilling all its poison? he wondered bitterly.

'Why the hell do women put up with toxic relationships?' he demanded suddenly, but naturally Miss Cool didn't react. She just tipped her head to one side and considered his question, as if he'd made a benign enquiry about the weather.

'Usually because they're poor and can't afford to escape.'

Was it her total lack of curiosity which made him pursue the subject further? Or the anger still simmering inside him which needed some kind of outlet? 'My mother isn't poor,' he said flatly. 'If she walked out of that farce of a marriage tomorrow, she'd get a large enough settlement to enable her to live in relative luxury for the rest of her life. Even if she didn't, I'd be happy enough to fund her lifestyle.'

'Maybe she's afraid of being lonely?'

'You think cruelty is preferable to loneliness?' he snapped.

Nicola met the angry blaze of his eyes, taken aback by the brutal candour of his questions, though this wasn't the first time such a thing had happened. Sometimes people came into the gallery and let slip the most extraordinary things and she'd often wondered if it was because power-ful billionaires had so few people they could confide in that they turned to her. Or whether it was a consequence of her ability to fade into the background—to be quiet and invisible—a convenient sounding board.

Yet this wasn't an anonymous patron, venting his spleen. She was here because she was being paid. She and Alessio were trapped together miles from anywhere and, because she was far from indifferent to him and all that brooding sexuality, she needed to put some kind of boundaries in place. She ought to return to that perfect little kitchen on the pretext of making more tea—in the hope he might stop asking these harsh and bitter questions.

But the pain which had hardened his brilliant eyes was difficult to ignore, and a lifetime of trying to fix other people made Nicola want to reach out to him, even though every instinct warned her not to.

'Talking can sometimes be cathartic,' she observed slowly.

Frustratedly, he shook his head. 'I should never have brought you here and subjected you to such a damned mess.'

She put her cup down on the table and looked at him. 'Why *is* it such a mess?'

There was a pause. 'Because my stepfather is a bully who gets his kicks from humiliating people—women in particular, though he isn't averse to hurting children.'

'So why...?' She bit her lip, wondering if he was talk-ing about himself. 'Why does she stay?'

'Why *do* women stay? I've asked myself the same

question all my life—only to come away with the same sense of incomprehension and frustration every time.' His eyes glittered. 'And now the visit for which you have prepared so carefully has been cut short and you find yourself in the unfortunate position of being marooned in the middle of the Italian countryside.'

'That much is true,' Nicola agreed slowly, wishing she could obliterate some of the pain etched upon his beautiful face. She glanced out of the window, where she could see the silvery wash of moonlight glimmering on a distant swimming pool. 'I could think of worse places to get marooned in.'

'What, even with a man you despise?'

Nicola met the taunting question in his eyes, knowing there was plenty about Alessio di Bari *not* to like. He infuriated her with his arrogance and high-handedness, yes, but she remained overwhelmingly attracted to him. She had taken on this bizarre job in order to help her feckless brother and his girlfriend, but something had happened along the way. Something she hadn't planned. With a single kiss the Italian billionaire had changed her, just like that. He had put a match to the bonfire of her senses and set them on fire, branding erotic images on her mind which wouldn't seem to go away.

The slow graze of his fingers creeping up towards her panties.

She swallowed.

The silken throb of her sex as she silently prayed for him to touch her more intimately…

Was it that blissful but ultimately frustrating experience which made her flirt with him, or just a desire to shake off all her responsibilities for once, and see what happened?

'I wouldn't say,' she offered, as lightly as she could, 'that I actually *despised* you.'

At first she thought he hadn't been listening, or had chosen to ignore her words. But when he looked at her... Nicola's heart missed a beat. When he *looked* at her, the pain in his face had become transmuted into something else. Something raw, and sensual and hungry.

'I want to kiss you,' he said, his voice thick. 'That's all I can think about right now. I want to blot out the world and ravish those delicious lips of yours. I want to carry on what we started this afternoon, Nicola—only this time I don't want to stop.'

It was the boldest thing anyone had ever said to her and as the silken heat of sexual awareness whispered over her skin again, Nicola felt dizzy with desire. It was weird. She felt lost and found, all at the same time. But it wasn't just her physical reaction which was so disorientating—it was the accompanying flutter of her thoughts. The absolute certainty that *this* was why she had waited all these years before having sex. Had she known on some subliminal level that Alessio di Bari was going to walk into her life and there was no way she would have wanted anyone but him to be her first lover?

But that was crazy thinking, from a woman who should have known better. If she wanted him, she mustn't frighten him away. She mustn't behave like every other woman in her family by being needy, or desperate. He had said he liked her because she was cool. Wouldn't he be appalled if he knew the real person who existed behind the serene exterior she had so carefully cultivated? The product of one of London's roughest estates, who was still a *virgin*?

She mustn't tell him that either, because she suspected that a man with his degree of experience would be horrified to learn how innocent she was.

But he's going to find out anyway…and then how is he going to react?

She didn't care.

*She didn't care about anything right then.*

Nicola reached out to touch the hard curve of his jaw, revelling in the rough rasp of new growth which brushed against her palm. Let her—and him—cross that bridge when they came to it. Hadn't she spent her whole life doing things for other people? The only reason she was here was because her brother had got himself into trouble yet again. Why *shouldn't* she have something for herself for once, even if it only lasted one night?

'So go ahead. Kiss me,' she urged, hoping she didn't sound like a faltering novice.

He took the hand which was still resting against his jaw and lifted it to his lips, taking each finger inside his mouth and sucking it. It managed to be innocuous and intensely erotic and Nicola gasped when he drew his mouth away. 'Oh,' she said, and he gave a slow smile as he heard the note of disappointment in her voice.

'I want to undress you. Very, very slowly. But not here. Not on the floor, or on that undersized sofa like a couple of teenagers with no place to go. I want you upstairs, Nicola,' he commanded. 'Now.'

'Okay,' she agreed, as if she regularly received such

propositions—trying to blot out her sudden rush of nerves. Her heart was pounding as he led her upstairs and she wondered why he was sounding almost *mechanical*. As if this were more about technique than feelings. As if he took part in this kind of detached seduction all the time.

Did he?

Nicola swallowed. Of course he did—and that was fact, not conjecture on her part. He might try his best to lead a private life but the Internet was full of stories about his conquests—women who were the polar opposite of her. The firecracker brunettes Lydia had spoken about. Women who had everything, while she had nothing.

Shouldn't that be enough to make her have second thoughts?

Probably. Especially as they had now reached the bedroom and all it symbolised. She stood on the threshold of the room, uncertain what to do, staring across the room at the neatly made bed, covered with exquisite white linen. The sunset was nothing but a memory and bright moonlight was streaming in through the unshuttered windows, coating everything in molten silver. But Alessio's expression was unreadable as he stared down into her face, and Nicola held her breath as she gazed up at him.

Had the journey upstairs been long enough to make him question the wisdom of what they were about to do? Had the billionaire financier suddenly realised he was about to have sex with ordinary Nicky Bennett and she was the last woman he should be holding in his arms?

But then he bent his head to hers and that first touch of his lips was enough to make her senses explode.

Oh, God.

She shivered.

It was like everything she'd read about, only this was for real.

Fire rippled through her veins, warm heat making her dissolve. Her breasts felt as if they were going to burst right out of her shirt and her tummy was tightening. She wanted to touch him. To feel him, and taste him. His arms slid around her waist and as she opened her mouth to him and swayed a little, she thought she felt him smile against her lips.

Should she be more restrained than this? More like the person she was supposed to be? Cool, unflappable Nicola Bennett who never let anything get to her?

But she couldn't.

And neither, it would appear, could he.

Wasn't Alessio di Bari supposed to be the self-professed master of control and wasn't he supposed to be undressing her *very, very slowly*? So why were buttons flying off her shirt so rapidly that she could hear them bouncing their way across the bedroom floor? Her shirt flew open and he slid it from her shoulders, letting it flutter to the ground in a silken whisper. He stared down at her, his eyes narrowed and smoky as her breasts strained towards him, pushing furiously against the black lace.

'Now that,' he murmured, 'is an invitation I can't refuse.'

He bent his head to trail his lips over her breasts and she tipped her head back.

*'Ohh...'* Nicola moaned as his teeth expertly grazed over the lace-covered nipples. Was that really her voice

she could hear? She was being so uncharacteristically loud. So *vocal* and *uninhibited*. But that was her last rational thought, because Alessio was undoing the buttons of her denim skirt and it was concertinaing to the ground, so that she was left wearing nothing but her bra and knickers.

'You are even more beautiful than I imagined,' he husked, his gaze raking over her silky black panties, slung low on her hips.

'I'm not.'

'Yes, you are,' he contradicted, tilting his chin so that their gazes were locked on a collision course. 'I'm not going to tell you any lies tonight, Nicola Bennett.' His lips hardened, his eyes gleaming cold in the moonlight— as steely as the sudden edge to his next words. 'Even if at times you might wish that I did.'

# CHAPTER EIGHT

'I'M NOT GOING *to tell you any lies tonight.'*

Alessio's words echoed round the bedroom and set faint alarm bells ringing but Nicola ignored them. All she could think about was this. *This.* She was going to have sex for the first time, after a lifetime of never having been interested before. She'd never even been alone in a bedroom with a man before yet she didn't feel in the least bit shy, despite being almost naked. How could she feel shy, when Alessio was gazing at her like that—the way she'd seen him look at pictures in her boss's gallery, his brilliant eyes smoky with appreciation?

Yet he still had his clothes on and she wasn't sure what to do next. What was the dress code—or rather, the *undress* code? Should she be touching *him*? She was terrified of messing up, of betraying her woeful inexperience—of disappointing, not just him, but herself. Because she'd waited too long to want to screw this up.

But surely she was capable of removing his shirt with some degree of skill. Sliding her fingers over his silk-covered chest, she started popping tiny buttons open. His torso tensed and she could hear his ragged breathing as she undid the shirt in silence, to reveal all the hard, silken flesh beneath. The garment whispered from his shoulders, joining her own on the floor before she bent her lips to his nipple, just as he had done to her.

'Nicola,' he said unsteadily as she circled the nub of puckered flesh with the flick of her tongue.

That sounded like approval, she thought, and was just about to turn her attention to the other one when he tangled his fingers in her hair and tipped her head back so that their eyes were locked on a collision course.

'No. Not like this,' he grated, his breathing still heavy.

Her heart beat with anxiety. 'Is something wrong?'

'Don't ask disingenuous questions,' he reprimanded sternly. 'I want you horizontal. I want to see all that golden hair spread over my pillow.'

He picked her up—he actually *picked her up*—and carried her over to the bed, laying her down on top of it so that she could watch as he undressed. His hand was moving to his zip and Nicola felt a sudden lump in her throat at the thought of seeing an aroused man for the first time in her life. But she wasn't going to waste a second with nerves or shyness, because sex was a natural part of life. She remembered the woman in the painting at the gallery—the way her face had been flushed with sensuality and satisfaction, and she wanted that, too.

She watched Alessio remove his trousers to reveal the silky boxer shorts but couldn't hold back her faint exclamation when she saw the formidable length of his erection—so pale and proud against his dark olive skin. It ran the risk of betraying her inexperience, but the strangled sound seemed to give him immense satisfaction, because he smiled as he came over to the bed and pulled her against his warm flesh.

'Yes, I am big,' he said, quite seriously, as his hardness pressed against her stomach. Reaching inside her panties, he brushed a featherlight fingertip over her quivering flesh. 'But you are so wet. So ready for me. I will not hurt you, Nicola.'

Nicola responded by covering his mouth with kisses and his laugh was low as he unclipped her bra, her breasts tumbling out into his waiting hands. And now he was sliding off her panties and she didn't know how much she could take as he continued to stroke her, with that barely-there touch of his finger.

'Please,' she whimpered as he increased the speed of his movements, making her soar towards something nebulous and sweet. 'Please...'

A spiral of intense pleasure was twisting inside her, like a wire being tightened and tightened and yet still it wasn't enough. When she writhed impatiently, he increased the pressure—fingering the slick flesh until she didn't think she could bear any more. And then suddenly she broke free, crying out her disbelief as she clung to him. As her body began to clench, her last rational thought right then was that he held her completely in his power and that, worryingly, she *liked* it. It didn't make her feel weak—it made her feel strong. Stronger than she'd ever felt before.

'Wow,' he murmured, after a moment, his lips drifting across her head to bury themselves in her hair. 'Who knew that the cool Miss Bennett could be so responsive?'

Through her blissful haze, Nicola felt him pull away from her. 'Oh,' she objected, in a heavy, slurred voice.

'This part is vital, *cara*. But don't worry. I won't be long.'

Nicola watched as he removed a condom from his discarded jeans and a feeling of horror swept over her as she realised she hadn't even checked whether he'd been carrying protection. What if he hadn't? Would she still have let him go ahead? The terrible thought swam into her mind that, yes, she *actually thought she might*—and the irony of that didn't escape her. Was she, who had always been so critical of other people's failings when it came to unprotected sex, not quite as strong-minded as she'd always considered herself to be?

But now all she could think about was the naked man who was getting back into bed, his powerful limbs gleaming in the moonlight. Restlessly, she writhed as he stroked on the protection, his mercurial eyes glinting with provocation.

'Impatience isn't a trait I would have associated with you,' he murmured.

It wasn't a trait she would have associated with herself, but all Nicola's usual certainties seemed to have vanished. He moved over her, his warm weight pinning her against the mattress, and as she tilted her hips in silent invitation it became important that she acknowledge him. To do something she had consciously refused to do before, for reasons which now seemed insane. As the blunt tip of his erection brushed against her molten heat, she gazed up into the charcoaled silver of his features and her heart pounded.

'Alessio,' she said unsteadily.

His eyes narrowed as if he had recognised the significance of the word.

'That's the first time you've ever said my name,' he observed.

As she nodded, his palm curved around her hip, anchoring it with careless possession. 'Had you been waiting for such a moment as this, Nicola?' he murmured. 'Is this all it would have taken? If I'd done this to you sooner, would you have whispered it? If I'd locked the gallery door and pulled you into the back room and taken you up against the wall behind that bronze statue, with your panties around your ankles, would you have said my name then?'

If she'd been hoping for romance it seemed she was to be disappointed, but somehow the Italian's gritted words were turning her on even more. So that what was intended to be a protest at his audaciousness came out as a shuddered repetition of his name and his own moan sounded almost helpless as he entered her.

And Nicola realised that he *had* lied to her, because it *did* hurt. He was so big and she was so tight that she couldn't hold back her startled gasp of pain. She saw Alessio's smile disappear, his look of disbelief turning into one of grim recognition, and for one awful moment she wondered if he was going to stop and she would never know what it was like. The fleeting thought occurred to her that she might die without ever making love properly.

But he didn't stop.

He just carried on, but now his movements seemed governed by deliberation, rather than the mindless passion of before. Little by little, he eased himself further into her body and little by little her muscles stretched to accommodate him, until he had buried himself so deeply it felt as if he were touching her heart.

His thrusts were slow and careful and despite it being the most amazing thing which had ever happened to her, she was aware of him watching her. As if he were an observer rather than a participant. Did that matter? Even if it did, Nicola was powerless to fight what was happening as sensation began to bombard her. Did he realise she was close to that mindless release all over again? Was that why he increased his rhythm, so that she was caught up in a frenzy of excitement?

'Alessio,' she whimpered, as wave after wave of bliss swamped her.

Only this time he wasn't listening—he was too intent on his own pleasure. His eyes were closed and his hard features shuttered as his body shuddered out its own release. She lay beneath him, trying to recover her breath along with her composure—but that wasn't easy when Alessio was still pulsing inside her. But this was exactly where she wanted him. She wanted him to stay inside her for ever.

Yet something was urging her to reclaim some of the power she had acceded to him and she sucked in a deep breath of resolve. Everything Nicola had learned in life had been by observing other people's reactions, because she didn't trust her own not to let her down. But if this silence continued much longer, she would start to fill it with her own worst imaginings. Or his. She didn't want him worrying that she was going to regard this as a big deal and reminded herself that she wasn't some hapless little victim. She had come into this with her eyes wide open—well, not all the time, obviously—and Alessio needed to know that.

'Are you disappointed?' she questioned slowly.

'Am I *disappointed*?' He pulled away and frowned. 'Wow. I've been asked a lot of questions after sex, Nicola—but that one is definitely a first.'

'How reassuring to discover that I can be original, even if I am just one of a crowd!'

Her cool words washed over him and Alessio felt a mixture of amusement and curiosity. Usually, he couldn't wait to roll off a woman's body and distance himself, yet for once he wanted to stay buried in her silken sweetness. But since avoiding pregnancy was the most important consideration of all, he carefully withdrew before turning back, his body tightening as he surveyed the wildness of her blonde hair spreading over the pillow, just like every fantasy he'd ever had about her. He tried—and failed—to reconcile the unflappable Nicola Bennett with the sweet virgin who had given him her innocence. He wondered why she had chosen to frame her question so negatively, instead of gushing out the breathless praise which always fell on his ears at such a moment.

Because the sex had been exceptional. Even for him. No, especially for him, he conceded reluctantly. Her swift transformation from ice to fire had first surprised him, then blown his mind. He had been entranced by her. He could never remember feeling so exquisitely aroused as when he had pushed into her molten heat. But there had been another surprise waiting...and Alessio was a man who was rarely surprised—especially in the bedroom. 'Why on earth would I be disappointed?' he drawled.

'Isn't it obvious?' There was a pause, which he had no intention of filling, before she gave an awkward shrug. 'Because I didn't tell you—'

'That you were a virgin?'

She nodded.

Alessio nodded. This kind of analysis was abhorrent to him, but she *was* inexperienced and maybe he needed to take that into account. It was better to ensure she wasn't harbouring any hopes which could never be realised—at least, not by him. He had been accused of many things by women—but falsely dangling the prospect of happily-ever-after had never been among them. But then, he'd never had sex with a virgin before. His heart missed a heavy beat. Nor expected to enjoy it quite so much.

'That would only be a problem if it were significant,' he drawled. 'If, for example, you thought I was so blown away by your innocence—which, incidentally, I was— that I would immediately demand you marry me. Well, then, *sì*, I would be disappointed. And so would you, for that matter, *cara*, because that's not going to happen. Not now, not ever.'

'Let me guess…because every woman you go to bed with is desperate to get your ring on her finger?'

Unapologetically, he shrugged. 'This I cannot deny.'

'Which I suppose implies that having a colossal ego must top the list of most women's marital requirements?'

He gave a slow smile. 'I don't think it's the size of my ego which accounts for my popularity with the opposite sex, *cara*.'

'Oh!'

He could feel waves of indignation radiating towards him, meshing with the far more tangible ripples of desire which were making him want to kiss her again. Tangling his fingers in the silky ropes of her hair, he pulled her towards him and her lips trembled as he grazed his own against them. 'Stop focussing on the unimportant,' he instructed huskily.

'I suppose you're going to tell me what *is* important?'

'You know damned well what's important.'

'How can I, when this is the first time I've ever done this?'

'Then why don't I tell you? Hmm? I want to be inside you again. I want to fill you completely until you can feel nothing else but me. I want to hear you cry my name when you come, like you did just now. That breathless little moan which seemed to go on for ever.' His voice dipped. 'Don't you want that, too, Nicola?'

She blinked at him—as if she couldn't believe quite how explicit he was being, but her eyes were wide and dark, the words rushing from her lips, as if she couldn't hold them back any longer. 'Yes. Yes, I do,' she whispered. 'I want that very much.'

This time he touched her with a deliberate lack of speed, though never had his control been quite so tested. Not a single inch of her flesh did he leave unexplored—first by his fingers and then his lips. Her body was so streamlined, he thought hungrily. So...*perfect*. He watched as her nipples hardened into silver bullets in the moonlight. He stroked his fingertips over soft, slender thighs which parted for him, and when he placed his mouth against her silken core, he could taste her honeyed musk.

As she whimpered beneath the flicker of his tongue, he could feel something unfamiliar—an alien sensation which rolled over him like a heavy wave and threatened to pull him under. Dampening down his own needs, he concentrated solely on hers, but by the time she pulsed helplessly beneath his tongue Alessio could deny himself no longer. His hands were unsteady as he eased on a condom and thrust into her waiting heat. Had he ever been this hard before? he wondered dazedly. Had he ever buried himself so deeply in a woman that it was difficult to know where he ended and she started? Pleasure caught him in a ruthless vice and his cry was wild as the seed pumped from his body.

He must have fallen asleep—unheard of—because when he opened his eyes, the milky wash of a golden dawn was lighting the horizon. Her skin and hair gilded by the rising sun, Nicola was lying on the far edge of the bed with her back to him, but her posture told him she was awake. And even though he had convinced himself he didn't care enough to pursue this particular topic, he broke the rule of a lifetime by doing exactly that.

'So why?' he questioned, stretching his arms above his head and giving a lazy yawn.

Nicola had been lying there wide-eyed while Alessio slept, preparing her answers for questions like these, like an ambitious pupil swotting for an exam. She turned to face him, unable to prevent the instant clutch of desire on seeing him naked against the snowy bedding.

The most important thing she needed to remember was

that this fling was going nowhere—and not just because he lived in Manhattan and she in London. Or because he was an eligible billionaire and she nothing but a glorified shopgirl. There wasn't going to be any kind of future for a couple like them, so why spoil what they had now with harsh reality? He wasn't really interested in her sexual history, or, indeed, any kind of history. He was probably only asking to be polite, or to pass the time. After all, they had to talk about *something* in between orgasms.

So she pushed away the kittenish mood which seemed to have crept up on her, the one which wanted to purr that she'd been waiting all her life for a man like him. Imagine how that would go down!

'You mean, why was I a virgin?' she verified slowly. 'Or why did I choose you?'

'Both.'

She didn't miss the brief nod of his head—as if her measured response was reassuring, making her think she'd pitched it just right. All she needed to do was to convince him that she wasn't going to read too much into this. 'I guess I was too busy with my career to have any time for men,' she answered truthfully, but didn't elaborate. She didn't tell him she'd been determined to avoid the social norms of the run-down estate where she'd been brought up, where relationships meant bust-ups and money problems. Bruised eyes and unplanned pregnancies. Or to tell him that her independence was vital to her and she was determined to never rely on men as her mother had done.

*Because none of those things were relevant.*

'You haven't answered the second part,' he observed.

Nicola hesitated. Neither was she going to tell him he was the most gorgeous man she'd ever met and it would have been easier to have stopped breathing than to have resisted his kiss. Would he be appalled to learn that she had melted a little to discover he'd lent his plane to his secretary for her sick mother? Probably. He might even accuse her of sentimentality, because lending a plane would mean nothing to a man like him. She could also confess that her heart had gone out to him after witnessing those awful scenes at his mother's house, but he might interpret that as pity. And Nicola despised pity— a smug emotion she'd been subjected to often enough in the past.

So she swept her fingers back through her tousled hair and told him a different type of truth—a statement she wouldn't have dreamed of sharing twenty-four hours ago. But what was the point of being naked in bed with someone if you couldn't say some of the things which were on your mind?

'Obviously, as time went on and everyone was—'

'Falling by the wayside?' he mocked.

'I wasn't making any moral judgements!' she answered quietly. 'But as I saw more and more of my friends having sex, I started wondering if I was missing out. I suppose I decided I needed a bit of an…an education.'

He still wasn't reacting.

'I w-wanted to find out if it lived up to all the hype,' she concluded, her stumbled words filling the awkward silence. 'That's all.'

'That's all,' he echoed, fixing her with a curious gaze. She saw the cold calculation which entered his eyes and wondered if she'd imagined his fleeting look of disappointment.

'And was it as good as you thought it was going to be?'

'Even better!' she said, with a rare fervour, and he laughed.

'You know, you really are turning out to be something of a surprise, Nicola Bennett,' he murmured. 'You make me want to do it to you all over again.'

'And what's…what's stopping you?' she questioned, with shy bravado.

'Nothing. In fact, I intend making love to you for as long as possible.' Pushing a handful of hair away from her face, he guided her hand towards one hair-roughened thigh. 'Though if you're still intending to catch that commercial flight in the morning, it's going to eat into the time we have together.' Curling her fingers around his growing erection, he pressed his lips to her ear. 'So why don't you stay on a little longer?'

# CHAPTER NINE

OF *COURSE* NICOLA didn't catch the commercial flight the next morning. Instead she eked out every last moment with the Italian billionaire. For two days and three nights, Alessio gave her a taste of paradise—there was no other way to describe it—and she wasn't someone with an overactive imagination. Yet even in her wildest dreams she had never imagined sex could be like this, or that she was capable of experiencing such pleasure, over and over again.

'You know—you are very, very good,' Alessio growled at one point, when she was straddling him on the very sofa they had rejected as too small the previous evening.

'You almost make that sound like a complaint,' she murmured, the experimental thrust of her hips making him groan helplessly.

'*Dio.* Are you out of your mind?' His smoky sapphire gaze burned into her. 'You are an exceptionally fast learner, Nicola.'

Yes. She always had been. It had been one of the things which had helped her leave her humble beginnings behind. And one of the first things she'd learnt was always keep your expectations realistic. So that when Alessio captured her lips and she shattered into pieces yet again, she didn't start imagining what this would be like on a permanent basis. Because that was never going to happen. None of this was real. She didn't really know him and he didn't know her. She didn't want him to. She was having fun in this delicious vacuum. She had pushed her worries about Stacey and the baby and her brother's release from her mind. She had left her cares back in England. Why shouldn't she enjoy this sense of freedom and this brand-new version of herself?

Which was why she kept her face impassive as their plane began its descent towards London and Alessio told her of his plans.

'As soon as we land, I'm afraid I'm going to have to leave you. I have a business meeting in the city.' There was a pause. 'And tomorrow I must fly back to the States.'

'That's okay.' Nicola smiled reassuringly. 'No worries.'

His sapphire eyes had narrowed. 'You're sure?'

What did he imagine she was going to do? she wondered caustically. Cling to his ankles and refuse to let go, just because they'd spent the last forty-eight hours having non-stop sex in the beautiful Italian countryside?

*And isn't that what you'd secretly like to do—hold onto him and never let him go? Aren't you going to miss those long days and nights, with Alessio feeding you scraps of delicious food which had been delivered every morning by some unseen servant of his rich sheikh mate?*

'I think I'll just about be able to cope,' she offered wryly.

His answering look conveyed both surprise and approval and Nicola realised that her refusal to try to pin him down was one of the things which made her attractive to him. He was a man who liked the chase, she recognised. An alpha male. A hunter. Maybe it was that which prompted his next drawled statement.

'But I'm going to be in London next week,' he said.

She wondered if he could hear the fierce beating of her heart as she attempted not to sound too delighted. Or too eager. 'Oh, yeah?'

Reluctantly, Alessio removed his hand from where it had been resting deliciously on her knee. There it was again—that familiar indifference. But whereas before her attitude had irritated him, now he was finding it beguiling. It added to her considerable allure and it was turning him on. In fact, *she* was turning him on, just by sitting there. He sucked in an unsteady breath. *Especially* by sitting there, with the sunlight streaming in through the aircraft window and transforming her hair into a shimmering cascade of gold.

He had planned to bid her a civilised farewell once they landed. Maybe give the Mayfair gallery a swerve for a while—at least until things had calmed down, which would obviously be the most sensible outcome. He'd even contemplated sending her something as a memento, because what woman didn't appreciate a new piece of jewellery? Grey diamonds, perhaps—to match her remarkable eyes. But now that the moment of parting had arrived, he was curiously reluctant to end things. At least, just yet.

As she gazed back at him with that unruffled expression, he found himself wanting to shatter her composure.

To see her come apart in his arms. He hadn't yet had enough of her, he realised hungrily. Not nearly enough.

'Why don't I take you out for dinner some time?' he said.

The pause which followed would surely have insulted any man—but especially a man who was unused to being kept waiting. But eventually, she inclined her head in a manner which was almost regal. 'Okay. Call me.'

*Call me?* Alessio could feel the urgent beat of his pulse and wondered if she was playing games with him. Didn't she realise he was aching so much right now that he wanted to dismiss the crew and tiptoe his fingers up her leg and push her panties aside, and…

'Alessio?' She was looking at him, mild concern in her eyes. 'Is something wrong? You almost look as if you're in pain.'

'Nothing's wrong,' he growled. 'I'll get my driver to drop you off at home.'

'No, honestly, I'll get the Tube.'

'I *said*, my driver will drop you off,' he repeated, with an impatient frown. 'There's a chauffeur-driven car at your disposal. Why do you have a problem accepting a simple favour, Nicola?'

Nicola wondered what he would say if she told him. If she explained she was frightened of getting used to this way of living. To his fancy cars and private jets. To *him*. Because wouldn't that make it harder to deal with when it ended—as end it must? She touched the sleeve of her silk dress, her fingertips whispering over the delicate fabric. So many beautiful garments which had gone un-worn because they'd spent almost every moment naked.

And he had paid for them, she remembered guiltily. He had clothed her from head to foot. Did that make her beholden to him in some way? 'What shall I do with the clothes?' she said.

He frowned. 'You keep them, of course. What else would you do with them?' His phone began to ring and, although he didn't pick up, he gestured towards the cabin door—clearly eager to get away. 'Come on. Let's go.'

At the foot of the aircraft, he deposited a brief, hard kiss on her lips, before opening the door of one of the waiting cars for her. She turned to see him slide into a second vehicle and lift his hand in a gesture of farewell as it pulled away. But he didn't look back, she noticed. His dark head was bent. He was already busy with something. A powerful man with more on his mind than a casual, sexual fling.

Despite his insistence, Nicola had the car drop her off at the nearest Tube station, and despite the driver's protestations that his boss had ordered him to deliver her directly to her front door. But that was the last thing she wanted. Alessio didn't have her address and that was how she wanted to keep it.

'I won't tell if you don't tell,' she said with a conspiratorial smile before ducking into the entrance of the London underground. Once home, she changed into jeans and a T-shirt and went round to see Stacey—panicking slightly when her brother's girlfriend regarded her with dull eyes. Weren't pregnant women supposed to be all glowing with health, with bouncing hair and bright eyes? The tiny bedsit felt stuffy in the oppressive summer heat and Nicola opened up all the windows before making a pot of ginger tea.

'I've got the money,' she announced, emerging from the poky bathroom, which she had briefly spritzed.

Stacey's face was sullen. 'Can't I have it now?'

'The thing is that it's supposed to be for you *and* the baby.' Nicola smiled encouragingly. 'So why don't we go looking for a new place together and you can plan your new home for when Callum is released?'

Stacey shrugged. 'S'pose.'

In a way, it was a relief for Nicola to get back to work and a routine which didn't give her a lot of time to think. By day she worked at the gallery and in the evenings she and Stacey checked out accommodation. Some options were way better than others, but by the following week they had found a clean, modern flat close to a nursery and park. With the proceeds of her Tuscan weekend, they bought a crib, bedding and a stack of tiny baby clothes, which were stored in the brand-new chest of drawers which Nicola managed to put together herself, even though the instructions were pretty incomprehensible. She visited her brother in prison and showed him pictures of the new place, and for the first time in a long time she saw him smile. He gave her a beautiful little wooden teddy bear he had carved in one of his rehabilitation classes, and asked her to give it to Stacey.

The relentless activity kept her days filled and she was often so tired when she went to bed at night that she fell asleep as soon as her head hit the pillow. But there was only so much displacement therapy she could do before the questions she'd buried in the recesses of her mind started to nag away at her.

Alessio had said he would see her this week and she hadn't heard from him.

Of course she hadn't. Was she a complete idiot? The sex had been convenient because they'd been trapped in a remote Italian cottage, but now he was back in his Manhattan playground and able to date his preferred movie star, or model—why *would* he bother contacting her? It had just been a polite way of saying goodbye.

On the plus side, she sold four paintings in quick succession and Sergio told her she was a genius.

'Hiring you was the smartest move I ever made,' he said thoughtfully. 'And the most incredible thing is that you're entirely self-taught.'

'Thanks,' she answered serenely.

But then, Alessio rang. A number she didn't recognise flashed onto her screen and every instinct she possessed urged her to let it go to voicemail.

She picked it up. 'Hello.'

'Nicola.'

She closed her eyes, an unsteady sigh escaping her lungs. How could that single word—that velvety version of her name—make heat instantly rush to her breasts like this? 'Alessio,' she said huskily.

'Ah! For a moment there I thought you were going to pretend you didn't recognise my voice.'

'And why would I do that?'

'Isn't feigned disinterest supposed to keep a man *on his toes*?' he mocked.

'Since we've already established that the sum of my experience with men could be written on the back of a postage stamp—how do you honestly expect me to answer that question?'

He laughed. 'I'll be in London on Friday.' He paused. 'Are you going to have dinner with me?'

Oh, God. Just the thought of it was making her pulse skyrocket. She caught a glimpse of her reflection and saw the huge, almost wild darkening of her eyes. Did he have this power over *all* women? she wondered helplessly. Could he make their bodies melt with desire, just by exchanging a few careless words on the telephone?

*Tell him you're busy. Tell him there's no point. Remind him that you live on opposite sides of a huge ocean.*

'Sure,' she said casually. 'I'll have dinner with you. Text me a time and a place and I'll meet you there, same as last time.'

He gave a sigh. 'Must we really go through this cat-and-mouse routine again, Nicola?'

She heard the faint impatience in his voice but had no intention of budging, because she needed to keep fantasy and real life separate. She *had* to. Because what if he wanted to come back to her place after dinner, to stay the night? Could she really imagine the powerful billionaire grappling with her plastic shower curtain? 'That's what I want, Alessio,' she said calmly.

But on Friday, a customer spent so long deliberating over a painting, that it was almost seven by the time Nicola closed up the gallery and she was running late. Casting a frantic look at her watch, she went to find her handbag. It was going to be a rush to get back to Peckham in time to change, but she should just about make it in time. Though, come to think of it…she picked up her phone and stared at the blank screen with a stab of disappointment. Alessio still hadn't texted her to tell her where to meet him.

And then, in that uncanny way which sometimes happened—of technology echoing your thoughts—a text came pinging through.

I've booked the Starlight Room at the Granchester for eight p.m.

Gosh. Nicola blinked. That was a bit *public*, wasn't it? She'd heard that the famous indigo ceilings studded with twinkling constellations made the lighting subdued, but there were always paparazzi lurking around the entrance, eager to snap the privileged clientele enjoying the hotel restaurant's exemplary food and wine list. Did he really want to take her *there*?

The gallery bell sounded and Nicola paused, rather irritated at someone ringing on the door, when it was obvious they were closed. But she couldn't just ignore it. The building was secure, but with so many valuable pieces on the premises you could never be too sure. Her finger hovering over the alarm button, she peered out into the golden summer evening, her heart missing a beat when she saw the distinctive figure silhouetted against the plate-glass window.

She darted back out of view, her heart now pounding. What the hell was *he* doing here?

Her text pinged again and she knew who it was from even before she'd looked at the message.

Open the door, cara. I know you're in there.

This was unacceptable. Completely and utterly unacceptable. Marching across the gallery, Nicola unlocked the door and stood glaring at him, trying not to be affected by his powerful presence. But the evening sunlight was making the dark gold of his skin seem even more luminescent than usual, contrasting vividly with the coal-dark hair and sapphire gleam of his eyes.

'What are you doing here?' she demanded.

'Isn't it obvious? I wanted to see you.'

'But you were going to see me anyway. We have a dinner date in exactly...' She glanced down at her watch before lifting her gaze again. 'One hour's time.'

'I couldn't wait that long.'

'Alessio—'

'Let me in, Nicola. Please.'

That final sexy plea was her undoing, and even though she despised herself for her acquiescence, Nicola did just that—though her fingers were trembling as she locked the door behind him before studying the arresting beauty of his face. 'You can't just...turn up like this, without warning.'

'I just did.'

'Why?'

'Because I want to kiss you.'

'Well, you can't.'

'You don't want me to?'

'There's CCTV.'

'Everywhere?'

'Not in the back, no. Alessio...'

'Shh. Just show me, *cara*. *Show* me.' He linked her fingers with his and she was leading him—she was actually *leading him*—towards the darkened recess at the rear of the gallery. As her footsteps faltered beside the bronze sculpture—which still hadn't sold—he pulled her into his arms and looked down at her, his bright blue gaze piercing through her rapidly crumbling defences. Could he detect her hunger for him? Was that why his lips grazed hers so lightly that a helpless shudder erupted from her lips, before he covered them with the kind of hard and possessive kiss she'd spent the last week dreaming about?

'Alessio,' she gasped, when at last she came up for air.

'Mmm...?' His lips were against her neck, his breath warm against her skin as he levered her up against the wall.

'We—' she whispered as he began to ruck up her skirt, but already her thighs were parting for him '—mustn't.'

'Do you want me?'

'Yes,' she gasped breathlessly as she skated her fingertips hungrily over his chest.

Alessio greeted her remark with a low laugh of triumph, but he realised that his hands were unsteady as he undid her black skirt and let it pool to the floor. His fingertips brushed against her moist panties and she moaned as he slid them over her hips. As they floated down to join her skirt, he unzipped himself and never had he felt so big, or so hard. 'Do you want me?' he questioned again, but her urgent kiss was answer enough.

'Yes,' she crooned against the thrust of his tongue.

He dealt with the condom—bitterly resenting the time-wasting element of having to protect himself and that realisation provoked a flicker of incomprehension. But then he was lifting up her legs and wrapping them around his hips and all his reservations were forgotten as he pushed inside her. Deep inside her. He swallowed. *Madre di Dio*. It was *incredible. Incredible.* Had any woman ever felt as tight as this?

Somehow he slowed the pace down—even though the primitive need to spill his seed was threatening to overwhelm him. Every sinew in his body was taut as he thrust into her body, until she began to come— making a series of small cries as she spasmed around him. And then he surged inside her, with soft words torn from his lips in a voice which didn't sound like his own.

It took a long time for him to move. He wanted to remain exactly where he was, lost in the slowly receding waves of satisfaction, but they couldn't stay like this all evening…because this was very definitely not his style.

'So. Now what?' he questioned throatily.

Nicola didn't answer—the intense pleasure still washing over her literally making her unable to speak. She couldn't believe she had responded to him like that—so rapidly and so…

She swallowed.

So shamelessly.

Had she really just had sex *at her place of work*? What if Sergio had returned unexpectedly, or if the *unusual* activity in the rear of the gallery had alerted the central security system to the possibility of a trespasser on the premises? She could hardly protest that Alessio di Bari was a bona fide gallery customer, when his clothing was in such telltale disarray and there was the small matter of the empty condom wrapper lying on the floor.

Her heart was pounding as she let her legs slide to the

ground, relieved to feel the earth beneath her feet again. As the potent aftermath began to recede she wondered how she could have been so stupid. All her life—*all her life*—she had worked hard to find a job like this—yet she had been prepared to risk it all for a quick thrill with a man who regarded her as nothing but a temporary diversion.

But any anger she felt she would direct at herself, not him. She had wanted that urgent coupling just as much as he had, and she didn't have a clue what to do next. What on earth was she supposed to *say*? Recognising the need to maintain her dignity, she began scooping up her crumpled clothes. 'I need to freshen up,' she said.

Alone in the lavish bathroom which her boss had installed during the gallery's recent refurbishment, she did the best she could with the limited resources available, thankful for the luxurious toiletries which were always kept there. Removing the clips from her updo, she gave it a brisk brush—because at least the thick curtain of hair gave her something to hide behind.

Afterwards, when Alessio wordlessly took her place, she went to the office and busied herself with emails which could have easily waited until Monday, but at least they kept her teeming thoughts occupied, so that when a shadow fell over the desk it took her almost by surprise. And so did the way Alessio levered her to her feet and lifted her fingers to his mouth, grazing his lips over them in a way which made her shiver with desire. But if that curiously old-fashioned gesture disarmed her, his next words put her instantly on her guard.

'My car is outside.'

'And?'

'I'll give you a lift home.' His gaze roved over her white blouse—now a little creased—and her black pencil skirt, and his slow smile was speculative. 'I assume you'll want to get changed before dinner? I'll get them to put the table back.'

A disturbing thought flew into Nicola's mind. Had he deliberately come here to seduce her so that afterwards he could snoop around to see where she lived? This was followed by an impatient sigh, because that really *was* being paranoid. As if he cared! As if he'd even given her that much thought. So take back control. Tell him what *you* want, rather than obediently doing what he says all the time. 'To be honest, I don't want that at all. Too much of a rush,' she explained, with a quick glance at her watch. 'Can't you cancel the booking?'

'Of course I can. Though most people wouldn't pass up on a table at the Starlight.' His blue eyes glinted from between shuttered ebony lashes. 'Unless you have something better in mind?'

'Obviously nothing's going to top one of London's most famous restaurants,' she said. 'But we could always go and…' Nicola shrugged, momentarily distracted by his bright gaze and trying not to read too much into what had just happened. But he had come to find her, hadn't he? He had even said that he couldn't wait until eight o'clock, which was a pretty big admission from a man like him.

So didn't that alter things, if only a bit? She had tasted his luxurious billionaire lifestyle—maybe it was time he sampled hers. And yes, it might emphasise the huge material differences between them, but surely it would also put them on a more equal footing. 'We could always...' She hesitated. 'Eat a sandwich in the park?'

'Eat a sandwich in the park,' he repeated, as if she had just suggested a solo mission to the moon.

'Why not? It's a lovely sunny evening and...well, autumn will be upon us before you know it.' Her confidence growing, she picked up her handbag, unable to deny her pleasure at seeing that look of bemusement crossing over his face. 'There's a great deli on the corner of Maddox Street. Come on, Alessio. Play your cards right and I'll treat you.'

# CHAPTER TEN

THE FAINT HUM of traffic was louder than the birdsong, but the air was warm, the evening was golden and for the first time in a long time, Alessio felt completely relaxed. Sated by sex and food, he stretched his arms above his head, his attention caught by the sight of Buckingham Palace, which stood at the far end of the park. But the gilded gates and imposing structure of the majestic building were far less arresting than the sight of the woman perched on the ground opposite him, her bottom nestling snugly on his suit jacket.

He narrowed his eyes, still faintly disconcerted by the position in which he now found himself. Had he really removed that expensive piece of clothing and thrown it carelessly onto the dusty ground for her to sit on? Indeed, he had. His throat dried as his gaze moved over her. She had kicked off her sensible work shoes and suddenly he found himself fixated by the sight of her bare calves. It was crazy. Just a short while ago his fingers had been inching up her legs towards her panties, yet now those slender ankles seemed to exemplify a very different but equally potent kind of eroticism.

The evening was, he acknowledged wryly, turning out like no other. Instead of enjoying the splendour of the Granchester Hotel's world-famous restaurant, he had eaten a crab sandwich on rye, followed by a punnet of strawberries, while sitting beneath the dappled shade of a London plane tree. And for once, Nicola Bennett didn't appear in the least bit cool, or shuttered. Her cheeks were tinged with pink. Her eyes looked dark and glittering—an aftermath, no doubt, of the rampant sex they had recently enjoyed. She looked vibrant and delectable.

'More to drink?' she suggested, offering him a frosted can.

He shook his head as he quashed his desire to pull her into his arms, because he always found public declarations of affection faintly distasteful. 'No, thanks.'

She glanced across at him. 'I don't suppose you do this kind of thing very often.'

'Have my offer of a dinner date trashed, you mean?'

A shadow crossed over her face. 'You're not enjoying it?'

Alessio let out a low sigh of frustration. Why were her teeth digging into the soft cushion of her bottom lip like that? He didn't want her to go all uncertain and *cute* on him. He wanted the old Nicola back. The composed, self-possessed woman who kept him a reassuring arm's length away. 'It's different,' he conceded drily. 'I don't think I can ever remember a spontaneous picnic being so heavily dive-bombed by wasps. But thanks for buying me dinner, Nicola. That certainly hasn't happened in a long time.'

She sat back on her heels and plucked a blade of grass from the dusty ground and he got the strangest feeling she was trying not to meet his eyes.

'It must be weird,' she said slowly. 'Being so rich that everyone always expects you to pick up the bill. I suppose you just grow up getting used to it.'

'Or not,' he corrected flatly.

She blinked. 'I don't understand.'

His laugh was tinged with bitterness. 'You think I was born rich?'

'It's a reasonable assumption to make. You're a billionaire.' She ran the blade of grass between two unvarnished fingernails. 'Your family own a vast estate in Tuscany. Your stepfather's an aristocrat. Somehow, I can't imagine you ever having been on the breadline.'

'Well, you're wrong.'

Her lashes shuttered her eyes. 'Am I?'

'Completely.'

She nodded but said nothing more and inexplicably Alessio found himself wanting to talk about it, despite his inbuilt aversion to personal disclosure. Was it his recent brush with the past which had seared it onto the forefront of his mind, along with the knowledge that his mother was refusing to extricate herself from her dysfunctional relationship? Or just that Nicola had fixed her incredible gaze on him, and he wanted to lose himself in the cool, grey depths of those eyes? 'I wasn't born rich,' he said slowly. 'My mother had nothing when I was born. No man and certainly no wedding ring.'

'Your half-sister told me you were illegitimate,' she ventured.

His eyes narrowed. 'But you didn't think to tell me that?'

'Why should I?' She shrugged. 'It was just before dinner and in view of what came next, it sort of slipped my mind. Also, it's none of my business.'

'True. I never even met my father. He was a sailor, according to my mother. She didn't even know his surname.' He gave a bitter laugh. 'Nobody could ever accuse them of being star-crossed lovers.'

But if he had intended to shock her or goad her into passing judgement, she didn't take the bait. In fact, she showed no reaction at all and something about her serenity made him continue.

'We lived hand to mouth.' He closed his eyes and as the evening sun warmed the lids, he took himself back to a very different life—a place he rarely permitted himself to visit. Had he thought that time would lessen its impact? Maybe. But to his surprise, the memory was still sharp. Still vivid. Painfully so. 'We lived with my grandmother in Southern Italy, in a tiny apartment in the mountains. And though we had very little, it was a good life.'

Or so he had thought.

Not so his mother. His beautiful, restless mother. Bitterly resenting the restrictions brought about by childcare, she had left most of the responsibility to his beloved *nonna*. He remembered her endless complaints that her youth was draining away as she regarded their remote, hilltop village with an aggrieved eye. 'I will never find myself a man,' she had moaned, glaring pointedly at her son. 'Not with all this baggage in tow.'

Harsh words for a little boy to hear, but Alessio had been willing to forgive the woman who had given birth to him. At least, in the beginning. Later, it became much harder to forgive.

'My mother felt trapped by her circumstances.' His lashes flickered open and he could see a crowd of tourists outside the gates of Buckingham Palace, their phones held high in the air. 'So she found herself a job as chambermaid in a fancy hotel in Lecce and an escape route, courtesy of a much older man who was staying there. She met an English aristocrat and quickly became pregnant by him.'

'Lord Bonner?' she guessed, and he nodded.

'Edward Bonner,' he agreed. 'It was a huge gamble, because she was running the risk of having two illegitimate children under four. But this time she wasn't deserted, because Edward badly needed an heir. He offered to marry her and take her to England to live in his stately home and begin a new life as Lady Bonner.' He paused. 'I'm sure you don't need me to tell you how delighted she was to be able to escape her life of poverty to become a bona fide member of the aristocracy.'

'But at least she took you with her,' she offered slowly. 'I suppose she could have left you behind.'

'Yes, she took me with her, although that had nothing to do with maternal devotion. I overheard her telling a friend that her refusal to be parted from her son would make her appear more caring to her new husband. At least I was never under any illusions about just how ruthless women could be,' he added harshly.

'So you were brought to England.' Her gaze was steady. 'That must have been quite the upheaval.'

'Sì.' He shrugged. 'From two rooms to a Palladian mansion with servants was a pretty big leap for a four-year-old boy.'

He read the empathy in her eyes and now he was beginning to regret having started this. Because knowledge
was power and she might be tempted to use it when their
brief affair ended. But, despite her expression of distaste
when he had handed her the pen, she had signed a con-
fidentiality agreement before travelling out to Umbria,
hadn't she? Was it that which made the rest of the story
come spilling out, as if he couldn't wait to purge himself
of the darkness which had lain within him all these years?
How long since he'd allowed himself to think about this?
He had been convinced that if you buried unsavoury
things deep enough they would rot away, like garbage,
but he had been wrong.

He stretched out his legs in front of him. 'When they
arrived in England Edward announced there could never
be any question of divorce and my mother was delighted
because it implied security. The reality was that it gave
him carte blanche to behave exactly as he saw fit—
and once my half-brother and half-sister were born, my
presence in the house became superfluous.' He paused.
'Edward and his legitimate offspring never missed an
opportunity to try to make my life a misery.'

'And was that…awful?'

'I'm pretty resilient, Nicola.' He gave a short laugh.
'Let's just say that my admission at seven to one of the
most brutal boarding schools in the country came as
something of a relief. At least, for a while. I wasn't a
natural fit for the English public school system, even
though I won the chemistry prize year after year. And
despite the entreaties of my tutors, when I was thirteen

I announced I was going back to Puglia to live with my grandmother.'

'And your mother didn't try to stop you?'

'Of course she didn't try to stop me,' he said softly. 'I was a constant thorn in my stepfather's side. A powerful reminder of his wife's other lover. There was never any love lost between me and Edward. That party in Tuscany was the first time I've seen them together in years.'

And suddenly it became important for her to understand there had been no handouts along the way. No deeds to expensive houses, or the promise of a large inheritance to cushion every decision he would ever make. 'Everything I've achieved has been through my own endeavours, Nicola. I've done it all on my own. Just a couple of years after I returned to Italy, my grandmother died—'

'Oh, Alessio.'

He didn't want to remember that time. His sense of helplessness and anger as the only woman who had ever really loved him slipped away—ravaged by her disease—had forged his determination that nothing and nobody was ever going to hurt him like that again.

'I knew what she would have wanted and so I worked hard at school and, against all the odds, won a scholarship to Stanford. America gave me the chance to reinvent myself and by the time I'd made my first million, I had paid off every cent my stepfather had ever spent on my education. And I've never looked back.'

He watched as she fiddled with the now-wilted blade of grass again, before lifting her head to look him full in the face. There were many ways she could have reacted to his story and Alessio was prepared for any of them.

She could have bitched about his mother, which would have been unacceptable—because everyone knew it was okay to diss your own mother but nobody else had that right. She could have stated the obvious—that his step-father was a bastard. What he hadn't been expecting was the quiet compassion shining from those extraordinary eyes. But as their gazes held, her expression changed. The softness in her eyes became edged with the quick-silver gleam of desire. He could see her nipples harden-ing beneath her white shirt and hunger began to pulse through his veins as he recalled what had happened be-hind the bronze statue.

'I think we've talked enough, don't you?' He rose to his feet, holding out his hand to assist her, before shak-ing off the dusty jacket on which she'd been sitting and slinging it over his shoulder. 'My hotel is just across the park,' he said.

And despite her inexperience, Nicola knew exactly what he meant by that careless remark. This was grown-up speak for *let's spend the night together* and she wasn't sure how to respond. Obviously, she wanted to go to bed with him but that mightn't be such a good idea. She was still in her crumpled work clothes for one thing, but that wasn't her main concern. More worrying was the cer-tainty that her feelings were changing. She was starting to care about him, and that had never been on the cards.

She hadn't expected him to open up to her like that. To tell her about his brutal boarding school and the hor-rible sense of exclusion he had encountered at home, or the break in his voice when he'd talked about his grand-mother's death. It was the things he *hadn't* said which had made his story so heartbreaking and it had shown her that nothing was ever as it seemed from the outside. Behind the glittering veneer of the successful billionaire was a man who had been badly damaged. And yet he had trusted her enough to tell her. Didn't that mean something? Were his feelings towards her changing, too?

Excitement rippled over her as she attempted to match his careless tone, because she certainly didn't want to put him off by being too *eager*. But she was. She wanted him so badly it was making her tummy tighten and her breasts were flooding with exquisite heat. 'Okay,' she agreed, pushing her too-hot toes into one of her suede court shoes. 'Though I'm not suitably dressed for a fancy hotel.'

'Who cares about that?' he questioned arrogantly.

They walked the short distance across Green Park to the famous Ritz hotel, where the white-gloved doorman greeted Alessio like an old friend. Inside was an abundance of gleaming marble and lavish flower arrangements and Nicola felt torn as they rode the gleaming elevator, her crumpled clothes making her feel out of place among the well-heeled guests, in their designer silks and diamonds.

But the moment they reached Alessio's suite and he slid his arms around her, she forgot everything. All her worries and insecurities trickled away beneath the seeking power of his kiss. She wondered whether this was going to be like that encounter in the gallery—all hot and raw and urgent—but it couldn't have been more different. His movements were tantalisingly slow as he began to undress her. Almost as if he was determined to demonstrate which of them was in control. But that was a good thing, surely, she figured as his fingertips brushed over her shivering skin.

She closed her eyes as he began to unbutton her shirt, slowly exposing her heated flesh, until she was practically going out of her mind with frustration. Her breasts were pushing hard against a bra which suddenly seemed insubstantial and she gave a gasp as he laved his tongue over her cleavage.

'Mmm...' came his throaty growl of approval as his teeth encountered the delicate lace and she worried that he might rip it. 'Is this some of the lingerie I bought for you?'

It was a question which jarred and Nicola stiffened.

Was he doing his best to remind her that she had been bought and paid for and carried her own particular price tag? Easy come, easy go? Would he have been less aroused if she'd been sporting her usual knickers which were three for the price of two? Perhaps if he hadn't chosen that precise moment to unclip the catch of her bra, she might have objected and pushed him away, but her aching breasts had now slipped free and he had captured them in his palms. And...

A shuddered sigh left her lungs. Sweet heaven. Who *cared* about who had bought her underwear? All she could think about was Alessio sucking on one nipple, while removing her panties. And then he was touching her just as he'd done before. Feathering his finger against her honeyed heat until she was coming apart, her knees buckling and her body bucking as he brought her to another swift climax.

The bed on which he placed her was enormous but all Nicola could think about was that, once again, Alessio's control seemed to have vanished—for he was tearing off his shirt with little regard for its fate. He was slightly more considered when unzipping his trousers and Nicola shut her eyes as the hard length of his arousal was revealed, suddenly self-conscious.

Because this wasn't like when they'd been in Italy and had come together like two strangers. Now she knew him better and somehow that made intimacy slightly more awkward. It was harder not to *care* about him, yet she didn't want to scare him off by revealing that. She wanted to grasp the familiar mantle of neutrality, but somehow it was eluding her. Was this what happened when a man started to invade your heart and your body—that your sense of self seemed to slip away?

'Look at me, *cara*,' he urged.

Reluctantly, she opened her eyes.

'Don't ever be inhibited around your lovers, Nicola,' he purred. 'Men enjoy seeing a woman gaze at them. They like to watch their eyes darken with desire.' His gaze was slitted with gleamed approval. 'Just as yours are doing now.'

It was no hardship to study his honed and golden flesh, but as she drank in his raw, masculine beauty Nicola was filled with confusion, his words sowing seeds of doubt in a mind which had always been a fertile breeding ground for rejection. Why was he talking about her *lovers* like that—when he was the only lover she'd ever had?

*The only one she could ever imagine wanting.*

But there was no time to dwell on her fears because

soon he had her moaning again as he filled her with his hardness.

His movements were deep and the confident thrust of her pelvis made him utter something helpless in Italian. And when she could hold back no longer, she began to spasm around him as he shuddered out his own fulfilment. And didn't that shared moment of orgasm feel extra special? Was that *tenderness* she could feel in his kiss? Was it that which made a rush of longing swell up inside her and stupid tears prick the backs of her eyes, so that she had to blink them away and turn her head away, praying he hadn't noticed?

The room was quiet and, with a lazy yawn, Alessio gazed out of the window at the green blur of leaves in the treetops. It felt good to look at nature for a change, he reflected, after years of the metal and glass view of his high-tech Manhattan penthouse. He stretched, unable to shake off this exquisite sense of lethargy as he tried get his head around what had just happened. The sex had been unbelievable, *sì*. In fact, he would go so far as to admit it was the best sex he'd ever had, which was saying something, given his extensive track record. But just before that last incredible orgasm, he had heard something which had hovered disturbingly on the edges of his mind and was coming back to him now with unwelcome clarity. Had that been a muffled sob choking from Nicola's lips? The telltale sound of unwanted emotion intruding?

He frowned because their chemistry was off the scale, *sì*, but was purely physical. He knew that and she needed to know it, too. Before she started to care. Before she fell in love with him, as so many others had done, even though he'd never given anyone cause to love him. Women like his mother, for whom a man's wealth was paramount. Women who would sacrifice a child's happiness as a means to an end.

But Nicola was different from other women, he conceded. And not just because she had chosen a sandwich in the park—which she had paid for—instead of eating in a luxury restaurant. He recognised that in many ways she was still an innocent and he respected her too much to break her heart. Turning over, he reached for her—the tantalising throb of an erection making him regret the inevitability of what he was about to say.

'You know I have to fly to Japan tomorrow?'

'I don't think you mentioned it, no.' That polite, gallery smile was back. 'I'm sure it will be lovely. Although I've never been there, of course.'

He frowned, because he had been expecting *some* sort of disappointment, not that shrugging acceptance. 'I was thinking that next time I'm in London—' he kept his voice deliberately casual '—we could see each other.'

Her wary expression didn't change. 'Sure. Why not?'

Her lips were so inviting that he might have left the subject alone and kissed her into sweet oblivion if he hadn't noticed the shiny streak of a dried tear on her cheek, which was enough to reinforce his resolve. Because if this was to continue in the way he intended it to, it was vital that he set down some rules, right from the start.

'I like you, Nicola,' he said slowly. 'In fact, I like you a lot. You're bright and funny and beautiful and one day you're going to meet an amazing man and marry him.'

He paused as he met the question in her eyes. 'But that man isn't going to be me.'

He waited for the inevitable storm. For fireworks and indignation. But there were none. That serene mask was back in place and, ironically, he wanted to shatter it—to glimpse the passion she only ever showed when he was deep inside her. But there was no passion on her face now. Just cool calculation.

'The first time I had dinner with you,' she said calmly, as if they were discussing nothing more controversial than the sandwich they had eaten in the park, 'I told you that I didn't want to marry anyone. Which remains true. I also remember saying, very explicitly, that even if I did—*even if I did*—you would be the last person on earth I would ever choose. Which also happened to be true. And my position on that hasn't changed.'

She flicked a thick handful of blonde hair over her bare shoulder. 'So I find it more than a little irritating to have been cast in the role of some sort of pining desperado—no, please don't interrupt me, Alessio—which seems more about feeding *your* ego than reflecting *my* feelings with any degree of accuracy.'

Taken aback by her objections and more than a little aroused by her cool logic and, of course, by the provocative movement of her breasts, Alessio held up his palms in a gesture of mock submission. '*Bene, bene!* You've convinced me. I just wanted to put it out there, that's all. So that there could be no misunderstanding.'

There was a pause and her eyes glinted with what might have been humour, but it might have been something else. Something both dangerous and alluring.

'You seem to be the only one in danger of misunderstanding, if you don't mind my saying so.'

He frowned. Would she consider it patronising if he admitted that it had been an unexpected feeling of *protectiveness* which had inspired his words to her? A desire not to hurt her, rather than a desire to feed his ego. He suspected she would. He met her shuttered grey stare. 'I still want you,' he said simply.

Nicola could see that for herself. The unmistakable outline of his erection was visible beneath the fine linen sheet and that realisation provoked an answering stab of heat, low in her sex. She could feel her breasts begin to flood and from the quick flicker of his sapphire gaze, she could tell that her reaction hadn't escaped him.

What would most women in this situation do? she wondered desperately. She supposed it depended on what they wanted. If they were holding out for commitment, then they might just cut their losses and leave. It would hurt for a while, but they'd get over it.

But she wasn't holding out for commitment.

She had lost her virginity to him. The only thing she had left to lose was her heart and that didn't *have* to happen—not as long as she guarded it fiercely. Because here was an opportunity to learn. The same kind of opportunity which had propelled her from abject poverty into one of the plushest art galleries in Mayfair. She had become an expert and, likewise, could learn from Alessio by watching and listening and, of course, participating. But this wouldn't involve studying by torchlight while everyone else was asleep, or juggling two waitress jobs while she studied hard at night school. This would consist of lessons in sex from someone who was unbelievably good at it.

'And I want you, too. Isn't that why I'm here?' But it still took a lot of nerve to actually come out and say it. 'Because you can teach me.'

He frowned. 'Teach you what?'

'Everything you know.' She shrugged. 'About sex.'

His eyes narrowed. 'You're not making any sense.'

'Think about it, Alessio,' she challenged softly. 'You're experienced and I'm not—but I've always been an excellent student.' The perplexed darkening of his blue eyes gave her a sudden heady rush of satisfaction, because this was a Nicola she felt comfortable with. Who saw what she wanted and went out to get it. 'And obviously—given my rather competitive nature—I want to be the best lover I can. And you can show me how to achieve that.' She paused. 'Can't you?'

His face was a picture. There was desire—yes, but it was the flicker of uncertainty in his eyes that made him seem more human. More accessible. And that was dangerous. She couldn't possibly make such a cold-blooded demand if she was then going to commit the cardinal crime of falling in love with him. There was no point in being bold and ambitious if she then came over as vulnerable.

But he had recovered his equilibrium and his faint consternation had been replaced by a slow smile of anticipation which was making her tummy tighten. 'You want me to teach you everything I know about sex, do you, *cara*?' he murmured, sliding his hand between her thighs to target her aching bud. 'It's certainly the most unconventional request I've ever received from a woman but rest assured, Nicola, it will be my pleasure. And yours, of course.'

*'Oh!'* she said faintly as he began to strum her aroused flesh and before too long she was contracting around his finger and choking out his name. As powerful waves of pleasure washed over her she pulled his head towards hers and her last thought before their lips met was that she could handle this.

Of course she could.

# CHAPTER ELEVEN

THE WIND WAS biting as Alessio emerged from his Munich flight and slid into the limousine waiting on the runway, ready to speed him towards central London. Lost in thought, he stared out of the window, barely registering the red-gold blur of autumn leaves swirling through the air. But for once he wasn't preoccupied with his latest project, nor the rapid global expansion of his chemical company, which had made him the wunderkind of the international markets.

No, his mind was consumed with one thing, and one thing only. His mouth grew dry. A woman with glacial eyes and a pale fall of hair, with an irritating habit of failing to return his calls.

Nicola.

Tantalising, aloof Nicola Bennett, who was driving him completely crazy.

He scowled.

He had imagined that her elusiveness might have dissolved a little by now, but he had been wrong. Her behaviour still perplexed him and he couldn't shake off the sense that, somehow, she was running rings around him. He wondered if she had any idea just how much he'd gone out of his way to accommodate her wishes. She wanted him to teach her about sex? Fine. He was more than happy to oblige. A muscle fired at his temple. Which meant there had to be a little give and take, since they lived on opposite sides of the globe.

What was so wrong with diverting his flight last week and ringing her unexpectedly at midnight? He had suggested she get over to his hotel as quickly as possible, promising that he'd be able to devote most of the following day to her, before returning to Manhattan. But her anticipated delight hadn't been forthcoming—and neither had his fantasy that she would arrive shortly afterwards, wearing very little underneath her coat. Instead, he had been subjected to an uncomfortable barrage of questions.

Was it too much to ask that he give her some notice? she had demanded coolly. Or was she just expected to cancel her existing plans in order to see him?

He had replied—with equal cool—that he didn't *expect* her to do anything and she should only cancel her plans if she wanted to see him, which it appeared she didn't. Because she had turned him down flat and told him to contact her next time he was in London!

At first, he had been disbelieving, then angry and then—bizarrely—curiously chastened. It had made him re-evaluate the way he treated women and think that maybe she deserved better. It had occurred to him that he might have to start doing things differently with her—but this realisation was cushioned by the reassuring rider that it wouldn't impact too significantly on his life. Because there was no perceived threat from Nicola Bennett. Their agreement had been straightforward from the start—a basic sexual compatibility which wasn't complicated by unrealistic emotional demands.

Which was why he had given her plenty of warning before arranging to meet her for dinner tonight. He'd offered to rebook the Starlight Room at the Granchester—the no-show destination of their first date—but to his surprise she had said it was too public and couldn't he find somewhere more discreet?

No, she definitely wasn't like other women.

Perhaps it was time he got to know her a little better. Would that lessen his fascination for her, he wondered idly—or simply increase it?

He leaned back against the leather seat and gave a soft sigh of satisfaction, because never before could he recall feeling such a heightened degree of anticipation.

Nicola flipped the door sign to *Closed* and turned to find Sergio watching her.

'Is everything okay?' he asked.

Nicola smiled at her boss, trying to reclaim the familiar sense of calm which seemed to have been eluding her these past few weeks—but it wasn't easy. Not when Sergio was hovering right beside the spot where she'd enjoyed that hot encounter with Alessio last month. Were they *ever* going to sell that wretched bronze—or was she doomed to endure a daily reminder of how decadent she had been?

'I'm fine, thank you, Sergio,' she answered politely, but didn't pursue the conversation. She didn't want to give him any opportunity to probe, but it seemed that, for once, his curiosity was roused.

'It's just that you seem…' He shrugged. 'It's hard to put into words.'

'Then don't even try!' Her words were bright. 'After all, I've sold three paintings this week, haven't I?'

'This is true, you have. With two more in the pipeline. Nobody could ever question your commitment or your success, Nicola. You just seem different, that's all.' He narrowed his eyes. 'Distracted.'

'Maybe it's the autumn weather. Chill in the air and all that. Look, I'd better get on. I've still got an email I need to send before I can go home.'

But there was truth in his words and she wondered what Sergio would say if she told him *why* she was so distracted. If she just happened to explain that she was conducting a clandestine relationship with one of his oldest friends and trying very hard to keep her feelings compartmentalised—a task being severely compromised by a lack of sleep and the constant gnaw of worry. Because Stacey had given birth three short weeks ago and the new mother was finding it a struggle. Actually, that was an understatement.

It had been a difficult birth and Nicola was discovering that nothing could really prepare you for the arrival of a screaming newborn. Little Jago was tiny and unbelievably cute, but solo parenthood was always going to be a challenge and nobody could take away the painful fact that his daddy was in prison—though Nicola had done her best to compensate for her brother's absence.

Some nights she'd slept on the floor of Stacey's living room, getting up to feed the baby to give the new mum a chance to rest. And of course, on nights when Alessio was in town, she got practically no sleep at all, though for very different reasons. But these late nights and early mornings were beginning to show. She'd used an inordinate amount of foundation on her face—but even the smooth matte finish couldn't disguise the inky shadows beneath her eyes.

Yet, despite the massive worry brought about by the birth of her new nephew, at times Nicola had felt almost *high* with happiness. Sometimes she wondered if it was wrong to enjoy such a giddy sense of well-being when Stacey was finding it so difficult to cope. But she couldn't help herself, no matter how much she tried to temper her feelings, or force herself to refuse Alessio's last-minute invite last week, because at the time she'd been dealing with dirty nappies. Bottom line—no pun intended—ever since she'd asked the billionaire chemist to teach her about sex, she'd been seeing him whenever he was in London. And every time she did, it just got better.

She felt the hard clench of her heart. Not just physically. That was the trouble. Everything about their affair was good. All the things she'd tried not to dream of were hers for the taking, because Alessio di Bari was an amazing man. Generous, intelligent and sexy—with a dry wit which often took her by surprise. Sometimes she wondered if he seemed so relaxed in her company because she'd been so adamant about not wanting a permanent relationship. Or did it all boil down to their insane chemistry—his specialist subject, as it happened—which combusted whenever they came close?

She glanced at her watch, realising there was no time

to waste on unanswerable questions. She needed to hurry so she would be ready in time to meet him. In the end it was all a bit of a rush—especially as she went home via Stacey's apartment, although she was still wearing her work clothes, which meant that, because Jago was full of cold, he covered her jacket in snot before giving another angry squall.

'He never stops!' wailed Stacey.

'Shh... Shh...' Nicola cradled the tiny baby and smoothed damp, wispy curls away from his forehead. 'Don't worry. He won't be like this for ever—and he's just got a bit of a cold, hasn't he? It's always difficult at the beginning, Stace. All the books say that.'

Stacey nodded, but her lips were working frantically as if she was trying very hard not to cry. Nicola's heart went out to the new mother as she made her a pot of tea and a sandwich, before rushing off home to get ready. Trying to fight off the plastic flap of the shower curtain, which kept sticking to her skin, she wondered what kind of future there would be for little Jago, with a father who was in and out of jail and a young couple with practically no prospects.

But *she* had done it, hadn't she? *She* had climbed out of the gutter and made something of herself without help from anyone else. And she would be around for Jago. Free of any family demands of her own and probably earning loads more money by then—there was no reason why she couldn't become a guiding presence in his life.

Her phone pinged, her heart giving a predictable leap when she read the message.

Where are you?

She replied, trying to emulate his terse style.

On my way.

She had requested a venue less public than the Starlight Room because she didn't want word getting back to Sergio on the grapevine—but the moment she walked into the restaurant Alessio had chosen as an alternative, she wished she'd kept her mouth shut. Because this was very private, yes—achingly so. Worse still, it was romantic. The flicker of tall creamy candles was the predominant source of lighting and it gave the room an intensely intimate feel. Rich brocade fabric lined the walls and there were heavy velvet drapes in darkly jewelled shades of emerald and crimson. It made her think of things she had no right to be thinking—about love and longevity and what was going to happen to them. About how much longer she could maintain this façade of not caring for him.

Alessio was rising to his feet, just as he'd done the first time they'd had dinner together. But things had changed. Back then she had been wary of him and he had been wary, too. She remembered the faint air of hostility which had radiated from his brooding frame. There had been calculating appraisal—from both of them—not this extended eye contact which managed to convey a wealth of repressed longing in a single moment. But nothing *had* changed, Nicola reminded herself fiercely. Not really. Only her own stupid mindset. *She* was the one who had started romanticising about what was only ever intended to be a functional relationship.

'Hi,' she said as she slid into her seat, slightly inhibited by the narrow skirt of her apricot silk dress. 'Hope I haven't kept you waiting.'

'Well, you have—but I thought that was your modus operandi,' he offered drily.

'I'm a busy working woman,' she returned, with a smile. 'How's life in Manhattan?'

'I've barely been there all month. Stockholm. Geneva. Munich.'

'That sounds like remarkably little down-time to me.'

'Isn't that what I'm doing right now?' He paused, his blue eyes slanting her a look of soft promise. 'How's life in London?'

'Oh, you know. Same old, same old.' Sitting back while the waiter filled their flutes with champagne, she wondered what he'd say if she told him she'd been acting as a quasi-mother since she'd last seen him. That the woman in the sleek apricot dress had been sponging the shoulder of her work shirt just an hour earlier. 'Are we celebrating something?' she questioned, watching as straw-coloured foam fizzed up the side of her glass.

'We could be.' He shrugged and smiled. 'The German branch of my company has turned in record profits for the first half of the year.'

'And does that…does something like that give you an inordinate amount of pleasure?'

'No, Nicola.' There was a pause. '*You* give me an inordinate amount of pleasure.'

Nicola's heart thudded, because when he looked at

her that way—with that smoky expression which made
his blue eyes smoulder—it made her feel dizzy with desire. It's sex, she reminded herself weakly. And because
that's *all* it is, you need to showcase some of your newly
learned expertise. He doesn't want a lover who's going
to gaze at him with her mouth open like a stranded fish,
while imagining what his first-born might look like. He
wants a sassy woman who's going to turn him on.

'Is this going to turn into some sort of verbal fore-
play?' she questioned quietly. 'Are you going to make
me want you so much that I won't be able to concentrate
on what I'm eating?'

'On the contrary,' he demurred silkily. 'I intend to feed
every one of your senses tonight, Nicola. And also—'
He halted as the head waiter arrived at their table, obviously keen to discuss the merits of the menu and wine
list, but Alessio simply raised his eyebrows at Nicola.
'Shall I order?'

She nodded and waited until the waiter had gone away
before looking at him quizzically. 'You were saying?'

What *had* he been saying? Alessio frowned. It was difficult to recall a word, let alone a sentence, when she was
dazzling him with all her fresh blonde beauty, which he
had missed during the fortnight they'd been apart. When
she had arrived here tonight, every man had turned to
watch her but she had been totally oblivious. She had no
idea just how alluring she was and he liked that about
her, he realised suddenly.

'I've been thinking—'

'Oh, dear. Could be dangerous.'

'It suddenly occurred to me how much I've told you

about myself,' he mused. 'Things I've never told anyone else.'

A sudden tension had crept into her shoulders, which was at odds with the lightness of her response. 'And should I be flattered?'

'That's up to you.' He put his glass down and studied her. 'But since the balance of information between us is so unevenly distributed, don't you think it's time we did something to redress that?'

Nicola couldn't compute his words and not just because he was talking in that analytical and scientific way of his. In fact, she was having difficulty catching her breath, because wasn't this what she had been secretly dreading for weeks? She might have limited experience of dating men, but she wasn't stupid. She'd been aware for a while that Alessio was relaxing his guard more and more, and that a closeness between them seemed to be developing. At first she'd put it down to sex until she was forced to acknowledge that they shared a compatibility outside bed, which she suspected was rare for him. But she had wanted things to stay exactly as they were, because it was safer that way. To preserve their transatlantic affair in aspic and keep it perfect. *This* had never been on her agenda. He wasn't *supposed* to want to get to know her better.

Like all men, he hadn't been interested in asking her any personal questions and she had been more than content for that state of affairs to continue. Hoping her smile didn't betray her sudden nerves, she tilted her head to one side. 'And how do you propose we go about that?'

'Oh, come, Nicola. It's not rocket science.'

'No, because I guess that would be your speciality.'

His eyes glittered. 'Just tell me something about your life.'

'My life?' she echoed weakly. 'Like what?'

'Parents. Siblings. Where you were born. Whether your mother used to bake you a cake for your birthday—that kind of thing. That's not such a big ask, is it?' He ran his finger around the edge of his crystal goblet. 'I thought all women liked to talk about themselves.'

Nicola plucked a bread roll from the basket on the table and proceeded to crumble it into a small pile of crumbs on her side plate. And all the time her mind was performing somersaults. She thought about what she could tell him about her growing-up years. Her mother baking a cake! It might have been funny if it weren't so sad.

Because even if Alessio were somebody ordinary—if he'd grown up in the suburbs, eating a roast dinner every Sunday—her story would still ruffle the feathers of all but the most liberal-minded. And Alessio was definitely *not* ordinary. Far from it. He wasn't asking because he *cared* about her, but because the distribution of information was unequal and he was a scientist who liked a sense of balance. What if she blurted out the truth about the current situation with Stacey and baby Jago? If she mentioned that she didn't know what would happen once Callum was released. Mightn't he respond in the same way he had done last time, with that slightly arrogant smile curving his lips as he reached for his metaphorical wallet?

*'How much do you need?'*

That would be unendurable.

Last time he'd offered her money, it had been nothing but a transaction. He had needed something from her and had paid for it accordingly. But now it was different. She was having sex with him. How would she feel if he offered her money now? Her skin grew icy. Like her mother? The mother she had vowed never to emulate, who would take whatever she could from a man in return for 'favours'. She stared down at the crumbled bread, knowing she had a choice. She could refuse to answer him, but she suspected that would create even more problems. Or she could shut the conversation down right now, leave—and never see him again. He was certainly too proud to demand to know why she had walked away.

But that was an over-the-top response because she didn't want to walk away. Not yet. Not when he was still giving her the kind of pleasure she'd never thought could exist for someone like her. It would end soon enough. So why not satisfy his curiosity and give him a *version* of her life? Because wasn't that what everyone did, when it boiled down to it? They edited their backstory to make it palatable.

'I was born in East London and, like you, I didn't ever get to meet my father. So, well... I'm illegitimate, too.'

He nodded as he absorbed this, but he didn't comment on it. 'And your mother?'

'She's still alive.'

'You still see her?'

'Of course. Not that often.'

'And brothers? Sisters?'

'I have one brother. He's...he's away a lot of the time.' Nicola knew she was playing with words, but what was the alternative? Ill-disguised horror as she exposed the brittle roots of the Bennett family tree? No. She wanted to keep this as brief as possible. 'His girlfriend Stacey has just had a baby.'

She chose that last statement deliberately, knowing his aversion to having children, but to her surprise, he smiled.

'So you're an aunt?'

'Yes, I'm an aunt.'

'Boy or girl?'

'A little boy. Jago.'

'Ah. His father must be pleased.'

She wanted to tell him to stop being so unpredictable. Why was he reacting with consideration on a subject which couldn't possibly interest him? Because it was confusing the hell out of her. When he was tearing off her clothes she knew exactly where she stood, but right now he was sending out mixed messages and she was terrified of getting the wrong idea. His brow was creased in a faint frown, as if her brief replies weren't what he had been expecting—but fortunately their oysters arrived and fussing with lemon quarters and raspberry vinegar gave her time to compose herself.

'Mmm…' she said, but even though she usually loved oysters, the cold mollusc felt faintly repugnant as it slid down her throat. Suddenly she heard her phone vibrating from the bottom of her handbag and some sixth sense urged her not to ignore it, because who would ring her at this time of night unless something was wrong? Knowing she was about to break a social taboo, she met Alessio's gaze across the table. 'Would you mind if I answered that?'

His sapphire eyes grew shuttered. 'Must you?'

But Nicola was already pulling the phone from her

handbag, her skin growing clammy as a picture of Jago flashed up and she saw the alert at the top of the screen. Four missed calls from Stacey.

'I've got to answer this,' she blurted out, rising to her feet and stumbling from the room, barely aware of the waiter she almost cannoned into, who narrowly avoided dropping a tray of cocktails. But the call had ended by the time she reached the restaurant foyer and when Nicola jabbed the 'return call' button, Stacey picked up immediately, her voice incomprehensible through the sound of Jago crying in the background.

'What's happening?' Nicola sucked in a breath. 'Is Jago okay?'

'I'm a bit worried, Nic. He's breathing a bit fast and won't take his bottle, and he's—'

Her words were interrupted by a snuffly wail and Nicola thought very quickly. It could be something or it could be nothing, but was it really a risk worth taking? And didn't Stacey need all the support she could get right now? 'I'm coming over,' she said. 'If you're really worried then call an ambulance, but if I jump in a cab I can be there in twenty minutes.'

'I'll wait,' said Stacey, her voice filled with gratitude.

With trembling fingers Nicola cut the connection and looked up to see Alessio standing in front of her in the restaurant foyer, his face shadowed and grave.

'I have to go!'

'I heard. My car will take you. You can tell me what's happening on the way.'

Nicola opened her mouth then shut it again as his car pulled up outside the restaurant, because only a fool would refuse his offer of assistance. All the barriers she had previously erected to keep him out of her life seemed irrelevant now as she nodded her head. Stumbling out the address, she was barely aware of the limousine door slamming shut, or the speed at which Alessio's chauffeur negotiated London's narrow side streets.

'Are you going to tell me what's going on?' Alessio demanded urgently.

'Jago won't take his bottle.' Nervously, her fingers played with the thin gold chain at her neck. 'He's all snuffly and I can tell Stacey's worried. If she needs to take him to hospital, it's much better if she has someone with her.'

He frowned. 'Isn't your brother with her?'

'No. My brother...' And suddenly the words just came blurting out. 'My brother's in jail!' She saw his lips flatten as he took out his phone and began punching out a number. 'What are you doing?'

'Calling a friend who's a paediatrician.'

'I don't—'

Imperiously holding up his hand for silence, he began to speak but Nicola barely registered a word he said, she was just wishing they would get there. Before too long the car was drawing up outside the flat and she was running upstairs and Stacey was letting her in, the baby cradled against one shoulder.

'Here. Let's put him on the sofa and have a look at him,' said Nicola.

She laid him down carefully, her heart contracting as she observed the rapid rise and fall of his tiny chest, and she was just about to phone an ambulance when the door opened and Alessio walked in, accompanied by a tall and incredibly good-looking man wearing motorcycle leathers and carrying a bag.

'What's going on?' demanded Stacey. 'Who are you?'

'I'm Alessio di Bari, a friend of Nicola's, and this is Harrison Drake, a friend of *mine* and one of the finest paediatricians in the country.'

At this, Stacey began to tremble. 'Just help my baby, will you? Please.' The urgency of her plea plunged the room into silence save for the sound of little Jago's breathing as the doctor began to examine him.

Nicola watched as Harrison gently unbuttoned the infant's sleepsuit and listened to his chest with a stethoscope, all the while directing a stream of questions at Stacey. At last, he straightened up, and nodded.

'He's got a mild dose of bronchiolitis, which is very common in young babies. You need to monitor him throughout the night and make sure you feed him less, but more often. I've got some nasal saline drops in my bag—you can give him those and they should help. If his breathing gets faster or more laboured then you should take him to hospital, but I think he's going to be fine.'

Close to tears, Stacey thanked the paediatrician and Nicola realised that sometimes just the positive words of a healthcare professional could be enough to reassure you when you were young and inexperienced. She helped Stacey prepare a bottle for Jago, dimly aware of Alessio leaving the tiny apartment to accompany the doctor downstairs and it came almost as a shock when he returned. Had she thought that would be the last she ever saw of him? That he'd be frightened off by all the chaos and the poverty he had witnessed? Yes, she had. He stood silently in the doorway as she cradled her tiny nephew and suddenly she felt acutely self-conscious about the way he was watching her.

'Thanks for that,' she said at last, laying the now-sleeping baby into his cot and straightening up. 'Your friend was brilliant.'

She wondered if he'd heard her because he didn't reply but then she realised he was looking round the apartment. And suddenly Nicola saw it through his eyes. The open pack of disposable nappies next to the TV, and the line of tiny sleepsuits drying on the radiator. Three dirty cups were sitting on the paper-strewn coffee table, along with the remains of a cheese sandwich. Why was Stacey so *untidy*? she found herself thinking.

He turned then and Nicola almost recoiled from the expression on his face, because Alessio had never looked at her like this before, not even at the beginning. His features looked as if they had been carved from some obsidian marble and his blue eyes were shuttered and cold. He was only on the other side of the small room, but he seemed so far away that he might have been on another planet. Was he *judging* them?

'I'm going to stay here with Jago and Stacey tonight,' she said, offering an explanation he hadn't asked for.

Afterwards she wondered what she'd been hoping he'd say. That he would see her tomorrow, as planned? Place his hand on her arm in a gesture of comfort, or even give her a hug? But he didn't. He remained exactly where he was—as if her proximity might contaminate him in some way.

But his features softened a little as he turned to Stacey and his deep voice was immensely kind—and something about both those things filled Nicola with a sense of wistfulness, which made her heart contract with hopeless longing.

'Goodnight, Stacey,' he said quietly. 'Take heart from Harrison's words, and, in the meantime, I will say a prayer for your son.'

# CHAPTER TWELVE

FENDING OFF QUESTIONS about the identity of their knight in shining armour, Nicola took the following week off work and moved in to help Stacey with Jago, who delighted them all with his rapid and robust recovery. It was good to be able to offer support she thought, and—importantly—it kept her busy.

She managed to track down Harrison Drake's address to discover he was a consultant at London's biggest paediatric hospital and sent a thank you card, as well as a contribution to his research project. She also attempted to demonstrate to Stacey the benefits of keeping a small space tidy and was surprised by the success of her endeavours—she'd certainly never seen the place look so neat before, nor the fridge stocked with so much healthy food. Her brother's girlfriend had even started talking about learning how to cook. Maybe Jago's sickness had been the wake-up call she'd needed. As if she'd suddenly realised she needed to make life as good as it possibly could be for her tiny baby—and for Callum, when he was eventually released.

But no matter how many questions Stacey asked about Alessio, Nicola blocked them all.

She didn't want to talk about him.

She didn't even want to think about him.

Some hope.

He was constantly on her mind. When she was making coffee in the morning, or forcing herself to eat a salad from the deli at lunchtime. In the bath, and in her dreams. Especially her dreams. Perhaps it was true what they said about absence making the heart grow fonder and that was the reason he was obsessing her thoughts so much. Because Nicola hadn't heard from Alessio since the night of Jago's illness—not a single word—and that had left her feeling hurt and bewildered. Was it over? Just like that? She'd known the relationship was always destined to end and there was never going to be an easy way for that to happen, but this felt unsatisfactory. Unfinished.

She remembered his cold and forbidding expression as he had surveyed her from the other side of the room. His failure to reach out and comfort her. Had he been appalled by that unexpected glimpse into the chaos of her private life? Had it driven home her complete unsuitability to be the lover of a man like him? Several times she picked up the phone to text him, but never followed through, aware that falsely cheerful messages were never convincing and ran the risk of making her look desperate.

But she knew from past experience that the only way to move forward was to learn from the past and grab at the present with both hands. It was pointless wondering why she had been ghosted from Alessio's life. It hurt more than she had ever imagined it would—but she would get over it.

She threw herself into promoting the gallery's latest collection of seascapes by an artist from South Devon, which had opened to great fanfare in the art world. She took a trip to Northumbria to advise on the hanging of a collection of paintings in a private home. Yet, despite all her best intentions, the days all seemed to bleed into each other until one was indistinguishable from the next. The autumn winds were fierce, the bronze statue *still* hadn't sold and the shorter, colder days filled Nicola with a gloom which wouldn't seem to shift.

In an attempt to shake herself out of her lethargy, she went hiking one Sunday morning, bought a newspaper on the way back and had just settled down to read it when the shrill ring of the doorbell disturbed her. Putting down the paper, she frowned. Because she hadn't invited anyone round. In truth, she never did. Old habits died hard. This was *her* space. Her refuge. It was small, yes, but it was all hers—so long as she kept paying the rent—and she felt safe here.

But when she peered into the door viewer, she froze. Shock iced over her skin, her heart squeezing painfully in her chest when she saw who was standing there. Tall, dark and indescribably sexy. The man who had been haunting her sleeping and her waking hours. Leaning against the wall for support, she closed her eyes and fought to control her rapid breathing.

Alessio.

Here.

She swallowed. Now what?

The Nicola she had been when she'd first met him would have quizzed him coolly over the intercom, but the Nicola she had become was aching to see him again... unable to stop her imagination from going into fantasy overdrive as she buzzed him in. But the moment she opened the door she realised just how stupid that fantasy had been. Alessio wasn't here because he had missed her, or because he wanted her—at least, not if his grim expression was anything to go by.

'How's Jago?' he demanded.

'Better,' she said, touched by his solicitude and softening a little. 'Completely better, actually. I... I probably should have let you know.'

'Yes, you probably should—although I gather you sent a note to Harrison,' he said, shooting her a blue bullet of a stare. 'Are you going to let me in, Nicola?' he questioned, with quiet, scientific precision. 'Or are you still intent on keeping me out of your home?'

'Of course,' she said, opening the door wider.

He stepped inside and, in a funny sort of way, the continued flintiness of his expression helped bring Nicola to her senses. Time to cancel the fairy tale, she realised. Time to let go of the dream. 'How *did* you find out where I lived?' she asked dully.

'I got your address from Sergio.'

She stared at him in dismay. 'You didn't tell him—?'

'That we've been having sex?' He gave a short laugh. 'No, I didn't tell him. Don't worry, Nicola. Your icemaiden status remains intact. He may have been curious but I certainly didn't enlighten him by explaining that up until recently I had been fulfilling a position as your occasional *stud.*' His mouth twisted. 'Good enough to sleep with but not good enough to share any other parts of your life.'

His abrasive words indicated the true depth of his hostility and Nicola wondered if it had always been there, simmering beneath the surface. She could feel herself slowly deflating, like a helium balloon being speared by a pin, and knew she couldn't allow that to happen. She had to be strong, because strength was about the only thing she had left. That, and her pride. 'Why are you here, Alessio?' she said quietly.

He nodded, as if he had been expecting this question a lot sooner, fingers dipping into his jacket pocket before withdrawing something which glittered like a coiled serpent in the centre of his palm. A modestly thin gold chain. Her only piece of 'real' jewellery and something she'd saved up for—fulfilling a stupid desire to fit in with the sophisticated world she sometimes inhabited. She blinked at it before looking up. 'I was wondering where that was,' she said, but couldn't deny the great stab of disappointment which speared her heart as she met his sapphire gaze. He'd come to return her necklace and that was the reason he was here. The only reason. Of course it was.

She took it from him gingerly and put it down on the nearest flat surface, knowing that she had to get rid of him before she did something stupid. Like breaking down, or begging him to pull her into his arms and kiss away her heartache and her aching sense of loneliness. 'Is there anything else?' she enquired coolly.

'Actually, there is. I'm curious and perhaps you can assuage my curiosity. I assume that the money I paid you was used to help your brother and his family—because I sure as hell can't see any of the new furniture you claimed to need.' His gaze flicked over her. 'I mean, why all the mystery, Nicola? The evasion and obfuscation? The double life you appear to have been leading… the brother who's actually in prison, not "away" as you euphemistically put it?'

She shook her head, stupidly wishing she'd had a chance to brush her hair. But it was pointless wanting his eyes to grow warm with desire or affection, because that ship had clearly sailed. Suddenly this became about defending her position. About battling for some kind of recognition and respect, as she'd done so many times before.

'You want to know *why*?' she demanded, her protective cloak of calm slipping away from her. 'You think I was ashamed of my past?' She nodded. 'Well, yes. Maybe some small part of me *was* ashamed and maybe you would have been, too, if you were me. Because while we were both born illegitimate, our circumstances couldn't have been more different. Oh, don't worry—I'm not trying to raise you on the poverty stakes. But the fact is I grew up in a *slum*, Alessio—with a mother who lived a very dodgy life. She went missing for long periods and we never knew where. My little brother and I were always cold and never had enough to eat and…' Her voice grew a little shaky as the harsh reality of those days came rushing back. 'Whatever food we had, I always gave to Callum, and sometimes I used to steal my classmates' sandwiches for myself, if I thought I could get away with it. There!' She looked at him defiantly. 'Are you shocked?'

But his stony features showed no reaction. 'Go on.'

Nicola sucked in another breath. She'd bottled this up for so long it was as if someone had suddenly shaken that bottle, so that all the words were pouring out. 'Most of my energy was spent battling the social services who wanted to take us into care. They threatened to split us up and I was never going to allow that to happen. Maybe I should have done,' she added bitterly. 'And then Callum wouldn't have ended up getting in with a bad crowd and forging a useless career as a thief. Or maybe I set him a bad example by nicking those sandwiches.' She walked to the other side of the room, hoping the movement would divert his attention from the fact that she was trembling.

'I had to fight for everything I've achieved,' she continued huskily. 'And I've done it by leaving that girl far behind. I had to learn to fit in with the new world I inhabited and was always terrified someone was going to find me out, and judge me. It was a bad case of imposter syndrome. That's why I felt safe here, in my own little place, because I'd never had that before. And okay—I never invited you round before, but you weren't exactly begging me to visit you in Manhattan, were you, Alessio? Our two worlds were never supposed to have met, let alone blended.' She stared at him, unable to keep the sudden flare of hope from her heart. '*Now* do you understand why I didn't tell you?'

But he shook his head—his expression stubborn and intractable. 'I would have preferred to have known the truth, no matter how unpalatable,' he said coldly. 'Remember, I told you so much about myself. I confided in you big-time, but you couldn't bring yourself to do the same, could you, Nicola?' His eyes were as icy as the deceptively blue autumn sky outside. 'When it came to the crunch, you just didn't trust me.'

His accusatory words stung her skin like tiny barbs

and it took a moment or two before she could answer, her words sounding small. 'Maybe I don't trust anyone.'

'Well, what do you know?' he said sarcastically. 'Mutual distrust. Not much of a basis for anything, is it, Nicola?'

And suddenly Nicola was scared by all these twisty *feelings* which were rising to the surface inside her, like scum in a pan of boiling bones. How dared he take the upper hand—as if he'd done everything right and she'd done everything wrong? Maybe nothing had really changed since her childhood, because no matter what she said, or did, she always seemed to be condemned for it.

'I don't understand why you're reacting like this,' she said, her temper beginning to flare. 'Because a woman with a messy life was expressly what you *didn't* want. How many times did you tell me you liked me because I was cool and aloof? The ice-maiden image turned you on—admit it! My supposed mystique was one of the things which attracted you in the first place, and my composure is what made you realise I'd be a good bet to take to Tuscany. And yes, it ended up being more than that—but our relationship was never intended to last, was it, Alessio? You told me that, too—in no uncertain terms. You spelt it out very clearly that you didn't want marriage, or children—in fact, you didn't want *any* kind of commitment. Was I supposed to ruin our brief affair by dumping a load of unsavoury stuff on you, which you didn't need to know?'

Alessio shook his head, unable to shake off the disappointment which was pressing down on his shoulders like a leaden weight. He wondered how he could ever have doubted his instincts. Not just his instincts but his experience of women. He had thought she was too good to be true and he had been right. Well, he had heard her out. He had listened to the reasoning behind her behaviour and it was difficult not to feel some compassion for what she had told him. But that didn't change the fact that he felt betrayed by her, and, surprisingly, that hurt.

Why?

Because he had mistakenly imagined some sort of bond to be growing between them? Maybe. At times his feelings had been behaving like cells on a Petri dish—multiplying and expanding in all directions without any input from him. And that was something he hadn't expected. Or wanted. His lips hardened. Because this was the reality of relationships—subterfuge and manipulation, smoke and mirrors—and he didn't need it. He didn't *need* pain and he certainly didn't need *her*. His life was easier without any kind of emotional complication. It was as simple as that. A sudden sense of freedom washed over him and he expelled a long sigh of relief. What a lucky escape he'd had. And he wondered if she had any idea how effectively she'd shot herself in the foot.

'You didn't tell me anything until you had to, until your back was up against the wall,' he accused softly. 'I wonder, would I ever have discovered more if there hadn't been a medical emergency?'

'Who knows?' A pulse was hammering at the base of her throat. 'I suppose I imagined that sharing secrets was the precursor to deepening a relationship—but ours was always flailing around in the shallows, wasn't it, Alessio?'

But Alessio shook his head because getting into pointless debate was a time-suck, when the only thing which mattered was regaining his freedom. 'I'm glad your nephew is okay,' he said, unable to miss the faint flare of light in her grey eyes and—just in case she thought he was leading up to something equally tender-hearted—he curved his lips into a smile he knew to be cruel. Because, despite everything, he liked her and she had been through too much to waste any of her precious life pining over a man like him. Better she hated him than imagined she loved him. 'And I wish you every success in the future, Nicola,' he finished softly. 'Please believe that.'

But it was with an unexpected wrench of his heart that he forced himself to turn away from her shimmering blonde beauty and let himself out of the tiny apartment.

# CHAPTER THIRTEEN

'*SOLD?*' NICOLA STARED at the glimmering bronze statue with a sense of uncertainty, before redirecting her disbelieving gaze towards Sergio. 'You mean, someone's bought it?'

'I do.' Her boss nodded, his lips twitching. 'That *is* what usually happens when something gets sold, Nicola.'

Dutifully, she offered an answering smile, telling herself that only a very stupid person would be sad to see the back of something which served as a daily reminder of the thing she was most missing. Not just the sex—though, of course, that was a pretty unforgettable part of it. No. A lump lodged in her throat. It was *him* she was missing most of all. Alessio. The brilliant chemist with the looks of a movie star. She'd tried telling herself it shouldn't be this hard to forget him, because he'd never been around that much. But he had always been a constant in her thoughts. If ever she'd felt low or wistful, it had been enough to conjure up the memory of his brilliant eyes and hard body, or something he'd said which had made her laugh. She had basked in the knowledge that he was part of her life and always looked forward to their next meeting.

Surely that emphasised the fact that theirs had never been a *real* relationship but simply a construct of transatlantic sex sessions. Yes, they had eaten dinner together and taken the occasional trip to the theatre or cinema and once, memorably, to Brighton, where they had walked along the pebbled beach and dodged the waves and she had confessed how much she'd always wanted to live beside the sea. But that shouldn't be enough to produce this intense level of heartache, which wouldn't seem to go away. She ought to be *glad* that the wretched bronze was finally leaving the gallery—and she could cut her ties to the Italian scientist for ever.

Even so, she was unable to quell the tiny splinter of hope which pierced her heart as she regarded her boss. 'Who's bought it?'

'Ross Fleming—a new client. Has a place by the sea in Cornwall. He wants it as a surprise for his wife, apparently.'

'Oh.' Her heart gave a lift-shaft plummet. 'How…nice.'

'It's being shipped out tomorrow—but he wants someone to supervise the installation and it's all a bit of a rush.' Sergio smiled in the manner of somebody just about to offer a huge bonus. 'You wouldn't mind going down to Cornwall, would you, Nicola? Tack on a couple of extra days and make a break of it, hmm? Put some colour back in your cheeks.'

Going to Cornwall was the last thing she felt like doing. She wanted to hunker down with a good book, or go and see Jago and watch him kick his chubby little legs in the bath. But Nicola recognised that Stacey was in the process of forging a deep relationship with her son as they prepared for his daddy's release and they needed to do that together, without her crowding them.

She gave a bright smile. Of course she would go. Sergio thought he was doing her a favour, and hadn't he been ultra-diplomatic for weeks now? Refusing to ask a single question about why Alessio di Bari had been so keen to get his hands on her address. He'd even resisted commenting on the unusual fact that she hadn't been able to sell a single painting since the Italian billionaire's departure.

Didn't she owe him?

Didn't she owe it to herself to get out of this rut and embrace what the world had to offer?

She packed a small case, took a stunningly scenic train journey along the Cornish Riviera and, after jumping in a cab, was driven to a low-key but unbelievably chic hotel, overlooking the blue-grey waves of the Atlantic. She showered, pinned up her hair, put on her working uniform of white shirt, black skirt, and matching jacket and slithered into the back of the taxi the hotel had ordered for her.

'You going up to Morwind, are you?' said the driver, when she gave him the address. 'Beautiful place. They say the sea views from there are the best in the county.'

'I'm looking forward to seeing it,' she answered politely, before lapsing into silence, because Nicola wasn't in the mood for conversation. She was trying very hard to compose herself for what lay ahead. Because the statue had been bought by a man for his wife and, stupidly, that hurt. How he must love her to have such an expensive piece shipped here, as a surprise. Suddenly she couldn't stop wondering whether she had sold herself short. Had she made herself too available to a man she'd always known would one day cast her aside?

But defining relationships in that way was insane. She hadn't been seduced beneath that gleaming bronze because she had *expected* anything from Alessio. She had done it because she hadn't been able to stop herself. Because he had consumed her senses in every way. Because she had adored him. Truth was, she still did. It wasn't *his* fault he didn't feel the same way. It wasn't anybody's fault. And even though her foolish heart was badly shattered she couldn't bring herself to regret a single second of it.

'Here you go,' said the driver, pulling up outside a large, contemporary clifftop house which somehow looked as if it had been there since the beginning of time. She could see at once what the driver had meant about the view, but it was more than that which made it beautiful. There was a sense of being close to the elements—of being part of the sea and the sky. As the cab drove away Nicola watched the swell of the crest-fringed waves and listened to them crashing on the rocks below.

But she couldn't stand there for ever. Time to meet the romantic Ross Fleming and, possibly, his wife.

Despite the modern architecture, there was an old-fashioned brass knocker. But her knock went unanswered for so long that Nicola wondered whether it could be heard in such a large house. She was just about to try again when suddenly the door opened and the sight which greeted her was so far off her scale of reality that she actually dropped her handbag and didn't bother picking it up as she stared into eyes as blue as a summer sea.

Alessio looked more casual than she'd ever seen him. His jeans were faded and a dark cashmere sweater clung softly to the honed definition of his torso. His hair was longer, too—ruffled ebony locks framing the slashed contours of his features, so that he had something of the pirate about him. But the blue eyes were exactly the same—brilliant and blazing and beautiful—and Nicola's first instinct was to cry and laugh all at the same time, because it was so incredibly good to see him.

But she didn't do either. She was too busy trying to stop herself from trembling. How *dare* he set up such a meeting? Was this intended to give him some sort of sadistic pleasure—extracting a cruel revenge for having deceived him? She set her mouth into what she hoped was a forbidding line, because he had hurt her once but he damned well wasn't going to get the chance to hurt her again.

'Is this some sort of set-up between you and Sergio?' she demanded coldly.

'Sergio knows nothing about it.'

'I'm looking for Ross Fleming.'

'I am Ross Fleming.'

'Really? I thought your name was Alessio di Bari.'

'Fleming is a pseudonym.'

'For the purchase of bronze statues, presumably?'

His sensual lips curved with the hint of a smile. 'Well, yes.'

She made herself say it and suddenly her cool mask slipped, because how could you remain composed while uttering words which felt as corrosive as battery fuel on your lips? 'For your *wife.*'

Alessio could see the incomprehension on her face and wondered whether his grand gesture might have failed spectacularly, particularly as the hurt in her eyes had been replaced by a growing anger. 'Nicola—'

'Have you brought me all the way out here to rub my nose in it?' she declared, giving a furious toss of her gleaming blonde head. 'You didn't waste any time, did you, Alessio? How long have you been married for? Did you find someone as soon as we'd split, or had there been someone in the background all along? Why, the ink must barely be dry on the certificate!'

From a purely aesthetic point of view, he thought how magnificent she looked when she was filled with rage, but suddenly Alessio realised he needed to act quickly if he wanted to appease her, and he did. He wanted that more than anything. 'Please, Nicola. The wind is strong. Come inside.'

'If you think I'm setting foot inside your house then you are very much mistaken. You really think I'm prepared to face your wife? What do you think I'm made of, Alessio, *stone*?'

On the contrary. Alessio swallowed. She was all magnificent creamy flesh and stormy grey eyes—and currently in the process of bending to retrieve her handbag from the step, presumably to ring for a cab to take her away as quickly as possible. And he realised then that half measures would get him nowhere. If he wanted her, he had to lay it on the line. To tell her. She needed to know how he felt. About her. About them. Yet how did a man break the habit of a lifetime and begin to articulate feelings he'd never dared confront before?

He sucked in an unsteady breath. 'There is no wife. The statue is for you, Nicola.' He paused. 'Only for you.'

She looked at him blankly. 'For me? What are you talking about?'

'I said it was for my wife and it is. But only if you are prepared to be my wife, for you are the only woman I would ever contemplate marrying. Because... I love you,' he said and suddenly his words were gruff. 'My clever, strong, proud, brave Nicola. I love you so very much.'

She was still eying him with frowning suspicion. 'Weren't you supposed to say that *before* you asked me to marry you?'

'I don't know what I am supposed to say!' he declared, lifting his hands in exasperation, in as vulnerable a moment as he'd ever shared with another person. 'Because you have thrown me into a state of confusion from the moment I first laid eyes on you. You are chaos theory personified! You fascinated me. Infuriated me. Intrigued me. I never knew where I was with you.'

'I know that,' she said woodenly, but there was no joy on her face—just that continued veiled look of suspicion. 'On some level I always knew that was my winning card and that's why I held onto it so tightly. You didn't want anything more than that.'

'You're right. I didn't. Until things started to change, without me expecting it. Without me even wanting it. I began to feel relaxed in your company,' he continued softly. 'To look in my diary to work out when next I could see you—but I forced myself to ration my time with you because I could not afford to let you become an addiction. But I was fighting a losing battle. And when I *did* rework my schedule in order to surprise you—you told me you were busy. Do you remember?'

'I was helping look after Jago that night.'

'Ah, Jago.' He nodded. 'That lucky little baby.'

*'Lucky?'*

*'Ma, certo,'* he said, with emphasis. 'To have an aunt like you. To battle for him. To help his young mother. That night when he was sick, my admiration of you knew no bounds. Do you realise that, Nicola? You didn't need to conceal anything about yourself, *cara mio*, because in that moment you were more amazing than I'd ever seen you.'

'You certainly weren't showing much admiration at the time,' she objected stubbornly.

Acknowledging her accusation, he nodded. *'Lo so.* I reacted badly because of the way you made me feel. Make me feel,' he corrected. 'Which is...'

Her grey gaze was steady, her features impassive. She was not helping him, he realised—and maybe that was a good thing.

'Scared,' he admitted at last. 'All my life I had vowed to never let anything scare me because for me that indicated weakness, which was a trait I could not tolerate. But I am living with that feeling now—all the time—and there is only one way to rid myself of it. I have tried to forget you, Nicola, but that is impossible. I have tried to contemplate spending the rest of my life without you— but that is unthinkable. With you, I want all the things I never imagined wanting. To build a home. To have babies. But I still don't know how you feel about such a prospect.'

Still she didn't speak and he nodded, knowing he

wasn't done yet—knowing he owed her more. 'I'm sorry for the way I behaved.'

She inclined her head. 'I was always taught that if someone offers an apology, then you must accept it.' She paused. 'But only if they really mean it.'

'From the very bottom of my heart.'

'Then I am sorry, too,' she said suddenly. 'I should have trusted you, but I was scared, too. I should have let you see that I loved you, but I was terrified you would reject me and push me away. Oh, Alessio.'

His heart was pounding as he asked her again. 'Does this mean you're going to marry me, Nicola Bennett?'

She glanced at the ground before looking up again and as he met her grey gaze he realised what she really wanted. And even though his scientific brain regarded such a desire with perplexity—bemusement, even—the man who loved her wanted it, too. For wasn't this the ultimate romantic gesture? Wasn't this what men had done since they first started losing their hearts to women? 'Marry me, *cara. Il mio unico grande amore,*' he said, as he dropped down onto one knee. 'My one and only love.'

And suddenly she was kneeling, too—not seeming to care about the damp step or the keen Atlantic breeze—and her arms were tight around his neck, her lips opening beneath his as she kissed him and kissed him, before breathing 'yes' into his mouth.

He wasn't really aware of the journey from the doorstep to the bedroom or how many items of clothing they dropped along the way, only that her stockings were ripped at the knees and he didn't feel complete until he had filled her with his seed. Quite literally. It was only afterwards that he realised it was the first time in his life he'd neglected to wear a condom.

'What if I've made you pregnant?' he demanded huskily.

Against his neck, Nicola giggled. 'Do you know, I think I'd be over the moon?'

'Me, too.' He gave an unsteady laugh. 'How crazy is that?'

'Totally crazy,' she agreed solemnly, turning to stare at the wide sweep of sea outside the window and thinking how beautiful it was. 'Why did you buy this house?'

'I haven't bought it—that would have been too presumptuous. I'm renting it, but it can be ours any time you want. You told me you didn't like skyscrapers and had always wanted to live by the sea, but we can live anywhere in the world. And, of course, we need to take your family into account.'

'My family?' she echoed tentatively.

He nodded. 'I can help your brother find work when he gets out of prison.'

'What sort of work? His CV is terrible!'

'He can learn a trade,' he said gently. 'He can find out what he's good at and use that. Because it's never too late to change. To start again. Or to fall in love. Life is whatever we choose to make it, Nicola—and I choose to make it with you.'

And suddenly she was crying, only this time he wasn't freaking out because she was displaying unwanted emotion—he was drying her tears with his fingers and his lips. And he was crying, too.

# EPILOGUE

THIS HOUSE WAS beautiful all year round, but Nicola loved it best in autumn. That was the time when the sun set straight in the west, dancing on the waves and flooding their bedroom with a rich, flame-coloured radiance. It was pouring in now, warming her skin and making it glow.

'Alessio?' she whispered, but he didn't answer and she shifted her position to glance down at her husband's sleeping form, wondering if life could get any more perfect. She smiled. Actually, yes, she suspected it could...

For almost three years now, they had been spending weekends in their beautiful Cornish home, following their London wedding. In an intimate ceremony, they had married in Marylebone register office with a small reception at the Ritz Hotel. It had seemed, as Alessio had whispered to her, an appropriate place to begin married life. They had honeymooned in Italy—touring the art-studded cities of Florence, Siena and Rome, which Nicola had always longed to visit.

But Alessio had surprised her yet again. He had taken her to the tiny mountain village where he'd lived with his grandmother and where he had retained his *nonna*'s tiny apartment above the bakery, having it religiously cleaned and maintained every week. They had spent two nights there—time enough for Nicola to experience the place he had come from, which he had left so long ago. But people in the street recognised him, and smiled—and the newly-weds lit a candle in the tiny church, where they had their vows blessed by the local priest. And maybe it was seeing their shining smiles of nuptial contentment in the photo Alessio sent to his mother which encouraged her to leave her mockery of a marriage at last. After a lot of thought, she had gone back to live in Italy, to Lecce—and they now visited her there, at least once a year.

Despite knowing she could branch out on her own, Nicola had continued to work for Sergio. She didn't want the hassle of starting up a new business and wasn't sure she had the necessary entrepreneurial streak. She was far more interested in devoting time to her precious marriage. Meanwhile, Alessio had opened his first English factory, which had brought so much employment to an impoverished section of the country.

Hearing a yawn and a contented sigh from beside her, Nicola looked down to meet the brilliance of her husband's gaze. 'You sound satisfied,' she remarked.

'That's because I am. You are very good at satisfying a man, *cara*.' He smiled and gave another lazy yawn, his gaze raking over her. 'It's good to be on our own again. Much as though I enjoyed the weekend.'

'So did I. Jago is so adorable, and Callum's so contented. Why, he's hardly recognisable as the same person. Even Stacey said so.'

'He has lost his prison pallor,' Alessio said suddenly. 'He has grown into a strong man.'

'And all thanks to you, my love.'

Because Alessio had helped her brother on his release from prison, getting him an apprenticeship as a cabinet-maker, the exquisite carvings he had made in jail pointing him firmly in the direction of his new career. Callum had married Stacey and they'd moved into a pretty cottage in Somerset, with a huge garden for little Jago to run around in. A place to keep chickens and grow vegetables and to live a quiet, rural life. It wasn't a life the young couple had ever anticipated, but it filled them with utter joy.

Yes, everything was good—more than good. Their only disappointment was that Nicola hadn't become pregnant. But they both had tried to keep this in perspective and count their many other blessings. Alessio had mentioned fostering, or adoption, or neither—if that was what they decided.

'What are you looking so pensive about, *mio cara*?'

The velvety voice beside her was curious, but Nicola closed her eyes, not wanting her expression to give her away. Wanting to savour her news for a few wonderful seconds more.

'I was just thinking—'

'Dangerous,' he murmured, her lashes fluttering open as his finger moved slowly down the side of her cheek. 'It wouldn't have anything to do with a baby, would it, *cara mio*? More specifically, *our* baby?'

She blinked at him, amazement and happiness written all over her face. 'How on earth did you know?'

Alessio smiled. He could list the physical signs of her condition, which had subtly changed a body he knew and loved so well. The slight tenderness of her breasts and almost imperceptible softening of her belly. With his scientific eye for detail, he had observed her refusing a bowl of figs for breakfast, which usually she adored. Her hair was even shinier, too.

But the reason behind his conclusion was simple. It was based on a principle which gave them both endless pleasure whenever he expressed it. His lips curved into a smile as he pulled her down into his arms.

'Because I love you,' he said.

* * * * *

# CINDERELLA AND THE OUTBACK BILLIONAIRE

KELLY HUNTER

MILLS & BOON

# CHAPTER ONE

'YOU NEED TO LEAVE.'

Reid Blake looked up from the computer that had only just started receiving emails and frowned at his older brother. Impressive as Judah was—with a murderous reputation to match the fierceness of his scowl—Reid wasn't the slightest bit intimidated by the bite in his brother's words. 'Why do I have to leave? I only just got here. And I'll have you know your darling daughter invited me to stay for an afternoon tea party in a cupboard beneath the stairs. She's making cupcakes for us and everything.'

Judah's face softened at mention of his daughter and so it should. Young Piper Blake was a whip-smart laugh and a half, with the face of an angel. It was a miracle daddy Judah could ever say no to her but say no he occasionally did, and nine-year-old Pip was better for it.

She certainly didn't get sensible guidance from her indulgent uncle Reid.

Judah sighed and leaned his impressive form against the ornate wooden doorframe. Many parts of the Jeddah Creek homestead were ornate—a testament to the peerage Judah held as an English lord of the realm, even if he had grown up in Outback Australia. 'If you're not leaving now, you'd best stay the night and sling a tarp over that mosquito you call a helicopter. There's a dust storm coming in from the west.'

'Aaargh.' Reid blew out a breath and ground the heels of his hands into his eyes as he pushed his computer chair away from the desk. Internet connections out here were sketchy at best and this was his last chance to download work emails before he went altogether off grid. 'Why is it that every time I clear a few days to head up to Cooper's Crossing the weather slams down? Do the gods not think I deserve a break from the insanity? Because, believe me, I'm looking forward to the solitude.'

'Then get off the Internet and go find it,' Judah countered.

'Can't. I'm waiting on feedback on a new engine proto-type I sent in at the start of the week. It's not easy being a genius with engines, a workaholic *and* a playboy billionaire bachelor. A princely catch. A stud. It's a pain in the heart, let me tell you.'

'Are you done?'

'Never knowing what a person wants from you. Your money or your love. Possibly the new solar engine proto-type that's going to revolutionise commercial flight as we know it. It's an existential crisis, I'm telling you.'

His brother eyed him impassively. 'You're no playboy.'

True, but irrelevant as far as world media was concerned. 'You know this, I know this, I like to think the few women I've seriously dated over the years know this, and yet the rest of humanity has other ideas.'

'Speaking of the women you've dated—'

'Let's not.'

'Believe me, I'd rather not. But your friend Carrick Mas-terton phoned here the other day, trying to track you down. Something about you being best man at his wedding.'

'And I've already told him no.' Never date your best mate's sister. Reid had broken that rule half a dozen years ago in the hope that Jenna might be the one. Instead, after six months' worth of intimate conversations, travel and attention, Jenna had sold the information she'd collected on him to the press and declared herself an environmental activist. She'd declared him an intellectually stunted free market capitalist who didn't give a damn about the environment, never mind his posturing. As a footnote, she'd disparaged his sexual prowess and labelled him the most emotionally unavailable person she'd ever met. The fallout had cost him several promising business associations and one of his oldest friends. 'Jenna's in the wedding party as a bridesmaid. Apparently she's willing to let bygones be bygones.'

Judah raised a sceptical eyebrow. 'Big of her.'

'Indeed. Anything else you want to know about my personal life?'

Judah held up his hands in a sign of appeasement. 'Butting out.'

'If Carrick rings here again, tell him you're not my social secretary.'

'Already done. I was more interested in where you were at with it.'

'Obviously still petty and wounded—at least, that's how they'll spin it.' Reid let his flippant façade drop momentarily. 'There was no good hand for me to play when it came to that invitation. Carrick and his bride are getting a two-week, all-expenses-paid holiday on a barrier reef island as my wedding gift to them. My secretary sent it through a couple of days ago. I suspect that's why he called here.' It would be interesting to see if Carrick ever took that trip, cashed it in, or ignored the gift altogether because he thought Reid was insulting him.

'You're sending him to *our* island?'

'Of course not. There'd be pictures of the beach house

splashed across the Internet within moments of their arrival. Carrick's fiancée is a social media influencer.'

'Joy,' Judah murmured dryly.

'I booked them some kind of high-end honeymoon island we have nothing to do with. They'll love it—should they choose to go.'

'Fair.'

'Keep an eye out for a headline exposing my unconscionable largess, my callous insensitivity, or both.'

Judah nodded. 'I'll have it framed and sent straight to the pool room.'

This raised a smile, as it was likely meant to do. 'Thing is, I do wish my old school mate a strong, nurturing, *happy* marriage. I want that for him. Hell, I want that for *me*.'

It was the closest he'd come in years to admitting his loneliness.

Judah sighed and wrapped a big hand around the back of his neck, a sure tell that he was uncomfortable with the turn the conversation had taken. 'You staying or going?'

'Going.' Right after he looked at the weather radar. Or maybe not, given how long it would take for that information to download. 'Going right now. Just as soon as I collect my cupcakes and say goodbye to your women. You realise they like me better than they like you?'

'If I truly believed that I'd have to shoot you.'

'You *say* that…but would you do it? Would you really?'

Judah smirked, cutting creases in his weatherworn face. 'They do say practice makes perfect.'

It was a testament to how solid their relationship was these days that they could talk freely about the incident that had put Judah in prison for most of his twenties. On the other hand, Reid had his own suspicions about what had gone down on the night of that shooting and, no matter how many times he'd tried to get Judah to reveal all, his older brother had never confided in him. When he was younger, that lack of trust had worn Reid down like sandpaper on sapwood. These days, Reid had a far more flexible under-standing of what people 'needed to know'.

'Dust storm incoming,' Judah said again. 'Didn't you say you were leaving?'

He was. He couldn't wait around for a weather map that might never download. Besides, wasn't as if he wouldn't be able to see a dust storm coming. 'See you in a week.'

'The homestead's all stocked up and ready for you.'

'Aw, you shouldn't have.'

'I didn't. Gert swung past last week.'

Gert had been Jeddah Creek station's part-time house-keeper ever since Reid could remember. She served two other remote Outback stations as well, driving a circuit around the three properties every two weeks. When Reid and Judah had bought the Cooper place to the north it had seemed only smart to keep that rotation in place for as long as Gert wanted the work.

'Fly safe.'

Reid nodded as he shoved his laptop and cord connec-tions into his carryall and zipped it closed. He'd been fly-ing helicopters since his teens and designing and building them since his early twenties. That 'mosquito' outside had a revolutionary engine design and a flight range more than double its closest competitor. 'I always do.'

Twenty minutes later, after a quick safety check and two cupcakes, Reid was in the air and heading north. There were no other passengers—he was on his own at last and happier than he'd been in a long while.

Judah was the reclusive rebel of the two Blake brothers,

which meant that Reid often doubled down when it came to fronting the various company holdings they held between them. Reid was the people person, the gregarious showman everyone could talk to without fear. No one—and that included his brother—knew how much he hated the constant scrutiny he was under twenty-four hours of every day, or how the flippant, indestructible, playboy veneer he'd cultivated over the years was beginning to seem like a bad idea. Mainly because after years of shielding his innermost feelings from absolutely everyone, he no longer knew how to let people in.

Every move one of his engineering companies made was scrutinised by the market, by other companies on the cutting edge of renewable energy, and by an ever-increasing array of lobby groups. Markets rose and fell beneath the weight of his words. It was enough to make him wish for the good old days when it was just him, alone at seventeen, with only a vast and fickle channel country cattle station to care for.

His parents recently deceased and his brother in prison for killing a man.

*Yeah, the good old days.*

There'd been no functional adults in the room when his brother had got out of jail and together he and Judah had bought up vast tracts of Australian channel country and set about turning it into a reserve. No one to stop Reid as he'd poured money into renewable energy research and prototype engines geared towards clean energy flight. No one to warn them that vast amounts of money, power and position attracted even more money, power, position and responsibility, ready or not. And they *had* proved ready. Reid was proud of everything he and Judah continued to achieve. But some days, and this was one of them, all he really wanted was blue sky all around him and the red dirt and saltbush scrub of channel country far below. After months of relentless hard graft—be it intellectual, social or political—and way too many people urging him to go faster, slower, sideways or over a cliff, there truly was no place like home.

He pointed the little helicopter north over familiar ground, his attention split between the harsh beauty all around him and the faint hint of dust in the sky to the west. Dust storms weren't that uncommon but flying into one was not recommended. Even the air currents ahead of a dust front were dangerous. If he had to land and let the weather front roll over him he would, but it wasn't his first preference.

Outrunning it was by far his preferred plan.

'C'mon, little darling, gimme all you got.' He maxed out the speed and felt a familiar sense of exhilaration slam through him. He'd been a lonely teen out here after his father had died and before Judah had been released from prison. Flying had been his first love and it still ranked right up there with sex as far as he was concerned.

Not that he'd ever mentioned it. The ridicule potential attached to his preference for flight above sex was high. He'd never live it down.

Billionaire Stud. The media ate that one up and people believed it, and for all that Reid joked his way around it, and used it as a shield to hide a tender heart, the description grated. Even before his disastrous experience with Jenna, he hadn't been able to tell if a woman wanted to get up close and personal with him because she actually liked him. Too many women over the years *had* wanted him for his money. That or they'd wanted him to use his influence to forward their political agendas. They'd used him to advance their careers or, like Jenna, claim a spotlight they couldn't command on their own.

Romantic relationships had been so transactional for so damn long…

Was it any wonder he preferred flying to sexual intimacy?

That wall of dust—and it *was* a wall, stretching to the north as far as the eye could see—was edging closer. 'Sweetheart—' he patted the console in front of him '—we need to go a little faster.'

Ari Cohen looked behind her at the wall of rapidly approaching dust and scowled. It had come up out of nowhere and was heading straight for her, and that meant breaking camp and getting as much of her stuff into the cabin of her battered old ute as fast as she could. Once that was done, she needed to find rocks to choc around the tyres and after that it wouldn't hurt to tie the vehicle down using rope and metre-long steel fence stakes hammered into the sandy ground as far as they would go. Only then would she feel safe while riding out the storm from inside the cabin of her ute.

She'd weathered dust storms before, ever since she was a kid, but she'd never seen a red wall of doom like this one before. A snappy wind whipped at her chestnut-coloured hair and blew the edges of her tent into the air as she collapsed it and quickly rolled it up, poles and all, and shoved it into the back seat of the twin cab. Her little gas cooking burner went in next as she grumbled about the 'too little, too late' nature of weather forecasts in general and the undisputed fact that no one really cared what kind of weather events happened out here in the middle of nowhere.

Not as if anyone actually *lived* out here except for the super-rich Blake brothers, who likely owned big chunks of Mars as well by now.

Ari was throwing tie-down ropes over her ute when first she saw the silver and black blob in the sky that turned out to be what looked like a muster helicopter—a tiny thing with a bulbous nose and slender rotors and next to no seating room.

If whoever was flying that thing thought they had any chance at all of outrunning the dust roiling towards them at what felt like a million miles an hour, they were sadly mistaken.

'Land, you maniac!' she yelled even though they'd never hear her. It felt good to say it. No one could ever say she hadn't told them.

Her heart caught in her chest as the helicopter lifted straight up and then arced to the right, as if flung about by the hand of capricious winds. She didn't want to be witness to tragedy. All she wanted to do was crawl inside the safety of her vehicle and ride out the storm as best she could, but she couldn't look away from the fight in the sky—helicopter against the elements, and how was man supposed to win against those odds? What fool thought they could? 'Come down!'

It was as if someone had heard her wish, because the little aircraft spun, tilted and headed for earth and— Oh, no.

'Not like that!'

*No! Oh, hell no!*

So much for rocks under wheels and big load tie-downs. When that little buzz box landed, it was going to land *hard*, and there was no one else around but her to go and see what—if anything—could be rescued.

She wasn't a doctor, nurse or medic of any kind. She'd never belonged to the SES or the military.

Driving towards disaster was so not her thing. But…

And why was there always a *but*?

She'd been born and bred out here on the edge of the desert and she *knew* what happened out here when there was no help on hand. This wasn't a forgiving land.

And whoever was in that blasted helicopter was going to need a hand.

She could curse with the best of them, and let loose as she started the engine. Who was to say her ute wouldn't be picked up and slammed down by wind that had slipped its leash? But she gunned the engine anyway and set out north, her hands loose around the steering wheel on account of the soft dirt that would send wheels one way or another, no point trying to resist that sway.

She could still see the way ahead. Still see the helicopter battling capricious winds. Not down yet but getting ever lower in the sky.

'Fight,' she willed whoever was up there flying that thing. Win.


For all his years of flying, Reid had never known weather like this. Any sense of superiority or confidence bestowed on him by humankind had long since left his brain. Getting the small craft on the ground was all that mattered now. Dying had to be factored into calculations. The efficiency of engines mattered nothing in the face of nature's reckoning.

He'd long since lost sight of the ground. None of his instruments worked.

He didn't know which way was up, and helicopters couldn't glide towards the ground and count on gravity to be their friend. Helicopters were the buzzy bees, the frantic winged. When something went wrong they plummeted.

And still he fought. Tried to feel which way was up, which way was down so he could edge ever lower. Easy. Easy, sweetie, as he fought the air and the dust that flung them this way and that with careless abandon.

This couldn't be the end.

It couldn't.

If he lived, he would definitely prioritise sex over flying. Make a solemn effort to give it all he had. *'I promise.'*

If he lived...

It was a miracle Ari even found the crash site, given the red dust blasting what was left of the paint from her vehicle. Never again would she screw up her nose at miracles, because there it was in front of her, the little helicopter of many scattered pieces, nose down and tail up and its rotors heaven only knew where. There was no one *in* the wrecked remains. No one she could see.

Where might a person land if they'd been flung somewhere?

Ari had no idea.

She cut the engine on her ute that might never start again after driving through this hellscape, but that was a problem for later. She had dust-free air here inside the cab, safe haven.

She could die out there.

Someone else *was* out there and whether they were already dead was anyone's guess, but, if they *were* still alive, they wouldn't last long unless they took shelter. That or someone *got* them to shelter. Meaning her.

What a thought.

She took a nylon strap meant for securing cargo rather than people and wrapped one end around her waist. She put her sunglasses on and wrapped a scarf around her head and mourned the lack of scuba-diving goggles because she could have used them too. Ari left the safety of the ute, hunched against the wind and the bite of dust against the bare skin of her ankles and hands. She tied the other end of the cord around her waist to the bull bar. The cord extended thirty metres at most and if she couldn't find anyone before that nylon stretched taut, she'd try again from a different direction.

'Fight,' she muttered from beneath the scarf now plastered to her head. 'I can *feel* you.' She truly could, another miracle, no matter the how or the why. 'I'm goddamn *coming* for you. Don't you give up on me now.'

# CHAPTER TWO

HE COULD BREATHE. The sound of fabric snapped all around him and he couldn't see a thing, but he could breathe and he wasn't alone.

'Who's there?' His voice sounded thick to his ears and the pain in his head threatened to drag him under, but he got the words out somehow.

'He speaks.' That voice held a faint edge of hysteria, but he'd never been so grateful for the company. 'Listen.' Her voice held compelling urgency. 'Was there anyone else in the helicopter with you?'

'No.'

The woman exhaled noisily. 'That's good. That's real good.'

'Where are we?' He still couldn't make his tongue work.

'In a tent next to your crashed helicopter. I didn't know if it was a good idea to move you so I brought the tent to you. There's a dust storm. It's bad in here but it's worse out there.'

'I can't see.'

'It's dark. It's the dust.'

'No. I can't *see*.'

Silence.

'Say something!' he demanded, reaching out towards the voice and clutching onto warm skin. An arm above the elbow, bare dusty skin, warm and alive. 'I can't see.' He felt a hand thread through his, calming him, grounding him.

'Pretty sure you hit your head,' she offered quietly.

Talk about stating the obvious. But he wasn't alone and he was still breathing and maybe he should start being grateful for small mercies. 'You'll stay?' It was vitally important that the pretty, panicked voice didn't go away.

'Yeah. Not going anywhere right now. It's brutal out there.'

'I can't see.' The blackness, the sheer *absence*, overwhelmed him.

'I hear you.' She brought his hand to her lips, their fingers still entwined, and her lips felt pillow soft and warm against his skin and he focussed on that above all else. 'I've found you.' And almost in a whisper, 'I just can't help you.'

He was clocking out again, consciousness fading beneath the agonising pain of…everything. 'Stay.' He was begging, and he knew it was a lot to ask but he didn't want to die alone.

'I don't think you're dying. Your pulse is pretty strong, yeah.' Raggedy raspy sandpaper voice chock full of dirt but so beautiful. Was she a mind-reader? How did she know his thoughts?

'You're talking out loud,' she said next, dry as dust, and he laughed, or tried to, but darkness ate at his consciousness moments later and he realised that any laughter, any movement, was a really bad idea.

'I'm not… I can't…'

'You're talking and you're alive,' she murmured. 'We can work with that.'

He squeezed her hand and she squeezed back. Right before the darkness took him.

When Reid next came to consciousness, he wasn't alone and for that he was grateful. His saviour had tucked in beside him, a warm presence and a soft breath against his shoulder, her fingers loosely folded over his wrist as if she'd fallen prey to slumber while checking his pulse. The tent—she'd said she'd put a tent up around them—no longer strained against a brutal wind but there was still a heaviness in the air and an unnatural silence all about them.

He could wiggle his toes and move his legs. His fingers moved and so did his arms. He could think. He could breathe.

He still couldn't see.

'How long's it been?' Might as well ask. The body next to his had tensed as he'd run through his body check. He knew she was awake.

'A while.'

'Doesn't sound as windy.' The tent no longer shuddered beneath the onslaught.

'I think it's because the tent's half buried beneath the dirt. The weight's pressing in on my body. You got the good side.'

She moved. Levered herself up on her elbow, he imagined, because the rest of her was still pressed against him. He tried to imagine what she looked like and came up empty. He had no idea.

Was she married? He wanted to fold her hand in his again, bring it close across his chest and search for rings. 'Will anyone mind if I never let your hand go?'

'I'll mind, at some point. But no one else is likely to mind.'

'How old are you?'

'Twenty-three.'

'Are you pretty?'

'Does it matter?' she chided.

'That a no?'

'Handsome, you are stuck with me in a tent in the middle of a desert in the middle of a dust storm and I'm just about to bring you food and water *and you can't see me.* Do you really give a damn what I look like?'

Well, when she put it like that... 'I'm Reid,' he said.

'I know who you are.' She let go of his wrist and moved away.

'No, wait!' Panic set in, fierce and overwhelming. He flailed for purchase, grabby hands that would have grabbed but for the stabbing pain in his head. That keening sound in his ears? It was him.

'I'm coming back.' She put her hand to his chest and pressed down as if she knew his heart needed holding in place. 'My ute's not far away and even if I can't see it for dust, I'm tied to it. I'll get there.' She fumbled with his hand and pressed it to her body. He could feel the knotted nylon around her waist. 'All I have to do is follow the line.'

'How will you get back?'

'I found you, didn't I? Went back for the tent, found you again and put the tent up around you after cutting the floor of it in half and tucking it around you. And if you believe that was fun or easy, I have a harbour bridge to sell you. I also have pain-relief tablets back in my ute. A few types. Does that sound good? Worth a round trip?'

'Get them,' he urged. 'Give them.'

'Let go of my hand.'

Now there was a problem. No way was he letting go of that hand, and he told her so using language his dear departed mother wouldn't have approved of. In his defence, he was probably going to be reunited with his mother sooner rather than later and he could apologise then. 'Stay.'

'Seriously?'

Manhood be damned, he wasn't letting her go. ''S dangerous out there. You shouldn't go.'

'What about the painkillers?'

'Who needs 'em?'

'I'm thinking you do.'

Maybe that was true. 'How come you're here?' This was nowhere land. People didn't live here. People didn't travel through here. 'Are you real?'

'I'm trespassing. Trespassing, unmarried, and not pretty in any standard sense of the word. My eyes are too far apart, my neck is too long, my nose has a bump in it from when I broke it as a kid and I'm skinny. I'm not that clever and most times I come across as too shy to bother with. But I am real.'

'Good. That sounds good.'

She laughed and it was the loveliest sound in the world. 'See? You're almost making sense—that's a good sign. You're following the conversation, your pulse is strong, your breathing's not rattly. I'm no medic but those are good signs. You're a tough guy.'

'That's me.' A great wave began to wash over him from the toes up, thick, visceral and dragging him under. Again.

'Reid? Reid!'

He couldn't hold on.

Not even to her hand.

Ari unzipped the tent flap and squirmed through the exit before zipping it back up from the outside. Concern for the wounded man had overridden her desire to stay inside the tent. She'd already lost her scarf to him when she'd wound it around his head to try and stop the bleeding, but she could lift her T-shirt up and put it across her nose and mouth so she didn't cop a lungful of dust, and she had a first-aid kit in the ute, and a pack of painkillers in the glove box, and enough water to see them through for days.

Please let his rescue not take days.

The man was a billionaire last she'd heard. Surely,

he'd have tracking devices all over that little helicopter or amongst his personal belongings.

They'd know where he was and soon as the dust cleared they'd come for him.

The dust was still so thick! He wasn't the only one whose eyes weren't working properly.

Pulling the T-shirt all the way up over her head, she took hold of the rope with both hands and pulled it taut and began to walk. She kept the rope tense and shuffled along and made it to her ute an eon later.

But her trusty old ride was right where she'd left it, even if it was now buried up to its axels.

She tried to shake the dust off before she got into the cabin, a stupid move if ever there was one, and finally settled for clambering in regardless and slamming the door shut behind her.

Better, much better as she brushed the dust from her face and tentatively opened her eyes, blinking hard. Grit everywhere. Up her nose. In her mouth.

*Don't rub your eyes, Ari.*

When instinct demanded she do just that. Don't move for a bit. Just…let the dust settle. She leaned back with her head against the headrest and slowly wiped at her face with the edge of the hand towel she kept just behind the front seat. It felt blissfully free of grit and she reached for the water bottle in the centre console next and unscrewed the cap with her eyes still closed and brought the bottle to her lips. Not cold, but very definitely wet.

She wet the edge of the towel and gently dripped some into her eyes until she could open them without feeling as if her eyelids were scouring pads. See? Easy as pie getting from the downed man back to her vehicle. She could do this all day.

Although it'd be nice to only have to do it once.

No phone service out here but she checked the phone's remaining battery and then set about filling her backpack and another carryall with supplies. If she was quick enough, she might be able to retrace her footsteps before the wind blew them away. She shoved her native plant identification book in the pack too—as a reminder of a wider world full of research and technology and all sorts of clever people. People who would come for the unconscious billionaire and make him well.

Until then, he had Ari, queen of nothing special, and she'd do her best to make him comfortable.

The trek back took longer because she lost track of her footsteps and the wind blew up again and so did the dust, and this time she couldn't keep her eyes closed and rely on the rope to take her where she was going. By the time she found the tent she'd begun making bargains with whoever might be listening.

*If you show me the tent, I'll stop swearing for a year.*

*If you stop with the dust, I'll study my heart out and top my horticulture course in every subject. Yes, even soil physics.*

*If he lives, I'll be grateful for ever that I don't have him on my conscience for the rest of my days. That's got to be worth a pledge to abstain from sex for at least a—*

*Oh! The tent. Hooray!*

Right in the nick of time.

'I'm back,' she said as she dumped her bags at the door and went around to her side of the tent and began scooping the fine red sand away from it with both hands. 'Are you awake?'

He groaned. Still in the land of the living.

'Awesome.'

Under other circumstances she wouldn't have minded seeing that handsome devil flat on his back and groaning just for her, but this was not that fantasy. She dug faster, wanting a little less weight on her side of the tent so that once inside there would be more room. For all that the tent was supposed to be a two-man job, Reid Blake had done his damnedest to fill it all by himself and the likelihood of them both having to shelter in it for the foreseeable future was high.

'Can you see anything yet?' Because she was of a mind to strip off most of her clothes before going inside, seeing as they were caked in dust.

'No.'

Not so awesome for him.

By the time everything but her clothes was in the tent, she'd broken her promise to not swear for a year.

Reid had somehow dislodged the bandage from his head and had likely been prodding at it with his fingers and then he'd used his fingers to examine his eyes. Either that or he'd started bleeding *from* his eyes. Either way, hello the stuff of nightmares.

'What is it? What's wrong?'

Did he sound sleepy or slurry and did it even matter, what with all the blood loss?

Don't panic, don't panic, don't panic, aaargh!

She was panicking.

She wondered if he could sense it.

'Nothing's wrong.' She tried to keep the fear out of her voice and failed miserably. What would she want from a protector she couldn't see? Reassurance of normality. Something to cling to. Humanity. The ridiculous nature of existence, even. 'Well, nothing except for the part where the dust is worse than ever so I left my clothes at the door and

I'm really hoping you can't see me because that would be awkward.' She dragged her backpack closer and unzipped it, spilling everything onto the ground, including her torch. He wasn't the only one who could barely see in this weird twilight world of dust and—

'You're...naked?'

'Almost,' she replied as she pointed the torch at the wall and turned it on. Great. Now she could really see the mess he'd made of himself and it was even more terrifying beneath the bright LEDs. He had no colour to his skin other than blood. His left trouser leg was soaked with it. 'Almost naked, yeah. Better still, I have painkillers. They're capsules so you'll have to swallow, but I have water here too. *Can* you swallow?'

He showed her rather than told her and she sent up a silent cheer as she dragged a sleeveless cotton sundress over her head. 'Okay, here comes the first tablet. You're getting three, with a sip of water after each, and then I'm going to clean up your face and do stuff to your leg.'

'What kind of stuff?'

'Good, lifesaving stuff.'

'And you're going to do this naked?'

'That's the way I roll, although I did just pull a dress over my head. But you...what a guy. Half dead and still with the sexy thoughts. I'm impressed.' She really didn't want to examine her own response to the wounded man she tended. What kind of woman came across a man in grave danger and thought to herself, *I bet skin-on-skin with you would be a glorious thing to experience*? She tapped the first tablet against lips that were softer than they looked, and warmer too, and that was a good thing from a first-aid perspective, even if the small contact sent a tingle of sexual awareness through her. 'Not going there.'

'Going where?'

'Straight to hell, most likely. Take your medicine. Don't make me shove it down your throat, because I will. Have you ever given a cat a worm tablet?'

He laughed weakly, and she caught a glimpse of teeth, a hint of tongue against her fingers and then the capsule was gone. She barely refrained from stroking him as she would an obedient moggy. 'I don't want to lift your head up, so get that capsule to the back of your mouth and I'll pour some water into your mouth and try not to drown you, and then you can swallow. Is that a good plan?'

It was her only plan and she hoped it had legs. Imagine trying to explain to a coroner her part in this man's death. Yes, your doctor, sir. He drowned in the middle of a dust storm in the desert. Lungs full of water. I've no idea how that happened… 'Are you ready?' She dribbled water into his mouth and waited way too many seconds until he swallowed. 'Did it work?'

'Yes.'

Twice more, he swallowed the pills, and then she ripped the wrapping from a bar of milk chocolate and took a big bite. This was *her* medication. Food for her frightened soul. 'Want some?'

'What is it?'

'Chocolate. I hear it chases away bad thoughts.'

His lips quirked upwards. 'Where'd you hear that?'

'I read it in a book. Possibly a book about wizards.'

'I'd laugh but laughing sends me unconscious.'

'Do you want some or not?'

'Yes.'

She broke off a square and fed it to him by hand. She had to stay snarky if only to balance the tentative tenderness of her touch. 'Your leg's bleeding. I'm going to take your trousers off.'

'Now you're just having a lend.'

If only. 'Yep, that's me. Injured man at my mercy and all I want is a look at his equipment.'

He paused as if listening to something she couldn't hear. 'Is it really that bad?' he asked, his lovely baritone little more than a rumble.

'It looks bad from the outside,' she admitted. 'But I have bandages and stuff.'

'Stuff.'

'All the good stuff. Please may I take off your trousers?'

'Stuff of my dreams.'

She laughed. Too high, all wrong, but his lips tilted up again.

'Now that's a nice sound.'

His words steadied her. She wouldn't panic if he didn't, and he seemed determined not to. If flirting got them through this without falling apart, surely she could embrace it? Chalk up this strangely intimate connection they were forging to extraordinary circumstances and keep doing whatever it was they were doing. She reached for the clasp on his jeans. Button-ups, all the way. Fancy pants, with plenty of weight to be going on with as she clenched denim in her fists and tugged them down his hips. 'We should try this again when you're feeling better.'

'We should.'

But his voice sounded thin and by the time she had his jeans off completely he was gone again, saying hello to oblivion.

She had gin in her carryall, don't judge, and she used it to clean up his leg before bandaging it tight. There had been no spouting artery fountain, just a deep seeping cut across thigh muscle, and she hoped her cleaning was thorough enough and that her fix would hold until proper medical care arrived.

She took care with his face. A bottle of water and her trusty towel removing the blood until she found the seeping gashes slicing up his forehead. She flooded the surgical gauze in the first-aid kit with alcohol and pressed it to the wound, and then picked up the long roll of stretchy bandage and slid her fingers beneath his head and bandaged it tight. There would be no prying this one loose. She'd smack him if he tried.

She tended to his other injuries next and tried to make sure he wasn't bleeding heavily from any other body parts.

He roused a little towards the end. 'How's your serenity?' he muttered.

'I'm predicting you'll live.'

'That's just hope.'

'I'm willing to embrace it.' She gave him more water. 'And now we wait.'

'Are you still naked?'

'Nope. I'm wearing a dress.'

'What colour is it?'

'Green.'

'What colour's your hair?'

'Dark brown.'

'And your eyes?'

'Also brown.'

'I'm picturing that actress from one of the James Bond films.'

'You do you, sunshine.' Who knew which actress he meant? She sure didn't. 'Where were you flying to?'

'North of Cooper's Crossing homestead. There are a couple of eco lodges up there.'

He really did seem functional in the thought department. 'Anyone expecting you?'

'No. The place is empty.'

'Will anyone be tracking your flight?'

Silence.

'But your helicopter has signals and stuff, right? An indestructible black box?'

'It's not a commercial passenger jet, angel. It's a prototype.'

'That's just disappointing.' She tried to let the reality of no one being able to find them using some kind of beacon sink in. 'Mind you, no one's coming for us in this weather anyway. How are you feeling? Is the pain medication kicking in?'

'Not even close.'

'It's not as if I can keep giving you more.'

'I know.'

She felt so useless. 'More water?'

'Please.'

One more pill couldn't hurt, surely. She fished one from the bottle and pressed it against his lips. 'It's just over-the-counter paracetamol. The first three were NSAIDs. I think I can give you both, but no more for another four hours after this one. You in?'

He was.

'How's the eyesight?'

'Frighteningly absent.'

She couldn't imagine a world of perpetual darkness.

'Keep talking,' he said gruffly. 'Please.'

She bit off another mouthful of chocolate, reached into her carryall for her textbook and stretched out next to him on her stomach, making sure they were connected from shoulder to toe as she spread her sleeping bag over them both. It wasn't cold yet but it would be later. Might as well get a head start on the warm and cosy factor.

She opened the book up to a random page and cleared her throat. 'Sturt's Desert Pea, Swainsona formosa. Family, Fabaceae. Named after the English medical doctor and botanist Isaac Swainson—he'd probably be pretty useful right about now. Formosa from the Latin for beautiful. I've never seen them this far north. It flowers from March to July but that's rain dependent. It prefers calcareous sandy soils. Calcareous—what does that even mean?'

'Who are you?' he murmured.

'I'm your dust-storm buddy.' She kept on reading aloud, one plant classification and description after another, while his body relaxed against hers and his breathing became slow and regular.

Gotta give it to her textbook—it *was* useful. She'd never again rant about the astronomical cost of it.

Because it had put sightless, seriously injured billionaire Reid Blake firmly to sleep.

# CHAPTER THREE

WAKING FELT LIKE rising through mud. So much mud weighing Reid down, wanting him to stay in that place where pain couldn't reach him and fear couldn't overwhelm. But fear had a way of tunnelling, and it roused him just enough to become aware of the stabbing pain in his head and an all-encompassing darkness. 'I can't see.'

He heard movement beside him and felt warm fingers circle his wrist. 'Do you know where you are?'

'I—' No.

'You're in a tent in a dust storm,' the sweet voice continued. 'Your helicopter crashed. You have a head wound and more.'

It was the voice from his dream. Or maybe it wasn't a dream after all. 'You were here before.'

'I found you. Put a tent up around you and gave you some painkillers.' He felt the press of a drink bottle to his lips and drank gratefully and ignored the trickle of water that escaped from the corner of his mouth and etched rivulets down his neck. 'Sunset was a couple of hours ago.'

He felt movement beside him and then the hand was gone from around his wrist. 'Put it back!'

'What?'

'The hand. Put it back! *Put it back!* Anywhere, it doesn't matter. Please.'

He now knew what startled silence sounded like. And then a warm, small hand pressed gently on his shoulder and he could breathe properly again. That touch, human connection at its most basic—it anchored him.

'Do you want my knees digging into your side too?' She sounded a little shaky—nice to know he had company in that regard. 'Because I want to sit up to check you over again, but if I do that, I'm gonna be all up in your space.'

'Dig in. Please.'

'You rich guys. So kinky.'

'You know who I am?'

'Yeah.' The hand stilled. 'Do *you* know who you are?'

'I haven't lost my mind.' Just his sight.

'Just checking. Far as I can tell, the bandage has stopped most of the bleeding from your head. I used up the rest of the bandages on you too, while you were out to it. There's one around your other wrist and hand—pretty sure you have a break there, and your shoulder looks out of place too. And I hope you didn't like those trousers too much, because I sliced them straight up the legs so I could stop the bleeding from the gash that runs from mid-thigh to your kneecap. And then I unbuttoned your shirt to check out your abs. Looking good, by the way. Then I slid my hand underneath you and groped all over your back and your butt—'

'Who's the kinky one now?' he murmured.

'And when my hand didn't resurface covered in blood, I decided you probably weren't bleeding out. After that, I kinda just tucked in beside you to wait. I figure your big brother will be trying to find you soon, but he's going to have to wait for the dust to settle first.'

'You know Judah?'

'I know of him. Same way I know of you. Hard not to around here.'

'So, you're local?' Was she being evasive with her identity or was he imagining things? 'I'm not about to sue you for trespassing, if that's what you're worried about.'

'Funny guy.' She patted his shoulder. 'I don't have any money for you to get and I doubt you'd want my ute. It's a relic held together with duct tape and baling twine and have you seen the cost of diesel these days?'

'So you're a broke horticulture student on an Outback camping trip?' Their earlier conversation was starting to come back to him. That blasted plant book.

'Sounds about right. I had a job mowing lawns and trimming hedges in Brisbane. Cleaning garden goldfish ponds and water features, keeping permaculture closed water systems in shape—I really liked that part of the job, but then my boss had a heart attack and sold the business and the new owners were a young husband and wife couple and there wasn't enough work to keep me on.' She sighed heavily. 'I have three thousand dollars saved—and if you do sue, I'll deny I ever confided in you. It's not in any bank.'

'Keep your three grand. And you shouldn't carry that kind of money on you,' he felt compelled to add.

'Who says I do? Okay, I'm grabbing my phone from my backpack so I can see what time it is.'

'You have a phone?'

'Yup. Phone, car, computer, and a good pair of secateurs. All my worldly possessions. See why you shouldn't sue me for taking cuttings of your rare plants without permission? Okay, it's eight fifty-two in the evening. Are you hungry? Could you eat a cow?'

'Do you have one of my cows in your backpack too?'

'Dude, I'm hurt by your extreme lack of faith in my essential goodness, but the answer is no. Not this trip.'

'You're not going to put pictures of me busted up all over the Internet, are you?'

'You think I could sell those for a mint and pay my uni fees?'

He absolutely did think that.

'Oh.' She paused, as if only just realising his accident would be of public interest. 'No, I'm not going to take pictures of you all busted up and sell them to the highest bidder,' she offered quietly. 'I wouldn't do that. If that's what people do in your world, I feel sorry for you.'

He felt the need to explain. 'You wouldn't believe what papers print about me.'

'So you're not crazy in love with your brother's beautiful wife?'

How had that rumour started again? 'Me and m'brother were trying to buy a national energy company a couple of years back. That rumour was a way to disrupt our takeover bid.'

She took her own sweet time thinking about that. 'Your world is brutal,' she declared finally.

'Yes.'

There was another pause, a bigger one, before the voice spoke again. 'She's very beautiful, though. Your sister-in-law.'

'She's also smart, kind and I've known her since birth. Still doesn't mean I'm in love with her.'

'I do have a macadamia and coconut bar I could share with you,' she murmured.

'Keep it.' He was angry with her for believing the lies they wrote about him.

'Hey, you were prepared to believe the worst of me too, Mr Take a picture of me all battered and torn and sell it to the papers and make a mint.'

He had no comeback for that. She was right. But maybe

they could start again, right here and now. He reached to-wards her and his fingers collided with the gently rounded flesh of what was most likely her rear end. He cleared his throat and withdrew his hand. She was a warm presence at his side from shoulder to toe. It was enough. 'Can we start over? I'm not…usually so…tetchy.'

'It's not just you. I'm on edge too and I'm sorry for re-peating what the gossip rags were saying. They make stuff up as they go along.'

'True.'

'Would you like some more water?'

'Please.'

She rose from her spot beside him and then he felt the cut of a plastic drink bottle against his lips. He reached up to close his fingers around the bottle and caught her fingers too.

'I've got it,' he murmured.

'Hang on, let me—there. It's all yours.'

He slaked his thirst, and he was uncommonly thirsty.

'Hey, easy with that.' He felt her palm against his fore-head, low over his unseeing eyes. 'You're hot.'

'I get that a lot.'

'I bet you do.'

Were they flirting? Was he reading the room right?

She cleared her throat. 'I meant you have a tempera-ture, which isn't exactly wonderful news. I don't think we should wait this one out until someone finds us. I need to go for help.'

'The ridge,' he murmured. 'You'll get a phone signal from up there.'

'Maybe.' The dust might make it impossible. 'But the track's a mess. I passed it on the way here. Thought about going up and decided not to. But I will get up it if need be,' she amended hastily. 'I've done it before.'

'*Have* you now?' No way was she a stranger to this land. 'Take me with you.'

'Hell no. You think I'm going to jolt that head of yours around any more than I have to? What if your eyes are hanging by a thread and the drive up the ridge breaks that thread? You'll never see again.'

He hated that she might be right. 'When will you go?'

'Not tonight. You aren't the only one who can't see two metres in front of them at the moment.' She sighed heavily. 'I'll leave at dawn. The dust should have settled a bit by then.'

'Don't leave without telling me.'

'I won't.'

She settled into what might have been a companionable silence if Reid hadn't been so hell-bent on filling up his lack of sight with other sensory input. He didn't want to be alone with his thoughts and the pain in his body that threatened to make him weep. 'Talk to me.'

'About what?'

'What's your favourite memory?'

'Why should I give it to you?'

'Because talking about it makes you happy?' He couldn't get to know her without her co-operation and it occurred to him that he really did want to get to know her. She was brave and resourceful. She didn't seem to have an agenda beyond keeping him alive and going for help as soon as possible. She was funny and sensible and unusual and…wonderful to listen to, and maybe it was just because they were under duress that he thought that way and maybe it wasn't. 'C'mon, work with me here. Tell me about the best day you've ever had.'

'Wouldn't you rather I read the textbook to you? We're up to plants beginning with the letter T.'

'Spare me.'

'You first, then.' She moved around and did whatever it

was she was doing—taking the blanket she'd had around him away so he could get rid of some body heat, he surmised. But her body stayed in contact with his and he was grateful he didn't have to ask for her touch again. She'd twigged that being without her touch made him panic. 'What's your favourite memory?'

'Watching my brother walk out those prison gates and smile when he saw me.'

'He didn't know you'd be there to collect him?'

'I told him I'd be there. I just don't think he believed it. We got half an hour down the road before I pulled into a service station that had a diner attached to it. I wanted breakfast and asked him what he was having and he just stared at the menu as if he was lost. My big badass brother needed my help with something and I was over the moon about it. I wanted him to like me so bad. He was my hero.'

'Your brother who killed a man was your hero?'

'Exceptional circumstances.' Reid heard his own voice hardening in warning not to press this line of questioning. 'He had to.' No point sharing that Reid was in two minds about whether his brother had pulled that trigger at all. Reid thought Bridie's father might have been the one with the gun in his hand and that Reid had taken the fall so that then sixteen-year-old Bridie wouldn't be left alone in the world. Not that Judah had ever confirmed this. 'He's still my hero—even after all these years.'

'Loyal.' She patted his shoulder as if to reassure him. 'I like that.'

'Why do you keep patting that shoulder?' Why not his chest or his arm or take his hand as she had before.

'It's the only piece of you that isn't bloody, bruised or banged up.'

'That bad?'

'Not good. Keep going with your best day ever. What food did you order in the diner?'

'So, I ended up ordering for both of us, yeah? I was eighteen, fresh out of boarding school and my father had just died and my mother had passed not long before that. I'd been alone on Jeddah station, running it, trying to make sure my brother had somewhere to come home to, and the only people I'd been around for months were Tom Starr from the cattle station next door, and his daughter Bridie, and Gert—the housekeeper who came in three days every fortnight.'

'I heard that story, yeah. You did a good job.'

'I didn't want to fail my brother. I badly wanted to prove to everyone I could do it.'

'I know that feeling.'

He could hear the truth in her quiet words, even if he couldn't see it in her eyes. His remaining senses seemed so much more acute. 'I couldn't have done it without them. I'm eternally in their debt.' He reached out towards her and she wove her fingers through his and held his hand.

'Touchy-feely guy.'

'Don't tell anyone. I have a reputation to maintain as an emotional desert.'

'Your secret is safe with me.'

Her hands weren't soft. Her nails felt a little ragged and she had calluses at the base of her thumb and fingers. He had the sudden urge to bring her hand to his lips and test the ridges of her knuckles with his tongue. Would she wrest her hand from his?

Or would she acknowledge a deep feeling of familiarity similar to his?

He contented himself with rubbing the pad of his thumb up and down her thumb instead. 'Where were we?'

'Ordering breakfast at the diner. On your best day ever.'

Right. 'I ordered two big breakfast combos, coffee with milk on the side, a banana smoothie each, apple pie, hot chips, tomato sauce, salt and vinegar, and a brownie each. Oh, and a couple of bottles of that blue-coloured sports drink. I had the station credit card in my back pocket and I likely would have kept right on ordering if the woman behind the counter hadn't said, "Son, I think that's enough."'

'Dead straight.'

He smiled, never mind his aching face. 'I dug in like a heathen when the food came and it took me a minute to realise Judah wasn't eating. I thought he wasn't hungry. I figured myself for a fool and started to apologise until he said stop. I told him I just wanted to make a good impression and I was sorry and again he said stop, so I stopped. I thought he was going to get up and walk out.'

'And this is your *best* day ever?'

'It gets better,' he defended. 'Judah had the biggest case of PTSD I've ever seen but he looked at me and somehow he decided to trust me. He said, "Reid, I'm hungry but this is a lot and I haven't made a decision for myself in seven and a half years. I'm gonna need your help."

'"Start with the smoothie and the banana bread," I said, and he laughed, but he did it, and I knew at that moment that he wanted me to stick around and that everything was going to be fine. Sometimes families fracture. I was scared that was going to happen to mine, and then what?'

'I get it. Trust me, I know that playbook by heart.'

Her voice held a wealth of sadness, bedrocked by maturity. He wondered how old she was and whether he'd already asked her that. Was he way off in thinking her a few years younger than him because she was still a student studying for exams? Didn't exactly matter. She understood, and that was enough to crack him wide open.

'The thing about the Blake family set-up is that the first-born takes all,' he told her gruffly. 'The British barony, all the land. Nothing on Jeddah Creek station or back in the UK was mine. And some time between the banana bread and the bacon and eggs I asked him outright if he wanted me to stick around. Almost lost my breakfast after I'd said it, although that may have had something to do with the way I'd bolted my food.'

'Maybe.' She had the driest laugh. He could listen to it for ever. And she was a good listener too, even if he had almost run out of steam for storytelling. His brain hurt. Everything hurt. 'So did he ask you to stay?'

'Mm-huh. Said there was no way he was walking through this world without me at his side. Best day ever.'

'I like it. Means he'll be coming for you sooner rather than later.'

He liked the way she thought. 'Now you,' he murmured. 'Share.'

'Ack, I don't have any memories like that. My world is small.'

'Tell me anyway.'

'Seeing the coastline for the first time was pretty spectacular. Water all the way to the end of the earth.'

'How old were you?'

'I dunno. About six? Seeing a man-made waterfall and swimming pool in someone's backyard also blew my mind. I would have been in my early teens then. Watching the rain come down out here, looking at the patterns the water makes as it finds its way along.'

He was sensing a water theme. 'Have you ever seen the Bay of Islands in Vietnam? Or the Weeping Wall on Mount Waialeale in Hawaii?'

'Never.'

'I'll take you when we get out of here.'

'Sure you will.' She sounded indulgent.

'I mean it.'

Maybe he did in the here and now, but Ari wasn't stupid enough to think he'd keep his word. They'd patch him up good as new and he wouldn't remember a thing about her.

'Give me another memory. Who's your favourite person?' he asked.

His words were starting to slur, and she desperately wanted him to stay awake, because every time he slipped from consciousness she thought he might never wake again. 'My mother. She passed.'

'Not your father?'

'He's not in my life. My mother never had much to say about anything, least of all him. He was a passing stockman from up north. A charming one-night stand. That's all I know.'

Ari squeezed his hand. He really did respond beautifully to touch. Maybe she'd respond that way too if she couldn't see anything. 'So talking wasn't her thing but she had the most expressive eyes I've ever seen. She could tell me she loved me and was proud of me with a glance. If I ever got a good mark at school, her eyes would show her pride. If I ever made something for her—kid stuff like a wind chime made out of a bunch of sticks held together with baling twine—she'd look at me with such love. When I was thoughtful and careful with what we had, her eyes would smile and she'd nod and I'd know I was loved. Even when—' Not so good, those later memories. 'Even when she married and got really busy and had my little stepbrother and stepfather to look after, she still loved me with her eyes.'

When she could. Ari's stepfather had been a jealous

man, always resentful of any love shown to Ari. As if there weren't enough of it to go around…

'I bet she looked at you like that a lot. You have a kind heart.'

'You think so?' Ari made light of his compliment, not wanting to reveal the truth of those later years when her mother would barely look at her at all for fear one of them would end up with a beating. 'Because I've just realised that I've been banging on about visual memories to a guy who currently can't see.'

'I can see blurry shapes,' he offered quietly. 'There's light and dark.'

She didn't have the heart to tell him she'd turned the light off long ago and they were talking in complete darkness. 'I washed some of the blood out of your good eye while you were out for the count.'

'I wish I could see you.'

She didn't know why those few words touched her so deeply. 'Yeah, well. Nothing fancy to see here, but I hope you see again soon. Mind you, if I'm being totally honest, there's something freeing about communicating with you in the dark using words and touch. I feel comfortable here with you like this. Almost as if I'm your equal. I'm not as self-conscious about my looks or the cheap clothes I've got on.'

'I don't judge people by their looks,' he growled.

'Yeah, you do. You were quite happy to picture me as a beautiful Bond girl.'

He swore softly, likely because she had him cornered. 'Well, I don't judge people by their bank balance,' he said next.

'Sure, you do. We all do, and the world is poorer for it.' She lay back beside him, shoulder to shoulder in the cramped little tent, and listened for his breathing. 'What's your favourite musical instrument? Mine's guitar. I can't read music or anything and I'm pretty sure I don't have perfect pitch. Nor can I listen to a song and play it from memory, but I like having a bash anyway.'

'Describe your mother's eyes whenever you played guitar.' His voice was getting weaker.

'Who knows? She always got as far away as she could so she didn't have to listen to it.'

'Funny girl.'

She closed her eyes and tried to figure out the blends that went into the making of his voice. Warmth wrapped around a core of pain that likely wasn't always present. Occasional sharpness that came with anger. A burr full of humour, pricking at a person's ears at unexpected times. Curiosity—how could a person explain the sound of curiosity? But it was there. She liked his voice a lot. Always had, even when she was a kid.

Not that she'd ever crushed on him as a kid—he'd been so much older, but still. The teenage boy with the ready smile hadn't lost his kindness.

'Who are you?' he rasped, and she was about to tell him she was Ari, Ari Cohen, his housekeeper's niece, and she'd tagged along with her aunt sometimes as a kid and met him way back when.

But he was already unconscious again.

Ari rose with the dawn and gently shook Reid semi-awake. He didn't seem to know where he was at all but she'd promised not to leave without saying goodbye and she also took the opportunity to feed him two more painkillers and get him to drink some water. She left the mostly full water bottle near his uninjured hand, although even that had swollen overnight.

'Reid, I'm heading up to the escarpment now. I'll be back as soon as I can.'

She rubbed his shoulder but he didn't rouse. One eye had swollen shut altogether and his other remained closed. His temperature had stayed up and she'd taken to pouring water on his bandages to cool him down, but it wasn't enough to stop his fever. He needed proper medical care.

She pressed her lips to his cheek for no other reason than if he died from his injuries, she wanted his last human touch to honour love.

In dawn's half-light she packed her ute and turned the key, and, after a few coughs and splutters, the engine roared to life. She'd been worried it wouldn't start because of the dust she'd driven through to reach Reid, but it seemed okay. *Sweetie, don't fail me now.* She set out towards the escarpment, following no track whatsoever, because she'd gone off road to find him and off road she would stay until she picked up the trail.

Five minutes later, she stopped to let some air out of her tyres before setting off again at a much slower pace.

Yesterday's dust storm had deposited a fine, silty covering over everything, and it was deeper than expected. Three hours, she estimated, before she got where she needed to go, and another three hours back to the tent.

Had to be done.

Reid's life depended on it.

She was two hours into her journey and she'd reached the foot of the escarpment and found the track that would take her to the top when she saw the helicopter in the distant sky. She skidded her ute to a halt, her heart thumping with hope that they would see the crash site uphill and the tent, or if they missed it that they would see her, and she could try and wave them down and give them directions.

But they didn't come her way, they circled back and forth in grid-like fashion, causing Ari to scream with frustration and begin mouthing directions they couldn't hear. She got out of the car and began waving her arms, before reaching back in the cab for a bright red pullover so she could wave that too.

*Head south, now southwest. That's it, you've got this. West. I meant west!* Now, straighten up and just keep going.

If she willed it maybe it would happen.

*That's it. Yes. Yes!*

They'd seen it. They'd found him.

Ari flung her fists towards the sky. 'Yes!' Hurry. 'He's waiting for you.'

The stress of the past twenty-four hours hit her like a truck, and she sank to the ground and put her hands to her face and sobbed her relief, letting go of the fear that whatever she did, it wouldn't be enough. He'd get the best of care now, and it *would* be enough.


Hours later, when Ari made it back to camp, there was nothing left but her tent on its side, her sleeping bag still wet with blood and a helicopter in pieces.

They'd come for him and taken him.

Wounded billionaire and test helicopter pilot Reid Blake was gone.

# CHAPTER FOUR

'I THINK YOU should come. You need the work and the Blakes can always use a spare set of hands.' Gert stood at her kitchen counter, packing cleaning supplies into neatly labelled plastic tubs. She looked up and arched a winged brow, as if daring Ari to refuse.

'You told me the caterers always bring their own staff with them.' The Jeddah Creek station ball, hosted by Bridie and Judah Blake, had become an annual event these past dozen years or so, getting grander every year. 'And they fly bar staff in as well.'

'True.'

'Then what is there for me to do?'

'None of them get to go back of house. You'll be helping me with the guest rooms and bathrooms and making the special guests staying at the homestead comfortable. You know the layout of the house and, more to the point, Judah and Bridie know you. They can trust you.'

Could they? Ari had never come forward to say she'd found Reid and looked after him until proper help arrived—that was six months ago now. Practically ancient history.

She'd been meaning to contact them as soon as she got back to town, but as one day had slid into the next and there'd been no word of Reid at all, she hadn't wanted to 'fess up and potentially be blamed for not doing more and sooner.

Or try to explain to big brother Judah exactly what she'd been doing out there in the first place.

It wasn't as if Reid would ever be able to identify her, even if he did have vague memories of her being there. Maybe she *could* go with Gert and see this dazzling Outback spectacle of beautiful people in an opulent setting for herself? 'So who are the special guests?'

Gert shrugged. 'Don't know for sure. It's all very hush-hush until they get there. We had a European prince and princess last year. Very polite.'

Ari blinked. 'Seriously?'

'Yep. And a grand dame of the English theatre—I can't remember her name, but you'd know her if you saw her. Barking, of course, but she told the funniest stories.'

'How many guest bedrooms do they put out for use?'

'Six. And two drawing rooms for only those house guests to retreat to, plus the library. So twelve guests in the house, maximum, and around five hundred outside in tents, vehicles and planes.'

'Five...*hundred*?'

'But you don't have to worry about them. Judah's station hands run herd on them.'

Still no mention of Reid or whether he would be present. Last she'd heard, he'd been released from hospital and was living in Sydney.

'You can sleep in my room with me, there's two single beds,' Gert continued. She'd had the use of that room for near on thirty years and had no qualms about treating it as her own. 'And you can give me a hand with the Sunday breakfast barbecue. Reid and his old boarding-school mates usually tackle that one, but not this year.'

'Oh, is he not coming?' See an opening and take it, guileless as you please.

'He'll be there, he just won't be helping out the way he usually does. But it's easy enough to do. Steak, sausages, bacon, eggs, onion, bread rolls, lettuce, tomato and a few different types of sauce. Hangover food. Breakfast is very popular.'

'I'll bet.' Ari risked another question. 'And how is Reid after his accident?' The Blake family had kept news of his recovery so hush-hush. It drove her nuts.

'Better than he was. It was touch and go for a while.'

'I didn't know that.'

Gert tucked half a dozen packs of cleaning wipes into the nearest container, alongside four litres of bathroom disinfectant concentrate. 'So, do you want the work or not? I'm getting old waiting for your answer.'

Gert was already old. She'd been doing the Devil's Kiss, Jeddah Creek, and Cooper's Crossing station houses cleaning run for thirty years. She spent two to three days on each farm, with a day's driving in between each. She would then return home for a long weekend break before loading up the van and looping around again. Gert and her van full of refrigerated foodstuffs and cleaning equipment and mail were as much a part of the Outback landscape as the cattle stations themselves.

'I'll even stop so you can collect plants along the way,' Gert coaxed.

'I'll believe that when it happens.' Gert drove as if the devil were riding her tail and rarely stopped for anything or anyone.

'Still waiting.' Gert smiled and the sternness bled out of her, leaving warmth in its wake. 'Don't make me start tapping my foot.'

'All right, all right, I'll come.' Ari could observe Reid Blake from afar as he mingled with the stars. And even if they did cross paths, he probably wouldn't speak. And what was the chance of him recognising her voice from their time in the tent, given he'd spent most of that time drifting in and out of consciousness? No, she had nothing to worry about on that score.

She could see for herself how he was getting on, lay new memories over more disturbing ones and then put him out of her mind altogether.

Maybe then she wouldn't be so obsessed with remembering every little thing about him. Fantasising. Measuring every other man she met against him and finding them wanting.

Not touchy-feely enough. Not interesting enough.

*Not vulnerable enough to seek out an honest connection,* her brutally honest conscience suggested.

*Face it, Ari. You liked being in a position of power over Reid Blake. It made you bolder and him more receptive.*

Which he wouldn't be now he was well again. He'd probably want nothing to do with her even if he did recognise her. The man in the tent probably didn't even *exist*.

Probably a good thing. That way she might stop *pining* for him.

'What's the pay rate?'

'As my trusty assistant? How about we ask for twenty-five dollars an hour from the time you get there until the time you leave, including when you're asleep?'

'Are you serious? That's a six-hundred-dollar day.' Before tax. And with her ute at the mechanic's and needing a new radiator, she could use all the cash she could get. 'How many days will we be there?'

That there was Gert's gotcha smile. 'Three.'

# CHAPTER FIVE

'YOU DO IT,' said Judah, as if his word were law. And, okay, maybe Judah was the oldest and this was his home and Reid was a mere guest here these days, but *come on*.

Reid had turned thirty last year. He'd been a billionaire in his own right since his mid-twenties, on account of his relentless quest to make solar-powered commercial plane travel possible. And he had absolutely no trouble whatsoever questioning his big brother's authority. Even if they had just entered the library, where several centuries of Blake family history lay gathering dust at every opportunity. He crossed to the unlit fireplace to lean against the mantelpiece, unwilling to show how much his leg ached this early in the evening.

Judah would only worry more than he already did.

Reid accepted the tumbler of twenty-year-old malt whisky Judah handed him and raised it to his lips for a hit of fortification before returning to the argument. 'You're the one with the title,' he said with possibly a little too much relish, because with that title came onerous responsibilities. 'You're head of the family. It needs to come from you.'

It was the afternoon of the twelfth annual Jeddah Creek station ball and already people were rolling in and setting up camp in the paddocks beyond the homestead. Caterers had taken over the mess hall and kitchen that the station hands usually used, and one end of the grand ballroom was in the process of being turned into a fully stocked drinks bar that would be the envy of any big city hotel. Every little detail concerning the glamorous society event had been hammered out months ago. Every last detail but for who would make the welcome speech and expose a family secret that had been hidden for years.

'If I make the announcement, no one's ever going to come forward,' argued Judah. 'They'll probably think I'll murder them.'

'Bull. You haven't murdered anyone in years.' If indeed his brother ever had been responsible for the loss of a man's life. 'Besides, it was self-defence.'

'The fact remains that you're far more approachable than I am.' Judah was having none of it. '*And* people want to see you in action after the accident. They want to know you're up and running, full speed ahead.'

'I'm here, aren't I?' Reid was beginning to lose this argument, he could tell. 'All you have to say is that it's recently come to our attention that we have a half-sister out there and we want to find her. Simple.'

The thud of something falling to the floor reached his ears and both he and Judah turned towards the direction of the noise. Was someone else in the room? He couldn't see anyone—not that his eyesight was all that reliable when the lights were dim. Or when the lights were bright, for that matter. But this part of the house was supposedly off-limits to the catering team, bar staff and musicians who'd flown in this morning, and as far as he knew Judah's house guests had yet to arrive.

'Who's there?' asked Judah sharply.

'Awkward,' came the muffled reply, and then a hand rose from behind the couch, followed by the outline of a young woman who looked to be barely out of her teens. When she stood up, she had a little dustpan and broom in her other hand, half full of broken glass. 'Hi,' she said weakly. 'Gert sent me to clear up a broken vase and so here I am. I was doing that when you came in so I just...' she waved her free hand about '...decided not to interrupt your very important conversation.'

'Gert sent you?' Something didn't add up. 'And who are you?' She seemed familiar. More than that, she sounded familiar. That bright, melodic voice was like a burr beneath his skin.

'I'm Ari. Ari Cohen.'

Was that supposed to ring a bell?

'Gert's niece,' she said next, looking from him to Judah. 'She said you wouldn't mind an extra set of hands back here today, so here I am. Bridie okayed it. I used to come here with Gert when I was a kid. She used to take us kids on her cleaning run sometimes in the school holidays and stuff.'

'And stuff,' he echoed quietly. It was true that Gert had often brought various nieces and nephews along for the ride, but that was a long time ago.

Memory pinged of a barefoot little girl who'd attacked dusty windows with a dirty dry rag and uncommon zeal. Once finished for the day she'd entertained herself by making racetracks in the dirt if she'd brought her matchbox cars with her. And if she'd forgotten those little cars, or lost them, she'd turn her hand to making pictures in the dirt using whatever came to hand. More than once, she'd ventured way too far from the homestead looking for different coloured dirt and Gert had sent Reid out to find her. He'd been in his teens and she'd been, what, seven or eight? 'You used to make the rock gardens.'

'That's me.' She smiled, and more memories came rushing in.

That smile.

That wide, cheerful smile she used to offer so freely for no good reason other than the sun was shining and she had company. He turned to his brother. 'Do you remember her? They might have been your prison years.'

Young Ari snorted and drew his gaze away from Judah.

'You didn't remember me either until I reminded you, hotshot, so don't go getting too carried away with how smart you are.'

Judah's cough sounded suspiciously like laughter.

Reid ignored his brother's rare lapse of composure. 'How much did you overhear?'

'All of it,' said Ari. 'I'm not deaf.'

Which for some strange reason set Judah off again.

Again, Reid ignored him in favour of the admittedly pretty young woman with the dustpan in hand. 'Who do *you* think should give the speech?'

'Hey, I'm just the hired help. Don't ask me.'

Her voice… He rubbed at the scar tissue at his hairline. It still gave him trouble, still itched abominably at the oddest times.

'Although your brother's probably right about people wanting to see for themselves that you're okay. You're kind of important around here,' she continued. 'Why can't you both stand up and have one of you welcome everyone and then the other one gets down to business? Everyone likes a united family front.'

Reid caught Judah's eye and spread his hands out, palm up. 'Makes sense.'

Something thumped against a solid surface and Reid sensed movement in his peripheral vision. 'What was that?'

Ari swung around towards a window with velvet curtains bunched and tied on either side. '*That* is the reason I'm in here in the first place. I have orders to lock him in the upstairs ensuite bathroom when I catch him. He escaped. We think human error was involved.'

Judah cleared his throat loudly.

Reid had no idea what was going on. 'Him? As in a person? As opposed to a…?'

'Kitten,' she said cheerfully. 'A fluffy, grey, tawny-eyed agent of chaos. He likes escaping from locked bathrooms, knocking over vases and hiding behind curtains.'

Reid turned to his brother. 'You have a house cat?'

'It wasn't my idea.'

Reid knew exactly whose idea it would have been. 'Does my niece have a kitten? Did the lord of the realm let the itty-bitty kitty out of the bathroom?'

Judah winced and scraped his weathered hand over his face. 'I don't want to talk about it.'

'Does the kitty have a name?'

'Fluffy.'

'I'm sorry, I didn't hear you on account of your hand being over your mouth.' Life was good today, what with Ari the desert nymph gracing them with her delightful presence and seeming so familiar, and now Judah wincing with embarrassment. 'What was that again?'

'Fluffy.' Judah silently dared him to laugh, but Reid would never. Not even a smirk. Okay, maybe Reid was wearing a *tiny* smirk to go with his white shirt, and immaculately cut suit. 'Does Fluffy have a last name? Fluffy Blake? Fluffy Woo?'

'No.' Judah looked truly pained by the turn this conversation had taken, which pleased Reid no end. 'Fluffy-Wuffy.'

Fluffy-Wuffy was currently being stalked by the lithe,

long-legged, black-trousers-and-T-shirt-clad Ari with the high ponytail. She moved with the grace of a dancer—maybe she *was* one when she wasn't cleaning houses, she was slender enough. Long neck. Delicate hands that parted the curtain and reached down and scooped up a little blob that meowed in protest.

'Oh, stop your complaining,' she murmured, and something about her *voice* was so familiar...

She was a local.

*The woman who'd found him in a dust storm and erected a tent over the top of him had been local.*

'What kind of car do you drive?' he asked as she tucked the kitten against her chest and headed for the door.

'I'm currently carless. I got a lift here with Gert. So... excuse me, it was nice to catch up, but I have to put the monster away.'

'Will I see you around, later?' He didn't want her to go. A familiar word sat on the tip of his tongue.

*Stay. Don't leave me.*

'I don't know,' she replied as she half turned and met his gaze and this time he was close enough to make out the colour of her eyes. They were an extraordinary shade of cognac and quite startling against her tanned complexion. 'I hope you find your sister.'

She took her leave, and he waited until he no longer heard her footsteps on the stairs before he spoke again. 'What colour would you say her hair was?'

'Brown.' Judah had grown used to Reid asking him to describe in detail those things Reid couldn't see properly.

'And her eyes? What colour are they?'

'Brown,' said Judah again. 'Why?'

'Just curious.'

Very, very curious.

* * *

Speech plans sorted, Reid downed his drink, abandoned his brother and made his way to the kitchen in search of Gert. The housekeeper had been a mainstay throughout his childhood and he was as sure of his welcome as anyone could be, even if she did greet him with a steely eye to match her greying hair and a curt, 'You're too thin.'

'I'm working on it, I promise,' and it was nothing but the truth. 'I do physio three days a week to strengthen my leg and drink the most disgusting protein shakes for breakfast every morning, along with my three-course breakfast.'

'Three cups of black coffee is not a three-course breakfast,' Gert countered. She knew him too well.

'Even so, I've picked up my calorie intake, on doctor's orders, and I'm feeling stronger for it.' He'd been incredibly lucky to survive at all.

'How's your eyesight?'

'Good as gold.' No one wanted to hear about the fuzzy vision in one eye and the tunnel vision in the other. The constant headaches. His dodgy balance. His chances of ever piloting a helicopter again were slim, even by his optimistic reckoning. Without bionic eyes.

As he was a man of unlimited resources, bionic eye research was now a priority for Reid Enterprises' newly created Medical Division.

'I met up with Ari in the library just now. I didn't recognise her, though, until she told me who she was.'

Let Gert make of that what she would. Could be his eyesight. Could be that he hadn't seen her in years.

'Did she find that cat?'

'You mean Fluffy-Wuffy?' He was never going to pass up the chance to say that name aloud, just to see his brother wince. 'She found him. *Fluffy-Wuffy* is on his way back to jail.'

'She's a good girl, Ari. The first in our family to study for a diploma, and it's not because learning comes easily to her—it's because she never gives up.'

'An admirable trait.' The acquisition of Ari information was going to be easier than he thought. 'What's she studying?'

'Some kind of land-care course. Landscape gardening. Horticulture too, which will be good for her. She's not one for staying indoors.'

It fitted. Everything about her fitted his mystery rescuer from the tent. 'I remember that about her.'

'She sits her last two exams in a couple of weeks and then there's a job waiting for her in Cairns.'

'Doing what?'

'She'll be a nursery worker in a big native plant nursery and landscaping business.'

'Does it have a career pathway for her?'

'Ask her,' said Gert as Ari swept into the room and stopped abruptly at the sight of him.

'Ask me what?'

'How wedded you are to your new job,' he said smoothly. 'Gert's been bragging about your studies.' Did Ari look a little paler than before? He couldn't trust his eyes. 'And it reminded me I've been meaning to advertise for a landscaper to extend the outdoor areas around the eco lodges. There's fifteen of them scattered throughout Jeddah Creek and Cooper's Crossing, mainly in groups of twos and threes.' His information was solid. Factual. But he was making up the job on the spot.

'I'm not set up to be an independent contractor just yet,' she said awkwardly as she reached for a tea towel and picked up a handful of wet silverware from the counter. Family crest and all.

'Is being your own boss a long-term goal?' he asked next.

She nodded warily.

'She wants to have a big Outback plant nursery one day and breed rare native plants. Tell him, Ari,' Gert urged. 'You talked about it enough on the way here.'

'Yeah, Ari. Spill.'

If anything, she grew even paler. 'It was just talk.'

It was her. It had to be her. His eyes couldn't confirm it, but his body seemed to yearn for the comfort of her touch. She was his mystery woman, his guardian angel. He'd been looking for her for months. Visiting her over and over again in his dreams and now here she was, pretending none of it had ever happened. Her reticence made him want to push and tear and, above all, touch. Why had she never come forward? He needed to know. He needed to fix this.

'So, you're a rare plant collector? How does that work?'

Her eyes flashed with a mixture of fear and defiance. She knew he was onto her.

Did she really think he was going to do anything but thank her? Reward her for her bravery? He wouldn't *be* here if she hadn't found him and kept him safe until the medics arrived.

'Blake Holdings—that's a company me and my brother formed—it provides research grants and accommodation for people who want to study habitat and wildlife out here. Landscape ecology and the like. That includes plants.'

'Yeah, for people with fancy degrees and doctorates,' she said, not meeting his gaze. 'I don't even have a tech diploma.'

'Yet,' he said quietly, and her pretty mouth firmed, and she nodded, even if she still wouldn't look at him.

'Yet,' she echoed.

He knew that voice. It kept him company in his dreams. 'You got the Cairns job, didn't you? Put down what you told them.'

'It's a *junior nursery hand* position.'

'Don't you want to jump in the deep end?' She hesitated and with that he moved closer to where he could see better. 'I couldn't see your eyes properly from over there.' They stood about a metre apart. Close enough for him to see her ridiculously long eyelashes and every emotion flitting across her expressive eyes. 'Is this too close? Tell me if it is.' It wasn't for him. They'd been closer in the tent, and not just in a physical sense. He wanted that again.

'No.' But she folded her arms across her chest, and he didn't need to be a body language expert to know that she was putting up barriers against him. He wanted to touch her so badly—one touch and he'd know for sure...

Instead, he kept his hands to himself, took a careful step back, and returned to his sales pitch. 'The way I see it, going into business for yourself requires three things.

'One: a bone-deep belief that you can do it.'

She lifted her chin and finally met his gaze. Had she really described herself as plain? Because between those eyes, that generous mouth, and her perfectly proportioned form she was anything but.

Was he really shallow enough to be pleased that the woman from the tent was brave, resourceful, *within his grasp* and beautiful in a way that was wholly unique and exactly to his taste?

Yes—yes, he was.

'Two,' he continued firmly, and shoved his shallowness aside, 'you need courage in the face of adversity and the ability to improvise. Anything happen to you lately to demonstrate that? Anything you want to mention? Anything at all?' That's right, Ari Cohen, I know what you're made of. I was there when you were tested.

'Is this a job interview?'

'And three,' he continued his pitch. 'It helps to have deep pockets.'

'Tapping out.' She huffed a laugh. 'Thanks for the tips. I'll keep them in mind.'

'If you don't have start-up money there are angel investors who—if you present a strong enough case—will invest in you and your business dreams.' Surely she could see what he was offering? 'You could ask me to back you.'

'No.' Her hands stilled on the cutlery. 'I'm not ready for that kind of responsibility. I don't know enough yet. I need to work with good growers and plant breeders and that's what I'm going to do. Then maybe I'll get to that bone-deep certainty you mentioned. I don't have it yet.'

'You know where to find me when you do. And if there's anything you want to talk with me about this weekend, I'm free.'

'I'm on the clock.'

He wanted to break the clock.

*Was she the woman from the tent? She fitted every memory he had of the event.*

He'd made no secret of the fact that someone had tended to him and then gone for help before the helicopters arrived. He'd put out a nationwide call for them to come forward and be rewarded.

Why hadn't she come forward?

'That's very generous of you, Reid.' It wasn't Ari who spoke. It was Gert.

Ari nodded but said nothing.

He made his way to the door, grateful he no longer had

to use a cane for walking and that he could see far enough these days to avoid walking into walls. A man had his pride, even in the face of rejection. Especially in the face of rejection.

*Why hadn't she come when he called?*

'What was that?'

Gert was no one's fool, no matter how wide and innocent Ari made her eyes. 'Kind of intense, isn't he?' she replied. 'Is he always so...helpful?'

'Reid always helps if he can, that's just his way. *Noblesse oblige*. He was born to it.' Gert filled an electric hot-water urn sitting on the counter with bottled water from a thirty-litre container. 'This has to go to the green drawing room on the ground floor.'

'Got it. Have you seen the paddocks?' Anything to avoid talking about her unsettling encounter with Reid. Or admitting to herself how much she'd wanted to reach out and take his hand and say something utterly ridiculous like *hi, it's me*. 'All those planes nose to tail in neat little rows. And there's a campground full of fancy tents with sisal carpets and solar fairy lights mixing it with farm four-wheel drives and campfires and swags. And the portable toilet blocks and the first-aid tent. It's like a festival.'

'It's grown over the years, just like everything the Blake brothers touch.' Gert studied her with a frown. 'Reid just offered you the kind of opportunity you've always dreamed of doing and you turned him down flat.'

'Didn't feel right.' Ari wrapped the cord around the urn and positioned the unwieldy cylinder for pickup. She'd barely wrapped her arms around the body, taps to the outside, when her aunt spoke again.

'They say he died on the way to the hospital.'

'What?' She had no air left in her lungs and the urn was far heavier than it looked. She'd convinced herself in the days that followed the accident that no one who talked and flirted and had shown up for her the way Reid had in the tent could be that badly injured. That thought had soothed her to sleep some nights. And she'd been *wrong*?

'Bridie told me. It's not general knowledge but his heart stopped three times while they were in the air. They got him back, obviously.'

Obviously.

'Reid's always been one for a laugh—even when the going got tough. Especially then,' Gert mused. 'He had a lot of responsibility laid on him at a young age, didn't have a choice, and I believe it was the making of him. But he was strong to begin with. I think he sees the same kind of strength in you.'

Ari slid the urn back on the counter. It was heavy. She wasn't ready for a Gert interrogation. 'He doesn't even know me.'

But that wasn't strictly true given their time together during the storm.

Reid had been having a whole different conversation with her from the one Gert had heard.

'Those eco lodges were his first business win. They still matter to him. You have two weeks until your exams and almost a month before you have to start that nursery job. You could do up garden plans for all those lodges before you go. At least take a look at them and submit something for his consideration. What if you wow him, and all those other fancy people who stay in them learn your name? You couldn't ask for a better start to your career.'

'He didn't mean it.' He'd been digging for a confession or maybe dangling a reward for services rendered. His 'investing' in her had nothing to do with her potential and everything to do with gratitude.

'Yes, he did. He meant every word. You should at least consider it.'

# CHAPTER SIX

IT WAS HER. The angel with the tent and the bandages and the painkillers that had saved his life and sanity. His rescuer who'd touched him when he'd needed it and spoken on demand, laying out pieces of her life for him to pick over, even as he'd offered up his most treasured moments for viewing. She'd left him to go get help, he knew that. But then Judah had arrived, and she'd returned to an empty tent.

There'd been no tent, no trace of anyone at all when a field team had returned to clean up the crash site. It was as if she'd never been there at all.

In the six months since the accident no one had ever come forward.

'I found her,' he told his brother when Judah rounded him up for speech time.

'Our missing sister?'

Judah was apparently not a mind-reader. '*No*, the woman from the tent.'

Judah eyed him warily and not without good cause. He'd sat through Reid's delirious ramblings about *the voice*. He'd sat vigil in hospital, baffled when Reid had finally roused and demanded the hand, only to be told *Not that hand... the other hand*!

Later, at Reid's insistence, Judah had given an interview

to the local paper expressing the family's gratitude to the unnamed person who'd tended Reid during the dust storm.

'I've found her. The woman who saved my life. It's Gert's niece. Ari.'

'She told you this?'

'No. Well, not exactly, but everything fits. If I could just get her in a dark room and touch her and make her talk to me, I could be absolutely sure.'

'There's a winning plan—if you want to go up on assault charges.' Judah laughed, short and sharp, and then caught his eye. 'Oh, hell. You mean it.'

'It's the only way to know.'

'Or you could just ask her if she was the woman with the tent.' Judah's voice of reason held no sway with Reid.

'I've given her every opportunity to come clean. I've baited her…'

Judah frowned. 'Why?'

'I've offered her work. Grant money. Accommodation. I *created* a position for her. Which she didn't accept.' Was his irritation visible? He thought it might be visible. He'd had so much less patience with the world since his accident. When opportunity came someone's way, the smart thing to do was grab hold with both hands and *take it*. 'Why wouldn't she *take it*?' His vision blurred.

'Reid. *Reid.*'

'*What?*' His irritation was very definitely visible.

'Chill. You don't even know if it's her.'

'I *do* know it's her.'

'You weren't conscious when we found you. Your temperature was off the charts. One of only two completely terrifying moments of my life. Three, if I count the birth of my daughter, which I should.'

He appreciated the sentiment, but… 'It's her.'

'Then sit down and talk to her. But not right now,' Judah added as Bridie joined them, a vision of woodland loveliness in her sleeveless ballgown that matched the colours of sunset over an Outback sky. 'We have a speech to make. I greet people. You tell people we have a sister out there somewhere and we're looking to find her.'

'Yeah, bring on the imposters.' There would be plenty of those. 'Hey, Bridie.'

His sister-in-law smiled gently. 'Ready to spill?'

It hadn't been an easy decision to reveal their late father's infidelity to the world and openly search for their unknown half-sister. They had one big-money withdrawal as evidence, along with two letters Bridie had unearthed last year when renovating the wine cellar. She could be anyone, anywhere. They'd debated long and hard about searching for her privately, but the truth was they'd run out of leads. 'I'm ready.' He pasted on a smile.

The sooner they got it over with, the sooner he could go find Ari.

With all guest rooms prepared, the library set up with extra refreshments, and the sitting rooms made over into mini retreats for the house guests, Gert let Ari loose to check on the caterer's preparations. Nothing to do with Ari wanting a glimpse of the beautiful ballroom all decked out and filled with beautiful people.

Ari found the event co-ordinator Gert had pointed out to her at the far end of the bar, counting cartons of wine and checking a list. 'Hi, I'm Ari, homestead staff. I've been sent to see if there's anything I can help you with.'

The woman smiled and tucked her pen through the top of the clipboard and then held out her hand. 'Lilah Connor, and thanks for the offer but I have the kitchen in the bunkroom running a treat and the ballroom, downstairs powder rooms and veranda areas covered. Anything beyond that is not my jurisdiction. There are parties out in the car park, *plane* park, and they're getting wilder by the minute. We are *not* the ones serving alcohol out there. Those planes flew in *stocked*.'

'Got it. I'll have a word with the bosses.' Meaning she'd tell Gert, who would relay the information upriver. 'The food looks like it's holding up well. Probably because of all those well-stocked planes.'

Lila shot her a conspiratorial smile. 'Maybe. Other than that, my team has everything under control. It's a fantastic setting for a party. The sunset and the red dirt and the fairy lights and the music and everyone dressed for the cover of *Vogue* magazine. I've never seen anything like it and I've catered a lot of A-list parties in beautiful locations.'

'Something else, isn't it?' A magical wonderland of beautiful indulgence.

A mini orchestra played from a wooden stage at one end of the ballroom. Elegant couples who knew how to waltz made the most of the floorspace available to them. Wall sconces splayed golden light around the edges of the room, throwing flattering light over those gathered around the edges of the dance floor.

'You, girl!' A florid man in a suit two sizes smaller than him waved her over and Lilah went with her. He turned towards the woman at his side. 'My wife isn't feeling well. She needs to lie down.'

'There's a first-aid station set up in the sitting room at the end of the veranda. It's this way,' said Lilah. 'I can escort you and we can get her checked out.'

'She needs a bed, not a Band-Aid,' he snapped. 'She almost fainted when they made the announcement.'

Ari hadn't been in the room during any announcement and looked to Lilah for help.

'You mean about the missing sister?' Lilah asked.

'Yes, yes! Look at her—don't you see the resemblance?'

Reid and Judah were both tall, dark-haired, and lanky. This woman was a tiny, generously rounded blonde.

'She needs a room in the *house*,' the husband insisted. 'We need to speak with *Lord Blake*.'

'I'll…find him,' Ari murmured.

'I'll stay here,' Lilah offered. 'Ma'am, let's find you a seat over by the wall, and a glass of water while we wait.' She and Ari shared a glance—they were doing their best to be accommodating but this was beyond what either of them had signed up for.

Ari plunged into the crowd and headed towards the front of the ballroom. She searched for Judah and Bridie.

Reid found her first.

'Ari.'

'Hey.' As if beautiful suit-wearing billionaires called her by name all the time. Her body tensed as she met his gaze and something clicked into place, some missing piece of the puzzle that could teach her about passion and obsession. Irresistible fascination with another human being. She had no doubt she could learn such things from him. She just didn't know if she *wanted* to go all in on him. He was Reid Blake and she was nobody.

'There's a guest with a sick wife who almost fainted at your announcement. They're over by the second set of French doors from the bar. He's belligerent and she's scared witless. He's demanding to speak with your brother and he wants a bed in the house for his wife.'

Reid passed a hand over his eyes, his fingers rubbing at a spot on his hairline. She could see the scarring, still puffy, not old enough to have faded to silver. 'I knew this would happen.' He reached inside his jacket and pulled out a phone. Ari began to drift away, job done, but he reached out and grasped her bare arm. *'Stay.'*

His gaze didn't leave hers as he spoke into the phone. 'We have our first contender.' He gave Judah the directions and ended the call. 'Come with me.' Without waiting for an answer, he slid his hand down her arm, laced his fingers through hers and began weaving through the crowd, with Ari at his side. The warmth and tingle of his hand in hers crashed through her defences, bringing with it memories of their time in the tent. That magical, terrible time when their defences were down and they'd connected with each other in ways she'd never imagined opening up to another person. *'I knew it.'*

'You sound like a crazy person.'

'You know exactly what I'm talking about—you're not that good an actor and unlike last time *I can see you*. I think you must have your mother's eyes. They're *very* expressive.'

He led her through to the long hallway that ran the length of the ground floor. Past the library, past the various bedrooms and sitting rooms until they reached the door at the very end. It was locked but the press of his thumb on a touchpad opened it to reveal an office decked out in burgundy velvet. Bookshelves, a massive walnut desk, an elaborate Aubusson floor rug and dozens of other examples of generational wealth.

'I hope this isn't your idea of cosy and informal.' Seriously, could there be a bigger contrast between this room and her tent? Did he really think she needed reminding of her *place*?

'This was my grandfather's office. Judah needs to redecorate.' He released her hand and Ari shivered at the sudden loss of warmth. He pulled the visitor's chair away from the desk. 'Sit.'

Did she want to defy him in this or save her fire for bigger battles? She sat, and he took the boss chair on the other side of the desk, but not before he'd shut the office door, plunging them into semi-darkness. The only light in the room came from the fairy lights in the trees outside the one narrow window at the opposite end of the room.

'Talk to me,' he commanded.

'I don't know what to say.'

'How about you tell me why you never came forward? Start there.'

There was no give in his voice. None. And she still didn't know what to say.

'You left without saying goodbye,' he continued. 'Not that I want to appear needy, but when it comes to you, I am diabolically needy-feeling. You promised to wake me.'

'I did wake you.' She'd kept her promise. 'You were delirious with fever. I did everything I could for you, you have to know that. I tried to help you. I did help you. What more do you want from me?'

'You left me.'

'To get help. I did not abandon you, I wanted you found. I was so happy when I saw them coming for you.'

His eyes blazed, caught on hers and held. A frisson of awareness snaked through her. She was craving his nearness, wanting his touch again, for reasons other than comfort.

Maybe this was way she'd never come forward.

She hadn't wanted to try and recreate the closeness they'd shared in the tent and not find it again. 'Can we turn on a light?'

He gestured towards the light switch by the door. 'Be my guest.'

The overhead fluorescent lights gave off a bright daytime glow. Ari blinked. Reid reached for a pair of sunglasses tucked into the handkerchief pocket of his jacket. Moments later the dark glasses hid his eyes from view.

'I'm still not good with bright light,' he offered by way of explanation.

'I'm really glad they fixed you. I've been wanting to know the details. I had that in the "reasons to reveal myself" column.'

'You made lists for and against coming forward? I'd like to see that.'

'It's not something I carry on me.' Or that he ever needed to see. 'How's your arm?'

'Pinned in two places, so it's a good thing I never have to rope another steer.'

'And your leg?'

'They used new surgical techniques to help with muscle regeneration.'

'And your head?'

He raked his hand through unruly hair, pushing it back to reveal a spiderweb of jagged scarring still pink against his otherwise tanned skin. 'They pulled a bunch of metal fragments from my head. It hasn't affected brain function so far, although after tonight Judah might beg to differ. The optic nerve in my left eye is permanently damaged but it could have been worse. If I'd stayed in the tent much longer it would have been worse.'

She nodded. 'I left at daybreak. The dust...' No way could she have left any earlier.

'I'm grateful, Ari. Why do you think I've been looking for you all this time? I want to pay you back. I owe you my life, and I am filthy rich and very well connected so if there's anything you want or need, *ask*.'

'I'm not really into payback. Look, I'm glad that you've made such a strong recovery and that I didn't do anything to make things worse. That's a load off my mind.' She still had nightmares about his face. 'If you don't mind me doing a bit of seed collecting in the area, and sometimes I might take cuttings—that'd be awesome. I'm not doing any damage and you said you wouldn't sue.'

'I won't sue.'

'Then that's all I need by way of thank you.'

'I don't believe you. Where's your ute?'

'Getting fixed. The radiator's busted but they found a second-hand one for me. It's under control.'

'Are you digging into your savings to pay for it?'

He remembered that conversation? 'Not after working for your brother this weekend. The hourly rate is generous.' She hated the sunglasses because they hid his eyes, so she stared at his hands instead. They were big and lean, much like the rest of him He kept his nails short and the watch on his wrist looked understated in a way that probably meant it was worth a fortune.

'Let me buy you a new twin cab,' he pressed. 'You'll need something reliable if you're going to be driving back and forth from Cairns.'

'No, it's too much.'

'It's pocket change for me.'

'La di dah, Reid. Stop throwing your money in my face. I don't want to be your little charity project that you check in on from time to time out of the goodness of your *noblesse oblige*.' Why had Gert put those words in her head? 'I would love for you to see me as your equal—for us to meet as equals—but I'm not. I never will have your kind of generational wealth or the status you enjoy. I really liked it in the tent when money and status meant nothing, and you needed my help. I had value—I think that makes me a terrible person that you needed to be practically dying for me to consider myself of value to you, but there you have it. I really liked the way we connected, and I still do like...you. I put that under reasons *not* to contact you.'

He leaned forward, elbows on walnut inlay, and steepled his hands. 'That makes no sense.'

She wished she could see his eyes. 'Yes, it does. Self-protection. Why fall for the unobtainable when I can avoid you instead? My reasoning is sound.'

'I'm not unobtainable. I'm right here.'

Yep, right there being deliberately wilful.

'Within reach,' he added helpfully. 'Looking for a woman who's brave and resourceful and who knows this land as well as I do and who won't drive me crazy. Big bonus points if she doesn't want me for my money or status. Sound like anyone you know?'

'No.'

'Now you're just being wilful.'

*'Me?'* He could talk!

He took off his sunglasses, possibly so she could quiver beneath his narrowed glare. 'I dreamed about meeting you again. This isn't how it went. There was touching—lots of touching and bonding. Definitely no arguing.'

'Hey, I have great dreams too,' she murmured dulcetly. 'And then I wake up.'

He blew out a breath and got to his feet. It didn't escape her notice that he favoured one leg. 'I think I know what the problem is.' He walked to the door and turned off the light, plunging them into near darkness again. 'Much better.'

'How is this better?' Every nerve-ending she owned was

waiting for his next move, his next breath. 'You can't just wish our differences away with the flick of a switch. It doesn't work like that.'

'Plenty of people think it does.' He stayed leaning with his back to the door, watching her, a grey cat in the dark. 'Let's experiment. Nothing too difficult or time-consuming, you have my word. I just want some clarity about what really went down in the dust storm.'

She was beginning to see why he was so successful in business. 'You mean besides your test helicopter?'

'I do like to run tests,' he murmured.

She got to her feet and eyed him warily. 'If I asked you to step aside and let me leave, would you do it?'

'Of course.'

But she didn't ask and he didn't move. A curse on her curiosity. 'What kind of experiment?'

'A kiss in the dark.'

# CHAPTER SEVEN

IN ARI'S EXPERIENCE, kisses were careful things, sparingly given. She was the product of a night of passion, raised by a single mother who trusted too easily, *loved* too willingly and time and time again had paid the price. Impressionable Ari had grown up wary. She wasn't against love, or trust, but they had to be earned.

'You're playing with me.' That was what playboys did.

'I'm not.'

'You're a playboy, and rich, and you can have anyone you want. So why me?'

'I'm not a playboy. I never have been, no matter what the tabloids say. I am smart enough to know when I'm onto a good thing. We found something in that tent.' He hadn't moved. 'I want to explore it.'

'What if it's gone?'

'It hasn't. Kissing you will prove it. It's a test. I'm an engineer. Engineers love tests.' He nodded, and the light from the window caused his previously shadowed eyes to glint. 'It makes perfect sense.'

She didn't know what to make of any of it.

Her gaze dipped from his eyes to his lips, with their strong lines and tempting shape, and she wondered what it would feel like to trace them with her fingertips, taste him on her tongue. No point denying that she was tempted.

'One—' She cleared her throat and tried again. 'One kiss and if it's not…right, that's the end of it.'

'Agreed.'

Honey smooth.

Too smooth as he touched a finger beneath her chin and with the gentlest pressure tilted her head upwards. Ari clenched her hands to fists and held them rigidly at her sides so she wouldn't reach for him if the kiss did measure up to impossible expectations.

'I don't know what you think is going to hap—' But the rest of the word had nowhere to go as his lips claimed hers and set off a cascade of sensation that lit her from within. That connection she'd imagined in the tent? It was there in his kiss. A warm blaze that promised home, with teasing hints of laughter and passion licking at the edges of her thoughts.

He reached for her, broad palms against her shoulders until he ran his hands down her arms and caught at her fists with warm fingers, teasing them open and bringing them to his chest to where his heart beat strong and sure. As the kissing continued, inviting her on a journey so full of promise she trembled with the need to take another step.

Deeper now, as her tongue tangled with his and he pulled her body closer to his, and she did nothing to discourage him. She loved the feel of being in his arms and pressed into his long, lean length and the way he savoured her as if they had all the time in the world.

It ended with a hushed quiet, his hands cradling her head and his forehead resting against hers as they traded ragged breaths and fiercely beating hearts.

And even though she didn't believe in love at first kiss, she was now a very firm believer in the lightning-bolt power of a first kiss.

'So.' She stepped away from all that hard-muscled warmth.

'So.' He sounded deeply, smugly satisfied.

'If I take up with you, chances are I'll end up with nothing. I have exams. A future I'm working hard for. I can't just...stop...because your kisses turn the world upside down.' Words spoken more for her benefit than his. 'I need to get back to work.'

'You really don't need to go back to work tonight, but I'm prepared to do this your way.' He moved aside and opened the door and bathed her in light from the hallway while he remained in the shadows. 'When do you finish your exams?'

'The nineteenth.'

'And the time?'

'Four p.m. Would you like to know where?' She could always put her snarky response down to sarcasm rather than a burning desire to set eyes on him again.

'Would you like a kiss for luck?' he asked.

'Best not. We could be here all night.' She was nervous now, because she truly had thought a kiss would put an end to his pursuit. She had nothing a man like him could possibly want. He'd been curious about the woman who'd kept him alive in the dust storm, that was all. And now that he'd found her he'd lose interest in her fast. 'I'm glad you've made such a good recovery. You deserve to soar.'

He smiled, slow and sure. 'See you 'round, Ari.'

'We'll see.' She wasn't part of his world at all. If he wanted to see her again, he'd have to come slumming in hers. 'I have to go to work.'

Ari scribbled down an answer she knew was wrong and set her pen down as the buzzer sounded. Her practical exam had involved classifying live plants, and while some had been familiar, others she'd only ever seen before in photos and botanical drawings. Growing up on the edge of channel country had given her a limited set of plants to know by heart. The rest she'd had to learn. Even her regular walks through Brisbane's botanic gardens hadn't given her the reach she'd needed for this exam.

She gathered up her exam booklets, made sure she'd written her name and student number on the top of each, and handed them to the supervisor with a sickly grimace. She might scrape through. Just. And if she didn't, it wasn't the end of the world. She'd just take the course again.

Ari breathed in through her nose and out through her mouth as she left the exam hall, hoping that the afternoon sunshine and a lung full of fresh air would help chase her grim thoughts away. Sarah, her plant classification partner, fell into step with her. 'How'd you go?' the younger woman asked.

'Touch and go.' No point pretending otherwise.

'A bunch of us are heading for the campus bar if you want to come too?'

Unlike Ari, Sarah lived on campus and was doing a degree course in horticulture full time. Sarah had study buddies and college tutors and friends to lean on. She'd been partnered with Ari for the practical component of two subjects on account of her last name being Collins. Cohen and Collins. Sarah had always gone above and beyond in her efforts to make Ari feel included, not just during coursework but within Sarah's friendship groups too.

It wasn't Sarah's fault that Ari had the social skills of a wary echidna. 'Thanks for the invite, but I'm just going to go and lick my wounds in private.'

'You sure?' They took the stairs together, in sync enough to reach the bottom at the same time. They stopped at the point the footpath split in two directions. The downward path led to the colleges. The upward path led to the car park. 'If you've passed all your other subjects with good averages and for some reason bomb this one, you can put in for special consideration,' Sarah continued.

'Good to know.'

'You sure you don't want to join us?'

'Yeah, I'm too old for all your partying ways.'

'You're, like, two years older than me!'

'Still not drinking with you, lovely.' They shuffled to the side of the paths so other students could walk past. 'Let's stay in touch, okay?'

'Yes!' Sarah beamed and hugged her for good measure. 'I have your number. Don't ghost me.'

'Go. Be merry. I promise I'll keep in touch.'

Ari didn't want to confess what she was holding out for this evening.

A long shot.

The promise of a kiss and a gravelly, *See you 'round.*

A fairy tale.

Reid leaned against the bull bar of Ari's battered old ute and waited for her to walk closer. She'd seen him from a distance—he'd noted the hitch in her step and the way she'd clutched the strap of her satchel tighter. She'd put her head down, her dark wavy hair swinging forward to partially cover her face, but she'd kept coming his way.

Granted, he'd planted himself right in her way but needs must.

He'd left her alone so she could study without distraction.

He'd found out everything he could about her.

He knew she had a stepfather and a younger stepbrother living in a house her mother had bought with cash twenty-five years ago. He knew from Gert that Ari wasn't welcome in her childhood home any more and that whenever she returned to Barcoo, the small Outback town she'd grown up in, she stayed with Gert.

No known father, dead mother, and yet somehow Ari had clung to the notion that if she worked and studied hard enough, she could make her own way.

Stubborn, resilient, driven, independent. She'd resisted his money, his gratitude, and made light of his kisses. She didn't want his help, even though it would give her a leg-up when it came to realising her dreams and securing financial independence. She didn't trust other people not to take away everything she'd strived for—he thought that might be one of the reasons she'd pushed him away, but when he pumped Gert for more information on Ari's upbringing, the older woman would only say so much. Ari's mother had married a bad 'un who'd chipped away at her confidence and self-respect until she was a shell of the woman she'd once been. Ari had copped the lash of her stepfather's belt and had the internal and external scars to prove it. Love had been scarce and trust non-existent. Gert had warned him against hurting Ari and he'd promised he wouldn't.

He wanted to make her life's journey *easier*.

Playboy, the media called him. Younger brother to dangerous, brooding, ex-con billionaire Judah Blake. Second son of a titled aristocrat—the feckless, charming spare, and once upon a time he'd done his very best to live up to that reputation.

He was the one who'd laughed and splashed his cash while beautiful women smiled prettily.

He was the one who'd wryly introduced those same women to unmarried billionaires and barons who were higher up the food chain than him. He'd crossed them off his *maybe* list as he'd watched them make their plays.

He'd met Jenna and thought she might be different. She hadn't wanted his money, she'd wanted his might, his reputation, his goals to align with hers, and when they hadn't she'd set out to destroy him.

He'd become even more jaded about relationships after that. He rarely trusted others to do right by him.

But this woman... Ari.

Maybe he could trust this one and in doing so get her to trust him. They already had a solid foundation—forged in a dust storm in a tent.

'I got your landscape plans for the eco lodges,' he said as she came to a halt in front of him. He would have searched her eyes for any sign of welcome if his eyesight had allowed for it, but she wasn't close enough for that and broad brush-strokes were all he had to work with. 'You added water.'

'I did.'

'It'll bring the wildlife and scare city people stupid.'

There was a smile, even if it happened to be a small one. 'You said the lodges were for scientists and ecologists. Surely they'll cope.'

'You'd think. Experience suggests otherwise.'

'Then don't use the plans.'

'I was thinking more along the lines of revise and resubmit.' She was in a mood and he couldn't tell if he was the reason for it, showing up like this uninvited. But he was an excellent mood-booster, and if that was to be his role this evening so be it.

When he'd been younger, he'd often had to coax his sister-in-law, Bridie, out of her house. And Gert could be curt, but Reid had always been able to get her laughing.

'How did your exam go?' he asked. Maybe that was the

problem. Maybe she needed to unload, in which case he could lend an ear.

She shrugged, and her perfect mouth turned down. 'Terrible.'

Okay. 'Care to share?'

'I really don't want to talk about it.'

There went his opportunity to showcase his masterful listening skills.

'So what do you want to do this evening? Because I'm here to make it happen.'

It wasn't as if silver-spoon billionaire Reid, with his genius IQ and revolutionary engine designs, would have any experience with failure. And even if she *was* underestimating his imagination, she still didn't want to talk about her exam. 'You came.'

'I said I would. I'm a man of my word.'

Also way too easy on the eye, in his moleskin trousers and polished leather boots. He wore a collared chambray shirt, frayed at the neck, with the sleeves rolled to his elbows. He wore his battered Akubra hat with the arrogance of long familiarity. He knew who he was.

For some people, that came easily.

His smile came easily too. 'Celebrate with me tonight. You finished your course. That's a big deal.'

'Not in your world.'

He pushed his hat back and now she could see his eyes more clearly. Hazel-green with a scar that cut one eyebrow in two and ran in shredded ribbons towards his hairline. 'I live here in Brisbane for part of each year. I'd like to show you my world here if you want to see it. But there is a catch. I need to get a lift back to my place with you.' He gestured towards his eyes. 'I can't drive. They're not ready yet.'

'Will they ever be?'

He shrugged and his engaging smile turned wry. 'No one knows. My eyesight's still in flux. I'm taking that as a win, and if it stops short of where I want it to be, at least I have the resources to work around it. But enough about that. Haven't you ever wanted to have dinner with a slightly damaged billionaire? We could do the whole *Pretty Woman* playlist.'

'You mean you flash your credit card around while buying me clothes, arrange for me to wear stunning jewels, take me to all the special places and then your friends call me a whore?'

'We could cut some of that out,' he assured her. 'I can't play the piano. And I'm not afraid of heights. That guy was a mess. Daddy issues.'

'Don't you have daddy issues too?'

'Nah. My father was a gambler and apparently a womaniser, although I never saw the womaniser part until after my mother died, when he went off the rails. I put it down to grief. When she was alive, my father treated my mother like the princess she was. Displays of affection between them were rarer than dolphins in the desert, now I come to think of it, but I chalked it up to aristocratic reserve.'

'You don't seem to have much. Aristocratic reserve, I mean.' Oh, hell. Was that an insult? 'I didn't mean that as an insult.'

He smiled. 'Thanks for clarifying. I won't take it as one.'

She'd never realised just how sexy confidence could be. 'Any luck finding your half-sister?'

'Not yet. Plenty of charlatans though. We did turn up something interesting. My father gave your mother a lump sum of cash around about the time you were born.'

Ari opened her mouth to reply, and then shut it again so

she wouldn't catch a fly. She felt hot then cold. She didn't *want* to be the missing Blake heiress. The thought of Reid being her half-brother made her feel ill.

She'd *kissed* him.

With feelings unbecoming to a sibling. 'My father was a stockman from the north.'

'That's what Gert says. She says she and your mother were housekeeping at Jeddah Creek station for a party of half a dozen high rollers—this was years ago—and my father was losing badly. He was about to bet Jeddah Creek station in its entirety when your mother fell to the ground while pouring them all more drinks. She told them her water just broke. It hadn't. You didn't arrive for another two weeks, according to Gert, but it did get my father away from the gambling table long enough to come to his senses. Your mother told him she'd overheard his guests discussing winning strategies. They were all in it together—against him.'

'Nasty.'

'He asked her what she wanted by way of thanks and she said, "Security for my baby." So he gave her enough money to buy a house. That's one story, anyway. I have others if you want to hear them. None of them suggest that we're related.'

'That's a relief.'

'You don't want to be the missing Blake heiress?'

'No. All the no.'

'We're not that bad.'

'We *kissed*.'

'There is that,' he murmured. 'Having to conjure up brotherly feelings for you would be difficult, given our smouldering connection.'

'It's not smouldering.'

'Incendiary?' He brightened. 'Explosive?'

'*Reid.*'

'Don't you want to hear the other stories about why my father gave your mother two hundred and fifty thousand dollars twenty-three years ago? I think you do.'

'I hope you don't want that money back. I don't have it.'

'Yeah, I heard that too.'

She didn't *like* that he seemed to know so much about her life. Had he asked around? Had Gert opened up to him about Ari's stepfather and stepbrother situation? Because, honestly, she didn't care any more that they'd turned their backs on her the moment her mother was cold. Even her mother had pushed Ari away towards the end as a way of keeping them happy. She'd never felt so alone and if it hadn't been for Gert stepping in and offering her a home, Ari didn't know what she would have done. She'd stopped thinking of them as family years ago. She was doing all right on her own these days, thank you very much, and she dared anyone to think otherwise.

'So that's your ticked-off look,' he mused. 'I wish I could see it better.'

'Do you? *Do you really?*'

'And I really like your *dire warning* voice. I promise I'll behave.'

'Are you always this jokey?'

'You're in a mood. I'm trying to cajole you out of it. I'm offering you the mood-lifting Cinderella experience. And all you have to do to get it started is give me a lift and your company for the evening.'

With a sigh that was more for show than for protest, she gave in. He'd already managed to take her mind off her study failures. His mood-boosting skills actually were as good as advertised. And there was also the not so small effort it had taken him to arrange to be waiting for her.

She'd told him about liking their time in the tent because

she felt useful, and here he was throwing himself on her mercy for a lift and ceding control. *Journey with me,* he might as well have said. *You drive. I trust you.* She'd never even *seen* a relationship dynamic like the one he seemed to be offering her. Did he realise how paper-thin her defences against him were? 'I'll do it. On one condition.'

'Name it.'

'Please don't dress me up and take me to the opera this evening. Or to a ball. Or to a fancy dinner with the flying snails and challenging silverware. Can we give that a miss?'

'As you wish.'

She headed for the driver's side door. 'How'd you get here?'

'Uber.'

'And how'd you know this was my car?'

'Gert said you drove a thirty-year-old Hilux. This one has red dust in its wheel rims. Calculated guess.'

'I wish there'd been more of those in my exam.' She blew out a breath. She wasn't going to think about that. Nothing she could do about it. 'My passenger-side door isn't locked. Jump in.'

He reached for the passenger-door handle. 'You don't lock it?'

'Who'd want it? Besides, the locks have been broken for years. I also need to drive us to the nearest mechanic. I was almost late for my exam because Bessie wouldn't start. I think it's the battery.' She didn't want to think about all the other things it could be.

She'd parked on an incline with the nose facing downhill and no other cars in front of her, and after two sluggish attempts at getting the engine to turn over, she blew out a breath, shoved the vehicle in neutral, released the brake and let it roll until she could clutch-start the beast.

It started with a jolt and she found second gear with barely a grind and then they were on their way. 'Atta girl.' She patted the dash.

'That is so sexy,' he murmured. 'Can you muster cattle too? Fix a broken five-wire fence?'

'Is that what turns you on?'

'It's never been a complete turn-on before. I'd have found it interesting but not necessarily a reason to pursue a woman. Maybe it's just you.'

No getting past his open interest in pursuing her. She was simultaneously grateful for his clarity and sure that his pursuit would be short-lived. 'You know what I'm going to do for you? I'm going to save us a lot of trouble and show you the real me.'

'I can't wait. How else are we going to get to know each other?' he murmured agreeably as they reached a stop sign and Ari prayed the ute didn't stall. 'What did you have planned for this evening before I turned up?'

'You mean after the trip to the mechanic? If I only had to buy a new battery, I was thinking I'd go home, get Thai takeaway from the restaurant down the road, put some music on and open a bottle of beer. Because that's how I roll.' She had her eyes on the road and couldn't see his reaction to her big night of celebration. 'There may have been a little sing-along and a toast to me for sticking to my education plan in the face of poverty. You're welcome to join me. I'm not wedded to the Cinderella plan.' They'd hit the main road. 'Can you bring up directions to the nearest battery place?'

'I have a better idea.'

Ten minutes later, Reid had directed her to a workshop of some kind on the outskirts of Fortitude Valley near Brisbane city centre. Huge industrial doors stood open and Ari could see several vehicles inside.

'Drive in. Bay three should be free.'

'What is this place?'

'It's where my team converts regular vehicles to electric ones.'

'Uh-huh.'

'Don't worry.' He'd caught her sideways glance. 'Converting this old dear is out of the question. Probably. But they're all mechanics or engineers of some kind and they can give it a once-over and get it running properly for you.'

She found bay three and parked as requested. By the time she'd collected her shoulder bag, Reid was already out and talking with a dark-haired man with grey streaks through his beard.

Both men turned towards her as they approached. 'Stan, meet Ari. Ari, this is Stan. He vets my engine designs and tells me I'm dreaming.'

'Sounds about right.' Stan nodded. 'Cheers. We'll take a look at the old girl and give you a call when she's ready. Meanwhile, we've got a replacement ride for you. Special order for Reid, here. Even better if you get to be the test driver while he's in it.'

'Told you I had a good idea,' he murmured.

Stan led them to what looked like a brand-new farm four-wheel-drive. 'Hybrid fuel, double cab manual workmate with a cab chassis, bull bar, front winch, towbar, lockbox, air pump in the lockbox, off-road tyres, and an air intake upgrade.' Stan patted the hood. 'Outback baby, as requested.'

Reid nodded. 'Torque?'

'Four hundred Nm max. Best we could do.'

Ari had no idea what they were talking about but nodded along with them, only to find two sets of eyes on her, expressing no little amusement. 'What? I can admire an

Outback baby when I see one. Long as it gets me where
I'm going.'

'Good, because I had it tricked out especially for you.'
Reid opened the driver's-side door for her. 'Even if I haven't
figured out a way to make you accept it. Yet.'

# CHAPTER EIGHT

ARI TOSSED HER bag on the seat, grabbed the handhold and hoisted herself up. How was she supposed to object to his gifting her this beautiful Outback vehicle when he hadn't even tried to give it to her? Yet.

Reid stayed where he was, arms crossed in front of him. 'You want a running board on this thing?'

'I'm only driving it for one evening, no matter what you think the future holds.'

'Maybe just a running *step*,' he mused. 'You're still going to need the clearance.'

'We are not even having the same conversation.' She took the time to absorb that new car smell and all the bells and whistles—phone slot, big screen. 'This thing isn't going to take over the driving, is it?'

'Not if you don't want it to—although I think the boys did add self-drive capabilities. Needs testing in the desert, though.'

'Huh. Another prototype?'

'This is me you're talking to. Everything that comes out of this workshop is a prototype.'

Hopefully not as life-challenging as his last one.

The truck was ridiculously easy to drive, and comfortable as well. Windows that sealed—no whistling wind. A dash that didn't rattle. No leaves fluttering in the broken air-conditioning vent. This air conditioning actually *worked*.

The air conditioning alone was enough to make her high-falutin' principles waver.

'How's it drive?'

'I feel like a princess in a golden carriage. Good job.'

Even the dratted man's quiet laughter made her feel happy. What was it about him that made her want to sign up for so much more?

But the car beeped whenever she got too close to other vehicles, and basically critiqued her driving the entire way to the inner-city warehouse apartment complex that Reid programmed into the car's computer.

'Okay, I'm over the helpful driving suggestions and my admiration for functioning air conditioning,' she said as she turned the vehicle into an underground car park with a rolling security door that slid open at the press of his keychain. 'You can keep the carriage, I'd like my old one back at midnight, please. Where are we?'

'Hamilton. I live here when I'm in Brisbane. A lot of my tech guys live here too—it's part of their wage package. There's a shopping strip across the road with a couple of clothing boutiques, restaurants and a bar.'

'Does that mean you own the whole woolshed apartment complex and the shopping strip too?'

His silence gave her a jolt. 'Oh. Hell. You do. I can't even—' She owned so little. 'We are so different.'

'Not that different,' he murmured. 'I aim to prove it to you. Park near the lift.'

She did.

The step down from the cab of the vehicle really was a bit steep for her, but she wasn't about to complain. Cinderella would have had a terrible time getting in and out of her carriage, would she not? In that gown?

She met up with Reid at the back of the vehicle but instead of leading her to the lift, he headed for the car-park entrance.

'So, we're heading for my place and takeaway and beer,' he told her, 'but there's water involved, which I think you'll like, and one of the boutiques across the road does swimwear and leisure wear. My shout for the swimwear and whatever you want to wear tonight. All part of the Cinderella deal. Payment, if you like, for holding my hand and tormenting me with your plant classification textbook.'

'I was *studying*.'

'I was barely conscious and unable to protest!'

Well, there was that. 'Sorry. I was trying to take your mind—and mine—off our situation. Which was *dire*.'

He had such a rich, rumbling laugh. 'Exactly. And you rose to the challenge magnificently, so whatever you want from the boutique is on me. Or you can swim naked. I wouldn't object.'

Or she might not swim at all. A far more likely option to her way of thinking.

But she walked with him to the swimwear boutique with its skinny mannequins and beach towels in the window, and Ari just knew by looking at the shop's high-end styling that the prices would be out of her reach. Who could afford hundreds of dollars for tiny brightly coloured bits of material, not to mention hundreds more for the various wraps and skirts that went with them? She headed for the specials rack. Reid headed for the counter and the smiling, sun-kissed woman behind it.

'Reid Blake. Fancy seeing you here,' the woman said, and her voice was warmly caressing but somehow not predatory.

'Rita.' He leaned against the counter. 'This is Ari. I've hijacked her evening, and she now needs a swimsuit and loungewear.'

'That I'm paying for, no matter what he says, so I'll be over here by the specials rack,' said Ari.

Reid sighed. 'See what I'm dealing with here, Rita? Insubordination. Help me.'

Rita looked aghast as she floated towards the specials rack. 'But Ari, darling, it's been a long day with very few customers. My commission is begging you to let him pick up the tab. He never comes in here flashing his big black credit card. The bike shop, sure. The Thai restaurant next door, often. Here, never.'

'Uh-huh.' Ari didn't believe a word of the woman's patter. He was probably in here every other week.

'Ari,' the woman said quietly, with a brief glance towards Reid. 'Not once.'

Ari didn't know what to do with that information.

'Reid, go order us some of those yummy little spring rolls from next door, while I open the champagne,' commanded Rita. 'Make yourself scarce. We're busy.'

'Rita's my next-door neighbour.' Reid fished a black plastic card from his wallet and set it on the counter with a snap. 'Ari is Cinderella tonight. You are her fairy godmother. We're going swimming later, and if you charge her for any of the clothes she selects I will double your rent.' He tapped the card. 'Got it?'

'Loud and clear, Your Lordshipness,' said Rita with a dismissive wave. 'Leave us.'

He left with swagger that Rita admired, right up until the door closed behind him, and then the older woman snorted, and Ari couldn't help but smile right along with her.

'That man.' Rita walked to the door and flipped a 'Closed'

sign outwards. 'He tries so hard to be a hard ass but it never sticks. He's a country boy with a lot of money and a burning desire to improve the lives of everyone around him. But I am telling the truth that he's never spent in here before. You must be special.'

'No.' Never special. 'I'm just…someone from home. Where he grew up.'

'Sounds special enough to me. One piece or two for swimwear?'

'Two? Or… I don't know. I don't swim much. I'm kind of a get-wet-up-to-my-middle if it's the ocean and an edge-clinger if it's a pool.'

'Trust me, he's not going to let you drown. I'm thinking a two-piece with a bespoke silk wrap and matching skirt. Coral reef colours with a bit of blue and seafoam. Trust me, I'm your fairy godmother and that there's a centurion credit card he's left on my counter. He can afford the designer silk.'

'But I don't want him to pay.'

Rita disappeared behind a curtain and returned with an armful of seafoam silk glory.

'Oh. That looks like nightwear.'

'Well, it is five p.m.' Rita held up the swimwear. 'You're a neat size ten and this will fit you to perfection. Try it on.'

'No.'

Which Rita somehow interpreted as *I'll take it*.

'The skirt is a wraparound—one size fits all. The wrap is gorgeous—so sheer, and there's a camisole and panties to go with it as well as a swimsuit. It's a honeymoon combo. From champagne and strawberries and ruffled sheets to a quick dip in the spa to soothe those aching muscles, it's got you covered, so to speak.'

'None of it look like it's going to cover very *much*.'

'Oh, sweetheart. You be you. I'll open the champagne,

and then we can really get started. We can cover more of you if that's what you'd prefer.'

Was champagne a thing on a Friday afternoon in a closed swimwear shop? Apparently, it was, and there were triple Brie cheese and fig jam and salted crackers too. By the time Reid returned, Rita had added pleated long trousers, a beaded silk sleeveless top, and pretty leather sandals to Ari's pile.

Reid had returned with enough finger food for ten people, and out came plates and forks and a guy dropped in with a big jug of beer and stayed for a satay stick with peanut chilli sauce and was this a bizarre way to spend a Friday evening in the river city? It didn't seem all that billionaireish.

Instead, Ari got to laugh as Rita and brew master Tanner, who owned the bar next door, swapped tall tales about customers and worked their way steadily through the food and beer.

By the time they left the shop and entered the old wool warehouse on the river's edge, Ari knew all about Rita's husband and one-year-old granddaughter, and brew master Tanner's experimental passionfruit beer pop that needed finessing because it tasted—he readily admitted—really awful.

The sun had started to disappear behind tall buildings, and coloured lights were beginning to wrap the city in their glow, and Ari felt pleasure sink into her skin. She liked this city with its moist heart and sticky nights. She liked Reid's company and not just because she was two glasses of champagne down and carrying a couple of thousand dollars' worth of almost-there clothing in two fancy recyclable carry bags. Apart from his dedication to giving her a Cinderella experience, his life and friendships seemed extraordinarily normal.

'I like your neighbourhood. And your friends. You're a people person. Who knew?'

'I knew,' said Reid as he unlocked an apartment door with the press of his finger on a door pad and ushered her into a soaring space with exposed brick walls and enormous glass doors at one end of the long narrow living space, lushly decorated with textured furnishings and dozens of paintings that shouldn't have worked when all piled together but they did.

Beyond the glass doors was a terrace that led to a delicately lit infinity pool that seemed to flow into the river. There was a spa section to one side, with a rock wall and spouts. Waterfall option, her brain supplied helpfully. She could picture Reid relaxing in this space. She could picture herself in it too, courtesy of the swimwear he'd just purchased for her.

'What do you think? Do you like it?'

She wanted to say something snarky about him not needing her approval. She wanted to chide him about having way too much money to spend on making his Brisbane crash pad a showstopper, but the words never left her mouth.

In truth, she didn't want to say any of that.

Why *shouldn't* he have a home full of beauty that instantly made people feel comfortable and welcome? Who was she to try and take him down with petty envy?

'I love it,' she said honestly. 'It's beautiful.'

'Guest suite is through that door to your left. My bedroom and a few other rooms are to the right, and my office takes up the mezzanine. I started this day aiming to whisk you away to an island tonight to impress you.' He walked to the big glass doors and again pressed his hand to a steel pad and the doors slid silently open until there was no visible glass wall left at all. This apartment was modest when it came to space and mighty with its bells and whistles. 'But there's water here too.' He looked back at her. 'I'm not backing out of our Cinderella deal, but we could stay here and order in and if it's beer you want, Tanner will deliver.'

'You say that as if we'd be slumming.' She couldn't figure him out. 'You have to know that my version of this evening comes nowhere near this standard of luxury. Isn't that what you want me to know?'

'Not exactly.'

She waited for him to continue.

'I want you to recognise that I get takeaway and beer and relax at home too. Just like you.'

Maybe her bedsit rental *was* the same as this place underneath. A place to cook, a place to sleep. She looked past the museum-quality paintings on the walls to the pool and spa and river and city lights on the other side of the bank.

Who was she to deny him his fantasy? 'So I go left, get changed, and meet you at the pool?'

'We could do that.' His eyes held so many smiles in them. She wondered what it would be like to be so full up with smiles that they tumbled out of her the way Reid's seemed to. Maybe if she stuck around, she'd find out. 'I'm sure you can figure out that there's a door leading from your suite onto a patio and from there you can access the pool area. You put a tent up around a severely wounded pilot in the middle of a dust storm in the desert. I'm pretty sure you can find a door.'

'You're still harping on that?' She didn't know why. 'You'd have done the same.'

'I like to think so. Doesn't make it any less impressive. I'm an awesome person. So are you.'

His confidence was contagious and he made her laugh. There were worse starts to an evening. 'Is this a date?' She needed to know. 'Or is this just you feeling beholden and thinking Ari's an awesome person?'

'It's a date. Although awesome Ari and grateful Reid are in play too. Do we need to overthink it? Because if we do, you should know that water helps. Have a problem? Have a shower. A heavy day? The spa pool is for you and don't forget to pummel your shoulders beneath the waterfall spout. I'm a believer.'

'I'm glad you don't take water for granted,' she said.

'You know where I grew up. Three-minute showers, no waiting for the water to warm up. Water is life. Which is why your designs for my eco lodges went all in on it. For you, luxury means free-flowing water available to all.' He tucked his hands into his trouser pockets. 'I came across some garden diaries written by an Outback farmer in South Australia. I bought them for you. Thirty years' worth. They're on your bed.'

*Her bed?*

And what a gift.

'Reid…' She didn't know what to say. *This* was what his money bought. Access to information that wasn't readily available. A step up that wasn't available to everyone. 'I don't know what to say.'

'Say you'll read them and resubmit your garden plans for my eco lodges. My north star is that we never stop learning and striving to respect the balance of nature.'

She was rapidly acquiring mad respect for this man, along with irresistible attraction, and she didn't know what to do with either. 'I'll read them. Thank you. See you in the pool.' She'd become a woman of choppy sentences. 'I'll be clinging to the edge or sitting on the step-in, if there is one.' Time to admit another of her failings. 'I can't swim.'

He took it in his stride with barely a blink. He shrugged and smiled warm and wide. 'Want to learn?'

Reid knew what women wanted him for. Access to his money and the high life, first and foremost. His name and nebulous ties to English aristocracy came second. His personality, his beliefs and values—too many women of his acquaintance didn't care about any of that. They didn't see him and never would.

That was why Ari was special.

She saw him—the boy who'd come looking for her whenever she strayed too far from the homestead. The one she'd sat next to at the kitchen table while Gert served up reprimand along with sweet biscuits and cold water. Those memories would compete with those from the tent and now he was showing her the meat of his world and he hoped she would layer them all together and come up with someone she liked, because he sure as sunrise liked her.

She knew where he came from. Same view when they travelled Outback roads. Same sunrises and sunsets and redgums and flash-flooding rivers cutting grooves through the earth.

He could teach her to swim, to soar, if she'd let him.

If she'd lower her guard and let him in.

# CHAPTER NINE

THE BIKINI SHE'D chosen seemed far smaller now than in the shop, but the colours were ones she knew well. Burnt umber, sky blue, wattle yellow and the bright red of Lilli Pilli berries.

The swimwear emphasised her slight curves and made the most of her legs. Garden work had given her lean muscle, and her wavy hair reached the small of her back. She had no gloss that came from beauty treatments and skilfully applied make-up, but what she did have going for her was her health, youth, a heart-shaped face, and good teeth. And when she slipped on the silky robe that matched her swimsuit, Ari felt almost beautiful.

It was hard not to feel special in such expensive surroundings.

Her Cinderella moment came with bare feet, an infinity pool and Reid Blake in all his near naked glory. Board shorts couldn't hide the scars that littered his body—he wasn't even trying to cover them up as he sat on the edge of the spa pool and waited for her to join him, his gaze bright and admiring as she approached.

Was she little more than a colourful shape? What did he see when he looked her way?

Why did his shortcomings embolden her?

'I usually start in the hot pool,' he said as she joined him.

'Seats and water jets are around the outside, it's deeper in the middle but you'll still be able to stand up and your head will be out of the water. All good? Feeling confident?'

'Yes.' She already loved the concept of spa baths. Now all she had to do was embrace the reality.

He eased into the water, and she shed her wrap and followed his lead and let the warm water lap at her skin.

'I've never been in one,' she confessed.

'Find a seat, rest your head against the headrests and let go,' he suggested, and she did just that, but there was nothing to hold onto and she couldn't relax.

And then he was easing his big body into the seat alongside her and taking her hand in his at the surface of the water and it was just enough to anchor her.

'Relax,' he murmured. 'If your legs and arms want to float to the surface, let them. If you want to put your feet down and your knees up, do it.'

'I think hand-holding's our thing.' She hadn't let his hand go but she wasn't squeezing it to bits either. She closed her eyes, tilted her head back against the padded headrest and sighed her pleasure. 'This is nice. We wouldn't have got this in my bedsit. It doesn't even have a bath.'

'How are you feeling about starting your new job?'

About that...

She'd heard from the nursery manager yesterday. 'You know how Gert was bragging about me already having a job to go to? There's been a slight change of plans.'

'I'm listening.'

'The owner's son came back from overseas and is "assessing his options", whatever that means. They don't want me just yet. They may not want me at all. They're going to let me know in a couple of months' time.' She blew out a breath. 'I think I'm done with them. Goodbye, Cairns.' She released Reid's hand to remove a wayward strand of hair from her face and tuck it behind her ear. 'I'm disappointed.'

'Work for me.' The confident way he said it mixed with the heat of the water and the gently rising steam and made her light-headed. 'Better still, I'll help you lodge the paperwork to create your own company and you can work for me as a contractor.'

'You hate my garden plans for your eco lodges.'

'Hate's a strong word.'

'You're not denying it.'

'I want to give you a proper project brief this time. I want you to move into one of my lodges and live there for a month or two. There's another lodge nearby and people will come and go. Get a feel for what my visitors respond to and how they interact with their surroundings and then submit a new set of landscape plans. I'll give you a three-month contract in two stages, development and completion.'

'You're serious.'

'Very. And you can look at it as charity or payback for saving my life if you must. There's no denying that your remarkably brave actions are what first got my attention.'

'You think I'm brave?'

'Yes.' And not just that. 'I had grit and determination and resilience when I took on Jeddah Creek station at seventeen. The same kind of grit and resilience and determination I see in you. And back then I had help, from Tom and Bridie and Judah and others, and I took it and it set me up for a future I never dreamed of.'

He wasn't finished.

'I don't want to take anything from you. I don't want to deny you the chance to work and grow and travel in directions you've never dreamed of. I want you to have help too, like I did. I want to pay it forward. I want to see you soar.'

Did she dare believe him? Trust him to do right by her?

Could she trust her own instincts when what he was offering sounded too good to be true?

He leaned back and closed his eyes, possibly to avoid her open-mouthed disbelief as she scrambled to sit upright. He'd left her with no defence against his generosity. 'Say yes.'

It was a chance in a million. 'You want to see me succeed?'

'Absolutely.'

'No strings attached? Regardless of whether I end up in your bed tonight?'

He lifted his head and studied her through narrowed eyes. 'I'm ruling that out for now. I'm playing the long game. But even if we do get romantically involved, my offer will stand. I want you to create a work future you're passionate about.'

He speared through the water to the opposite corner of the spa pool and turned to face her with the arc of an eyebrow. 'Say yes to the contract.'

Gert had vouched for him.

It really was the opportunity of a lifetime. 'What happens if we have a *very intense, very short-lived* affair and discover we're not that compatible after all?'

'You'll still have a company that has nothing to do with me and a lucrative, high-impact landscape-gardening project under way or completed. Your work will speak for itself, and you'll have other projects lined up, none of them connected to me.' His quiet words carried across the sound of bubbling warm water. 'I'm trying to empower you, Ari. Place you in a position where, no matter what happens, you win.'

'Even if you lose?'

'I'll have had my chance with you and taken my shot. How is that losing?'

Did he have no fear at all? What if he lost his heart to

her and she trampled on it? What was he *seeing* when he gazed at her so steadily? 'Aren't you scared of giving your heart to the wrong person?'

'You and I, we have a lot in common. We don't trust easily. Stands out a mile. People have let us down. Which means that one of us has to blink first and say I trust you and I want you and I'm ready for whatever that brings. I don't think you'll let me down, and I sure as hell won't let you down. It's a good start to whatever kind of relationship we forge, don't you think?'

Could she really walk away from Reid's captivating confidence?

No.

No, she could not. 'I'll work my butt off until you're happy with my work. Like that blasted exam, I'll do it over and over until I get it right. I won't let you down.'

'I know you won't.'

'And we probably shouldn't ruin my golden opportunity with…y'know…sex right now. Too soon. Like you said.' *But, oh, how she wanted to ruin it.* 'That's very chivalrous of you.'

'Long game, remember?' And then he was looking straight at her, with a glint of challenge in his eyes. 'Swimming lesson number one. Push off the edge of the seat section with your feet, arms out in front of you and let your body glide through the water towards me. I'll catch you.'

'But it's all bubbly in the middle.'

'So it'll tickle. Believe me, your body can do it. Don't overthink it. Push off and glide. Believe.'

It was so *easy* to believe around him.

Moments later her hands hit his chest and she tried very hard not to scramble for purchase and cling to him like a vine. She found her feet and blushed as she snatched her hands away. 'You just wanted my hands on your hot bod.'

'Former hot bod,' he countered dryly. But you're right in thinking I like your hands on me. 'Now turn around and push off again and glide back to the other side. Don't put your feet down until your hands touch the wall.'

Pretty soon she was gliding all over the place while Reid drawled lazy suggestions to go faster, slower, and change direction midway across without putting her feet down.

'Taking control is addictive,' he said at last, when she'd settled into her spa seat with a great deal more confidence than she'd had to begin with. 'Whether it's taking control of something you're doing, or directing others, it can be a buzz. After a while it becomes second nature, and you start to think you know more and make better choices than anyone else. It's rubbish, of course, but no one tells you that to your face because you're the boss with the endless line of credit. Eventually that way of thinking bleeds into every part of your life, romance included.'

'So you're…bossy in bed?'

'Would you like me to be?' He had a wicked grin.

She eased lower, up to her chin in bubbly water because maybe then he wouldn't see the blush that felt as if it went all the way from her cheeks to her chest.

'I like teasing you,' he said next. 'You take the bait so beautifully.'

She retaliated by splashing water in his face, and she really should have thought that through because moments later they were both splashing each other for all they were worth, as if they were twelve.

Fifteen at the most.

It ended with a drenching and Reid pinning her against the side of the pool, with his arms beneath her shoulders, holding her up, and her body bumping against his and finding all sorts of interesting developments.

'You see, this is what I *don't* get from the women I date,' he murmured.

'Told off?'

'Scolded. Taken to task. Given a tongue-lashing,' he added.

'Are you *sure* you don't get that last one?'

'Cinderella!' He sounded delighted. 'You're *raunchy*. Bawdy. Risqué. I love it.'

'Cinderella was not raised a lady, Reid. Do keep up with your fairy tales.'

'I have to kiss you.'

He had quite the flair for drama, or was it silliness? She loved it. 'Because you're unbearably smitten?'

He angled closer until their lips were almost touching and she didn't pull away. 'Mainly to shut you up,' he murmured, and then his lips were on hers, cool and sure, tempting and teasing until she opened for him and let the heat take hold.

It wasn't like their last kiss. He didn't see the need to ask more wordless questions he already knew the answer to. He turned playfulness into searing desire so fast she was in danger of drowning.

Ari clung to him, her heart tight in her chest as his hands caressed her skin, wove through her hair and he cradled her close.

He'd been living rent-free in her head for so many weeks now, but the reality of being in his company again was so much better than anything she'd imagined, and she'd imagined a lot.

Water had long been one of her favourite things. Reid was fast becoming her favourite person. Put the two together and she had no defences left.

Ari didn't end the kiss, Reid did.

He took a step back, leaving her clinging to the pool edge as he ran not quite steady hands through his already soaked hair.

'Think I need a cool-down,' he murmured, and turned and climbed from the hot pool and entered the larger lap pool. Sexy guy. Even with his carved-up leg and visible injuries.

Sexy guy who wanted her, Ari Cohen—nothing special—in his life and was going to quite some lengths to make it happen.

Which in Ari's opinion made him *even* more desirable.

She rested her forearms on the side of the spa and watched as he swam a couple of laps, his movements slow and precise. Still recovering, her brain supplied helpfully.

'You're a pretty good date,' she said when he surfaced at the side closest to her and didn't attempt another lap. 'More of a fairy godmother than Prince Charming, though.'

'I'll take it under advisement.'

He left the pool and reached for a towel from a pile sitting on a small side table. He scrubbed his face and hair dry and wrapped the towel around his waist. When she made her own exit from the water, he handed her a towel too.

'It's a lot to take in.' She didn't look at him as she dried off and reached for her pretty silk wrap. 'I've never thought much beyond having to take care of myself. There's never been a Prince Charming on my horizon until you dropped from the sky.'

'I thought you said I was the fairy godmother.'

'Yeah, well, maybe you're both.' She wanted to make another confession, so he would know all her limitations up front. 'I've never been in a relationship. Never even tried to trust a man to put my well-being on equal par with his. I didn't exactly have good role models for that.' She was looking for a reaction from him, but he didn't flinch. 'I've had sex. No strings. One-offs. They fit my sense of self-worth.'

'Work on that,' he commanded gruffly.

'I will. I am. You're helping with that by offering me options I've never dreamed of, and it's a lot. *You're* a lot to take on, this world you inhabit isn't one I've lived in, even though you're doing your best to make it seem mostly normal. For me it's a lot, so thanks for taking it slow.'

'All part of my plan for world domination, but you're welcome.' He'd finished towelling his hair dry and it stuck up in tufts, going every which way. 'How about we have that beer now? Or food. You hungry? There's a riverfront restaurant a short walk from here if you feel like dining out. Or we can have it delivered. Your call.'

She had wet hair, no make-up, and beautiful casual clothes to change into. She didn't want to add anyone else to the night's mix. 'I'd like to hang around here and eat in. We could put together that design brief you mentioned earlier. I could cover your gorgeous outdoor table in scribbled notes and drawings while you describe what you want to achieve. There could be half-eaten plates of food and boutique beer on the table that no one's rushing to clear away. And maybe at the end of the evening as I'm walking out the door to catch a ride home, there could be farewell kissing and a promise to catch up again soon.'

'That's your wish for the evening?'

'Yeah.' Pretty simple. And yet every moment of it had the potential to make her heart sing. 'Too lame?'

'Not at all.'

The evening unfolded with a magic born of stunningly beautiful surroundings, the prioritising of creativity, imagination, and the feeding of the senses.

Not to mention the teasing, flirting and touching.

When Reid finally walked her to the Cinderella truck that he insisted she drive home, there were plans afoot for her new landscape-design company and for her to take up residence in one of the Cooper's Creek station lodges from next week onwards.

Whatever this was that flowed back and forth between them like gossamer strands of an ever-growing spiderweb, she'd surrendered to it.

She would shelve her defences and see where it led and maybe *that* was the greatest takeaway gift of the evening.

Not the pretty clothes or the access to information, but her willingness to believe in possibilities of her own making. With a little help from a friend.

# CHAPTER TEN

A WEEK LATER, with the contents of her bedsit sold to strangers and her more prized possessions stored at Gert's place, Ari set out for her new accommodation. She had her faithful old ute back in her possession and it was running better than ever on account of its new engine, new tyres, and some kind of satellite link that had been added to the dash. The satellite technology gave her GPS, Internet and music, no matter which direction she travelled or how remote her destination.

It was amazing.

When she'd wanted to pay for the upgrades, Reid had waved her offer away with a steely glare. When she'd broached the subject of paying rent, he'd countered with, 'I broke your tent, now you get to use my accommodation. It's a fair exchange. Besides, there's a brown boronia, a Sturt's desert pea, and half a dozen grafted grevilleas waiting for you at the lodge and I'm challenging you to keep them alive.'

*Go with it. Just go with it. Accept the challenge and give it your best shot.*

And here she was, parking her car outside the fancifully named Red Gum Lodge, given that it consisted of rammed-earth walls and a corrugated-iron roof covered in solar panels. The only timber she could see was on the north-east-facing deck, and the framing of the tall, narrow windows set deeply into the walls. The cabin would be cool inside, even with the evaporative air-conditioning unit turned off. Large concrete water tanks had been buried in the ground and the tops provided a large open area between the two lodges. The tanks had been outlined with rock walls and in the centre, the remnants of a campfire. People, yes. Vehicles, no. It was functional space, but not beautiful. The bones were there but it had been let go.

Someone had made an effort to plant trees and shrubs around the buildings, and the extensive notes Reid had given her about the original design revealed that there were grey-water recycling systems in place. A quick lap around both lodges told her that water capture didn't seem to be happening.

Each apartment had two or three bedrooms, one bathroom, two toilets, and separate living, dining and kitchen areas. No open-plan beauties for this build—the architect had wanted inhabitants to be able to close off different areas of the house for better temperature control. The furnishings were high end and the colour scheme was earthy and relaxing. Gorgeous landscape photographs, taken by Reid's sister-in-law Bridie, hung on the walls, bringing the outside in.

Her apartment, a two-bedder, was the nicest place she'd ever lived in. She didn't have much to bring in and after that she stood on the deck and looked clear to the horizon as a playful wind whipped at her hair and rustled narrow leaves.

She couldn't resist stretching her arms wide and twirling in delight at her good fortune.

Even if it had come at the expense of Reid's misfortune.

The thought sobered her, and she stopped twirling and lifted her face to the sky and pleaded for Reid's well-being.

Gert had confided that Reid's latest health check hadn't brought with it the good news he'd hoped for. Ari had only spent that one evening with him in Brisbane, but towards the end of it she'd begun to get a feel for how hard he worked to make his stride look normal, his eyesight seem normal, his recovery appear complete.

It was a charade he'd kept up until the very end and it had troubled her, even if she'd chosen not to confront him about it.

Unpacking felt like coming home.

Boxes in the spare bedroom and her toiletries cluttering up the bathroom. She opened windows to take the stuffiness out of the air, and turned on the hot-water system and pump, and the air con as well. Groceries in the kitchen and her clothes in the bedroom cupboard.

Clothes that included the dazzling casual outfit Reid had bought for her, and she showered with the water still cold and slipped the top and trousers on and the pretty sandals too, before heading outside and taking a selfie with the sunset in the background, her hair whipping around her face and her smile as wide as it ever got. It was a good picture, even if it wasn't up to Bridie Starr standards.

Trusting her instincts, she sent the selfie to Reid. Maybe he could make it big on his computer screen if he couldn't see a smaller phone version.

*Tease,* he texted back a couple of minutes later. *Settling in?*

*Beautiful home,* she wrote back.

Moments later another message announced its arrival with a ping.

*Not too isolated?*

*No.*

Solitude had long been her friend and she had plenty to be going on with. Cairns would have been a nice change, she was sure, but this stark, unforgiving landscape was her happy place.

Thank you for the push. And for believing me.

My pleasure.

Her pleasure too.

Thank you again.

By the end of her first fortnight at Red Gum Lodge Ari had driven thousands of kilometres from one corner of Cooper's Crossing station to the next, following waterways and rocky outcrops, stock routes and wildlife corridors. She journalled wildlife sightings and plant species, and if Reid had begun to feature in her daydreams, maybe it was because she'd expected him to turn up one day, out of the blue, and he hadn't yet, and she was getting edgy.

Her 'Reid will appear like magic' scenario that she returned to every night was wishful thinking right up until the afternoon it wasn't.

She pulled up outside her lodge to find the other lodge occupied and a familiar white work truck parked alongside it.

Bridie Starr stood on the deck of the other dwelling and waved as Ari approached. Lady Blake these days. Award-winning photographer and wife of Lord Judah Blake. Cat-walk model in her teenage years, mistress of Devil's Kiss pastoral station that had now been folded into Jeddah station reserve. Between Jeddah Creek, Cooper's Crossing and Devil's Kiss, the Blake Family controlled thousands of acres of south-west Queensland. No mining, only eco-tourism, limited grazing. Conservation.

Bridie turned away from Ari as another figure joined her. Not her husband Judah, as Ari had expected.

Reid.

Ari approached them with a skip in her step, digging deep for a confidence she was far from feeling. 'Visitors!'

'I told him you wouldn't be far away,' Bridie countered with a smile. 'We've come bearing fresh-caught barramundi, lemons, salad greens and your favourite biscuits from Gert. I was going to stay overnight, but I've been spying on a red-backed kingfisher family all week, and Judah's just spotted one of the chicks. He's swinging by to pick me up.'

'If you ask me, he can't bear to part with you overnight,' said Reid, his eyes hidden behind dark sunglasses and his gait a little stiff. He didn't attempt the trio of steps that would have brought him from the deck down to her level.

Which left her looking up at them.

'Either way, Judah's picking me up in the helicopter in half an hour,' said Bridie cheerfully. 'Ari, promise me you won't let Reid drive the truck.'

'It's self-drive,' Reid protested.

'And we know how well *that* works out here, don't we?' countered Bridie.

'It needs a little tweaking,' replied Reid, and although he didn't sound defensive he did sound kind of strained.

Not about to get in the middle of *that*, thought Ari. Although... 'Hey, Reid, if I drive you wherever you want to go while you're here, and never stop running my mouth because I haven't spoken to anyone in a week, that would be a fair exchange, right?'

'Totally fair,' Bridie answered while Reid stayed silent.

'Ari, do you want to do a walk-around while I take some *before* shots of the outdoor areas for your website?'

'My…what?'

'You can tell me what you have planned for the place. I'd love to know. I'm a silent partner in these lodges.'

'*So* far from silent…' murmured Reid.

'My design's still in the planning stages.' Ari felt compelled to explain her lack of progress. 'So far, it's been all about the plants. But good to know I don't just have Reid to impress. Who else do I need to worry about?'

'It'll come together,' said Reid, as if he refused to doubt it for a second, but she noticed his white-knuckled grip on the wooden railing of the deck, and the pinched grooves around his mouth. 'Although practise your presentation on Bridie, by all means.'

'You're not joining us?'

'Later.'

Something definitely seemed off with him, but she couldn't put her finger on it. Did he not want to be here?

Why had he come if he didn't want to be here?

And then Bridie joined her, camera in hand, and started walking and there was nothing for it but to give Reid an awkward wave and catch up with the other woman.

Ari began to outline her plans while Bridie nodded and took photos, sneaking in a couple of shots of Ari.

'Don't do me,' Ari protested quickly. 'I'm a hot, sweaty mess!'

'Nope, you look beautiful. Very authentic.' Bridie took aim again. 'They'll be perfect for your website bio. I'm a website whizz if you need any help setting one up.'

It was on her list of things to do. Later. 'I need to do a good job first, otherwise the best landscape-design website in the world isn't going to help build my business.'

'I'll mock one up. I'd be happy to. Photos speak.'

Bridie Starr's landscape originals sold for thousands. 'I know what your pictures are worth. I can't afford you,' Ari stated bluntly.

Bridie pointed the camera right at Ari and the camera took a dozen or so shots in rapid succession. 'I'm doing it for free.'

'Why? I don't even *know* you.'

'Yeah, but I know Reid. He's one of my favourite people. Which, by the way, I'm so glad I get to speak with you in private, because I want you to keep an eye on him. He's been told to rest and take it easy. No bright sunshine in his eyes.'

'And you brought him *here*?'

'Sunglasses,' said Bridie, waving Ari's protest away. 'He even has goggles; provided you can get him to wear them in public. Not too much physical exertion for him either. And maybe some of these outdoor areas could be developed with shade cloth and roofing. Deep, deep shade and sensory stuff. Scents and textures and the like.'

'You mean a garden for the blind?' That definitely hadn't been in the brief. 'Just how bad *is* his eyesight?'

'Reid's guarding that knowledge pretty closely. He's so good at adapting that it's hard to catch him out, but I think it's worse than he's letting on.' Bridie offered a quick smile. 'Most of all I wanted to warn you that he's grouchy, frustrated with the slowness of his recovery, and don't be surprised if he disappears into the darkest bedroom every now and then because his head or his leg or his arm is killing him. Not that he'd ever dream of mentioning it. He's Outback tough.'

'Uh-huh.'

'Judah's the same—weakness must never be shown.'

'Uh-huh.'

'And here comes my darling man now.' Bridie looked to the sky. 'He's early.'

'How long is Reid planning to stay? You said something about being here overnight?'

'That was his original plan. A quick trip to see how you were getting on, little bit of fresh-food delivery, a little bit of flirting if I know Reid, although Gert's given him strict instructions to behave. It'd be great if you could keep him for a week. A week of rest would do him the world of good.'

'You want me to keep a grumpy billionaire occupied here for a *week* when he thought he was staying a *day*?' The woman had way too much faith in Ari's powers of persuasion.

Bridie's smile turned into a beatific grin. 'Everyone needs a challenge. And I can't wait to see the new landscaping you come up with. It's going to be brilliant.'

'You don't know that,' Ari protested as Bridie turned and headed back the way they'd come. 'This is the first real landscape I've ever been let loose on.'

'Yeah, but I have the best feeling about you. You've got this, Ari. I'm a believer.'

Reid watched the helicopter rise with a sharp pang of envy as Bridie and Judah flew away. He'd taken the freedom of being a pilot with an endless supply of aircraft at his disposal for granted and now he was grounded. Couldn't even drive a farm ute, according to Bridie, never mind that he'd had this particular work truck kitted out with the latest self-driving features. He'd been all for testing its off-road capacity this morning on a solo run to visit Ari, but once Bridie had got wind of his intentions she'd invited herself along for the ride.

She'd come in handy, though, he had to admit. Getting

bogged in loose sand twice within the first five kilometres of the trip hadn't been encouraging.

The self-driving system hadn't been able to navigate a vaguely visible track through loose dirt and sand with any degree of clarity.

Bridie had insisted on driving them after that second off-road adventure, while Reid had to sit there and mime being okay with not being able to contribute in any meaningful way. He'd been so very patient when it came to his rate of healing, but as improvement slowed his confidence had started to erode.

With Ari, in particular, he wanted to stand before her as a vibrant, physically robust man who could see every little bit of the world around him. How could he read her emotions when he could barely recognise a smile at twenty paces? If he wanted to read the expression in her eyes, he had to get within kissing distance, and what if she didn't want him to smash through her personal-space boundaries?

But if he didn't get close enough to see her expression, how could he know whether Ari was glad to see him?

She'd kept contact with him to a minimum during the time she'd been out here.

Was she simply a doggedly independent soul or actively avoiding him?

She was treating him like the client he was, with a progress report at the end of her first week, but he wanted to be so much more.

Just knowing she was out here made him want to be here too. Sure as hell, *that* had never happened to him before, although he'd seen it before in Judah when it came to wanting to be where Bridie was.

Reid wasn't quite ready to admit to being head over heels for Ari, but he couldn't stop thinking about her.

She'd had to get the plant cuttings she'd taken from channel country earlier that day out of her ute, she'd said awkwardly once Bridie had left. Did she need to plant them as well? Put their stems in water? He hadn't asked. He'd been too busy trying to ignore the spiking pain behind his eyes.

An hour later she still hadn't returned and his vision was shot and his leg ached so much that he was seriously reconsidering his flat-out refusal to use a walking aid, and... *Dammit, why was he so weak?*

A knock sounded on the screen door between kitchen and deck. 'Can I come in?' Ari asked.

'Of course.'

She'd changed her clothes and now wore a yellow T-shirt and a plum-coloured skirt instead of khaki work trousers and shirt. She'd pulled her hair back into a ponytail and wore a colourful chunky bracelet on her slender wrist.

The fact that she'd changed clothes and added jewellery had to mean she was glad to see him, surely?

'Come in.' She hadn't found him flat on his back, and his ego liked that. Granted, he was only filling the ceramic water dispenser that sat next to the sink. The tap hose was one of those stretchy ones, so it wasn't exactly difficult. All he'd had to do was remove the lid, point and shoot.

'They're good, aren't they? Those water-filter set-ups,' she said as she entered the room.

'You want a glass?'

'No, I'm good.' She came closer, resting her pert behind against the side of the counter on his other side. 'You didn't tell me you were coming. I'd have baked a cake.'

'Are you pleased to see me?' If he couldn't rely on his sight for information, he'd have to get it some other way.

'I am *extremely* pleased to see you. But I do have a confession to make.'

'Tell me.'

She smiled in his direction. 'I hurt my shoulder this morning, trying to pull out a—um, probably not a great idea to tell you I don't know the name of the plant. The point is it took a lot of pulling and I have a sore shoulder.'

He wasn't sure where this conversation was going but he tried to pre-empt her, nonetheless. 'You want a massage?'

'No, the hot shower did a world of good but now I want to lie down on a bed and move my arm around and find my shoulder's happy place. I used to dislocate it all the time as a kid.'

'You have a dislocated shoulder?'

'No, but it's about to pop, I can feel it, and I'd rather it didn't. You could lie next to me while I see to it. We could hold hands, just like old times. And if need be, you can grab my arm above the elbow and pull.'

It sure as hell sounded like a dislocated shoulder, but he was up for it. 'Whatever you need.'

They ended up side by side on their backs on the bed, with the window shutters closed to the heat of the day, and at last he could close his eyes and drop the pretence of being able to function normally. He could feel her moving her arm about but she didn't encroach on his space, and he didn't reach for her hand.

He wasn't needy.

Not like before.

He didn't want Ari to think him weak.

But her hand—presumably the one attached to her good arm—reached for his and chivalry demanded he reciprocate. That was what he told himself as simple contentment invaded his body. For all the many ideas and projects that had consumed him over the years, all his restless travelling, he'd never felt so at peace as he did with Ari's hand wrapped in his. 'How's your shoulder?' he murmured. 'Do I need to pull?'

'I think it's okay. How's your headache?'

He made a feeble attempt to muster his defences, but he was too far down the contentment hole to rally more than a mental shrug. 'How did you know?'

'It's written on your face.'

'Bridie didn't notice.'

'You keep telling yourself that, precious. She's lovely, and she cares about you, and believe me she noticed. She asked me to persuade you to stay a week.'

'What did you say?'

'Told her she was dreaming if she thought I could get you to do anything you didn't want to do. But I'm not against the idea of you being here for a while. I'll still have to work—my client deserves something extraordinary and I'm determined to give it to him, and I'll probably put you to work on that too, but my evenings are free. Afternoons too, if I make an early start. Of course, there's no lap pool or health-spa facilities, but I have thoughts on turning an old water trough into an outdoor bath, so there's that. I think an outdoor shower after a hard day's work would be another welcome water addition. It's dusty out there.'

'Exactly how soon do you expect this outdoor bathing area to appear?'

'Well, my client needs to approve the concept and after that it depends how much money he's got to throw at the proposal, y'know? There are budget versions that any stockman from around here would appreciate.'

'And the water? Where's that coming from?'

'The boss's last landscape designer put a gorgeous grey-water filtering system in place but didn't understand the soil out here. I can make it work. Am I putting you to sleep?'

Maybe she *could* read his face after all. 'Almost.'

'Sleep. I'll be around when you wake up.'

'Last time I did that I ended up in a hospital bed two thousand kilometres away. *Without you.*'

'Well, you will choose the best surgeons.'

She made him laugh and his head ached because of it. 'How's your shoulder?'

'You're going to have to sit up, put one of your feet in my armpit, and pull on my arm.'

'Let's do it.' Before he lost the will to move. He got into position—he'd done this before—and within moments it was done with barely a whimper on his part.

Ari didn't whimper at all, just sighed when he eased back down beside her and took her hand.

'Have you taken pain tablets yet?' she asked.

'Half an hour ago.'

'Do you need more?'

'Can't.' He was under strict directions to take them *only as directed*. Maybe he *had* been pushing his body a little too hard in an attempt to camouflage weakness. Maybe now was a good time to stop.

'I'll get you a cold pack from my cabin.'

'Are you trying to heal me again, with whatever you have lying around?'

'Hey, whatever works.' He could feel her getting up but he didn't open his eyes. 'Back in five.'

'Five minutes, you say?'

She squeezed his hand. 'I promise.'

# CHAPTER ELEVEN

REID WAS FAST asleep when Ari returned. She put the cold pack and a glass of water on his bedside table and left him to his healing.

Returning to work, Ari picked up where she'd left off, planting cuttings into circular hollows in the ground, lined with fallen leaves and a thin layer of clay soil she'd found a few hundred kilometres east. Busy work, but she'd never felt more confident about her choice of career and the possibilities in front of her.

Reid was here, and while this was very much his world, it was hers too.

He found her as the sun hit the horizon, sending hot streaks across the sky. He took a long look at her plant nursery pits, and then looked at her and said, 'Okay, I'm a believer in the outdoor bathing idea. You're covered in mud.'

'Knew you'd see it my way. Your scientist and researchers also come back covered in mud at the end of the day. I've been stumbling upon them and doing informal surveys. If there was an outside shower area, they'd use it.'

'Tell me more during dinner.'

He then coaxed her to dine with him once she was presentable by promising baked fish, fresh salad, and mangoes for dessert.

She showered quickly and made her way to the lodge

he'd claimed for his stay. There were only two lodges at this site, with the other one remaining empty until his arrival.

'Iced tea or something stronger?' he asked as she entered his kitchen. 'I'm sticking to water.'

'Because of your medication?'

'That and a heartfelt desire to avoid another head-cracker.'

Made sense. He'd lost the tension in his body and his eyes had lost their haze of pain. She watched him plate up the baked fish with a surety born of long practice. 'How's the sister search?' she asked, when he set the meals on the table and held out a chair for her.

'Full of dead ends. Judah's taken the lead on it,' he admitted as he took a seat and waited for her to start eating before picking up his cutlery. Pretty manners that she didn't fully understand—they served mainly to emphasise Reid's social class and her lack of any.

And then she remembered the story about him taking his brother to the roadside diner and nervously ordering everything on the menu. And how she'd been with him when he'd wolfed down Thai starters and terrible passionfruit beer at the swimwear store. He was the same man.

And this time the food was great, and she wanted his company and so what if she didn't quite know where the fishbones would be found? It was barramundi. Wasn't as if the fish bones were going to be small.

Ari favoured eating over talking—probably another no-no in polite society, but it had been a big day and she was hungry. Only once she'd cut grooves into the juicy flesh of mango cheeks and flipped the skin and devoured her half—and Reid's half too, when he declined his—did idle chat turn serious.

'So, no progress on the sister hunt but I did discover something interesting about the money my father gave your mother just after you were born. Could be nothing. Could be something. Want to hear it?' he asked.

Ari paused, sweet mango juice dripping down her chin as she put the fruit back on her plate and attempted to clean her sticky face and fingers with a napkin the size of a tissue. Reid wordlessly handed his napkin to her and waited for her answer.

She'd loved her mother dearly—but there was no pretending that her mother's life choices had always played out in Ari's favour. The stepfamily situation was a classic example of that. 'I don't know if I want to hear it. Is it going to shatter all my illusions?'

'Maybe.'

Again, he waited for her response. 'I guess I could stand to know more.'

'We have a forensic accountant looking through old financial records,' he told her. 'The money my father gave your mother came from a bank account owned by an Australian business called FNQ metals. My father held that money in his account for just under twenty-four hours before passing it through to your mother. At first, I thought it was a one-off transaction—a gambling debt paid in full, say—and my father had simply flipped it to your mother as thanks for not letting him gamble his home away. But there were other deposits from that account over the years, smaller amounts, same day each year, and they were all passed through to your mother within twenty-four hours. Is there anything special about the twenty-fourth of May?'

'It's my birthday.'

'Ah.' He seemed pleased. 'Figured it might be.'

'Meaning…what, exactly?'

'I think someone used my father to deliver money to your mother on your birthday. Still want to hear more?'

She took a quick sip of her iced tea, for courage. 'Is there more?'

'FNQ Metals is a publicly traded company these days but before that it belonged to a guy called Deacon Murray. He started out as a travelling stock contractor through Far North Queensland and the Northern Territory. He married at nineteen and he's still married to that same woman. He has three sons, now in their thirties. He made enough money out of cattle to buy himself a mining lease. It coughed up not just iron ore but copper and zinc as well. This is all public knowledge. My father had no business dealings with him at all beyond the money that went to your mother.'

She knew where this was going. 'You think this Murray guy is my father?'

How much of her could Reid actually see when he looked at her so steadily? Could he see her panic? All the hope and pain and years of wondering? Trying to discover clues in her dead mother's belongings?

'I think you should go online and look at some of the pictures of Deacon Murray and his kids. Then, if you want me to put an investigator on his whereabouts around the time your mother got pregnant, I will.'

This day was just full of surprises.

She traced her finger down the side of her glass and studied Reid from beneath her lashes. She needed a bit of a shield while his information sank in. 'Do I look like him?'

'A bit. You look like one of his boys more.' Reid sat back. 'I think he took his mining business public so he could get the money to set you and your mother up. I suspect he did it through my father because your mother refused his direct offer of financial assistance.'

She took a deep breath. 'That's a lot of wondering.'

'Like I said, I can put someone on it and get you some facts. You could be a rich man's daughter.'

She'd always wanted to know who her father was. She'd never imagined him rich or successful. In her eyes he'd always been a handsome no-good drifter who'd known nothing about siring a daughter.

If Reid's speculations were true, then Deacon Murray had known all about Ari and hadn't come anywhere near her. 'You're absolutely brutal when it comes to making me question my identity.'

'Is that a bad thing?'

She pushed away from the table and headed for the deck. She wanted the cover of darkness as she worked through her emotions. Reid joined her, wary and watchful.

'Talk to me,' he said as he leaned against the railing.

'He knew about me. He's never been near me.' That was the most devastating revelation. 'And maybe he tried to help financially, and it did a bit and got spread around between others too. All to the greater good, right? But I'm an adult now and he owes me nothing, and your father's been dead for years and surely money can't still be coming in. I don't know what to do with this information.' She leaned against the railing of the deck and looked to the stars in the sky. There were millions of them in an Outback sky. On most nights a person could see them very clearly.

But Reid wasn't looking at the stars. When she glanced his way, he was looking at her. 'You could reach out to him.'

'And say what? All that money you sent amounted to *nothing*? He's not going to want me.'

'I wouldn't say that.'

But Ari was past listening. 'He made his choice when I was born. *Money's not care.* It's just a convenient way to paper over guilt.'

Reid blew out a breath. 'I thought you'd be pleased.'

'Well, I'm not! Your family history probably goes back hundreds of years. You know who you are. Everything's legit. You don't understand what it's like to not know who your father is and dream about some day connecting with him. In the good dreams my father is thrilled to discover he has a daughter. He's a wonderful man and he's thrilled to meet me.' She choked back a bitter laugh.

'What happens in the bad dreams?'

'In the bad dreams he's known about me from the beginning, and he just doesn't care.' She couldn't stand to let Reid watch her fall apart. 'Thanks for the meal. I have to go now.'

'Ari, wait. Let me—'

*'You can't fix this!'* He didn't deserve her anger. 'I'm sorry. I have to go.'

'When you say go, do you mean get in your ute and drive away?' he asked carefully.

'No.' She waved a hand in the direction of her cabin. It was too dark to drive without getting lost. She wasn't insane. 'I'm just going to my—your—' Aw, screw it. 'I just want to fall apart somewhere you can't see me, okay? I'm going to my room.'

'Okay.'

*Okay.*

She'd made her way to the steps when he spoke again. 'Ari, the money's not nothing. Murray wasn't so wealthy back then that he could fling it around without a care.'

She bit her tongue in an effort to keep harsh, hurtful words like *You would know* from tumbling out.

*Don't shoot the messenger. Don't lash out with words you don't mean. Stick to the ones you do mean.*

'I'm sorry you get to see this side of me. I'm bitter and ungrateful and I don't give a damn about any money he might have sent. Money on my birthday? Why didn't my mother *tell me*? She didn't want me to know anything about him and he didn't want me at all.' So much for retreating to her room before hot tears threatened to spill. 'That's just betrayal.'

'Feelings are messy and very, very real,' he countered quietly. 'For some people, myself included, it's always tempting to run off and try to deal with them alone.' He favoured her with a crooked smile. 'You should talk to Bridie about hiding in your room. She hid in her room for years.'

Teenager Bridie Starr had been the beautiful, traumatised shut-in, forcing herself to step outside so she could take photos to send to the imprisoned man who'd saved her life—Ari knew the story. 'I'm not going to hide in my room for years because my father never claimed me.' It was probably too late to hide her emotions from the man in front of her, too.

'I'd like to walk you to your room,' he said gently. 'If I may.'

'Bad idea.'

'Is it?'

'I'd probably drag you inside and shamelessly demand that you help me forget all my lineage and make me feel wanted.'

His eyes gleamed. 'Oh, *really*?'

That was a yes from him. Ari suddenly felt very short of breath and it wasn't because she was about to start weeping.

'Happy to help,' he offered gravely. 'In fact, as a gentleman, I *insist*.'

Hell, yes. And she was going to take him up on his offer. To hell with muddying the waters between contractor and client. She wanted this. No, she needed this.

Ari *deserved* this.

He'd only wanted to help. All the digging he'd done, all the tracking down of information that he hadn't outsourced to anyone else… In all sincerity, Reid had imagined he was helping Ari. It had never once occurred to him that this new knowledge would hurt her.

All he wanted to do now was fix her.

They walked to her bedroom in silence, and once there Reid drew her into his arms and sought her lips with his. It started off as apology and comfort, but all it took was Ari's passionately uninhibited response for it to spiral out of his control and become something else entirely.

Gentle caresses became greedy ones as he slid his hands beneath her clothes and honoured the warmth of her skin and the shape of her body. So smooth and warm, utterly responsive as he set his lips to the underside of her jaw and traced his way to her collarbone. Her scent a tease, the way she melted against him an aphrodisiac.

He'd never been so invested in a woman's pleasure as he picked her up and she wound her legs around him. He tumbled them onto the bed and began shedding clothes, and so did she, and that first full slide of skin against skin was almost Reid's undoing.

Women liked him and he liked them. He'd made a point of knowing how to please them. But none had ever wielded the power over him that Ari did. Undoing him so completely that he struggled to think, let alone plan ahead.

He would taste every inch of her—was that a thought worth following? It worked for a while, until he reached her breasts and discovered that the edge of his tongue could make her wild with need. He let her roll him on his back as he closed his lips around her and suckled, and moments later soft warmth covered his hardness as she rocked against him seeking friction.

*That* plan worked brilliantly for both of them—maybe from now on he would let Ari make all the plans all the time when it came to bedroom contact. That fleeting thought lasted the time it took for her to line him up so he could slide into her tight heat, an action that ripped a groan from the depths of his soul as he rolled with her until she lay beneath him and let purest instinct take over.

When Ari crested, he was moments behind her, and it wasn't his finest, most considered performance, but it was hands down the most intense sexual experience of his life. His brain was fried, his body exhausted, and he couldn't stop smiling.

It was his first, fumbling experience with sex all over again—dialled up to a hundred.

'That was—' no way was he about to admit he might have been doing sex all wrong...until now '—illuminating.'

'I'll say.'

Was she smiling? He turned his head and when he couldn't quite tell, he reached out and traced her lips with questing fingers. 'Stop it,' he murmured when she nibbled them. 'I'm trying to tell if you're satisfied. Are you smiling?'

She flowed into his arms and tucked her head beneath his chin and placed her hand over his heart. 'With all my heart.'

'Because you're satisfied?'

'Because you make me happy.'

'Because I want to be sure you're satisfied. If you're not, I could do other things to you until my poor, broken body is ready for more.'

'Oh, well, then.' This time he could *feel* her smile against his chest. 'I could probably be *more* satisfied. I wouldn't want you to have any doubts.'

'You're sure?' He ran his fingers over her body until he reached her knee and then he scooted down and let her leg below her knee drape over his shoulder as he pressed a teasing kiss against her inner thigh.

'Do what you have to do.' Her words ended on a gasp.

He flicked her centre with his tongue and felt her arch against his hands so he did it again, exposing her with his thumb to better access his target. 'You're sure you're sure?' Her hands clutched at the bedsheet beneath them as he blew against the sensitive, swollen flesh.

'I'm sure!'

And still he hesitated, because teasing her was just too satisfying. For him.

'Would you like me to beg?' she demanded, and now there was a thought he could get behind in full.

'Yes.' Satisfaction laced his voice at the wonder that was Ari Cohen in his bed. 'I certainly would.'

Reid stayed on for five more sex-soaked days. He spent his spare time dictating extra parameters to the self-drive programming so that his ute didn't drive off into a sand bank every five minutes. Ari spent her days working on a landscape plan, eventually abandoning her idea of presenting him with computer drawings in favour of explaining what she wanted to do with various areas as they walked through them—once in the morning, once at noon, and then again at night. He approved the plans with all his heart, rejected any suggestion of her doing the hard labour required, and together they put together a team of former stockmen, fencers, and tradesmen willing to spend two weeks on the job and get it done.

They butted heads on whether Ari should stay on or turn both lodges over to the team of workers.

Ari argued there was absolutely no reason for her to leave and every reason in the world to supervise. Reid claimed she should take Gert's old room at his homestead and let the guys have their privacy, and *sure* it would mean a four-hour round trip every day but those were the breaks.

He knew he was being ridiculous as they fought about trust, and security, and stereotypes. He didn't know how to swallow his concerns until Ari picked up the phone and called her former lab partner, Sarah, who might well be looking for a bit of work or know of someone who was. Half an hour later, Ari had two more female labourers in place and Sarah's sister, who was a plumber with her own earthmoving equipment, had been signed up to the job too.

Reid tripled the labour costs on the contract Ari had prepared, signed it, and the arguing stopped, and the lovemaking resumed.

Reid was utterly, irrevocably putty in the hands of Ari Cohen.

If it hadn't been for a raft of medical appointments with specialists far busier than him, he'd have stayed on.

Instead, he arranged for Ari to come to Brisbane at the end of the following week to view the copper birdbath she wanted to install, never mind that she'd already ordered it.

'You just want to see me again,' she teased, but he had absolutely no defence against her words.

It was nothing but the truth.

# CHAPTER TWELVE

'HMM.'

Reid hated the *hmm*s of eye specialist Fink with a vengeance.

It wasn't that the man was a bad conversationalist; the doc could string long sets of words together when he wanted to. And given that Fink was the best eye specialist the country had to offer, Reid trusted that the man knew what he was talking about, even if Reid sometimes needed a dictionary.

Had Reid thought his eyesight was improving, those *hmm*s during this latest examination would have registered as confirmation that all was coming along as expected. They might have been tolerable.

But Reid's vision had not been improving, his headaches were becoming more frequent, and no amount of 'positive thinking' and 'mindful recovery' was going to wish those undeniable facts out of existence.

Reid kept his chin on the rest pad and stared at the bright light he'd been told to stare at as the slit lamp machine clicked and whirred and took pictures of the inside of his eyeballs.

'Okay, we're done.'

When the doctor rolled away, still in his chair, and turned towards a wall-mounted computer screen, Reid came to stand alongside him. Not that Reid had much chance of seeing what the older man saw unless he stood a whole lot closer, but if it helped Fink make his diagnosis and explain what was happening, Reid was all for staring at the screen right along with him.

'I haven't made any headway at all with my eyesight this month, have I?' asked Reid as the doctor studied the screen and said nothing.

'Correct.'

Not the best news he'd ever heard. 'Why not?'

Fink turned to look at him. 'Best guess? Your original head trauma and cranial nerve damage was too severe for you to ever fully recover. You've made remarkable strides, Mr Blake, but the body's repair system has its limits. Your vision in your right eye is always going to be better than your left. The tunnel vision you now experience may not improve. Wear your eye patch again, doesn't matter which eye, and see if your headaches subside. Wear wraparound sunglasses day and night and note whether that too helps with the headaches.'

'I guess getting my driver's licence back is out of the question?' Initially, he'd believed he'd get there eventually but any last hope of that happening had been quietly fading.

'Son, I know what you want to hear. And I know some fool mental-health expert likely dangled that possibility in front of your nose like a carrot, but I'm going to go out on a limb here and stake my professional reputation on the notion that no one with any sense is ever going to let you control a vehicle again.'

'Noted.'

Hated.

'Would you like a second opinion on that?'

'No.' They were his eyes, after all. He was intimately acquainted with what they could and couldn't do. 'Did I tell you I've found the prettiest girl in the world?'

'Have you now? Well, it sounds like those eyes of yours may be good for something after all.' There was a smile in Fink's voice. 'I don't see any neurological evidence of deterioration, so don't be too disheartened by these latest results. No improvement may mean that your eyesight is stabilising and this is your new normal. Your eyesight test results may go back and forth a bit from now on, depending on the day and how tired you are. Do you have a headache now?'

'Yes.'

'Pain scale?'

'Five.'

'Have you taken any medication for it?'

'Not yet. Didn't want to juice my test results.'

'Stick to inventing engines, Mr Blake, and get the nurse to give you some ibuprofen on your way out.'

'Nah, I'm good. I'll take some when I get home.'

The doctor sighed. 'I know you Outback types have a built tough reputation to uphold, but do yourself a favour and next time you get a migraine take the medication I'm prescribing you.'

'Thanks, Doc, but I still have the last prescription you gave me. How about I just get that one filled?'

'Hmm,' said the good doc. 'Do.'


R and R. Rest and recovery. The only people who thought that was a positive thing hadn't endured endless months of being told to throttle down, kick back and relax, and hand control over to others.

Even Reid's Brisbane apartment that had been especially set up for rest and relaxation couldn't soothe him this morning.

Reid had found it especially hard to hand over the reins of the engineering company he'd built, never mind that the 'others' in question were reliable, visionary, and didn't *need* him at the helm. Reid had chosen his executives a little too well, and even people-shy Judah had stepped up to shoulder some of Reid's workload. This morning while eye doctor Fink had been telling Reid to take his pills like a good boy, Judah had been presenting the quarterly forecast to Reid's board of directors. Judah, whose knowledge of solar engines was sketchy at best, but who believed unconditionally in Reid's timeline for bringing those developments to the market.

Judah's strategy had been alarmingly simple. 'I go in, I tell them this is what you want, and they approve it. Easy.' Oh, to have been a fly on the wall at that meeting.

Judah meant well. He was working his arse off keeping all the Blake family enterprises running smoothly while Reid *recovered*. Stock prices were up, milestones were being met.

Business was booming along without him, and he shouldn't feel resentful about that, he just shouldn't. It was a measure of how good he was at building strong business foundations that they stood strong without him.

And yet…the longer his recovery, the more sidelined and useless he felt. Reid's confidence, his place in his family, was based on his ability to be the wunderkind. The kid who held it together. The young man with vision and work ethic. The mechanical genius who'd built a billion-dollar company using the contacts and start-up money his family had afforded him. He didn't want to be put out to pasture like a lame racehorse. He wanted to be part of something bigger than himself.

He needed to be sure of his worth.

And for the first time since he was seventeen years old and sitting across from his brother in a petrol-station diner, he questioned it.

Even Ari had taken the reins of her fledgling business and *shone*. She and her crew were busy creating an outdoor utopia on their sixth and final set of lodges. After that, Ari had another few weeks of rotating around the work sites as she made sure her gardens were growing as they should, and then she'd be gone. Her work was getting noticed, what with Bridie featuring it in her social-media stream, and magazines always keen for editorial featuring what was happening within the mystical Outback Blake empire.

A leg-up had well and truly been given, and Ari was now perfectly positioned to succeed.

Which left Reid's fairy godmother gig superfluous to requirements, and his Prince Charming feathers charred because he didn't waltz that well any more.

He'd tolerated being a wounded prince as best he could.

He actively hated the thought of being a permanently broken one.

He leaned against the kitchen counter of his Brisbane home and watched as Judah slung his tailored jacket over the back of a chair and headed for the fridge. Judah could still stare at a dinner menu for a long time before making his selection, but he had the contents of Reid's drinks fridge well and truly sorted. Kiwi and leafy greens go-go juice if he wasn't drinking alcohol, Crown Lager if he was. Apparently, it was a green juice kind of day.

'You have the board's backing, and the shareholders voted their approval,' Judah told him, and all Reid could do was nod listlessly, because this latest achievement didn't really have anything to do with him. 'Are you listening?'

'Yeah, of course. Good.'

But Judah wasn't having a bar of Reid's fake enthusiasm. 'I thought you'd be pleased.'

'I am. Hey, you want to go rock climbing at Kangaroo

Point this afternoon?' The cliffs were a local climbing spot with great views of the city. 'We should celebrate the good news.'

Judah halted in the process of ditching his tie and un-buttoning the top few buttons on his pristine business shirt. 'You're climbing again?'

'Yeah.' Reid tried to inject a little confidence into his reply. This would be his first attempt, but Judah didn't need to know that.

'Are you cleared to do that? What did the eye doctor say?'

'Yeah, he's really pleased with my progress. Everything's on the up.'

Judah shot him a sharp glance. 'And the headaches?'

'All part of the process.' Not lies, exactly. More like spin. He'd been cleared for moderate exercise. They sent begin-ners up Kangaroo Point all the time, no former climbing experience required—and Reid's climbing skills were well beyond that. His leg was getting stronger all the time and his dislocated shoulder had been an easy fix. As for his eyes... tunnel vision could only help him focus on the cliff face in front of his nose. Reid wanted this challenge. He needed it.

'Who are you climbing with?'

'Jules.' Professional climbing instructor and indoor-climbing champion. 'She won't mind if you turn up.' Reid paid her enough not to mind, and Judah had climbed before, even if he hadn't taken to it the way Reid had.

Judah made a face. 'I can fit a climb in tomorrow morn-ing. I still have a meeting with the EPA to get through this afternoon.'

'No drama. You do you, I'll do me.' Reid wasn't about to admit that Judah's presence had been a bright spot in a week full of medical appointments and increasingly bleak health news.

Reid needed a win. One tiny boost to help him feel functional again and *worth* something. 'It'll be fine.'

Ari didn't know if Reid had somehow set a satellite to hover over her location. She didn't know if satellites could do that, but not once in the past two months had Ari or any of her team lost phone or Internet connection.

Her team. She'd put together a core group of people who wanted to keep working for her and her next project was to landscape a visitors' centre for a small town with a big grant geared towards it becoming a tourist gateway to channel country. After that, she'd locked in a job on Queensland's Sunshine Coast for a local celebrity. Five acres of hinterland scrub to tame and Ari was there for it. And maybe it was the generous pay or the travel or the way people had clicked, but her trade crew were there for it too.

End of day meant getting online and checking out the weather report and whatever was trending by way of news. Ari usually did it while throwing together something to eat, but today her appetite was skewered by the headline on her phone.

'Billionaire Tycoon Takes Another Fall.'

There were two photos to go with the headline—one was of a group of people gathered at the top of a cliff. The other picture was an old headshot of Reid in a tux.

He'd fallen off a cliff? No, a climbing accident. No. According to a spectator there'd been no dramatic fall. He'd been nearing the top of the climb and had seemed to pass out. His climbing partner and others had been on hand to help and eventually he'd finished the climb and been bundled into a waiting ambulance.

According to the reporter, he was in a stable condition.

The rest of the article was fairy floss about his numerous accomplishments, his ex-con billionaire brother, and his sister-in-law the world-class photographer.

Ari's hands shook as she dialled the number Reid had given her, but her call went to an answering machine and she didn't leave a message. She phoned Bridie next, and when the other woman answered, Ari could barely find the words.

'Hi.' Her voice shook, she sounded rough. 'It's Ari. I—' She didn't have any right to query. 'I saw the news.'

'You want to know about Reid?'

'Yes, please.'

'We're at the Princess Alexandria hospital. He's undergoing tests. He seems fine. He's beyond cranky—at the world and everyone in it—but fine.'

'What happened?'

'Hey, feel free to try and get medical information out of a grown man who doesn't want to talk about it. No, go ahead. I dare you.' Bridie sounded at the end of her wits.

'That bad?'

'Judah's on a tear because he's worried out of his mind. Reid's telling us to go away because he's *fine* but he can't sign his name on a hospital form because as far as I can tell he can barely see the lines.'

'I—' Would he want her there? With all that was going on? He'd never talked much about his injuries or his recovery. Beyond that first evening at the lodge when she'd lain down with him and he'd slept for a couple of hours, he'd acted as if he had no medical issues at all beyond some fuzzy or tunnel vision every now and again—he never had come clean on what he could and couldn't see. He'd never admitted to another headache. 'Can you tell him I called?'

'You want him to call you back?'

'Yes!' Too eager by far. 'I mean...'

'You mean yes,' Bridie said dryly. 'I'll let him know.'

'Thank you, I—' She wanted to be there so badly, but didn't know if she had the right. 'I'd like to come and see him.' The way she hadn't last time. Their relationship was new but surely she had the right to reach out by phone. Cheer him up in person if that was what he wanted from her. 'I'm worried about him.'

*You're in love with him.*

That too. All it had taken was the thought of never seeing him again to make that inescapably clear to her. 'Is it wrong to want to yell at him a bit?'

'By all means, *do*. We're all just tippy-toeing around being stoic and supportive and it's not working. I'm no doctor, but if you want my opinion he took on more than he could chew and doesn't want to admit it because he's embarrassed, and, Ari, I'm trusting you with this information because I know you'd never use it against him or take it to the press—'

'I would never.'

'I know.' Bridie sounded so *kind*. 'Reid's struggling to accept that he'll never be as fit and healthy and active as he was before. You're welcome to try to talk some sense in him but that might just put you in the firing line.'

'I'm used to being in the firing line. My stepfather was a mean drunk and he wasn't especially fond of me. Not that I want to bore you with baggage, or that I think Reid's anything like that. He's not,' Ari added hastily. 'But I can hold my own in an imperfect world. I'm not afraid of facing up to problems head-on. Unless it's about my birth father. Still picking at that big gaping wound, but I'm working on it. I'm tough and resilient and I get where I'm going eventually. I can start driving now. Be there in the morning.' Did any of that make sense? She didn't know.

'Anyway,' she continued quietly. 'I'll wait for his call.'

'He's having an MRI and I'll tell him you called. And when I get home I'll come find you and we'll catch up for a cuppa, okay?'

'Okay.' Ari had the sinking feeling that the only thing she'd accomplished with this phone call was to expose her crush on Reid for all to see. What if he wanted to keep their relationship a secret? What if it was just a fling—too new or too casual for Ari to be worming her way into his family unit and he didn't want to see her at all? 'Sure.'

He didn't ring back.

It took Ari another week to realise that Reid wasn't *going* to ring back.

The crew had finished their work on the last of the eco-lodge locations and were packing up to return to Brisbane. Ari was in two minds about heading there too, but indecision had taken hold. What was she going to do? Knock on Reid's door and demand he let her in?

*Yes.*

*He told you to trust him.*

*What if he's waiting for you to value him and be there for him the way he's been for you?*

When her work crew headed east in raggedy convoy, Ari went with them.

Reid Blake wasn't expecting company, so when his security system pinged to let him know someone wanted in, he took his time getting out of the spa and grabbing a towel and heading for the security screen on the patio to see who it was. Bridie and Judah had finally headed home this morning after days of hanging around and making sure he had everything he needed to be going on with.

He saw doctors daily. He had a physio come and tend him twice a week.

Eye doctor Fink had seen him in the hospital and again at Reid's apartment two days ago. He'd toured Reid's loft workspace, asked questions about work and his daily routine, and then dictated a list of aids and devices for the sight impaired. He'd sent the audio file to Reid and told him to investigate new ways of getting on with it.

He'd asked Reid where the prettiest girl in the world was and *hmm*'d when Reid answered, 'Working. Doing her own thing, *like she should.*'

He didn't want Ari to see his weakness and his fear. He'd get around to seeing her again when he was good and ready, and that might be a good long while. Reid finished towelling off and leaned closer to the screen so he could see who was at the door.

And yet here she was.

Shorts and boots and T-shirt and backpack slung over one shoulder, dark sunglasses shading her eyes and her hair pulled back into a ponytail. She looked tired and dusty and strong and healthy and his heart just about split in two because he didn't want her here almost as much as he did want her here. And he didn't know what to do.

'Hey,' she said brightly when he opened the door. 'You've been swimming.'

His wet trunks were a dead giveaway, he supposed. 'Ari.' He pitched his reply just shy of cool. 'What brings you by?'

He didn't need to see the expression on her face to see the tensing of her shoulders or the straightening of her spine. 'I realise our relationship…friendship…whatever this is, was built on you turning up out of the blue unexpectedly. Do I not have leeway to do the same?' The words themselves weren't her only challenge. Her steady, forthright delivery called him on his less than enthusiastic greeting too.

Silently, he stood aside so she could enter. If he was truly going to go through with cutting her out of his life, better he didn't do it at the door with an audience potentially lurking nearby.

She headed for his kitchen, slinging her backpack on a stool before turning to face him, arms crossed in front of her and her feet planted wide as she surveyed him from head to toe and back again. 'You don't look like you're at death's door.'

'I'm not.'

'Good to know. You haven't been taking my calls. Not even my business ones.'

He hadn't been taking anyone's calls.

'Wallowing in a pit of self-pity and despair, Bridie called it.' She walked around him in a slow circle, as if studying a sculpture, and it was all he could do to stay still and relaxed. 'You can understand my concern, although I'd like to point out that your arse is still very fine, as is the rest of your appearance. Not that I'm shallow and attracted to you solely because of appearance, but I've seen you looking worse.'

'I'm fine.'

'I don't think so.'

'What do you want me to say?' he snapped. 'That my eyesight's shot?'

'Yes.' Her calmness was not rubbing off on him. 'Let's start there.'

Hot temper flashed in his eyes, and good. She was angry too, and if he couldn't see her well enough to see the signs, she'd simply have to provide him with verbal cues. 'You said you trusted me, and I believed you. You called me resourceful and resilient and worthy, and I believed that too.

I needed a hand, and you gave it, unconditionally. We're friends and more.'

So much more and in such a short time. Maybe that was part of the problem.

She took a step closer. 'Why can't you trust me to be there for you?'

He took a careful step back. 'I don't want to argue with you.'

'I'm not arguing with you.' Even if she did sound fried. 'I'm arguing *for* you. For us, and a future we might share.'

And he couldn't let her win. 'I don't want to saddle anyone with having to stick by someone with my limitations. You're just starting out. Every good thing in this life is out there waiting for you.'

'But not you.'

'You'll be fine without me. Better than fine.'

'And here I thought I was going to be the reluctant one in this relationship,' she said. 'Never quite believing I was good enough. I've got no money. No connections. No unshakeable belief that I'm smarter or wiser or more talented than most other people. And yet somehow you made me believe that I can pull my weight and be valued and loved and wanted because I'm me. Ari. Why can't you be just you, battered and not seeing too well around the edges but whole—and lovable too?'

She was battering away at his defences as if they were matchsticks. He had to push her away before he crumbled in a pile at her feet, a pitiful, broken shell of a man who couldn't let a good woman go. 'You have a stepfather and stepbrother who drove you from your home. A father you won't go near,' he snarled. 'You can't even fight your own demons. What chance would you have against mine?'

'Is that the argument you're going with? You're pushing

me away because I'm not used to fighting for every scrap of love I've ever been gifted?' She stepped forward and poked a pointy finger into his chest. 'I can and will fight my own demons. You'll see. And then I'll be back for you. Maybe you can slay a couple of your own demons while I'm away.'

She headed for the door.

'You forgot your backpack.' But she didn't turn around. 'I built you a garden at site six. A sensory garden full of texture and shadows and water and sounds. It's a haven for relaxation and renewal, a place of majesty and tranquillity and I built it with all the love I have in my heart for you. The plans are in the backpack. Drawings, notebooks, pressed plants, jars of different coloured dirt that I used. Pictures of all the birds I've seen in the garden so far. Waterway plans and drainage. Pumps and pipes and everything else. So what if you can't see everything I've written? You're the one with endless resources. If you don't want to go and experience it for yourself, try getting someone to explain it to you.'

His doors didn't slam. They drew quietly closed with a good-mannered huff.

He leaned his back against it and pressed the heels of his hand against the sudden sting in his eyes.

She argued passionately, and for him, and he loved her for that. He loved her full stop. He'd figured that out at some point between the slaying of demons and the building of a tranquil garden just for him. But how could he keep her, and keep her happy, if he couldn't even see his own way forward?

He had to let her go. His shortcomings were not her responsibility.

She'd see that he was right.

Eventually.

# CHAPTER THIRTEEN

ARI WAS HEARTBROKEN and Reid was a jerk, but she wasn't giving up. Sometimes growth came with reckonings and putting one step in front of the other and trudging through bad weather until blue sky broke overhead. Reid had his journey and she had hers, and as she drove west, out of the city, she reasoned that he had been right in some ways. She did still have personal problems of her own to tackle before demanding he tackle his. She was a successful, confident woman with a whole lot of love, energy and encouragement to give. She could do this.

Ari picked up her phone and put a call through to the one living person who'd never let her down. 'Hi, Gert, I was wondering if I can come and visit for a few days?'

'You know you can.' Gert's voice grounded her. 'When?'

'Tomorrow? I'm heading back from Brisbane. I'll stay in a motel overnight.'

'I thought you were still at Cooper's Crossing.'

'We finished up yesterday and lit out. It's all done. I wanted to give Reid the good news.'

'How is he?'

'Grouchy. Finding it hard to come to terms with what his accident has taken from him.' She might explain more when she got there. She wasn't sure how much Gert knew about Ari's relationship with Reid. Ari hadn't been hiding it—she'd simply been working hard and out of reach of the real world for most of it.

'Had to happen eventually,' Gert said with a sigh. 'That boy always did present his bright side to others, even after taking some mighty hard knocks. As if people wouldn't tolerate having him around if he wasn't all sunshine and light.'

She hadn't thought of it that way. Something else to chew on during the long drive home and take with her when next she saw him.

'I want to drop in on Patrick and Jake.' Her stepfather and stepbrother. 'Clear some air if I can. Put the whole lot behind me if I can't.'

'About that.' Gert paused as if choosing her words carefully. 'You might want to reconsider. Patrick's been on a bender for days.'

Ari closed her eyes. 'What set him off this time?'

'Who knows? He's not a good man.'

'He might have been once upon a—'

'No, Ari. That man drank the money set aside for your education, threw you out of the home your mother owned the minute she died, and threatened his son with a beating if they so much as acknowledged you.'

'Jake's been nodding at me when he sees me these days. He's almost eighteen. I can be there with a helping hand if he wants out.'

'He spat on you.'

'He was *ten*.' Ari had never expected her little stepbrother to defend her when Patrick had turned mean. Granted, she'd never expected her step-sibling to spit on her either, but if it had kept him in his father's good graces, she could understand the why of it. Neither her nor Jake had been driving the animosity. Someone else had been directing the roles they had to play.

'I want to help. I want to offer Jake a labouring job on my crew when we do the gardens at the visitors' centre.'

'That'd be like asking him to declare war on his father.'

'I know. And maybe he'll spit on me again, but I'm still going to offer him a way out of his father's grasp, same way you offered me one.'

There was a long, long pause. 'I'll back you,' said Gert finally. 'Let's fight for him.'

'Gert…' Her aunt waited for her to continue. 'Have you ever heard of a man named Deacon Murray?'

'Doesn't ring a bell.'

'Look him up on the web. See if his face is familiar.'

'Why?'

'I think he might be my biological father. I think I'm going to write to him. Ask him what happened and why he sent money—a lot of money—via Reid's father, but never came near me. See what happens.'

'Are you expecting anything from him?'

'Not a damn thing beyond answers—if that's who he is. I'm just…building the me I want to be, going forward. I owe it to myself to face my demons head-on, right? And clear the way to move forward with confidence in my own value. Enough self-esteem to let love in. Lead by example, even.'

That was what she wanted out of all of this.

'I'll see you when you get here,' said Gert. 'Drive carefully.'

Ari dialled the next number as she paced a three-star roadside motel room. It was clean enough for the faint smell of cheap disinfectant to tease her nostrils. Good enough for her even if she had spent the past few months living from one lovely architect-designed eco lodge to the next. She didn't need access to luxury. Not from Reid, not from the father she'd never met. She wanted honesty instead.

She had no private number for Deacon Murray, but she did have a business number.

A female voice answered. Receptionist? Personal assistant? Wife? Who knew? 'Hi. My name is Ari Cohen and I'd like to speak with Mr Deacon Murray, if he's in.'

'Is he expecting your call, Ms Cohen?'

Ari could work with polite professionalism. 'I expect not, but if you could tell him I called, that would be great. Ari Cohen, from the Barcoo. I'd like to email my contact details through to you as well.'

'Not a problem, Ms Cohen. I can certainly let him know you called and get those details to him.'

Applause for the super-efficient woman, whoever she was.

Ari tossed her mobile on the threadbare bedspread and pushed her hair from her face. She wasn't finished facing her fears by any means. But it was a start.


It was ten past six in the afternoon and Ari still had a hundred kilometres of dirt road to drive before she reached Gert's when her mobile phone rang and an unfamiliar number lit up the screen. She eased her foot off the accelerator and let the vehicle ease to a stop. No need to get off the road, not out here. No need to even stop, she decided, as she picked up and said hello. It could be a potential client, and, if so, she needed to be available to them. 'ARI Landscaping, Ari speaking.'

Nothing.

'Hello?' Her reception was iffy.

'Ari Cohen?' The man cleared his throat and Ari held the

phone a little further from her ear as she brought the car to a halt. 'This is Deacon Murray returning your call.'

Oh. Now it was her turn to get tongue-tied. 'Right.'

'I believe I know why you called. I've been waiting for it for a long time, wondering what I'd say when the moment came.'

He was going to say no.

'The thing is, I have three sons.'

Who needed a daughter when they had three sons?

'And a loving wife who's stood by me for over forty years.'

He was definitely going to deny ever knowing her mother.

'And I love them all very much.'

Why would he confess to giving Ari's mother any money? He'd pretend it was all Lord Blake's doing and that he knew nothing about it. She could see it coming a mile.

Deny. Deny. Deny.

Well, *bring it on.*

'I'm listening, Mr Murray.' To hell with giving him an out.

'What is it you want?' he asked with quiet deference and made her frown.

'I want to know who my father is. If that person is you, I'd like to meet you in person so I can count that question answered once and for all.'

He'd never agree to her request.

He cleared his throat again.

Men were cowards.

Honourable cowards were the worst.

'On behalf of my entire extended family, and myself, I'd like to invite you to an informal barbecue lunch this Sunday at my home.' Quiet words that rang with sincerity. 'We'd all like to meet you very much.'

* * *

Ari was still in shock when she walked into Gert's kitchen two hours later. She'd said yes and hung up, because her feelings were threatening to strangle her into silence. She had two days to get her act together before meeting them all in person. The man had eight grandkids, for goodness' sake. Three daughters-in-law. His wife bred dachshunds and there were puppies on the ground, did she want one?

It was all just a little too soon and definitely too much but no way was she letting the opportunity slip away. Regardless of whether they truly were as loving and accepting as they sounded, Ari would be there for it.

She'd almost forgotten what other wheels she'd put in motion—it had been one hell of a day—but the young man in Gert's kitchen brought her back to reality with a start.

'Jake.' She sought the older woman's gaze. 'Gert. Sorry I'm late. I got held up.'

'Perfect timing,' Gert replied with a wave of her arm towards the oven. 'I'm about to dish up.'

Ari dropped her duffel beside the door and went to the bathroom to clean up, and when she returned, Jake was carving meat while Gert added serving spoons to salad greens and cheesy potato bake.

It wasn't until halfway through the meal, with Gert providing most of the conversation, that Ari stitched together the scattered remnants of her will and turned to her silent stepbrother, who'd eaten quickly, with his eyes lowered and his head down, giving clear signals to those who knew how to look for them that he had no idea where his next decent feed was coming from.

'I have a landscaping business now and a really good team of tradies who work with me.' Her goal was to put the offer to him, tell him why she was making it, and leave the rest up to him. 'I need a labourer for a job we have coming up at the visitor information centre at Black Ridge.'

'What's the pay?' He didn't look at her.

'The award wage for someone your age plus a living away from home allowance that all my employees get. I can send you the job description and the wage breakdown if you're interested.' She'd be calling the shots. 'It's pretty simple garden labour, but if you won't take orders from me and have no intention of working hard, don't take the job. You won't last a day. I'll make sure of it.' She refused to let him disrupt her crew with family angst.

She wondered whether or not to touch on their not so happy past. Probably best to open that wound wide and see if she could flush out the rot. 'You were only a kid when I left home. I don't know you very well and you don't know me. But I do know your father's faults and his fury and what he does to drive people away. I'm trusting Gert's judgment when she says you're not like him.'

His head came up, his brown eyes direct and his boyish jaw hard. He was well on his way to becoming a strong, handsome man who looked a lot like his father. 'I'm not like him.'

'Be sure.'

She saw fierce determination and hope in his eyes. 'I'm not like him,' he repeated. 'I'll work hard for you. I want the job.'

'You'll start next Tuesday, helping me source plants and order materials.'

The faintest of smiles crossed his lips. 'Looking forward to it.'

'Eat up,' said Gert, her expression warmly approving.

Maybe taming demons of old wasn't so difficult after all.

# CHAPTER FOURTEEN

THE PROBLEM WITH arguing with Ari and watching the door close behind her was that Reid still had business ends to tie up and they still needed to deal with one another on a professional basis. Reid had promised her she wouldn't be disadvantaged should a romance between them go bad. So far, he hadn't lived up to his promise at all, but he would.

Soon.

For the first time in his life he'd allowed his sister-in-law to sweep into his life and scoop him up and take him home to Jeddah Creek station. Not that it was his home any more but as the family seat in Australia it held all the treasures and memories of his childhood home.

In retrospect, his Kangaroo Point climb had been a terrible idea, useful only for exposing his physical frailty for all to see. Business had suffered. He'd pushed friends away, craving solitude and room to heal outside the public gaze. He'd even tried to push Judah and Bridie away, but they were having none of it.

He appreciated their efforts to make him feel essential to the family unit, but more than anything he'd wanted to lie on a bed with Ari and hold her hand and say *I don't know how to be who I used to be* out loud. He wanted to say *I need to create the new me but I'm tired for the first time in my life and there's a black dog licking at my heels.*

He wanted to turn her into a what? A nursemaid? A whipping post for every frustration? What kind of person would he be if he did that to someone he—?

Someone he loved.

Far better to lie around in dark rooms and pretend he was doing just what the doctor ordered. Resting. Relaxing.

Spiralling into the darkest depression.

His bedroom door opened but he made no move to open his eyes. Bridie wouldn't have entered without knocking first. Judah wasn't home. It could only be one other rather small person with no notion of the boundaries he was so desperate to enforce. 'Uncle Reid,' a little voice whispered. 'Are you awake?'

'Yes.' He tried to make a point of not lying to minors.

'Are you hiding?'

'No.' So much for telling the truth. 'What's up?'

'Have you seen Fluffy-Wuffy?'

The grey terror? Bane of his brother's life? Currently fast asleep on his back on Reid's bed, and using Reid's leg as a hot-water bottle? It was tempting, very tempting to say no. 'He's here.'

'He naps a lot.' Piper ventured closer. 'So do you.'

This was true. Maybe Reid could ease back into truth-telling after all. 'Yes. I'm resting and relaxing.'

'Mum says that just because you look better, doesn't mean you are.' She'd reached the bed, her hand reaching out to pat the cat, who started purring up a storm.

'She's right.' A pox on truth-tellers young and old.

'Can you see good any more?'

Had she heard Bridie discussing that or had her own observations led to the obvious conclusion? 'No. But I'm a rebel. One day I'll make a robot eye that can see for me.'

'I'm going to be a rebel too,' Piper declared, and Reid

smiled at her confident declaration. He had no doubt that his niece would test boundaries all her life. Judah tried to hold a strong and sensible line, Bridie less so, but this child was already such a force to be reckoned with. As an heiress to billions, would she grow up to resent people seeing her as a bank teller machine, wanting to be around her as a pathway to wealth and status? Or would she weed them out, as Reid had done over the years?

Would she find the Aris of this world without having to land at their feet in a broken heap?

He hoped so.

'Do you want to play truck drivers with me?'

Did he have anything else to do?

Reid eased up onto one elbow, just as the cat decided to open those golden eyes and stretch his claws. 'Try me,' Reid told the formerly sleeping feline. 'I dare you to use those on me. Make my day.'

Cats were smart. Fluffy-Wuffy merely rolled to a sitting position and began to wash his face. 'What does playing trucks involve?'

'We find an empty truck and get in and pretend to drive. You can give me a proper driving lesson if you want,' his niece declared with a winning smile.

'You're *nine*.'

'And I can almost reach the clutch.'

'Piper, what did I tell you about not bothering Uncle Reid?' A new voice had joined the throng, but Bridie didn't venture any further than the doorway.

'You said never wake a sleeping tiger but he was *awake*. And he'd kidnapped Fluffy-*Wuffy*!'

'Lies. All lies,' he mumbled in protest. 'By all means, take the cat.'

'I've just had a call from Ari,' Bridie said. 'She mentioned she'd been trying to reach you.'

'Uh-huh. I've been asleep.'

'Her contract terms state that someone needs to do a final inspection of site six and sign off on it. I've done the first five. You want to take this last one? You could organise a pilot and get up to the site this afternoon. She tells me this one is the crew's favourite. Her favourite too. She's incredibly talented. Her outdoor spaces are such sensory escapes.'

'Then tell her we'll waive the inspection clause and sign off on it and she can be on her way.' A pillow hit him in the head and sent an unexpected jolt of adrenalin through his system. 'Hey, mind the skull!'

'Tell her yourself. Get up.' It was Bridie as he'd never heard her before. 'Piper, take the cat to the kitchen and give him some food. And stay downstairs until I return, okay?'

Surprisingly, her daughter did what she was told.

Reid warily sat up and put the pillow behind him, out of easy reach. 'Something you want to say?' He'd never been at the pointy end of Bridie's displeasure before. He didn't like it.

'Yes, I have something to say. I've been wanting to say it for a while. Stop sulking around feeling sorry for yourself. Get up, get active, and go and sign off in person on the job *you* set up, and give the woman *you* pursued some kind of praise and closure when it comes to the enormous project she took on for *you*.'

Ouch.

But he did have decent arguments to present in his defence. 'One: Ari has benefitted from my patronage, and I don't owe her anything,' he declared coolly.

'And two: I don't see how it's any of your business to tell

me how to run *my* business.' Never mind that those lodges were half hers and they were in business *together*.

Bridie glared at him. 'I say this with love in my heart for you, Reid, but you're being an arse.'

'Playboy, remember? Not a good bet when it comes to women wanting anything more than a quick once-over. I saw, I conquered, I'm done.' Surely that load of steaming excrement erupting from his mouth would get Bridie gone?

His sister-in-law merely tossed her hair behind her shoulders and crossed her arms. 'Bull.'

'You've just never seen my playboy ways up close.'

'If you mean I've never seen you happier than when I went to collect you from Ari's work site five weeks ago, then no. I've never seen that before. And then you pass out on a rock face and decide you're no good to anyone—which is blatantly untrue—and ghost the woman you're in love with and who is in love with you! So, you tell me…what's going on?'

'She's not in love with me. I was a means to an end, nothing more. It's fine. She's fine.'

'I'm not buying it, Reid. You care for Ari more than you're letting on. I can see it in you. You're letting good things go because of a minor…physical…' she waved a hand towards him '…glitch.'

'Does this pep talk have a point?'

'Yes, and I've made it. Get out there and engage with Ari. Sign off on her work. Tell her it's genius, because it is.'

'I said I'd sign off on the job and I will.'

'And *don't* leave her hanging on a personal front,' said Bridie. 'You're better than that. I don't care what playboy hat you think you're wearing. One way or another, clear the air.'

'The air is clear.' He'd scorched the earth while he was there, but surely the air had cleared. He was letting Ari go for her own good!

'Good.'

'Are we done?'

Bridie hovered uncertainly. 'I do love you, you know. I don't think you're useless or unworthy or whatever's going on in your head. So there are things you can't do any more. So what? Reorient towards what you can do.'

So they weren't done… 'Bridie, you've had your say and I love you for it. I've heard you out. And I think I've taken advantage of your hospitality for quite long enough. I'll be on my way home within the hour.'

'Which home?'

'Cooper's Crossing.'

Her eyes narrowed. 'There's no one else there.'

Reid smiled mirthlessly. 'Exactly.'

An hour later, an anxious little girl stood in front of the screen door that would lead Reid to the waiting helicopter and pilot. He had his carryall in hand and his wraparound sunglasses in place and did he not look like an uncle who was going somewhere?

Whoever said the blocking of one sense would stimulate other senses knew what they were talking about. He'd added another sense since his eyesight had dimmed. He now had the unwanted ability to read other people's body language.

He refused to call it reading someone's emotional aura.

'Are you coming back tomorrow?' Piper asked.

'No.'

Agitated arm swinging ensued. How did a person keep a child they adored at arm's length? 'But I'll be back.'

'Will you be you again?'

What a question. 'I might be a little bit new. But people always change. You'll have changed a lot by the time you grow up, and even after that. We all do.'

'But I can still love you, even when you're new,' the little princess said. 'You don't have to teach me how to drive, you know. We can do other things together that are fun.'

'You're right.'

'I can read to you.' She shuffled from one foot to another, her anxiety spiking his. 'If you like.'

He hated the very thought. 'I'd like that.' There he went again, lying to a loved one. 'And I'm learning to sing. You could have lessons too.'

Shoot him. Shoot him now. 'I could.'

'Do you want to take Fluffy-Wuffy home with you for company?'

He'd found his line in the sand. 'No!' Hell, no! 'Thanks, Pip, but no. He'd miss you too much.'

'Not if he had you.'

How he got out of that house without crumbling in a heap, he never knew.

'Take me to the eco lodges at site six,' he said to Judah's new helicopter pilot who'd been brought on six months ago after it had been made clear to all that Reid's days of being a flying taxi service had come to an abrupt end. The man was more than competent and, beyond a nod and a gruff, 'sure thing' didn't feel the need to fill the air with conversation.

So what if Reid didn't have his hand on the joystick of the helicopter as it ate up the ground between Jeddah Creek and Cooper's Crossing? He could still appreciate a blue sky all around him and the feeling of going somewhere. He had red dirt below him and a work site to inspect and a part of him relished having something concrete to be responsible for. He wasn't completely useless. If all else failed, he could while away the hours by torturing his nearest and dearest with his singing. Maybe he really did just need to re-examine his priorities in the face of this latest health setback and set a new course and get on with it. Maybe Bridie *had* managed to pillow-slap a little sense into him after all.

He was even looking forward to being in Ari's garden space. It wasn't as if she would be there. He'd checked with Bridie, who said Ari was hundreds of kilometres east, working on another job.

He'd texted Ari in reply to her missed message and said he was inspecting site six today and expected to sign off on it later this evening. She'd sent him a single line in reply.

Thank you for the opportunity to shine.

An hour or so later, the pilot set the little aircraft down a short distance from the new landscaping, and they waited until all was still before getting out and securing the blades.

'Not sure how long I'll be,' said Reid.

'I brought some paperwork with me.'

'Use one of the cabins if you like. I'll find you.'

They set off together towards the trio of buildings. Of all the sites where the lodges had been built, site six was by far his favourite. It had been built on the curve of a permanent water channel and huge river redgums dominated the landscape to the southwest. Even with his limited eyesight, he could appreciate the pale glow of the tree trunks and branches when the late afternoon sun hit them just right. Tendrils of the mighty Diamantina river cut the floodplains to the west, bringing birds and wildlife close.

Before Ari, a couple of waddi trees and random mounds of saltbush had dotted the area between the three cabins, and basic walking tracks had been stomped into place between one cabin and the next. The cabins had provided refuge from the heat of the day or the winds that whipped dust into every crevice and there had been little reason for anyone to gather outside, but now…

While the pilot headed for the nearest cabin, Reid turned left and followed the circular dirt track surrounding all the buildings—its edges now defined by scrubby acacia trees and flowering understory plants he'd only ever seen during a big wet.

Ari had ringed the entire garden area with thick Corten steel posts planted close enough together to let small creatures in and the hungriest herbivores out.

He turned inwards and crossed a narrow walking bridge over a shy, trickling stream filled with rocks and grasses and alive with the sound of frogs and other insects. Snakes and lizards too, he'd bet, although he didn't see any.

Ari's answer to that had been that there would always be snakes in paradise and that the balance of nature demanded it. She'd assured him she'd made every effort to keep people on the walking tracks and had made the outdoor gathering areas as uncluttered as possible, with no spots for creatures to hide without being seen.

She'd kept the waddi trees and the circle theme and added paving and places to sit, and curved shelters, half wall half roof, that provided various levels of shade. There was a sunken fire pit. A viewing deck with a curved back wall and not one but two porcelain bathtubs open to the sky and sunset views, with a rustic wooden table sitting between them.

The ground beneath the tubs was some kind of smooth concrete mix set with tumbled stones and pebbles from a riverbed. They'd been laid out in snakelike curves, and he remembered from her notes that the idea was for people to walk on them barefoot and massage their feet while their bath was filling up.

Reid turned on the taps to one of the tubs and let the

warm, clear water run through his fingers as he stared at the outline of his favourite river redgum in the distance. He could smell eucalyptus and a fainter scent of something sweeter. He heard the buzz of insects nearby, but they seemed to have other things to do than bother him.

The water reticulation overhaul Ari and her team had given this place was genius, cobbled from a research paper outlining ways in which the Israeli desert had been turned over to food production, and a regional zoo's schematics for a closed water system that grew endangered turtle species.

The whole set-up for growing plants and redefining habitat here was ambitious, possibly foolhardy, and he anticipated no shortage of scientific minds wanting to track the system's progress for years to come.

He didn't notice her presence at first.

He hadn't heard her approach over the splash of the water into the bathtub. But he sensed something, maybe just the stirring of the air, and when he turned, there she was, leaning against the wall, silently watching him. She wore cut-off shorts, a short-sleeved yellow top, and work boots and she looked relaxed and not at all surprised to see him.

He, on the other hand, was extremely surprised to see her. Glad too, if the sudden leap of his heart before it settled into rapid drumming was any indication. He wished, more than anything, that he could see her face and the expression in her eyes. Then again, if he could still do that, he wouldn't have turned her away in the first place. He would have still had enough to offer her. 'This is unexpected.'

'Bridie told me you were on your way here, and I was in the neighbourhood so here I am.'

'Trespassing.'

She put her hands in the pockets of her shorts and nodded agreeably. 'Again.'

He loved the sound of her voice and the ease with which she navigated uncertainty. He relished her dry wit and sheer practicality when it came to traversing this Outback landscape. She belonged here, more than anyone he'd ever met.

Her spirit called to his.

He'd never been so tongue-tied or so fanciful.

'What do you think?' she asked. 'I have a morning tour, a midday tour and a sunset tour all planned out.'

'It's half past five.'

'I know,' she replied dryly. 'You will be difficult and turn up in the in between. But even if you don't want the tour I can stand here and tell you that I planted the area around this bathing ledge with tea trees with antiseptic properties, and wattle that helps with aches and pains, and she oaks whose cones are said to help with rheumatism. In times to come you'll be able to pick a posy and add it to your bathwater. The aloe in the pot over there is good for sunburn, you probably know that already. Gert has a recipe for a cream. I thought it might be fun to make up a batch and leave it in the cabins, along with the recipe, but that's overstepping my brief by a few hundred kilometres or more. That sweet smell is brown boronia. I found a guy who'd been grafting it onto different root stocks, so I went a bit mad and planted hundreds of them.'

He could listen to her talk about plants until the end of time. Maybe he'd imprinted on that particular pastime in the tent. 'Will they live?'

'So far so good.'

'I had my workshop engineers read your water schematics out loud to me. They added supersized whiteboard visuals and that helped. They're fans of your work now. So am I.'

'Thank you. I've been tweaking the water reticulation systems all the way along but this was the first time I had a permanent water supply to dip into. I think it went to my head.'

'The results speak for themselves.'

'I'd really love a maintenance contract that covered an entire year, but I guess putting something together and then handing it over to others to care for is all part of the business.'

'It's going well? The business?' So stilted and formal, but he didn't know how to be anything else without reaching for her.

'Very well. I've been getting more enquiries than I know what to do with. I feel like I'm on a runaway road train. I'm sure as hell not the one driving it.'

He'd felt that way too, early on in his career. Of course, he hadn't admitted it quite as readily. She would need good people around her for guidance and support. He could—

No.

He could step back and let her soar.

'Been slaying any demons lately?' she asked lightly, but it wasn't a careless question. She was signalling a move from business conversation to the personal.

'None. You?'

'I'm employing my younger brother as a full-time labourer—he's a hard worker, it's going well. And I've been to a barbecue at my father's place with all his family present. They were all terrifyingly friendly, even the pregnant dachshund. I may have said yes to one of the puppies. I'm not entirely sure what I said, to be honest. Fear of rejection brings on the crazy talk in me. Like now, for example.'

'Did you tackle your stepfather as well?'

She shook her head. 'Too risky. He's too deep in the bottle right now. That's not my fight.'

'Wise.'

'I have a healthy sense of self preservation. Unlike some.'
He deserved that.

'Do you ever wish we could go back to the tent and just talk?' she asked quietly. 'Because I've been wishing that a lot. Whatever else, we were honest about our needs back then. We wore our vulnerability with ease.'

'It was memorable.' On that he could agree.

'I keep wondering what I'd say or do to let you know how much I respect and treasure you.' He stilled and she drew a quick breath and kept right on speaking. 'I'm crazy in love with you, but I might have forgotten to mention it last time we spoke. I wondered whether you'd missed that about me, what with your no longer excellent eyesight. I mean, do you really need to see me light up like Sydney Harbour bridge on cracker night whenever I see you?'

He wanted to see that so badly.

'You should ask my crew about the way I behaved the day I found out you'd been in that cliff accident. So much stomping around and staring tragically at my phone in between trying to call you. I already knew you were smart and generous and could make me feel good about simply being me, but that was the day I realised how much I wanted to have the *right* to be there for you.'

'You want someone to need you, that's all. And I refuse to be your patient.' Finally, some spoken words he actually *meant*.

'I've thought about that.' She crossed her arms in front of her, classic defensive posture. 'Another demon I wrestled with while I tossed up whether to track you down again or not, because I do like being needed, yeah. Trying to fix you while you were hurt made me feel that I had something of value to offer. And afterwards, you went out of your way to make me feel good about simply being me. You made me believe I had plenty to give, so here I am. Making my play for your love and attention. Again. Just in case I didn't give you enough information the first time.'

She took a deep breath—he could hear the inhale even if he couldn't see her chest rise with the effort. 'I can't make you love me if you don't—it would be foolish to try. But if you're pulling away because some of your body parts don't work the way they used to and you no longer believe that what you have to offer is enough, just *stop* with that way of thinking.'

She unlocked her arms and spread them wide as if offering him her all. 'Your dodgy eyesight isn't going to keep you down for long. It isn't going to prevent you from loving someone with all that you are. There are so many ways to connect. A million ways to show and feel love. What's one more curve to navigate? That's what I really came all this way here to say. If this is the end of us, I didn't want to finish it by being cranky with you. You deserve better than that. I can *be* better than that.'

'You're going to go a long way, Ari Cohen.'

'Maybe so.' She tapped her heart. 'But this? For better or for worse, this is yours. And you know where to find me, if ever you want to get in touch.'

'May I kiss you goodbye?' His words came out all cracked and torn.

She took a step back. 'Best not. I'll cry.'

He closed his eyes and turned away.

And she was gone.

# CHAPTER FIFTEEN

AFTER ONE WEEK of solitude, Reid was second-guessing his decision to let Ari walk away. After two weeks, he'd taken to living in one of the cabins at site six and walking the tracks she'd laid out for him several times a day. In the mornings he listened for the birdsong. At midday he sought out the shady rest areas. Come sunset, he could be found in a bath, watching the colours of romance and fire light up the sky.

He found a carved wooden walking stick hanging from a tree branch on one of his walks. Oiled and knotted and handy should he ever encounter a snake he wanted to send on its way without getting too close.

He found an ice pack for migraine sufferers that covered a person's forehead and eyes in every freezer in every cabin.

He found a single lens binocular, a monocular, in the bird hide that had been built in the curve of the channel bank and used it to bring the moon close enough to see every colour with his one good eye, with its pinpoint tunnel vision.

His phone did not stop ringing, with his key employees asking for his opinion on one thing or another, and he came slowly to the realisation that he wasn't superfluous to requirements and his brain worked as well as it always had. He was a linchpin in a world he'd spent many years building and that wasn't about to change because his vision was no longer twenty-twenty.

Demons were being slayed. Time was taking care of them.

Time and the slow realisation that he was still capable and needed.

Ari's landscape worked its magic on him and brought him back to his senses, and those senses were stronger now, stepping up, getting a workout here in this garden of sensory engagement.

Ari was like no one else he'd ever experienced.

It would be his pride and his pleasure to walk through life with her, and she was right there, waiting for him to catch up and recognise what she already knew.

Happiness was spending a lifetime with someone you loved and who loved you right back, no matter what the limitations or challenges ahead.

The day he discovered the tiny Matchbox car racetrack hidden beneath a sprawling saltbush—with tunnels and cars parked in finger-made caves—and it took him straight back to Ari as a child, and the challenges she'd faced and the way she'd created worlds using nothing but wonder and imagination—he knew that letting her go was going to be impossible.

He loved her.

He needed her.

He wanted her, and every adventure that came of it.

Beyond belief.

Reid sat at the outdoor table between three cabins, the visit from his brother and sister-in-law not exactly going to plan. His medical records lay spread out in front of them, and Judah, for one, was relishing every bit of being a big brother hell-bent on making the most of his little brother's discomfort.

'Tell me again what we're looking for?' Judah asked silkily.

'Anything I might need to explain in detail to someone

who…' *loves me* '…might want to be with me romantically. A future wife, for example.' He refused to be embarrassed. His question was legitimate. If he was going to track Ari down and lay his medical future out before her and beg her forgiveness for ever turning her away, he wanted a second opinion on what information to include.

Would he lead with his healthy sperm count, for example? Or the metal in his head that still needed to come out? Or a comprehensive explanation—or demonstration—of the limits of his eyesight?

'Start with your eyesight,' said Bridie. 'It's a lot worse than I thought.' Worry laced her voice and she reached for his hand and threaded her fingers through his. 'I'm cross you didn't tell us how bad it was.'

'I thought it'd improve.' His defence was threefold. 'I didn't want to worry you. And I didn't want anyone to fuss.'

'Tell me again how Ari came to you and told you none of this matters and you turned her away,' murmured Judah.

'She should have tied you up and convinced you,' said Bridie firmly and Judah just about snorted his coffee.

Dearie me, was there a story there that Reid could use to throw a little shade Judah's way? Could something useful come out of Reid's hasty decision to call in the troops to help him plan his offensive on Ari's emotions? She deserved a grand gesture, and he was working on it. 'What was that, big brother? You agree?'

But Judah recovered fast, his momentary splutter replaced by steely composure. 'And *after* coming clean about your eyesight, and future changes to it, you might want to mention your artificial hip, missing spleen and the not so insignificant repairs they had to do to the artery in your groin. You could finish with this little gem from your team of specialists. *"Mr Blake's speedy recovery has been noth-*

*ing short of miraculous.'"* Judah's curt voice effectively conveyed his displeasure, no need for Reid to see the finer details of the other man's scowl in order to get the message. 'Why didn't you *tell* us?'

'We all had a lot going on and I didn't want—'

No one jumped in to put words to Reid's thoughts. 'I didn't want to appear weak in front of you. That was why it hit so hard when I went climbing and came unstuck and photos of my unconscious self being lowered to the ground by a bunch of helpful strangers got splashed across social media for all to see. There it was. My frailty exposed for all to see.' Reid appealed to his brother who'd spent over seven years in prison being a badass so that other inmates left him alone. 'Judah, you *know* there are times when a man can't be seen to be *weak.*'

Judah ran a frustrated hand through his hair and looked to Bridie, who huffed and threw up her hands. 'He needs us. This is very clear.'

'Do you think grovelling should come before the facts or after the facts?' Reid asked, gesturing with his hands towards his medical records.

'Before.' Bridie sounded very, very sure.

'Not even sure you need the facts,' Judah murmured.

'I need you to help me craft an email regarding my ongoing health challenges,' Reid told them. 'That's step one. And I want your thoughts on step two, which is seeing her again.' He didn't want to fail Ari again. Never, ever again.

His beloved sister-in-law sent him a wide, sunshiny smile that he'd long since learned to associate with outrageous ideas. 'I have an idea.'

# CHAPTER SIXTEEN

WHEN ARI HAD received Reid's email, with a dozen attachments containing medical records and a brief explanation that this was why he'd tried to end their relationship, she hadn't known quite what to think.

The brief had been brutally matter-of-fact and his medical records had been stomach-churning. He'd had a far harsher time of it than he'd ever let on. He'd be grateful if she took the time to consider the information and get a good notion of what choosing to love someone like him would mean for her future, should they decide to embark on one together. Full disclosure was obviously needed, he'd written, in order for her to make a fully informed, rational decision.

Definitely an engineer, she thought. Since when was love rational?

He'd finished the email 'Reid'.

Below that, though, had been a treasure trove of words.

Your Reid.

She liked that one.

It had been followed by:

What if she doesn't reply? How long should I give her before I call? I should say, 'I'll call in a couple of days'. Or, no, too needy. I should ask her to call if she needs more information—write that down. 'Call if you need more information.' Or, no. Just my signature will do. Just Reid.

Dammit, Judah, why are you grinning? What do you mean, how can I tell? You have a mouthful of teeth as big as a corn cob and whiter than the moon. I can see them! Yes, I will practise my poetry before I see her next, you tool. Just help me write the goddamn letter.

Respectfully Reid?

What do you mean too many Rs? I always sign my letters 'Respectfully'.

Who in the world uses the word 'felicitations'?

You call this helping?

Just finish it and press send!

Your Reid.

Felicitations, Judah.

Ari had read that spiel at the end a hundred times over and it still made her grin like a woman with a corncob mouth. It gave her the confidence to wait a day and fully digest the information in those attachments before replying.

Dear Reid,

This explains a lot, although not quite everything. Your brother is awesome, btw. Would you like to meet to discuss mutual future prospects? I'm crazy busy prepping for my next job at Black Ridge, but I'm free on Saturday.

Your Ari

When an email reply came through for her with an invitation to meet him at Jeddah Creek station homestead at four p.m. and prepare to stay for dinner and that she was welcome to use Gert's old room if she'd like to stay the night, Ari agreed to everything. He was obviously back at his brother's place for a while and there were more than enough rooms for them to speak privately.

She definitely wanted another look at that bonkers family library.

Saturday morning brought a phone message from Bridie, saying she was sending a helicopter for Ari to save her the bother of driving.

Ari had been back at Gert's by then, dropping Jack off, before getting back on the road.

She didn't say no.

When Ari saw that the field next to the homestead was full of light aircraft, luxury jets, and Outback vehicles and tents of every kind, she turned to her taciturn young bush pilot. 'What's going on down there?'

'It's for the ball.'

'Ball?'

'Spring Fling charity ball for rural health services? Ring any bells?'

Not one bell was being rung. 'And it's on...tonight?'

'Starts at six p.m.'

'Oh.' Bridie had neglected to mention it. Last time a ball had taken place here, Ari had been *staff*. 'Fancy that.'

It was hot, dry and dusty in the aircraft parking lot. People were bringing out the sisal mats and fairy lights and setting up their luxury and not so luxurious camping spots. Piper was sitting on the steps, a little grey cat lounging regally beside her. The girl jumped up and waved to her enthusiastically. 'Mum, she's here!'

And then Bridie appeared, dressed in a sleeveless yellow cotton frock and enough sparkly jewellery on her fingers and wrists to make it clear that the mistress of the house was dressing to impress. Her hair was up and make-up expertly applied and made the most of her flawless features. Ari felt altogether plain in reply. 'You're just in time.' Bridie hugged her, and since when were they on hugging terms? 'The stylist has just finished my hair and you can slot in next.'

'Um, Bridie? Hello. Thank you for sending the helicopter to collect me, and I can see you're really busy, and I'm pretty sure I missed a memo because I had no idea this was a ball weekend, but if you need a hand—'

'No! No hands. All will become clear in time. Come in. Please. I have a gown for you, I had to guess your measurements, it came in this morning, and if you don't like it, we'll raid my closets.'

'A…gown.'

'*Very* modern-day ballroom elegance. Valentino. Full confession, I *did* help with the selection. Reid paid.'

'Where *is* Reid?'

'He was with Judah earlier, but I've lost track of them. We don't need them yet.'

Bridie gave Ari no time to protest as she led her into a beautifully appointed guest bedroom set up with two beauty stations. 'Ladies, this is Ari. Ari, this is Darla, magician hair stylist, and Casey, make-up artist extraordinaire. They're here to help. And this is your gown, and a few pairs of shoes to choose from—I wasn't sure how high, but I do remember you wore heels when you were here before, so I didn't stint.'

Ari stared in wonder at the gown displayed on the headless mannequin in the corner. It was a deep, dusky blue festival of froth, shot through with gold and silver meteor streaks originating from one side of the seriously tiny waist. It was strapless at the top, the chiffon skirt caressing the ground. It was the most elegantly romantic confection she'd ever seen. 'That's for *me*?' she squeaked.

'Do you like it?'

How was that even a question? 'I don't understand.'

'Reid wanted you to have the full Cinderella experience. Apparently, he owes you one.'

'He doesn't.'

'Ah, well. Work it out between you,' Bridie said blithely. 'We have two hours before we have to be ready, and I still need to see to a few details before I have to become Lady Blake of the Outback for our overseas relatives.'

'You have overseas relatives attending too? Fancy relatives?' Ari had barely got her head around being friendly with Reid's regular billionaire and altogether famous family members.

'A very special one,' confirmed Bridie. 'Reid doesn't know yet, but Judah's been corresponding with her for weeks.' Bridie's smile broke as she leaned in close to whisper in Ari's ear, 'We found the missing sister. And she's magnificent.'

Wide-eyed, Ari stared at the other woman with dawning delight. 'Really?'

'Yes. But it's a secret. This night is full of them so zip lip, buckle up and enjoy the ride. Are you with me?'

'Yes!' Abandoning all objections, Ari spread her arms wide and let happiness take hold. Although, hands. Hands that had been scrabbling around in the dirt all week. 'My nails belong on a troll.'

Casey held up a packet of something and rustled it gently. 'Got you covered, sweetie.'

'We good?' Again, Bridie left no room for argument. 'Yes, you've got this. Enjoy. See you soon.'

It was what Ari had always imagined getting ready to be married would be like. The fussing and the primping. The detailed discussions about smoky eyes versus dewy innocence. Given that stunning gown in the corner, Ari's hair would of course be styled up. Audrey Hepburn in *Breakfast at Tiffany's* got a mention and they ran with it. Ari had not a scrap of jewellery to complete the look, but that dress was its own shining star and didn't need any accompaniment.

By the time they were finished with her, and Ari stood staring at her reflection in front of a wall full of floor-to-ceiling mirrors, her transformation was complete.

Ari Cohen was no more.

This person was someone new, and Ari couldn't wait to take her for a turn in the ballroom.

'How does it feel?' asked a voice from the doorway, and there stood Reid in full black-tie regalia.

'Excuse us,' said Ari's magic helpers and Reid smiled at them as they slipped past him and out of the room.

'It feels like a fairy tale,' she told him. 'I will never trash the Cinderella experience again. I'm a believer. Although…' It was probably time to come clean. 'You know how I can't actually swim?'

'Mm hmm.' He sounded dreadfully indulgent.

'I can't waltz either.'

He laughed at that, and she flung herself into his welcoming arms, and he held her tight and buried his face in her neck. She could feel his ragged breaths against her skin and the rapid tattoo of his heart against her chest. 'Missed you, Ari,' he murmured. 'You wouldn't believe how much.'

'I might believe it.' She'd worked her fingers to the bone hoping that exhaustion would stop her from missing him. 'I missed you just as much.' She breathed out a sigh at the solid, all-encompassing strength of his embrace. 'I want whatever future you're imagining for us. I don't care what it is, I just want to be there for it. With you.'

'I want everything you have to give.' He released her and stepped back and reached into his pocket and brought out a small velvet box. 'This was my great-grandmother's. I had it sent from England. You're going to love England when we finally get there. So many gardens.'

He opened the box and held it out to her with both hands. 'I'd get down on one knee but I'd need a cane to get back up, or you could heave me up but that's not the effect that I'm going for. I'm vain enough to want to camouflage my failings, but I hope to hell I'm smart enough to hold onto the best thing that ever happened to me. I won't ever turn you away again. I will be there for us. I'll show up and do the communication work needed to offset the things I cannot see. I will never let you doubt my love for you. I'll wear it out loud and it'll be there for all to see.'

He looked into her eyes and she could have sworn he saw clear through to her soul. 'Ari Cohen, I love you. Will you do me the honour of spending your life with me, marrying me, being with me for all the turns and twists ahead? I can't promise a smooth and easy road, but I can promise that I will love, honour, and cherish you for as long as I draw breath.'

'Yes.' She sought his lips with hers and fed him love, make-up ruined by the tears in her eyes and the fierce tenderness of his lips. 'Let's do that, yes.'

Drinks flowed, music played, and the ballroom was full of people who'd dressed up and turned up to get a little Outback dust on their heels, admire a tangerine sunset that stretched on for ever, and enjoy an evening of outrageously opulent Blake hospitality.

Ari's diamond engagement ring glittered in the lamplight as Reid introduced her to friends and business partners, rescue workers and support staff with the ease of a born people person.

No one could tell the extent of his injuries hidden beneath his expensive designer suit. No one had any inkling of the emotional journey he'd undertaken and the changes that had been wrought.

Strong man, to have recovered from such injuries.

Smart man, to have confronted his insecurities and examined them and laid them bare for his loved ones to see.

Her man.

'You're glowing,' he murmured, leaning into her for a moment before straightening again.

'Lit up like the Thames on New Year's Eve.'

'Have you ever been to London on New Year's Eve?'

'No.'

'We're going.'

No objections were forthcoming. Ari's world was ever expanding, beyond her imagination, and she was ready for it. With Reid in her arms and his love to keep her safe, she was ready for whatever the future held for them. And then a willowy blonde woman walked up to them and commanded attention.

Was this the super special guest? It must be.

'Reid Blake? Please allow me to introduce myself.' She had a charming English accent. Crisp. Aristocratic. Wary rather than warm. 'My name is Victoria Colby-Jones. *Lady* Victoria Colby-Jones. Your brother found me, after some rather unorthodox digging.'

Reid's expression swung from shock, to disbelief, punctured by a couple of rolls of amazement, before he finally settled on a kind of kid-under-a-Christmas-tree delight. 'Vic! You even look like me, I can tell. Only female, and shorter.'

Lady Victoria's generous mouth firmed. 'Quite.'

'Look, Ari. It's Vic!' Ari wondered whether an elbow to the ribs would dampen his joy. 'Vic, this is my future wife, Ari.'

Lady Victoria looked her up and down and finally pronounced judgment. 'The pleasure is mine. Is Ari one of those hideous Australian nicknames and your given name is Ariel?'

'No. I'm just Ari.'

'Ah.'

Judah and Bridie joined them and formed a tight circle. Reid was quick to commandeer his brother.

'Does she need a hug? Does she look receptive to hugging?'

Judah leaned closer to his brother, but his eyes didn't leave his newfound half-sister's face. She could hear every word and everyone in the small standing circle knew it. 'No.'

'Got it,' said Reid as Ari took the opportunity to grind her stiletto heel into the toe of his gleaming leather shoe. 'Darling, mind the toes,' said Reid at his most injured. His thousand-watt smile brightened as he returned his attention to the newcomer. 'Lady Victoria, do you waltz, by any chance?'

'Of course I waltz, Ree…'

Everyone waited for the end of Reid's name to drop. It didn't.

'May I call you Ree?' his half-sister asked in dulcet tones. 'I'm doing my very best to fit in and failing miserably, I can tell.'

Ari's estimation of the haughty lady rose exponentially. 'Have you seen the sunset yet?' she asked.

'Vulgar,' Lady Victoria proclaimed. 'And yet somehow captivating.'

Bridie lured a hovering waiter forward and rescued three champagnes from a sparkling silver tray. One for Ari, one for Lady Vic. The other one she drained.

'Lady Victoria. Sister,' said Reid at his warmest. 'Have you ever tried to *teach* a woman to dance in the middle of a crowded ballroom?'

'No.'

'Would you like to?'

'No. I far prefer to make a fool of myself and other people in private.'

Which was how, at the end of a beyond perfect evening, Ari found herself in clearing ringed by ancient stones, beneath a giant redgum tree, barefoot in the dust in a Valentino dress, and with a couple of strings of fairy lights and a waxing moon to guide her way. Five people. Two brothers, a newfound sister, and the women those brothers had chosen to love.

And no one else to witness them making a spectacle of themselves.

They'd been learning how to waltz beneath Victoria's steely gaze. Swapping partners. Learning how to touch and to move together in acceptable ways. Someone to lead and not always the male partner. Someone to follow. Give and take and perfect moments of togetherness to be found in there somewhere.

'Waltzing is respect wrapped in gossamer,' Victoria declared. 'It's intimacy tempered by society. Waltzing properly with someone you love is perfection.'

Ari and Reid found their perfection as they shuffled closer and simply held each other close. 'Is she real?' asked Ari.

'I think so, but I'm exhausted,' murmured Reid. 'If I don't lie down soon I'll fall down and I've done quite enough of that lately.'

Ari had an idea but she didn't know if it would fly. Not in these clothes, but the stars were right there, millions of them in an inky sky. 'Do you trust me?'

'For ever and beyond.'

She was doing this. Stepping out of Reid's arms, she raised her hands in a bid for attention and took control. 'All right, people. Line up. Lady Victoria in the middle, Reid and Judah on either side, Bridie, you're next to Judah on that end, and I'm here next to Ree. Now hold hands.'

'Is this a dance?' asked Lady Victoria suspiciously.

'Kind of. It's a soul dance. It's how Reid and I first met, and it's an ice breaker. Hold hands, please, and lie down.'

'You mean in the *dirt*?' Lady Victoria wanted clarification.

'Yep. Right here. Right now.'

'But our gowns will be *ruined*.'

'But you'll see the stars like you've never seen them before and feel the weight of your body pressing into the earth and you'll get to say hello to this place in a way you'll never forget.' She took Reid's hand. 'They're just clothes. Beautiful clothes, granted, but they've done their job this evening, haven't they? They're just clothes now.'

Ari couldn't make anyone comply with her wishes. The men weren't moving. Everyone was waiting on Lady V.

And then, with a dancer's grace, Lady Victoria sat down and everyone else followed. Bridie laughed. Judah snickered. Reid cursed, and then they were all on their backs in the dirt and it was visceral and magical for those who knew how to lie back and close their eyes and feel.

Ari felt Reid's hand tighten around hers. Silence had never been more serene.

'Welcome to the family, Victoria,' Judah said gruffly. 'We might not be what you're used to but there's love for you here if you want it and beauty and truth and openness beyond imagining.'

Victoria was silent and time seemed to stop as everyone waited for her reply. Would she want what they were offering?

'Thank you, Judah, and Reid, and Bridie and Ari. Thank you so much for your hospitality and welcome.' Her voice cracked on that last word. 'I want it.'

# EPILOGUE

IT WAS A wedding small and intimate, with red dirt at people's feet and brilliant blue sky overhead. Gert was there as auntie of the bride, wearing a burnt-umber-coloured silk dress and hat that she and Ari had shopped for together. Bridie and Piper were matron of honour and young bridesmaid, stunning in deep ivory silk with red and orange accents. Ari's stepbrother Jake was there, wearing his first ever suit that he'd begun saving for as soon as he'd received his invite. He'd turned into a startlingly handsome young man and he stood quietly beside Gert and winked as Ari passed them by. Judah had been pressed into service as Reid's best man and stood strong and firm next to his brother.

And then there was Reid, his wild curls almost but not quite tamed and the eyepatch over his left eye giving him a rakish air that he did his very best to live up to. While the sight in one eye had faded, the other eye had strengthened. With that one bright hazel eye in play, he still saw more than most.

He thought her beautiful, even when she was up to her elbows and knees in dirt and surrounded by flies, and he told her so every day, using his words and his gaze and in a dozen other tiny ways.

It was in the cup of tea he placed at her elbow on the

early mornings when he had to attend one of his numerous business meetings.

It was the way he closed his eyes and drew her into his embrace just to breathe in her scent.

It was in his touch when, finally, she stood in front of him in her wedding finery and he reached for her hand.

She'd chosen to wear a simple white sheath of a wedding dress with off-the-shoulder sleeves and a tiny waist. No veil, no gloves. She carried a wedding bouquet of all her favourite native flowers. Flowering gum and flannel flowers. Lamb's ear and banksia cradles.

She wore her hair loose and her make-up was flawless courtesy of Bridie, who'd helped her dress.

On her bedside table this morning, Reid had left a long velvet box and in it was a diamond bracelet that matched her engagement ring. Something old, his note had said. Her something borrowed was a handful of delicate opal hairpins that Bridie expertly slid into place after twining several strands of Ari's hair into an elaborate flower shape above one of Ari's ears. Her something new and blue had come from Gert—a gossamer-thin wrap of sky-blue silk to drape across her back and over her arms and dance with the afternoon breeze.

Piper stepped forward to take her bouquet and Reid immediately reached out to capture that hand too, a smile breaking over his handsome face as he studied her.

'Your eyes are telling me you love me,' he murmured. 'Best day ever.'

'I've words of love for you too, so you can remember them in the dark.'

'Perfect.' He leaned forward and pressed his lips to her cheek. 'You're absolutely perfect for me. I have so many words of love for you too. Want to hear them?'

Happiness bloomed, strong and sure. This beautiful life and this brilliant, loving man were hers, and she would cherish them from this moment forward.

'You know I do.'

\* \* \* \* \*

# COMING SOON!

We really hope you enjoyed reading this book. If you're looking for more romance be sure to head to the shops when new books are available on

# Thursday 8th June

MILLS & BOON

# MILLS & BOON®

## Coming next month

### PENNILESS CINDERELLA FOR THE GREEK
Chantelle Shaw

'I had the impression on the beach a week ago that you want us to be work colleagues and nothing more.'

His dark blue eyes were unfathomable, but she noticed a nerve flicker in his cheek. He sipped his wine before he said softly, 'Is that what you want, Savannah?'

She was about to assure him that of course it was. Anything other than a strictly work based relationship with Dimitris would be dangerous. But she was transfixed by his masculine beauty, and when he smiled she felt more alive than she'd done in ten years. 'I don't know,' she admitted huskily.

The band had been playing smooth jazz tunes during dinner, but now the guests had finished eating and the tempo of the music increased as people stepped onto the dance floor.

Dimitris pushed back his chair and stood up. He offered his hand to Savannah. 'Would you like to dance?'

*Continue reading*
**PENNILESS CINDERELLA FOR THE GREEK**
Chantelle Shaw

*Available next month*
www.millsandboon.co.uk

# LET'S TALK
## *Romance*

For exclusive extracts, competitions and special offers, find us online:

**f** MillsandBoon

**𝕏** @MillsandBoon

**O** @MillsandBoonUK

**♪** @MillsandBoonUK

Get in touch on 01413 063 232

# MILLS & BOON

## THE HEART OF ROMANCE

---

## A ROMANCE FOR EVERY READER

---

**MODERN**

Prepare to be swept off your feet by sophisticated, sexy and seductive heroes, in some of the world's most glamourous and romantic locations, where power and passion collide.

**HISTORICAL**

Escape with historical heroes from time gone by. Whether your passion is for wicked Regency Rakes, muscled Vikings or rugged Highlanders, awaken the romance of the past.

**MEDICAL**

Set your pulse racing with dedicated, delectable doctors in the high-pressure world of medicine, where emotions run high and passion, comfort and love are the best medicine.

*True Love*

Celebrate true love with tender stories of heartfelt romance, from the rush of falling in love to the joy a new baby can bring, and a focus on the emotional heart of a relationship.

*Desire*

Indulge in secrets and scandal, intense drama and sizzling hot action with heroes who have it all: wealth, status, good looks…everything but the right woman.

**HEROES**

The excitement of a gripping thriller, with intense romance at its heart. Resourceful, true-to-life women and strong, fearless men face danger and desire - a killer combination!

# JOIN US ON SOCIAL MEDIA!

Stay up to date with our latest releases, author news and gossip, special offers and discounts, and all the behind-the-scenes action from Mills & Boon...

 @millsandboon

 @millsandboonuk

 facebook.com/millsandboon

 @millsandboonuk

*It might just be true love...*

# MILLS & BOON

## MEDICAL

*Pulse-Racing Passion*

Set your pulse racing with dedicated, delectable doctors in the high-pressure world of medicine, where emotions run high and passion, comfort and love are the best medicine.

# MILLS & BOON

## *Desire*

Indulge in secrets and scandal, intense drama and plenty of sizzling hot action with powerful and passionate heroes who have it all: wealth, status, good looks…everything but the right woman.